NEW CITY

Lauren Barr

Cover designed by Cathy Helms; Avalon Graphics
www.avalongraphics.org

For Stephen Barr
The world changed without you in it

Chapter One

She lifted the axe above her head and brought it down with a thud. Starting to rot, the soft timber gave under her blade, sending up a shower of woodchips. The scent of fragrant pine filled the air as she split log after log into firewood. The muscles in her arms flexed easily with the repetitive motion; she was used to the work.

As her thick dark hair slipped out of the elastic holding it back, Evie stopped, cursing. Setting down the axe, she brushed her hair back with brusque hands, catching stray strands before twisting it into a knot at the top of her head. She passed the sleeve of her plaid shirt over her face, flushed and damp from exertion.

The sun was still bright but provided less warmth than only a few days earlier, and the summer air had morphed into a cooler breeze that would soon become deadly. Evie listened to it sighing through the trees. It was the sound of sadness and longing for days — and loved ones — gone forever. The air held the tang of overripe leaves and last-minute flowers, and the foliage was starting to blaze. Evie shivered, and not only from the chill, as she told herself she had to face facts. The seasons continued, no matter how much she wished the world would spin backwards and return her to the time before.

She looked across the yard to where Kit was working in the garden. Kit had been gifted with the ability to nurse plants to life, a gift that Evie did not share. She always admired the way Kit's long fingers could turn the dirt, picking what needed to be purged and feeling which plant was thirsty.

Now that Evie had broken her rhythm, she was reluctant to continue working. Leaning against the handle of the axe, she contemplated her sister, digging in the thick wet dirt. Despite being only sixteen, three years younger than Evie, Kit was already several inches taller. This irritated the hell out of her, although she admitted the height suited her sister better. With her dancer's build and sunny blonde hair that fell straight to her shoulders, Kit took after their willowy, graceful mother. Evie had a compact, curvy figure and was dark, like her father. She was proud of her wavy brown hair. She hadn't cut it since before and it now reached halfway down her back.

The sisters had similar faces, though, with matching serious, dark brown eyes and a stubborn set to their mouths.

Kit wore a patterned apron over a pretty ruffled shirt and jean shorts, spotless even when working in the mud. Though no one was around to see, Kit always made sure she looked her best, not allowing her clothes to fall apart or let her hair get unruly.

Shaking her head at her sister's proper ways, Evie turned and hoisted the axe again. She had been chopping wood for over an hour, and this time her arms and back complained at the movement. As she brought the axe down the second time, a pile of vegetables landed at her feet. She hadn't noticed Kit come storming over to her from the garden.

"What the hell?" Evie shouted at her sister, letting the axe fall to the side.

"This is it!" Kit motioned to the pile of onions, tomatoes, beans, and lettuce she had thrown down. "This is what you expect us to survive on."

One of the tomatoes was overripe and had burst when it hit the ground. Now its oozing seeds leaked over the pile of woodchips. Even Evie with her limited knowledge of produce could see that the meager vegetables were undersized.

"It's not the only thing we're going to survive on," she said. "We can re-stock in town. There's still plenty left for the two of us."

"And then what?" Kit tossed her hair back, something she did when she was angry. "We will be finished our vegetables in a matter of weeks, even if we try to preserve them. Then we'll be down to canned goods and dried food, and even those supplies are running out. Evie, there is nothing left for us here. What are you waiting for?"

As her sister stared down at her, Evie could feel something start to crumple inside. She looked at the squished tomato for a long time, avoiding Kit's furious eyes.

Finally, Evie nodded. "You're right. It's time."

Kit's expression melted, from anger to astonishment. "Did you just say I'm right?"

Evie shrugged, defeated. "I've been thinking about it for a while. We shouldn't wait any longer. I know there's no reason to stay, other than ..." she trailed off, lifting her hands to cover her twisting mouth. "I don't know what is out there. I'm afraid we will be worse off," she finished from behind her hands in a small voice.

"I don't know what's out there either," Kit said, looking over Evie's head and pretending she had not seen her cool, calm sister give way to emotion. "But I know what is here — nothing. There's nothing for us here."

Evie nodded, trying to get her thickening throat under control. "I know. We need to get ourselves prepared and ready, but we need to go. Sooner than later, before winter sets in. We might not survive another one."

"Evie, that's fantastic!" Kit jumped up, pulling her sister in for a hug. "This is it. We're going to the city?"

"Yeah." Evie let her sister hug her, but her mind was racing. "We're going to Greater Havern. Are you okay with that?"

"Are you kidding?" Kit bubbled over. She seemed tense, like a spring on the verge of letting loose. "I have been going crazy here, just the two of us all alone, not knowing how many other people survived or where they are. I mean, not literally crazy, like in a talking to my sock puppet kind of way, but it's not good for us to live like hermits."

Evie drew her dark brows together. "I thought you didn't mind. You always seemed so peaceful when you were reading or gardening ..."

"I read and I garden because there is nothing else to do. I don't mind those things, Evie, but we are not *living*. We are only ..." She stopped as she searched for the proper word. "...

abiding."

"But we are *surviving*."

"Hey, big sis, we're doing awesome. All things considered. But come on, we're young. We both need to have a life beyond this." Kit gestured to the quiet forest surrounding them.

"If there *is* something beyond this," Evie said in a low voice, her throat aching. She pulled away from her sister. "There's lots to get ready, I'm just going to go in and check on a few things. Start some lists and that." Ignoring Kit's puzzled look, Evie stumbled away from her, running up the steps of the house and in through the back door.

The house was dark in comparison to outdoors; Evie tripped twice as she hurried up the stairs to the upper level. She found her way into the bathroom and collapsed to her knees, breathing hard. Panic pressed in on her from all sides; she could feel it squeezing her chest, hammering in her head. With no escape, she lay down on the tiles. The cold seeped onto her cheek and chest.

She took one deep breath, then another. The feeling of being consumed by uncertainty started to fade as the pressure relented. She rolled over onto her back. In the dim light, she could just make out the water stains on the ceiling. They had been there for years. *Dad was going to fix the roof but* ... She looked away. One more deep breath and she started to contemplate what was going to come next.

Leaving their quiet farming community of North Pine was risky, but they had stayed long enough, probably too long. The idea that some sort of government still existed and was searching for survivors in remote communities had come and gone.

Evie knew there were others out there, and she clung to the hope that some of them would want to help. But the only people who had come to their door were predatory men. She shuddered at the memory. Without laws, without order, they had become animals. She was terrified that more marauders like them would find her and Kit, and the next time she might be helpless. The thought made her want to retch. She couldn't go through that again. They had to leave, for their safety and their sanity.

Evie hated thinking about last winter. It had passed in a

blur, with the sisters too numb to feel the cold. There was no central heating, no electricity, so they made do with a healthy pile of firewood they chopped themselves. On the worst nights, they slept in front of the fire in sleeping bags, getting up every few hours to make sure the embers never went out. But, thank god, those nights had been few. The winter hadn't been as harsh as it could have been, otherwise they would have frozen to death.

Evie stirred, bracing her weight against the sink as she rose. She could barely see herself in the light, so she rummaged in the top drawer to pull out candles and matches. As she lit the candles, the sharp smell of sulphur filled the air. The unsteady light reflected in the mirror, casting her silhouette on every wall.

Shadows flickered across her face, making her appear drawn and hollowed out. Dark shadows stretched under her eyes, skeletal, her full mouth pressed into a grim line. Her pale skin reflected back the light. Sighing, she reached into the drawer again, pulling out a pair of scissors. Her chestnut hair fell around her face and down her back, gleaming in the candlelight.

"You can do this," she whispered to her reflection. She wasn't entirely sure what she meant: to set out into the unknown or to cut her hair, but it didn't matter. It felt like something that had to be done.

Her throat tightened again and this time she let the tears overflow and slip down her cheeks. She clutched the front piece of hair in front of her eyes, taking a deep breath before chopping the strand at chin length. Her hand didn't shake, but worked in one smooth motion. The space filled up with the quiet rasping of the scissors. As she continued, her tears slowed and stopped, letting her concentrate on the task at hand.

She paused in her snipping to sneeze. The candles were scented with a heavy floral smell, lilac or jasmine, she could never tell. Kit must have picked them up. The scent made her head spin, making the moment feel surreal.

She started hacking at the hair at the back of her head, without thought to precision or care, while she thought about the food problem. Without phones, computers, or newspapers for a year, they had no idea what was out there or how they would feed themselves.

After their community had been demolished by the Sickness, the sisters had ventured to every town within a day's drive looking for other survivors. They found only more death, more corpses.

Evie choked back the feeling of panic again. That was the root of the problem. That's why she had put off the decision for so long. She had no idea whether moving on would save them or hasten them along to death. They could be murdered. They could starve. Or they could discover that they were alone in the world. She simply had to trust the logic that in cities with populations of hundreds of thousands, some people — some good people — must have survived. Anything else would be unbearable.

The logistics of travelling had to be arranged now. Their logical destination was Greater Havern, the bustling city that lay a day and a half south by highway. It was warmer there, with temperate winters free of snow. Surrounding the city was nothing but desert, but the Eastern Havern River twisted through the city, creating the oasis they were looking for. To the west was a range of mountains, wild and impassable without proper transportation. On the other side lay fertile valleys, filled with orchards, lakes, and fields of grain. It would be the ideal place to go, but there was no guarantee of safe passage.

She had enough gas stockpiled to get their large pickup to the city, and if she had miscalculated she would simply find more. She seemed to have a talent for that. Greater Havern wasn't unknown to her. She had visited the city many times as a child; it would have been her home if she had been given a chance to attend university.

Evie put the scissors down and stepped closer to the mirror to admire her handiwork. Her hair laid in short cropped layers around her jaw and cheekbones. The short cut sharpened the angles of her face, giving her an elfin look. She wiped away any evidence of the tear tracks on her face.

Looking down at the mess she had made, Evie scowled. Most of her hair had fallen into the sink, but some had dropped over the sides, scattering on the floor. What had once been so lovely was now nothing more than tangled garbage. Blowing out the candles one by one, she left the darkened bathroom and started down the stairs.

Kit waited for her at the bottom of the stairwell. She took in Evie's new appearance, aghast.

"What did you do?"

Evie shrugged. "I just thought it was time for a change."

A moment of silence passed, Kit's solemn eyes intent on her sister. "You okay?" she asked, her eyes showing more understanding than Evie could bear right now.

Evie nodded. "I'm fine. There's a lot we need to do, so we had better get started." She began listing items off on her fingers, disregarding the solicitous look. "We need to pack and get supplies for the trip. We'll need to make sure our gas stock is good to go. We'll need to load up Dad's guns. And I think we should go to the hospital." She lifted her chin, meeting her sister's direct gaze.

Kit nodded along with her, but cringed at the mention of the hospital. "Why do we have to go to the hospital? I've spent enough time there to last me all my lifetimes."

"I know." Evie eased around her on the stairwell. "It'll be hard, but we need to raid it. We might need drugs and bandages at some point. We'll stop by on our way out of town." She turned and started walking into the kitchen.

"Oh my god!" Kit cried.

"What?" Evie whirled around, wondering if her sister was suffering from the same misgivings she had.

Kit looked horrified. "I don't care if nobody other than me will ever see you. I am not letting you go anywhere until you let me fix the back of your hair. Did you cut it off with a hacksaw?"

Evie stared at her sister for a moment, then a giggle burst out of her. Kit gave her a tentative smile and Evie gave in to her impulse. Within seconds she was helpless with full-throated laughter. It was higher-pitched than usual, and teetering on the verge of hysteria, but it was better to laugh than to cry. Kit was always able to help her stay on the lighter side when things got too grim.

"No, seriously," Kit said, grabbing her arm and herding her back upstairs. Evie obediently followed, still laughing.

Over the next two days, they prepared for their journey. While the physical trip would not be very long, they knew they would not be returning to the house and community they grew up in. Evie found herself picking up mementos from her former life, then putting them back down, scolding herself. There was no room for that, in the truck or her new life. Deciding what to take and what to leave was hell.

Finally, it was time to load up the truck and go.

"Kit, I told you, only one suitcase of clothes," Evie shouted when she saw Kit dragging three cases towards the truck.

"Why can't I bring more?" Kit yelled back in anger. "It's not like we're coming back. These are the only clothes I'll ever wear again."

"Don't be so dramatic." Evie rolled her eyes. "We'll get more clothes in Greater Havern. We don't have room for everything in the house."

The bed of the truck already held a tent, blankets, their father's guns, canisters of gas, and all the non-perishable food left in the grocery store. As Evie loaded the food into the back, she remembered the guilty pleasure they felt every time they had gone to the store during the past year and taken whatever they wanted without paying. She stuffed the last of their many bottles of vitamins between a can of tomatoes and a box of pasta and let out a sigh. There would not be room for the drugs; they would have to go in the cab. She and Kit threw a tarp over the top and tied it down, then they climbed into the cab.

Jostling down the pockmarked dirt road, away from the only home they had ever known, Evie and Kit resolutely kept their eyes on the road ahead. They drove to the hospital in silence. Evie brought the truck to a stop right in front of the wide entrance with the intimidating NO PARKING sign, seeing as there was no one to complain.

The small parking lot was full; most people who had checked in had never left. This did not make the hospital feel busy or bustling in any way; in fact, the crowded cars seemed to enhance the silence, make it lie heavy and expectant around them. Evie wished there were no cars at all, no sign of others, that the place appeared as abandoned as it was. Even the ambulances sat docile in their bay, as if at any moment they would be called into action.

The girls entered the echoing hallway. The hospital was by no means large, but it had two storeys and three wings. The sun was now slanting in through the large windows at the front, providing them with lots of light, but the corridors darkened as they stretched away into the interior of the building. Evie shuddered at being back. The pungent smell of antiseptic surrounded them, but beneath that, there was another, fainter smell — sweet and rotten at the same time.

As if reading her mind, Kit whispered, "Evie. Do you think there are still bodies here?"

Evie didn't want to think about what they would find if they went poking around. Everyone had helped out where they could during the Sickness. Both Evie and Kit, young as they were, were fitted with masks and helped care for patients in the beginning. But the trickle of sick became a stream, and the stream became a flood, until the community was consumed. Once the true extent of the Sickness was realized, people began to take care of their own, leaving others to deal with theirs. Evie buried her own father. But for those left behind? She hadn't thought of what remained.

"It's okay, we're not going far," she whispered back. "Do you remember the way to the supply room?"

"Yup. Stay on this floor. Straight ahead to the back and then turn left."

"Great, I'll follow you."

As they moved down the hallway, both girls switched on their flashlights. It made their surroundings more eerie. Once they turned the corner, they could see only what the thin beams of light illuminated. Seeing everything in quick light flashes, thinking of what surrounded them, Evie found she was holding her breath. She released it.

A cold touch grazed against her forearm. Evie shrieked.

"Holy crap, Evie, I'm right here!" Kit cried in exasperation. The echoes of the scream rang down the hallway.

"I'm so sorry," Evie said in a tense shaking whisper. "You just have very cold hands."

"Well, I think this is the door." Kit pushed down on the metal handle of an unmarked door, which looked like every other door along the hall.

As the door opened, their lights flashed on shelf after shelf, row after row of medical supplies.

"You start over there." Evie indicated the right side of the room with her flashlight. "I'll go over here."

"What are we going to put everything in?"

"Um." Evie looked around the room, flicking her flashlight over the shelves. Her light settled on a pile of cloth laundry bags near the door. "Oh, this is perfect. Just fill these up. Take anything you think people might need ... bandages, sutures, needles ..."

"Antiseptic?" Kit asked as she perused the boxes in front of her.

"Yes, good."

Evie was looking at a wall full of medications. She didn't recognize any of the labels. The names seemed to run together — ephedrine, lithium ammonia, gluburide and metformin, oxacillin. She had no real idea what many of them were for. The neat sterile boxes seemed to look back at her blankly. With a shrug, she started emptying the shelves. The important thing was she had them; she would figure out what they did later.

Soon the girls had two overflowing bags each.

"What do you think?" asked Kit as she held her bags up.

Evie looked at her sister, uncertain. "I don't know how much to take, or if any of this will be of any use." She considered the bags. "I do know that this is pretty much all we can fit in the truck, so I guess it will have to do."

"Good." Kit was as relieved as Evie to be leaving the hospital. They took their stash and headed out, back towards the sunlight.

"So this is it," Kit said, her eyes shining, as they pulled out of the parking lot.

"This is it," Evie echoed, trying to sound as happy and confident as her sister.

Chapter Two

Evie shifted again, trying to find a comfortable position in the passenger side of the cab. She'd been awake for hours, and although she was still exhausted, she knew she would not be able to go back to sleep.

They had driven for eight hours after leaving the hospital the day before, taking turns at the wheel. Too tired to set up camp when it started to get dark, they just pulled off the road and dined on cold canned spaghetti. Then they crawled back into the truck and slept in the uncomfortable upright seats.

No wonder I can't sleep, Evie thought in irritation as her head hit a bag of medical supplies sticking out over the top of her seat. The sun was just starting to lighten the sky as she sat up and peered out the window. The September air was so chilly she could see her breath when she yawned. It hung in a puff in front of her face before dissolving.

Kit was curled up in the driver's seat, a blue crocheted blanket from home wrapped around her. Evie reached over and jiggled her shoulder. Kit stirred then nuzzled further into her blanket.

"Kit," Evie said, voice soft, as she nudged her sister with more force. "Kit, I'm going to start driving. I need you to get into the passenger seat, and then you can go back to sleep."

Evie got out and ran around the truck then climbed back into the cab. After much encouragement, a sleepy Kit got herself settled in the passenger seat and was soon breathing deeply again.

She had wrapped the blanket so high around her face only her eyebrows were visible.

Blinking her bleary eyes, Evie started the engine. She could have made a fire and brewed coffee, but she was anxious to get going. They might not reach the city before nightfall, and she didn't want to spend another night on the road.

They had passed several small towns yesterday. They had explored them all during the last twelve months, so Evie kept her gaze straight ahead and tried not to think about the horrors they had seen.

Now, as they drove farther south, she noticed there were fewer and fewer trees and more fields and pastures. The land was flat except for the occasional valley. She saw only one river and wondered whether it was the river than ran through Greater Havern.

Birds rode the air, the sunlight catching them as they drifted by the clouds. Geese had started their habitual migration south, not a bit bothered by the plague that had ended civilization. Evie watched their passage overhead, craning her neck to see them through the windshield. Their wings beat in constant time in their haste to get away from the cold north. For them, escape was so easy. She wondered what it would be like to pick up and fly away from this place, from this life, without fear or regret. Leaving everything behind and taking off into the endless blue …

The car drifted towards the side of the road and a hard bump jostled Evie from her reverie. She swung the truck back on track, avoiding a trip into the ditch.

The road had been a well-maintained busy highway before the Sickness, often congested with cars. But after a year with no maintenance, potholes and cracks roughened the surface. It would only get worse as nature took her course.

Evie squinted against the rising sun and wished she had her sunglasses. She flipped the sun shield down and shook her head, trying to stay awake. She drove on, disregarding lanes or former rules. There were no more speed limits, since there were no more police officers. And, of course, there were no other people driving the roads. Evie wondered what she would do if she saw another vehicle driving towards her. It would be shocking but miraculous.

Movement along the side of the road made her slow down with a smile. She reached over and shook her sleeping sister.

Kit straightened up. "Are we there yet?" she mumbled through her hair. Brushing her blonde tangles out of her eyes, she saw the empty skyline and frowned in disappointment. "Why are we stopping?"

Evie pointed across the highway. In the fields, a herd of horses was galloping along, free and joyful. Kit gasped at the sight, her sleepiness falling away. Her hands clapped together in delight. "They're so beautiful!" she breathed.

The animals that had survived the Sickness had always been wild. Those that depended on humans for their care died from exposure or starvation.

Neither of the girls had tasted meat since being on their own; neither had the heart to slaughter anything. After being surrounded by so much death for so long, it seemed criminal to kill another living creature. And their need had not yet reached that point.

Kit gave a contented sigh as they pulled away again, leaving the horses behind. "We wouldn't have seen anything like that *before*, would we?"

Evie shook her head, still smiling at her sister. "I guess not. How are you feeling? Would you be ready for some breakfast?"

Kit perked up at the thought of food and shifted, stretching out her back. "That sounds great. You want to have a fire and everything?"

"If we can manage it, that would be excellent."

Evie started to slow down then saw something up ahead. It was a car, pulled over to the side of the road. Looking down at the gas gauge, she saw the needle flickering too close to empty for her liking

She pointed to the car. "Why don't we stop there? Looks like it's been abandoned. I think we should check and see if it has any gas left. Our supply is starting to run low."

"We still have canisters in the back."

"I know, but what if it doesn't get us there? Or to the place we may have to go after that? Might as well take what we can get." *Running out of gas on the road would be death*, she thought.

At one time, the car had been expensive — a black Mercedes Benz. The three-legged hood emblem still showed a hint of dull glimmer. Two of the tires were flat and patches of rust were starting to appear around the doors. It wasn't uncommon to see cars pulled over to the side of the road; they had already passed several on their journey south. Sometimes the Sickness had struck so suddenly, the victims died within hours. If they were driving, they pulled over to the side of the road. Some managed to get out and try to walk away, but most just lost consciousness and died.

"Evie," Kit said with reluctance. "Do you think that the — owner — is still …" she trailed off with a look of wariness and disgust.

"It's likely." Evie had already thought of that and was trying to prepare her stomach for what they would find. She had seen so many bodies already. But one that had been sitting in a car for a full year was entering into a whole new realm of disgusting experiences for her.

Evie pulled up next to the Mercedes and got out of the truck, her mouth set in a thin line. Kit hesitated and then followed Evie to the luxury car. They both peeked through the driver's side door. Kit screamed and looked away, while Evie grimaced and took a bracing deep breath.

The body was slumped over, face down on the passenger seat. It — he — had been a man, maybe a businessman, judging by the tailored suit he was wearing. He was probably older; the wispy hair trailing around his collar was yellowy-white. Evie was thankful they couldn't see his face. She didn't want to know what he looked like at this stage.

"How do you know if there's any gas left?" Kit asked.

"Well, if the door is unlocked, I could turn the car on to find out." Evie peered into the car again, shading her eyes against the glare. "Yes, the keys are still in the ignition."

Kit stared at her sister with a look of complete horror. "I'm … going to be over here." She dashed around to the other side of the truck, gagging.

Evie gave a bleak smile then tried the car door handle. The door swung open, bringing with it a smell that made her eyes water.

"Urg." She clapped a hand over her mouth and nose as she leaned into the car. There were bugs everywhere — on the body, on the seats, and burrowing into the carpet. Evie pulled the neck of her T-shirt up over her face and reached around the body to the ignition, desperate not to disturb the corpse. She fumbled with the keys, grimacing at the squish of a bug as she crushed it under her thumb, then turned them with a little prayer. To her immense relief, the engine roared to life. She checked the gas gauge — it showed half a tank. Turning off the engine, she popped the gas tank then levered herself away from the car and slammed the door shut. She stumbled a few steps away before taking a deep breath, gagging at the smell of putrefaction coating her skin and her lungs. She batted at her hair, checking for bugs.

"Oh crap, oh crap," she panted. "That was gross."

Kit came towards her with an apologetic look on her face. "Well? Was it worth it?"

Evie nodded, still bent forward, coughing.

"Good. Here's the stuff." Kit held out an empty gas can and the hose they had been using to siphon gas.

Evie glowered at her. "Why do I always have to do the gross things? I don't know if you noticed, but I just crawled into a car with a corpse, and I'm pretty sure that you hid on the other side of the truck. Now I have to do the siphoning too?"

"You're just so much better at it than I am," Kit replied with a sugary sweet smile.

"Fine." Evie snatched the hose and canister. "But you're making breakfast."

Evie fed the hose into the gas tank. Then she sat on the ground so the other end was lower than the car and held the empty canister between her knees. She looked at the hose in distaste, mentally preparing herself. She hated this part.

"Remember not to swallow!" Kit chirped from the other side of the truck.

Evie rolled her eyes, muttering, "That only happened once," then began sucking hard on the open end of the hose. She tasted gas and placed the hose into the canister. Once the gas flooded out, she spat onto the ground. "Bring me some water, Kit," she yelled as she settled next to the car. She leaned back as she held the hose in place. *Other than the taste, it isn't so bad*, she thought. The fumes made her head swim in pleasant waves, and she liked the smell. It always brought back memories of lazy hot days by the lake, the smell of gasoline drifting up from their boat. She and Kit used to stay there every summer when they were kids; outside from the minute they woke up until long after the sun had gone down. They wore their bathing suits all day, and ran around with a gang of children from nearby cottages. They stopped only to eat or to sleep.

When Evie was twelve, her mother passed away from complications of diabetes. Her father never recovered from the loss, and they stopped going to the lake. He said he was too busy, but Evie knew it was just too painful to be reminded of what they once had. But for Evie, the memories remained, precious long lost moments of happiness, where everything was sunlit and golden.

"Are you okay?" Kit was holding a bottle of water out to her, concern etched on her face. Evie realized she was sitting there with a misty smile on her face, the hose held in a haphazard way, nearly missing the can. She reached up to take a sip of water.

"Thank you," she said after she rinsed her mouth out. "And I'm all right. I think I just forgot where I was for a second."

"I don't blame you. I always wish I could forget where I am. " Kit straightened and surveyed the bleak landscape around them. "I've started to set up breakfast, over there, so soon you'll have a decent meal." She gestured to a point far away from the car and its grisly contents. "You look exhausted, so I'll drive the next leg."

The countryside continued to change as they got closer to Greater Havern. Farmland and open prairie was replaced by desolate semi-desert. The untended land was barren. Even the ground was baked and cracked. The whole area was parched.

And it was getting hot. The temperature was rising so quickly, it felt as if someone had turned on an oven. Their old truck had no air conditioning, and Evie found herself longing for the early-morning chill. They wound the windows down as far as they would go, but the wind was hot so it didn't cool them much. Sweat trickled down Evie's bare neck, and she gave a moment of thanks that she had cut her hair.

"I know the city is on the edge of a desert," Kit said, gazing around at the scorched earth. "But I don't remember it looking so ... so much like a desert."

Evie looked at a square of fenced-off land, which might once have been a field. There was no sign of old crops. The bare earth was dotted with occasional patches of tall coarse grasses blowing in the dusty breeze. "I know what you mean. I don't remember any desert until farther south of the city. I think the fields used to be kept watered by irrigation from the East Havern River. I guess that now, without anyone to run the irrigation system, nature is taking its course."

"It's just so different. I have a hard time believing that human kind had such a huge effect — that we could change the world so drastically."

"And that the world would change back so quickly after we are gone," Evie finished her grim thought. "This is what the world looks like without people."

The girls sat in silence, sharing a moment of desolation. Kit, wanting to break the stillness, reached over to turn on the stereo.

"Wait!" Evie cried, grabbing her arm. "What are you doing?"

"I was just going to put on some music." Kit gave Evie a puzzled look. "I put some CDs in before we left."

"Oh." Evie relaxed. "I thought ... for a second, I thought you were going to turn on the radio."

Since the radio stations had stopped broadcasting, every once in a while the girls had tried the radio to see if they could pick up a signal. Any station they had access to had long since been off the air, leaving only empty static behind. It was morbid curiosity that made them try, as their absolute aloneness was always confirmed. Every time, though, Evie held her breath, thinking, *maybe, this time, someone is trying to get in touch with us.*

"You know," Kit said, stretching out each word as she thought about what she was going to say, "we are pretty close to the city. If there is anything out there, we might be able to pick it up."

"Right," Evie nodded. "I guess we should try." Her hand still hesitated over the dial. *What if no one is there and the city is empty.*

We are alone; we will drive until we run out of gas, and then what? What's the point? Evie looked at her sister in dread.

Kit gave her a little frown. "I know what you're thinking, but we should still try. If we don't find anything, it doesn't mean a thing. We could still be out of range, or there could be lots of people who just happen to not be on the radio waves. Don't you dare freak out, just give it a try." She paused, and said under her breath. "It's better to know."

Is it? thought Evie, but she turned the radio on anyway. She held her breath as she listened, flipping through the channels. All she found was shapeless static. There was nothing to be picked up. She let out a sigh.

The noisy static did nothing to ease the forlorn feeling that had been creeping in around them. The world was an alien place, unfamiliar and hostile, and — most of all — empty. Evie wanted to pinch herself, to just wake up, but this nightmare had gone on too long for her to believe it could be anything but her reality.

"I don't remember that," she heard Kit mutter to herself. Evie shook her head and tried to stave off the feeling of desperation growing inside her.

"What?" she asked, focusing on her sister.

"I don't remember those hills over there. Wasn't it pretty flat all the way to the city from here?"

Evie squinted. Off in the distance to the right she could see three hills rising above the rest of the flat land. They stood proud of the baked ground, rising up in a gentle slope and tapering off at the top. They were almost identical in shape and size.

"Those were never there before. Those are new."

"But what are they?" Kit asked. "They don't seem natural. They're too smooth."

Evie stared at the hills, wide-eyed, and felt a shudder run down her spine. "No, whatever they are, they are definitely not natural." She had a suspicion, something horrible, but she didn't want to say it out loud.

They drove ever closer. With every minute that passed Evie's sense of revulsion grew. Something about the hills was *wrong*, she was sure of that. When they were near enough to make out what they were, Kit took her foot off the gas, rolling to a stop. She let out a low moan.

"Oh, no," she whispered. "How could they?"

The hills were man-made piles, layer on layer of bone and scraps of blackened leathery skin. Thousands of human bodies had been incinerated. Evie felt like her eyes were going to pop out of her head. She wanted more than anything to look away, but it was impossible. Finally she lowered her gaze to the scorched earth and wept.

"Oh, no," Kit said again, her voice shaking. "We shouldn't be breathing this air." She tried to close her window, but in her panic kept on missing the handle. "This can't be good for us!" She covered her face with her hands and burst into tears.

Evie brushed away her own tears and put a hand on Kit's shoulder. "It's okay, we don't have to worry about them. These people must have died from the Sickness. If we were going to be infected, we would have already. We are immune. We're safe from them. Come here," she said as she wrapped her arms around Kit and let her sob into her shoulder. "We knew that things would be bad, no matter where we went," she said into her sister's ear. Kit nodded but continued to shake.

Evie admitted to herself that nothing could have prepared her for this grisly sight. There were thousands and thousands of bodies there, probably first dumped into a hole, then piled high and set on fire. What kind of people could do that? Yet in a city with a population of over a million, how many had died? Where could they all have been buried or disposed of, and who would be able to do it?

All her questions since the Sickness began with *who*. Now there was another one. Who had burned the bodies? Who continued to live? Their only chance at survival, at finding any sort of life in this world, lay with finding these people, the *who* in all her questions. But what kind of people were they?

Kit's sobbing had quieted. Evie sat her up and brushed back her hair. "It's okay. I'm going to drive for a while, all right?"

Kit nodded, tears still streaming down her face. Evie reached for the door handle to get out, but Kit grabbed her arm in alarm. "No! Don't get out of the truck."

"But —"

"I mean it," Kit said in a fierce voice. "This is not a good place. Do not get out."

"All right." Evie eased back into the seat. "We'll do it the hard way." The girls struggled to shift around each other in the cramped cab, even though it was so tight there wasn't much room to move. Evie was happy to hear Kit snort with laughter when her leg got caught on the stick shift and she fell. *She'll be all right. It was just a shock.* Still, once Kit had settled in the passenger seat, she rolled up the window in jerky movements, refusing to look outside at the piles. Evie followed suit, rolling up her window despite the baking heat.

They drove in silence for an hour. Evie was watching Kit out of the corner of her eye. Although she had composed herself, she continued to brush away tears.

"There's some tissues in the glove compartment," Evie said.

"I'm okay." Kit's eyes were on something ahead of them. "Evie —" she hit her sister in the arm without looking at here. "Look!"

Off in the distance, at a point at the end of the road, was the silhouette of the city, shimmering in the heat haze. It was almost imperceptible but unmistakable — the outline of buildings reaching up into the sky. Once again the truck stopped in the middle of the road as the sisters looked at each other.

"Are we doing the right thing?" Kit whispered.

Evie hesitated, then nodded, jerking her head a bit. She stuck out her chin. "What other choice do we have?" She gestured around them, taking in the landscape. They were surrounded by bare earth, empty and flat, stretching out for as far as they could see. The sky was even bare of clouds, an endless expanse of blue. There was one road, leading to the speck in the distance. "This is it, little sister. We have to keep on going."

As Greater Havern was the only thing of note on the landscape, it was impossible not to focus on it, obsess over every detail as they approached and the city grew. The road they drove on grew wider, but remained empty. There still were no other moving cars, no sign of life. By this point, the sun was lower in its daily arch, deepening the sky to indigo as they approached the outskirts. The highway was elevated in the suburbs, so Evie and Kit were able to look down at the row on row of identical houses. They were all dark, with cars parked in the driveways as if still waiting to be driven. There was no sound or movement anywhere.

Evie continued driving towards the centre of the city, holding her breath. Evening started to set in and the air cooled. She was beginning to think they would drive right through the metropolis without seeing a soul when she saw something that caused her heart to somersault in her chest.

Chapter Three

Lights. A halo around the buildings. The downtown of Greater Havern was emitting a haze of electric light against the darkening sky. There was no mistaking that there was power in those buildings.

After driving for several more minutes, eager eyes taking in the glow, Evie changed directions, taking a right turn onto a smaller road that followed along the north side of the East Havern River. The girls looked in awe as the downtown buildings came into view across the river — every window blazed with light. As they approached a massive arching bridge, Evie came to a stop and looked at the twinkling reflections in the broad expanse of water.

"I can't believe it," Kit said, eyes shining. "They have lights — electricity! There must be hundreds of people here, maybe even thousands. We're not the only ones. We're not alone. It's going to be all right. Evie, we're going to be all right. What do we do now?"

The flicker of hope Evie felt while gazing at the lights was overwhelmed by the rising lump of panic in her throat. She didn't have the answer. She hadn't planned this far ahead. How could she? They had no idea what they would find. All she had thought about was finding other people, not how to approach them. Perhaps they would not be welcome. Maybe she and Kit would be considered intruders. Were the citizens of Greater Havern worried about newcomers infected with the Sickness?

She swallowed hard, forcing down the dread threatening to boil over, and lifted her chin. "We'll drive around until we find someone. There's electricity here, so the people must be organized. And if they're organized, there must be someplace we can go to, maybe report to," she said, surprised at how quickly the logic came to her. "They must expect people to come here, like refugees. We'll find some people and ask them where we're supposed to go." She tried to sound more confident than she felt.

"What if we don't find anyone?"

"I don't know!" Evie yelled, her anxiety showing. "We'll sleep in the truck and look around again tomorrow."

She put the truck into gear and started driving, leaving the dark northern suburbs. When they reached the south side of the bridge, they gaped at what they saw in the glow of the street lights. It was obvious that Greater Havern was in bad condition. The streets were dirtier, grittier than Evie remembered. Garbage was strewn all over the place — tin cans had been overturned, their contents rummaged through, and plastic bags blew across the sidewalks and plastered themselves to the walls of the decrepit buildings. There was a stink in the air, the definite smell of raw sewage floated around them. Kit wrinkled her nose in disgust. Dirty grey buildings, each one more nondescript than the last, hemmed them in. They crept along the road, craning their necks, looking for signs of human life.

They drove past several blocks of warehouses and older office buildings. The windows were smashed and the lower walls covered in graffiti. The city seemed empty, abandoned.

Evie turned a corner and Kit gasped, grabbing her arm. She pointed to the right side of the street. From behind an overflowing dumpster, a man peeled himself from the shadows, walking towards them with both hands in the pockets of his slouchy pants.

Evie braked so hard both she and Kit were jerked forward. They stared at the man, open-mouthed. Aside from the unwanted intruders who had visited them last winter, he was the first human they had seen in months. Kit let out a small noise, a look of wild joy on her face. Evie gave her a tight smile, daring to hope that everything was going to be okay.

Then the hand around Evie's bicep tightened. Evie looked around her, checking the side mirrors. Two more men had followed the first and another one was behind the truck. Evie's elation was abruptly replaced by wariness. The way the men surrounded the truck made her feel threatened, as if she was prey. On an instinct she reached behind her. Her fingers groped around the floor of the truck until they brushed against something cold and metal. With the tips of her fingers, she inched the crowbar forward until she had a solid grip on it. Her eyes never left the man approaching them. He was taking his time.

"What are you doing?" hissed Kit.

"Where are the guns?" Evie said through her teeth, trying not to move her lips.

"The guns? They're in the back. You said you didn't want them pointing at our heads as we drove. Do you think we need them?"

Evie cursed her lack of foresight. "It's just in case." She put the truck in park but left the engine running. "Lock your door."

Kit responded, slamming her hand down on the lock. The man was at Evie's window. His eyebrows rose at the sudden movement and Evie bit her lip, hoping her sister could keep it together.

"Kit," Evie said, still not looking at her. "Try to relax and act natural, okay? I'll take care of this." She settled the crowbar next to her thigh, hidden from view, her right hand wrapped around it. The fingers of her other hand fiddled with her door lock, although she knew it was broken.

The man tapped on her window with his knuckles, once, twice. Up close he looked seedy and hungry. His skin was chalky, with pale stubble covering his cheek, chin and neck in patches. With bloodshot eyes and greasy matted hair, he appeared to have not slept in days. His clothes, jeans and a T-shirt, were covered with mud and what looked like dried blood. If she had met this man in other circumstances, Evie would have avoided him. But he was her hope of finding out what was happening in this city. She took a deep breath and rolled down her window, trying for a brilliant smile. *Might as well give it your all*, she thought.

"Hello!" she chirped in her brightest voice. "We just arrived in the city. I was hoping you could let me know where it is we should be going if we are, um, newcomers." She winced at her awkward words, not sure she was making any sense.

"Well hello there," the man replied. "You do look new to town." His voice was light and his tone polite, matching Evie in friendliness. He gave her a smile that might have been pleasant, if all of his darkened teeth had been present. His eyes told a different story, though. They were flicking all over the inside of the cab and the truck bed. She gave a silent prayer he couldn't see everything they had under the tarp. He rested his arm on the open window. Evie tensed and gripped the crowbar tighter.

The man noticed her tension. "Hey, now, easy there. You're strangers to the city, are you? Well, there's no need to worry, because we're the welcoming committee."

As soon as he had uttered the last word of his unconvincing speech, his face twisted into a scowl. He wrenched open Evie's door, grabbed her, and pulled her out of the driver's seat. With a cry, she went flying, sprawling face first on the dirty cement. She landed with her left wrist at an awkward angle underneath her and gasped with pain. She still had a firm grasp on the crowbar. She looked up as she heard Kit screaming in the truck.

"Shut up, you little bitch, it's your turn next." The man slammed the door hard. Evie heard his heavy footsteps right behind her. She pushed herself up off the ground and lunged at him with the crowbar. By some lucky chance, she managed to land a blow on his forehead.

He fell back a step or two and hunched over with his hands to his face. The other men took uncertain steps towards him, but stopped when he waved a hand at them to back off. He straightened up and brought his hands down from his face, laughing. The sound was ominous. Even though blood ran down one side of his face from the gash, he turned to her with the same amiable smile he wore before. The smile was chilling the first time. Now, with blood flowing down his cheek, it was gruesome.

Evie straightened, slow and stiff. She looked around her. The men had tightened their circle, surrounding her. She counted six. Two others had appeared out of nowhere. *News travels fast in the city*, she thought in panic.

Evie's left wrist was useless, but she again raised the crowbar with her right hand. Some of the men grinned at this. A man to her left with dark skin and leather pants made as if to lunge at her.

The first man, the leader, swaggered into the circle. "Aren't you a pretty thing. You know, it's been a very long time since there's been any pretty girls round here. Why don't you put away your little toy and come join us for a while. Your friend can come too. We'll show you the ways of the city." He leered at Evie while his cohorts laughed. He was so close she could smell his sickly breath. She glared at him in defiance, swinging her arm back to strike again. She had no idea what she was doing and was no match for six men anyway, but she'd be damned if she would go down without a fight.

The leader smirked and narrowed his eyes at her. "That's all right. I like them feisty."

Kit screamed again.

Before Evie could react, someone else strode into the circle behind her. He stood at her back, out of reach. A quick glance back at him showed that he was large, with skin so dark it seemed to absorb the light. She blinked then looked back at her would-be attacker.

"Gentlemen," the unidentified man called in a booming voice. "Is there a problem here?"

The man behind Evie radiated heat and confidence. It made her nerves tingle. He had the same effect on the thugs. The tension spiked, and the men who had been crouching around her and grinning just seconds ago looked stiff and uncomfortable. The leader of the gang lost his fierceness as his gaze travelled over Evie's shoulder.

"Does somebody want to explain to me what's going on?" the black man rumbled. The sound of his deep melodic voice rolled up Evie's spine. No one in the group answered.

"Ryson," he snapped. The leader bowed his head further. "I should have expected you to be in the middle of trouble. I'm going to ask you one more time; what's going on?"

"Nothing. No trouble here, sir," Ryson mumbled to his shoes.

"No trouble?" The man laughed, a slow, low chuckle. "Is that why you're bleeding?"

Ryson looked up then, blinking away the blood that still trickled into one eye. "It's nothing like that. See, there was a small misunderstanding between us and these ladies here."

The man strolled around Evie, coming into her sightline. Now that she could make out his features, she understood why the hoodlums were so intimidated. He was built like a lineman and his large head, shaved bald, gave him a look of bullish ferocity. She was thankful he appeared to be on her side. He was wearing an impeccable suit, with a crisp white shirt underneath and a dark tie. He looked as though he was going to the theatre. His skin was so black it was hard to distinguish his features. He gave Evie a sidelong look then stared at Ryson.

"I'm guessing these young ladies are newcomers, and you were of course ..." He let the statement hang in the air.

"Welcoming them, of course," Ryson finished, looking eager. Some of the other men nodded in agreement. "See, like I said, there was this misunderstanding. Then this girl here just attacked me, with a crowbar. We were just trying to help, that's all."

Evie heard Kit's squeak of indignation from the truck. She tightened her grip on the crowbar, keeping it raised at her shoulder.

Evie's protector laughed again. It was a humourless sound. "That's one hell of a misunderstanding. And she's got quite the swing." Some of the men in the background tittered. "You weren't trying to sample anything, were you?"

Ryson looked aghast. "We would never do something like that. We were just trying to be helpful. We were going to take them directly to Lachlan's."

The man shook his head, looking disgusted. "Of course you were." He didn't even try to hide the sarcasm in his voice. "Ryson, get out of my sight. I don't want to see you out here at night again. The streets aren't safe, and you're not making them any safer."

Ryson took a few steps backwards and tripped over his feet. Stumbling, he turned, looking back over his shoulder at the black man with a wary look. His buddies melted back into the alleys, lost to sight and sound, the same way they had appeared. Soon it was only Evie and the huge man standing together in the street. He turned to look full at her.

"Welcome to New City," he said. "You can put that down now." He indicated the crowbar she still held up at shoulder height. It came to his waist. "I'm not going to hurt you."

Evie hesitated and shifted her grip. "How do I know I can trust you?"

He laughed, and this time the sound was warm and genuine. "I like a girl who's not too trusting. I don't know how to convince you that I won't hurt you. I can tell you that I can take you to a place where you'll be safe."

Evie stared up into his face, trying to read him. He had just saved her and Kit from god knows what, but the adrenaline was still pumping through her veins and she couldn't think straight. She had no idea what to say, but knew she was not ready to trust him yet.

He put his hands up. "Or, you can keep the crowbar, I'm okay with that. I do want to get you girls off the streets though. As you have probably figured out, it's not a very safe place to be, especially not for girls like you, new to the city."

"You seem to be safe enough."

"All the more reason you should stay with me."

Evie finally let her arm drop. It seemed a little ridiculous to be threatening a man twice her size. "I'm sorry, you must think I'm a crazy person." She loosened the grip on the crowbar, letting it fall to the ground with a clang. She gave a shaky laugh and looked away, trying to pull her thoughts together.

"You must be pretty shaken up after what you just went through."

"What —" Evie was cut off by her shrieking sister, who had jumped out of the truck and leapt on her.

"Evie, I was so, so scared! Oh my god, I thought you were going to die, and you were so brave, and I wasn't doing anything, and those men were awful." She looked at Evie, tears streaming down her cheeks. "I didn't know what we were going to do. Until —" She turned and threw herself at the man, "you showed up and saved us. Thank you so much. I don't know how we can ever thank you enough."

The man looked down at the blonde girl wrapped around his middle, bemused. Evie couldn't help thinking, even in her state of shock, that her little sister certainly had a flair for playing the damsel in distress.

"It's nothing," he said, untangling himself from Kit, who flung herself into Evie's arms again, sobbing.

"Kit," said Evie, chuckling in spite of everything. "It's fine — Ow!" she yelped as Kit hit her injured wrist.

The man was scrutinizing them. "Are you hurt?"

"It's just my wrist. I fell on it, but I don't think it's broken." She tested it, rolling it a few times and wincing.

"I know someone who can help with that. The man I work for, he's a doctor. He'll be able to take care of you. Only we really should get out of here."

Evie looked at him. "To go where? Who's in charge of the city? Is there some kind of government we should report to?" She didn't want to run into a situation blind again.

He looked her up and down and sighed. "My boss, he's in charge. He's the person to talk to if you want to get by in this place. But I'll let him explain that for himself."

"How do I know we'll be safe?"

"As far as I can tell, lady, you've got no one else to trust. If I wanted to hurt you, you would be hurt by now, crowbar or not. And I'm the only person you've met in this city who hasn't attacked you, so I think I have that going in my favour as well." He smiled at her, his dark eyes warm. "You can trust me, I swear."

Evie held his gaze for a long time. Finally, his warmth turned to impatience. "It's kind of a limited time offer. We need to go."

She drew in a breath. "Okay, I guess. We'll go with you for now."

"Good." The man was all business. "Get into the truck, I'll drive."

Kit bounded along to the passenger side. Evie followed behind at a slower pace, keeping her eyes on the man as she picked up the crowbar.

They squished themselves into the cab. Evie sat half on Kit's lap, with her legs over her, cradling her injured wrist. The man folded himself into the front seat. His legs were considerably longer than either Evie's or Kit's, so his knees were wedged around the steering wheel. He couldn't push the seat back because of the four bags of hospital drugs jammed in behind him. Evie prayed he would not ask what was in the bags.

Knowing he looked ridiculous, he muttered to himself, "The things I do." He shook his head and started the truck.

Evie sat in silence, still trying to work out whether the guy was genuine or whether she was being conned. She didn't have to worry there would be an awkward silence. Kit was bubbling over with curiosity, peppering the man with questions. "Who are you? What do you do? Where are we going?"

The man looked over at Kit in annoyance. "You ask a lot of questions, you know that?" She continued to look at him with her bright face. He sighed. "They call me One."

"I'm Kit, and this is my big sister Evie."

"Kit. And Evie." One's eyes flicked over the girls as he said their names. It made Evie uncomfortable and she sank back into the seat a little.

"You're called One?" Kit said. "That's a weird name."

He wasn't able to suppress a look of irritation. "It's a nickname."

"Huh." Kit thought about that for a bit. "So, like, other people call you that."

"Yes, they do. Can we leave it?"

"Sure, One."

"Since you're in a particularly chatty mood, maybe you can answer some questions for me. Where are you from?"

"We come from a place way up north called North Pine. Have you heard of it?" Kit asked, then shrugged when One shook his head. "Not surprising, it's very small."

"I assume that your town was hit by the Sickness, same as everywhere else?" Both the girls gave automatic nods. "Any other survivors?"

"No one but us," Kit answered, losing her cheerful tone. "We've been on our own for a while. We've only seen a few other people since ... until today."

"Did either of you show any symptoms of the Sickness?"

"Not at all. We ended up working as nurses for everyone at the hospital, but we never even caught a cold."

"That's consistent with what we've seen in the city," One said. "Lachlan, my boss, has been keeping a careful eye on things, to make sure there's no re-infection, but as far as anyone can see, those that survived the first and only wave of the Sickness are immune."

He shifted in his uncomfortable position. He seemed unused to talking so much. "What else do you want to know?"

"Why aren't there any cars around?" Kit asked.

"Because they're not really necessary. New City isn't that big, it's just the former downtown. The boundary pretty much is where you see the electricity. You can walk or cycle anywhere you need to go. I'd say the whole powered city is roughly twenty-five blocks in any direction," he said, waving his hand to indicate their surroundings.

"Also it's a matter of fuel. Oil is a very precious commodity around here, and there are some who would go very far to get it. After the fallout of the Sickness, we collected most of the cars on the streets, keeping them for use later or for their gas. No one drives anymore, which is why those guys back there pounced when they heard your truck. I heard it from four blocks away. I knew strangers were on the streets, so I came to investigate. I figured there would be trouble."

There were a few moments of silence while the girls realized how lucky they had been before Kit broke in again. "You call it New City. Why?"

He shrugged. "No real reason, I guess. It's just what everyone calls it. Life is very different now from what it was before the Sickness, and Greater Havern changed a lot. So many new people came here, we eventually got to calling it New City."

"Yes, we've been here — before," Kit said. "It looked nothing like this. It's so dirty now."

"Where are we going?" Evie asked as they took another turn through the grim streets. She felt disoriented by all the lights around her and couldn't figure out where they were.

"I'm taking you to the safest place in the city. My boss has turned it into something of a refuge for survivors of the Sickness. There's lots of room and lots of food. As you can see, we have electricity as well, and running water. It's safe and comfortable, so I think you girls will like it."

"What does your boss get out of it?" Evie asked. The question came out harsher than she intended and Kit hissed under her breath, "Be nice."

Evie didn't take her eyes off One. He looked over and stared her down. "Lachlan is a good man. He's taken this city and rebuilt it into a place where people can actually live. He started the power plant going again, and he's given people jobs."

"And he does this all out of the kindness of his heart?" Evie couldn't help herself; she wanted to challenge the big man.

"He does it because he wants to see our civilization rebuilt. Judge his motives for yourself, but right now he is offering you a haven. Here we are."

Chapter Four

One turned the truck into a square courtyard. At the end of the paved expanse was a building that stood out for its sheer size and beauty. Built in a faded cream brick, with a classic Victorian façade, the building soared above the concrete apartment blocks. Two wings stood on either side of the main building and decorative ledges marked each floor. The windows, all framed with decorative wrought iron, were ablaze. Small white lights — the kind used to trim the outside of houses at Christmas — silhouetted the entire front of the building.

The portico light flooded out over the red carpet leading up to the wooden front doors, carved in intricate detail. Near the top of the building, two words were lit up like an old-fashioned movie theatre, spelling out The Grand. The building was so majestic, so over the top, so clean, it didn't belong in its squalid surroundings. It looked as if it was still waiting for the jet-setting crowd to swan in.

The girls disentangled themselves and got out of the truck, blinking in the lights as they craned their necks to take it all in.

One chuckled. Evie gave him a sharp look, trying to see if he was making fun of them.

"As you can see, it's called The Grand," he said. "It used to be a hotel."

"I remember," she said. "I had heard about it, but I've never been here. It was supposed to be the nicest place to stay in Greater Havern."

"Movie stars and royalty would stay here," One agreed. "Now it's mostly a private residence and a gathering place. New City administration happens here as well. Think of it as the city hall. As I said, it's also used as a refugee shelter for anyone who needs a place to stay."

Kit was still twirling around under the building, eyes and mouth wide as she tried to see the whole thing. One stepped away from the truck and motioned to the entrance.

"Ladies, please allow me to show you in," he said, stepping up to the door.

"Wait," Evie called. "We need all of our stuff."

One gave her a stern look. "All of that will be taken care of for you. We always want to ensure you're as comfortable as possible here." He acted as if this was still a hotel. Evie gave him a level look.

"And I would be most comfortable if I had all my stuff with me."

"I can assure you that everything will be brought up for you. We don't steal here in New City."

"And I can assure you that ever since the Sickness, any assurance I've ever gotten has meant jack, so I'll be taking my stuff now."

"Evie," Kit hissed under her breath.

One didn't take his eyes off Evie. "And the truck?"

"What of it?"

"Well, I was going to arrange to have it taken to the underground garages. Or would you like to bring it up to your rooms as well?"

Evie narrowed her eyes. "Don't be ridiculous. I'll drive the truck to the garage myself."

One sighed this time. "That won't be possible. Lachlan insists that his employees park the vehicles and that all of his guests enter through the front doors. That would include you."

"What if we don't want to stay here?" Evie squared her shoulders.

Kit grabbed her sister's arm and said, "Listen, Evie, I think we should stay here. It seems nice, and he said it's safe. Where else are we going to go?"

One gave her a derisive smile. "Yes, Evie. Where else are you going to go?"

Evie relented, taking out all the bags from the truck by herself and piling them around her feet. The bags from the cab, filled with their supplies from the hospital, she kept closest. The biggest sticking point was when One saw the hunting rifles and canisters of gasoline.

"Ah, yes, these are going to be a problem," he said, not without satisfaction, Evie noted. "You see, no one is permitted firearms in New City."

"What? How do people protect themselves?" Evie asked, indignant at the thought.

"Well, I'm sure you can hang on to that crowbar if it makes you feel tough." One looked down at the weapon Evie still held. She glared at him.

"Why is that? Where do all the guns go?"

"They are dismantled and the parts are used to make useful products. The reason, if you haven't figured that out yet, is that once the Sickness hit, there was anarchy. Mass looting, theft, rape, murder," One expanded, warming to the subject. "There can be no order if every man and woman can kill you as soon as say hello. Lachlan instituted the law that no firearms are permitted within city limits. You'll see, it's made the city a much safer place."

"Why don't I feel any safer?" Evie muttered.

Kit piped up, "What about the gasoline canisters? Those are safe enough. Provided they don't catch fire or anything," she corrected herself.

"Gasoline is so precious that it has become public property," One explained. "You need a permit to use it. It's all stored in one place."

"Let me guess," Evie said. "All right here at The Grand. What is this, a commune?"

"Really, Evie, what did you expect? As you can imagine, this really is the best place for anyone to be. It has all the amenities." One gave her a smile, but it didn't reach his eyes this time. "Now, ladies, if I can escort you in. I will park your truck for you later, safe underground, until you need it again," he said, over Evie's objections. "Please, come in."

Burdened by their bags, the girls trudged up the steps. One held the door, bowing them in with a mocking gesture. Evie stuck out her chin as she passed him.

The lobby was as luxurious as the exterior. Dark hardwood floors were scattered with antique rugs of blue and gold, woven with elaborate patterns. They were so soft and deep Evie felt her feet sinking as she trod on them. She looked across the cavernous space, past the intimate groups of plush blue velvet chairs and the unmanned reception desk to a white marble staircase that swept up to the second storey. Her eyes took in every detail of the curlicued railings that edged the balcony and of the gold trim on the ornate plaster ceiling. She marvelled at the luxury. She had never been in such a place. She shut her mouth when she realized it was hanging open.

It was spectacular, but it was empty.

"Where is everyone?" she asked, trepidation in her voice. She could hear music coming from deeper in the building, a deep rhythmic bass she could feel reverberating in her chest.

"That's for you to find out," One said, his growly voice full of amusement. "Now, you girls be good and wait here. Someone will come for you." With that, he headed down one of the hallways, leaving the girls alone in the posh, lonely lobby.

"What do you think?" Kit asked, her eyes huge.

"I don't know," Evie responded, feeling like a stain in the beautiful room with her laundry bags surrounding her like a pauper. "This is all a lot to take in."

"You must be the newcomers," said someone with a high nasal voice. The girls spun around, looking for the source.

A man appeared from under the balcony to the right, striding towards them with purpose. He was dressed the same as One, in a dark suit and white shirt. He was nearly as large, but the similarity ended there. He was as pale as One was dark. His hair was long and so blond it looked silver. His thin lips were indistinguishable from his pale face. Evie wondered whether his eyes had the pink cast of an albino, but she couldn't see them; they were hidden behind a pair of designer wrap-around sunglasses. His hands were encased in leather gloves.

"Another one," she breathed. "Let me guess," she called out to him. "You must be Two?"

He took no notice of her sarcastic tone. "I go by Three."

Kit smiled at him. "I'm Kit, and this is Evie. It's nice to meet —"

"I'm sure it is," Three cut her off.

Evie stepped forward. "So, what happened to Two?"

Three raised a translucent brow over his sunglasses. "Two is no longer with us. I'm here to show you to your rooms. This way."

The two girls, in a rush to follow the retreating man, tried to pick up all their bags, but Evie cried out as she twisted her hurt wrist once again. Three sighed and stopped, then came back to pick up half their luggage. The bags did not slow him down.

At the top of the marble staircase they came to a set of dramatic double doors with ivory inlay. Three opened one door and held it open. The thumping bass poured over them.

A short hallway led them to another balcony overlooking a ballroom. Evie blinked, trying to make sense of what she was seeing. She felt Kit's hand on her back.

Multi-coloured flashing lights swept the room in time to the pulsating music. The sides of the long rectangular dance floor were lined with bars where young women wearing next to nothing were serving drinks. They leaned over the bars, smiling at their customers, breasts precariously hanging out of mesh tops. Behind them were walls of liquor, lit up from behind, looking like works of art. At the far end, enormous speakers were set up, with boards of electronic equipment tied together with a confusing array of wires.

The dance floor was a crush of people, more people than Evie had ever seen in one place. They were pressed up to one another, dancing and pulsing to the music. The dancers seemed not to notice that there was no physical space around them. The impression was not of individual people, but one organism, grinding to the beat. Evie saw a few couples break away, still grinding into each other. She looked away, feeling like a voyeur, but what she saw next was also upsetting: scantily dressed women dancing on raised platforms.

Trying to hide her shock, she turned to Three and said in a neutral voice, "There must be hundreds of people here." He either didn't hear her over the music or chose to ignore her.

She was relieved when Three continued along the balcony and went through another set of doors. The music faded as they trotted along behind their silent guide, bags bumping against their sides as they struggled to keep pace.

It seemed to take forever to walk the long bright corridor. It was decorated in the same stately style as the front lobby, and the walls were lined with watercolour paintings, but there was no time to pause and admire them. When Three finally stopped in front of a bank of elevators, Evie was panting and glaring at him, although she said nothing. Kit was looking around her, bewildered by the opulence. Three pushed a button for the elevators and then stood staring at the patterned wallpaper. Without looking at them, he intoned, "Lachlan will want to meet with you, but I will show you to your rooms first. You can get settled, and when Lachlan is ready, you'll meet him."

"What if *we're* not ready to meet *him*?" Evie couldn't keep the insolent tone out of her voice. Three said nothing, just smiled at her with his tight, thin lips.

The elevator arrived with a soft ding and the gold doors slid open. They stepped inside, letting the bags spread out at their feet. Three hit the button for the seventh floor and they rode up in silence.

Their floor was indistinguishable from the one they had just left, except the carpets here were a chocolate brown. Three stopped at room 713.

"This will be your suite for now, ladies. Make yourself at home."

"Do we get keys or anything?"

Three gave his thin smile. "We don't have locks on the doors so that we can keep an eye on any undesirable activities."

"It also means that anyone could just walk in on us," Evie said, affronted. "What kind of place is this?"

"A safe one," Three simpered.

"Yah, I've heard that already. What if I don't like not having a lock on my door?"

"Then you can always leave."

"Can we?" Evie's voice was low. Her dark eyes stared into his sunglasses, wishing she could see past them.

He laughed, high and thin. "Of course you can. The door is downstairs, where you left it. You can leave any time you want. I'll be back to show you to Lachlan when he's ready, if you're still here, of course." He pushed the door open for them and walked away, still laughing.

"Evie, why are you being such a bitch?" Kit turned on her the minute they closed the door.

Evie turned on her sister and exploded. "You saw what was going on in that ballroom. All the women looked like hookers and —"

"I think you're overreacting. That's probably just the way girls dress in the city.

"What, like skin is the new post-apocalyptic style? I don't think so. I haven't liked a single person we've met here so far and something about this whole set up at the hotel seems really sketchy."

"What's our alternative?" Kit said, voice going up. "Hang out on the streets with that Ryson guy? I think we need to stick it out. We should meet Lachlan. One said he's in charge of the whole city. I'm sure he'll be able to explain everything."

"Fine," Evie muttered, knowing it would be foolish to leave.

Kit came forward and put her hands on Evie's shoulders. "Come on, let's look around. I can't wait to see running water again."

The suite was entirely predictable, but to Kit and Evie it was full of marvels. First they looked into the kitchen then moved back to the living room. It was furnished with a couch and armchairs. The centrepiece was a wood-burning fireplace. It reminded them of home.

The fireplace was surrounded by an ornate wooden mantle and side panelling. Evie thought it was a little overdone, but she couldn't help admiring the craftsmanship. She ran her fingers over the carvings then caught her breath when she felt the panelling give a little. Shifting it forward, she could see an empty hollow behind the wood. It was some sort of hidden compartment. She looked up at Kit, who had already moved on without seeing anything, and decided to keep that to herself for the time being. She followed her sister into the bedroom. It had two queen sized beds and a walk-through closet that led into a large bathroom. Kit shrieked when water came crashing out of the faucet. "Oh, feel it, Evie, it's warm! We can have showers." Kit was as excited by the flushing toilet, which Evie had to admit was a luxury she had not expected to see again.

"I guess we're rooming with each other," she said to Kit, as Kit started to open up their bags. She took a few items to the closet. "Don't unpack too much. We're not staying long."

Kit frowned at her. "I don't see why we wouldn't take advantage of a place like this when it's being offered to us."

Evie shifted, looking around at the room. "Like I said, I just don't trust anyone here."

"Oh, you don't say," Kit snapped, then softened her tone. "We need to trust somebody, sometime. We can't do this all alone. And look at everything we've been given."

"That's just it," Evie said. "I'm wondering what the catch is."

"Why can't you just trust people?" Kit turned and walked into the bathroom. "I'm going to take a hot shower, in case this Lachlan comes looking for us. I'll want to look my best, of course."

Evie's lips curled into a wry smile. She felt a restless energy pass through her and she started to roam around the suite. She went into the kitchen and ran the water cool, filling a glass for herself. "This doesn't suck," she admitted to herself.

The small fridge was still stocked as a mini-bar, with tiny bottles of alcohol and oversized chocolate bars that probably once cost a fortune. She took some chocolate out with a thought to eating it later, when her stomach wasn't churning with anxiety.

Walking back into the living room, the plush carpet under her bare feet, she eyed the television with interest. It flashed to life when she flicked it on, but it showed nothing but channel after channel of static. Apparently, New City did not have a TV station yet. She shrugged and walked to the floor-to-ceiling windows. She looked out at the dark and dirty streets and shuddered. Maybe Kit was right, she should try to trust people. If they had not trusted One, they would still be driving around those mean streets, easy prey to packs of men.

Kit was still humming in the shower, so Evie wandered back over to the fireplace. With careful hands, she felt all over the wooden mantle, pushing and prodding with her fingertips. As far as she could tell, there was only one loose panel. She pressed in the right place and it swung inwards, revealing a space the size of a small cupboard. It was deep enough that she could reach her whole arm in without hitting the back. The walls of the space were cement, cool to the touch.

With as much haste as she could manage with a hurt wrist, she grabbed the two hospital laundry bags filled with medications and emptied them onto the hearth. Then she arranged the contents along the back of the hiding space, box after box forming towers and rows. The lines were so straight they looked like little soldiers. She closed the panel, checking that the small hinges were undetectable. Pressing her palms against the mantle, she wondered whether the men who ran the hotel were aware of the hiding place. She couldn't even trust this one secret.

Taking the other two laundry bags, filled with medical supplies like bandages and syringes, she spread their contents over the four bags, so it wasn't obvious she had emptied two of them. All of the drugs were hidden from sight. She turned away as Kit came out of the bedroom with a towel wrapped around her head. "What are you doing?" she asked.

Evie looked up with innocent eyes. "What do you mean?"

"I mean, you're going to meet this Lachlan guy, the head of the city, looking like that?"

Evie tossed what remained of her hair back. "What are you trying to say?"

"I'm trying to say you look like a homeless street urchin."

Evie was about to respond when there was a loud knock at their door.

Chapter Five

Evie rushed to the door, wanting to open it herself, not liking the idea that anyone could just walk into their room. Waiting in the corridor, hands clasped behind his back, was One, looking even larger in the elegant hotel than he had on the streets.

"I've taken care of your truck — it's parked downstairs. Here are the keys." He held them out to her and she snatched them out of his hand.

"What about our guns?" Evie asked, unable to keep the sharpness from her tone.

"They have been put in a safe place."

"What if I want to keep them?"

"You don't have a permit to carry firearms."

Evie was about to argue, but he cut her off. "You'll need to speak to Lachlan about that. Which, incidentally, is why I'm here. He wants to see you now."

"Oh, he summoned, did he?"

One just took a step back from the door, inviting them to follow. Kit went out first, giving Evie a look that said *be nice*. Evie closed the door tight behind her, wishing there was a way she could lock it. She didn't put it past One and his cronies to search the room as soon as they were gone, looking for other things that weren't permitted in this city. She was worried that her stash would be discovered. Perhaps all the rooms had secret cupboards in the fireplace so they would know where to look. The drugs were her safety net, something she could use to trade. She couldn't bear to think she would lose them.

They followed One down the corridor. It was lit by electric sconces that cast an eerie orange glow reminiscent of torchlight. One stopped in front of the elevators, pressing the up button.

"Do many people live in the hotel?" Kit asked him, hoping to start a pleasant conversation.

"Quite a few," he rumbled without looking at her.

"Who were all the people in the ballroom?" Evie wanted to know.

"The good people of New City."

"Do they all live here?"

"Do you two always ask this many questions?" he shot back at her. "Some live at The Grand and some don't, but they all come here to the nightclub to have a good time."

"But why —"

One cut Evie off. "Look, don't you want to have a good time? People come here to have fun, and to forget. Lachlan thinks that everyone who survived the Sickness has been through a lot, and they deserve to forget every now and then."

"And Lachlan just lets people party here."

He looked down at her, amused. His smile chilled Evie. "Every person pays for the privilege of enjoying Lachlan's hospitality," he said as the elevator slid open and he stepped into it. "You'd be best to remember that."

The girls followed him in and he hit the top button.

The doors opened not into another corridor but into a luxurious office. An enormous oak desk stood in front of floor-to-ceiling windows. The velvet drapes were open, showing the starlit sky. In the middle of the room, two delicate chaise lounges upholstered in saffron silk sat facing each other. The walls were panelled in a dark cherry wood. As Evie stepped onto the plush maroon carpet, she again felt her feet sink into the thickness.

Sitting behind the desk, giving off a vital sense of power, a man watched them with a stern look. He was large, although not as immense as One and Three.

He stood as they entered, showing off a sophisticated three-piece charcoal suit and grey shirt. As stylishly as he was dressed, it was clear there were well-used muscles being constrained underneath his clothes. He was too rugged to be handsome, his features harsh and bulky yet somehow still appealing. Clean shaven with a ruddy skin tone, he had very short brown hair, showing the beginning of a receding hairline. Evie guessed he was in his late thirties. His presence filled the room, leaving Evie wishing she could leave and be allowed to breathe again. She felt Kit press in closer to her, arm to arm.

As the girls were sizing him up, Lachlan was inspecting them. His stare was so intense, Evie fought the urge to hide. Finally, he seemed satisfied. Adjusting his silver cufflinks, he smiled then gestured for them to sit down.

"These are the newcomers, then?" His voice was deep and well-modulated. "Make yourselves comfortable. I love to meet all the new people who come to my city."

Evie and Kit sat in the leather chairs facing his desk. Evie perched at the edge, while Kit sank back into hers, arms crossed over her chest. Glancing back, Evie saw One standing by the elevator, hands clasped in front of him, face impassive.

"Now, I understand you've had quite the adventure getting into the city. Set upon by a gang?" The girls nodded and he sighed, shaking his head. "It's terrible what people have become. There's no need for civility to fall apart. We're all of us survivors of the Sickness — we should be coming together, not attacking one another."

One spoke to Lachlan while motioning to the girls. "They might have been okay. This one here faced down six men with nothing but a crowbar."

"Did she really?" Lachlan's gaze fell on Evie with interest. "That was very brave of you, my dear. I'm sorry, we haven't been introduced properly."

He stood and came around to the front of the desk, standing just in front of Evie's chair. The feeling that she couldn't breathe intensified. *Too close, too close,* something in her brain was screaming at her.

He held out a large hand, dressed with silver rings, large heavy ones on his first three fingers. "I'm Lachlan."

Evie reached up to take it. Her small white hand disappeared into his as he held it with steady pressure. "I'm Evie. And this is my sister Kit."

"Ah, Kit." He reached out to take her hand. Evie saw that Kit touched him with only her fingertips. Evie risked a searching look at her sister. She was much quieter than normal. Kit's eyes were fixed on Lachlan's face. "Both of you such beautiful girls, and sisters. How lucky for both of you to have each other." He turned back to Evie. "You must have strong survival instincts to still be around after all that happened. One tells me you have been on your own for a year. So what on earth were you doing taking on six men with a crowbar?"

Evie shrugged. "Seemed like the thing to do. We weren't exactly given much choice in the matter."

Lachlan threw his head back and gave a crowing laugh. "Seemed like the thing to do? How fantastic. I can see how you've gotten along." Still chuckling, he looked down at her. "Are you all right? Hurt in any way?"

"I'm fine," she said, at the same time that One responded that she hurt her wrist.

"That won't do. Let me see it." Lachlan held out his hands. "It's all right," he said when she hesitated, "Before the Sickness, I was a doctor. I suppose I still am, although other priorities have taken me away from my first profession. I can set you straight in no time."

Evie placed her wrist in his hands. He jerked her hand back, sending a flare of pain up her arm. She gasped at the intensity of it. Lachlan didn't even notice, pressing on her wrist with bruising force.

"Doesn't seem to be broken, lucky you, but that's a nasty sprain. I'll wrap that up as soon as I can."

Evie took her arm back, cradling it against her. "It's fine. I can take care of it."

Lachlan's eyes sharpened. They were light brown with flecks of green. "Don't be ridiculous. I said I would do it."

Uncertain, Evie gave a little nod. He relaxed and moved back behind his desk. "Well, I think as a welcome we should all have a drink. May I offer you some whiskey?"

He went over to the cabinet built into the wall next to his desk and took out a decanter filled with amber liquid. He poured a large drink in one of the glasses and looked up at Evie. She was surprised to see a challenge in his eyes.

She raised her chin. "Sure, that sounds great."

He smiled. "And how about you, Kit?"

Evie shifted in her seat, frowning at Kit. She still wasn't comfortable with her younger sister drinking. "I'm fine," Kit said in a small voice.

Pouring an equally large drink for Evie, he brought it over to her. Taking it in her unhurt hand, she brought it up to clink against his offered glass. With a smug look, he wandered back around to his chair and again sat across from them.

Evie took a sip of the liquid. It was strong and tasted like smoke. She felt the heat of it slide down her throat to her belly, warming her. Her eyes closed and she smiled. She looked up to see Lachlan giving her an approving look.

"I see you're a woman with fine taste."

Evie took another sip. "Hardly. We're from up north, far north. There's not much to drink up there other than what people have made in their garages, like moon shine. This isn't as strong as that, but tastes much better."

He gave another crowing laugh. "I'm glad it meets with your approval. It's often too strong for many of the girls staying here."

Evie leaned forward and set the glass on the desk, her head a little spinny from the drink. "We saw some of the girls here tonight. The servers in the club. They seemed to be, um, dressed for a good time."

"You saw the club did you?" Lachlan gave One a small frown. "Well, I don't police what the residents wear when they are working. What we really want to do is make sure that people are entertained. We've all earned the right to that. Don't you think?"

"I thought it looked a little shady."

Lachlan turned his hard look on her and she gave her head a shake, wondering what she was thinking. "I'm really thankful that One saved us tonight and that you are giving us a place to stay, but I'm not really sure we can stay for long. We haven't decided exactly what we're doing yet. This is the first civilization we've seen in nearly a year."

He set his glass down as well, mirroring her body language. He looked serious now. "Evie, I understand what you're saying. We're not trying to keep you here against your will. I can assure you it is your safest option, but if it makes you uncomfortable, you are entirely free to leave. I suggest you at least spend the night here to rest and recuperate. Tomorrow I'll fix up your wrist and you can be on your way — if that's how you feel in the morning. Many people in New City enjoy the protection and relative luxury of The Grand."

"Don't get me wrong, it's beautiful here. It's just, I have no way of paying you back."

He gave her a gentle smile. "It's not about payment. People are welcome to stay here. I've had the good fortune of coming into this property since the Sickness. I can assure you that it is safe and that you'll be taken care of."

"Then how does the whole thing work?"

"Everyone pitches in. We all work together to make this a wonderful place to live."

Evie took another sip. "It sounds really nice. So, if we stayed, would you give *us* work?"

Lachlan's smile took on an edge. "You would want to work for me?"

"Of course. I mean, if we do decide to stay here, of course we'd want to pitch in to earn our keep, just like everyone else."

"Well, I'm happy to hear it." He set his glass down. "I'm sure we could find something for you to do. But for now, please don't even think of it. For the moment, you are my guests. You've earned it after your ordeal."

Evie gave him an uncertain smile, wondering what the "something" would be.

The phone on Lachlan's desk rang, making Evie jump. She hadn't heard a phone ring in a long time. Lachlan picked it up and listened for a moment then said, "All right. Bring him up." He hung up with a satisfied smile. He looked to One. "It's James, he's been apprehended. Three is bringing him up."

One looked more grim than usual. "Shall I show the ladies out?"

Lachlan's gave the girls a perfunctory glance. "It's been a pleasure, but I have some unfortunate business to attend to."

Kit stood up as if to leave but turned back to him and said, "So, like, are you the mayor?" Evie noticed Kit's voice was deeper and softer than normal.

"What was that, my dear?" he said, seeming as though he wished the girls would leave now he had other business to attend to.

"You seem to be in charge of the city. How does that work, exactly?"

A slight roll of his shoulder indicated it was of no major concern, but he was giving Kit his full attention again now. "Well, I would say that over the year I've gradually developed a place of leadership in New City, certainly. I've spearheaded some major development projects that have added to everyone's safety and comfort. You have me to thank for the electricity. I've gotten the hydroelectric plant up and running again. It brings power to most of the old city's core, which makes up what is now New City. I won't take all the credit for it, though, many other people helped me. We are all happy we have been able to bring some comfort to our fellow survivors."

"Did you organize the body dumps outside the city?"

"Excuse me?" Lachlan was surprised at the question.

"The body piles, outside the city. People were burned there. Did you do that?"

"I did." His eyes narrowed and he pressed his lips into a thin line. He seemed to be reappraising her. "I was acting chief medical officer of Greater Havern General Hospital at the time. Once it became clear that I was not going to succumb to the Sickness, survivors looked to me in matters of the health of our population. Grisly as the body piles are, they are nothing close to the sight of a city lined with corpses. I'm sure I don't have to tell you how dangerous it would have been to let the bodies rot. We couldn't risk more disease."

"Were they even dead yet?" Kit asked, so quiet Evie could barely hear her.

"Kit! What kind of a question is that?" she hissed at her sister.

Lachlan grimaced. "I know it's been an exceptionally hard day for both of you. You need to rest. Things will look better in the morning, they always do." He stood up and walked towards the elevator, indicating that the interview was over.

The elevator dinged and the doors swished open to show Three gripping the arm of a younger man whose hands were cuffed. Three pushed his ward into the office. The scruffy young man stumbled then righted himself, looking up at Lachlan with a feral grin. "Lachlan. Wonderful to see you again," he said, giving a comical bow.

Lachlan seemed furious, glaring at the man. "I wish I could say the same for you, James."

One walked forward and gave the young man another shove, causing him to fall to one knee with a grunt.

Evie and Kit looked at each other in alarm. Who was this James and what had he done to deserve such treatment? They had not expected to see any violence in these gracious surroundings. Evie instinctively pulled Kit back. She stared at the reluctant guest as he righted himself. Tall, but much slimmer than the other men, James wasn't much older than Evie. Dark tangled hair was tied back from his face with a piece of string. Torn jeans sat low over his hips and a black leather jacket sat crooked over his shoulders. The two bright scarves looped around his neck seemed incongruous against his sombre, rumpled clothes; they were pristine and looked expensive. He stood with a cocky arrogance, still grinning up at Lachlan like a dare.

Lachlan turned to the girls. "I'm sorry you had to see this. Being in a leadership role sometimes means dealing with the unpleasant aspects of society. Please, leave now, make yourselves comfortable. One will show you to the kitchens if you're hungry." He stopped the big man as he turned to go. "But, One, Keep them away from the general riff-raff that sometimes gets into the hotel. I wouldn't want them to get the wrong idea."

One looked uncertain but gave him a nod.

Evie turned to Lachlan. "Is there anything in particular we should avoid in the hotel?"

He turned back to her, his eyes kind. "After the Sickness, people tended to be a little less civilized than they used to be, as I'm sure you can imagine." He looked James up and down with a baleful eye. "Sometimes they get a little rowdy, that's all, and I wouldn't want that to be your first impression of The Grand. Not on your first night here."

James snorted. He was white and strained, as if ready for a fight, but bright dark eyes looked at her with such curiosity he reminded her of a bird. Straight as a razor, his nose was a little too long, but a full mouth softened the hawkish look. He winked at her. Evie blushed, turning away.

Kit crept around James and walked into the elevator without saying a word. Evie was about to follow but turned back to face Lachlan.

"You're not going to *hurt* him, are you?" she asked in a soft voice.

Both Lachlan and James turned to her in surprise. James gave her a wide wicked smile. "Don't worry about me, love. I can take care of myself."

"No, Evie, we're not going to hurt him. He just owes me something that needs to be repaid."

"Okay." Evie's eyes were very serious. "Thank you for everything."

"See you tomorrow."

There was something taunting in Lachlan's voice that sent a chill down her spine.

James was still watching her, his mocking expression mixed with something else. "Listen," he called to them as they stepped into the elevator. "Don't —"

The last thing she saw before the doors closed was One stepping forward and striking James across the face, cutting him off. Lachlan continued to hold her gaze until the doors closed.

Chapter Six

Evie ignored One and his superior smile as they rode the elevator; her eyes were riveted on her sister. Kit's face was drawn and white, and she wasn't her bright, bubbly self. Evie was dying to ask Kit what was troubling her but didn't want to say anything in front of One.

When they got off the elevator, One led them towards the back of the hotel. "The kitchens are over here. Cooks come in most days to prepare for the functions and they always leave food for everyone to snack on. You'll be able to find something to eat any time of the day or night," he said, with a glance at Evie's thin frame.

"That would be nice," she said.

They walked in through swinging double doors to the back of an institutional kitchen that seemed to stretch the length of the hotel. The only illumination, apart from dim strip lights along the floor, was from a huge fridge with glass doors. The girls ogled the cafeteria-style shelves filled with plates of cheese, sliced beef, fruit, drinks, and baskets of bread.

"You can help yourself, but try to leave some for the rest of us." One sounded bored. "Residents often come in late for snacks. The booze is along the side in the cabinets. You can have as much as you like. Now, can you find your way back to your suite?"

The girls nodded in silence. With a final smirk, One turned to go. "Don't go wandering too far. We wouldn't want you to end up in trouble already."

Evie turned to Kit as soon as the heavy doors swung closed behind him. "Are you okay? You look awful."

Kit looked at Evie and stammered, "You were right, Evie. This isn't a good place."

"What do you mean? You were all rah-rah hot water before, telling me it was safe and comfortable and better than being on the streets."

"But there's something about Lachlan that's off. I can guarantee it. He frightens me," Kit said in a shaky voice. Then, looking around at the kitchen full of free food she added, "And look at all this. Maybe I'm just used to things being harder. At least when we had to steal our food, I knew where it was coming from. This all seems … a little too convenient."

"Since when does the queen of hot baths have a problem with convenience?" Evie said. Her stomach grumbling, she turned to the food. She grabbed some bread and beef, holding them out in front of her. "Look at this. When was the last time we saw meat? It will be good for us; we can get healthy. We're definitely not going to starve here."

"Fine, I'm not going to argue that it's a good set up," Kit said, finally following suit and finding a cold cola in the fridge. "I already told you that, and I haven't changed my mind, but what's Lachlan getting out of all this generosity, and why is he so interested in us?"

"He's being civilized," Evie said, mocking Lachlan's pompous tone. Kit laughed and choked on her cola. Evie continued in a more serious tone. "Look, Kit. I think I was wrong to say we should take off right away. I was in panic mode and it was a kneejerk reaction. I don't trust Lachlan either, and his lackeys are beyond scary, but he doesn't have any reason to hurt us. I think we should stay until we've had a chance to explore New City and find out if there's anywhere else to live and work. It might take a couple of days. Are you okay with that?"

Kit did not reply. Instead, she put a slice of roast beef onto a hunk of bread and bit into it like a savage. She sighed around the bread. "Oh, that's good. It's dry and it's still good." As soon as she had devoured the sandwich, she looked at her sister and smiled. "Wow, did both of us ever just change our minds. My question is which one of us is being the reasonable one right now? I guess I'm okay with staying for a while. Let's make the most of this while we can," she said, reaching for more bread and cheese.

Evie gave Kit a hug then pulled out a jug of milk. Examining it, she whispered, "I think this is fresh." She poured some into a glass and took such a deep swallow she almost gagged on the creamy liquid. "Wow, I was not ready for that," she said, wiping her lips. "That is really rich."

"You better drink more than that if you want to get any flesh on those bones of yours," said a smooth voice from the front of the kitchen. Both Kit and Evie turned, squinting into the darkness at the form coming towards them. "Starvation is just not in anymore. Haven't you heard? Men like a little something to hold onto, a woman with real curves."

Her low, rich voice was like honey, which matched her looks. As the girls distinguished her from the darkness, they saw she was one of the most beautiful women they had ever seen in real life. Her skin was the colour of dark roast coffee. Her black hair was in tight curls and pulled back, with some of the front pieces loosened and floating around her face. Her almond eyes were a shade of warm amber.

She was wearing a short layered dress in fiery reds and oranges, with matching red stilettos that displayed her long, graceful legs. Tall and statuesque, she was showing off more than enough of the womanly curves she was talking about.

"Hi there, honeys, I'm Millie," she said as she sashayed over to the floor-to-ceiling liquor cabinet filled with bottles. She opened it and took out a large bottle of clear liquid. Taking the top off, she took a long swig. She smacked her lips and came over to inspect them. "So, you new around here? You look it, but I hadn't heard that anyone had come in. Nobody's come to the city for months, so I expect you'll be big news," she said to Evie, looking her up and down with open curiosity. Not hostile, but not warm either.

With her starved skinny figure, rumpled two-day old clothes and scuffed skater shoes, Evie felt clumsy and childish next to this elegant woman. Millie turned her attention to Kit and gave a little smile. "Both of you such pretty girls. Definitely big news."

"What do you mean?" Kit asked, putting down her food as if it had gone bad.

"Nothing, honey. It's just that men like pretty girls. There's nothing wrong with that, is there?" She hummed to herself while waiting for an answer.

"Do you work here?" Evie asked, wondering about Lachlan's comment that everyone pitched in.

Millie snorted. "For as long as I can remember, it seems."

"Are you a waitress at that club?" Evie eyed her outlandish outfit.

"Yup. Lachlan gave me a job as a waitress. Funny the things that people have decided are important since the Sickness. Right now it's lots of booze and short skirts." She took another long slug from the bottle and turned to leave, wobbling on her heels. This wasn't the first drink she'd had that day. She left with the bottle. "Ta-ta to you both. I'm sure I'll be seeing you around." With a flippant wave over her shoulder, Millie was swallowed up by the blackness.

Kit looked at Evie with wide eyes. "Yikes. You think everyone who works here is like that? You know, I don't think I want to find out tonight. Let's go upstairs."

Evie agreed but grabbed more bread and cheese. "We'll be hungry tomorrow. We have to get our strength up." Each with an armful of food, they headed back out the way they came. Kit paused to grab a handful of chips and candy that were sitting out on the countertop, making Evie snort.

Once back in their suite, Evie threw everything on the table then dragged a chair towards the door, propping it under the door handle.

"Does that really work?" Kit asked.

Evie shrugged. "At the very least, we'll know if anyone comes in."

The girls got ready for bed in silence. Evie jumped into the shower, enjoying her first taste of hot water in ages. She stayed in way too long, letting the water pound onto her, warming every inch of her skin. There were little soaps everywhere, the kind you would expect in a fancy hotel, and she used each of them, smiling at the feeling of being clean and smelling good.

By the time she slipped into her bed, Kit was curled up under the blankets in the other. The sheets were clean and warm, but Evie couldn't find a comfortable position. She shifted to one side then the other, finally ending up on her back staring at the ceiling. "What are we doing?" she whispered to the blank white space.

"It'll be okay," came the whisper from the other bed. "It's been worse."

Evie remained silent, thinking back over the past year. *It's been much worse than this*, she thought. Unwanted images drifted past her closed eyes, taking on a life of their own as she drifted into uneasy sleep.

Shuddering with cold in front of a fire that wouldn't light; willing herself to stop shaking. Pressing her forehead to an icy glass window, tracing idle patterns into the frost, looking blind out into the white of the storm. Of course it was going to storm. *Her breath forming a patch of fog that grew with each exhalation.* We should have been better prepared. What did we expect? *Something catching her eye in the blowing snow.*

She shifted in the bed, trying to wake up before sinking back into the dream.

Listening, quiet, tense for no reason. Under the roar of the wind, the whine of snowmobiles.

People! It's been months.

Voices floating up from the white — male and laughing. Or was it a trick of the wind?

Men in high-tech outdoor gear, faces covered by goggles and beards grizzled with snow. Yelling at her, laughing. Kit pleading.

Glass spraying out over the front porch. Glass shards lost in the snow and ice. The numb disbelief and the never-ending cold.

Gloved fists, embedded with metal.

The sound of a fist against wood broke into her consciousness. "No!" Evie yelled, ripping herself out of her nightmare. She was sitting bolt upright, tangled in her sheets from the overnight thrashing around. Cold sweat covered her, causing goose bumps to rise on her uncovered arms.

She heard a knock at the door, the startling sound that had woken her. She looked around, confused. The large window to her side showed the sun was barely up and her sister was still asleep in the bed next to her. Memories of the previous night flooded back to her — driving to New City, seeing the lights, being attacked. Finding themselves in this strange luxury hotel that housed refugees from the Sickness.

Standing, she tried to shake off the nightmare that stalked her. She walked over to the door, moving the chair carefully so it didn't scrape on the floor. The knocking had turned to pounding. The sound made her shudder. She opened the door and peeked out.

Three stood there looking annoyed. He was dressed the same as the night before, in a black suit. His white hair stood out against the collar. He wasn't wearing sunglasses this morning, and Evie could see that his eyes were as colourless as his hair — they looked like glass. She drew back, averting her eyes.

He smiled at her discomfort. "Lachlan is ready to see you."

"Now?" she said. "I'm not ready to see him."

"Lachlan doesn't like to be kept waiting." The smug amusement was still on his face.

"Well, I don't like being summoned to see people while I'm in my pyjamas, so he's just going to have to." She shut the door in his face.

Stumbling back into the bedroom, Evie rustled through her bag for some proper clothing to wear, coming up with a pair of clean jeans and a grey sweater. She pulled them on as Kit woke up, blinking sleep out of her eyes. She looked confused as to where they were then took in the fact that Evie was dressed. "Where are you going?" she asked, her voice still hoarse from sleep.

"To see Lachlan," she whispered. "Three is at the door."

"Oh, Evie, no." Kit sat straight up in bed. "I don't think you should go."

Evie smiled at her sister's dishevelled appearance, avoiding her worried eyes. "It will be fine. Besides, I don't think I have much of a choice. We can't just ignore him while we're staying in his hotel. It will just be for a few days, remember."

"I'm going to do my best to ignore him," Kit grumbled.

"Don't let anyone in. Put the chair back under the door as soon as I'm gone. I'll knock to get back in." Evie turned to leave.

"Evie? Be careful."

Evie gave her sister a smile. "When am I not?" Her smile faded and became a scowl as she left the room. She didn't say another word to Three as he walked her down the hallway towards the elevators. He ignored her as they rode to the top floor then held a hand out for her to exit. The office was empty and Three didn't follow her. "Wait here," he said. "Lachlan will be back shortly." The doors closed, leaving Evie alone in the elegant room.

Feeling restless, she paced the room, feet padding across the plush carpet. Most of the panelled walls of the rooms contained bookshelves or closed cabinets. The elevator was cleverly hidden in the wooden inlay, the doorway concealed unless you knew what you were looking for. Glancing at the other blank walls, she wondered what was hiding behind them.

Nosiness overcame her mounting anxiety, and she started to explore the room. Passing each wood panel, she pressed and prodded, not sure what to expect. When she was at one side of the office, a door on the opposite side opened to reveal Lachlan. She let her hands drop.

He frowned at her. "What are you doing?"

"What?" she said, hoping to not anger him. "I ... was pacing. I get restless. I'm not really one for being cooped up indoors."

"You prefer to have the run of things, do you?" There was a gleam in his eye that made Evie feel uncomfortable. She remained silent.

"Well, no matter. Come over here. I want to have a closer look at your wrist." He was holding some bandages, which he then set down on the desk. Evie winced, remembering the bruising force he used the night before, and her slim hand encircled her wrist protectively. But she moved towards him. He looked into her eyes and smiled. "Don't worry, I'm not going to hurt you," he said.

Once again Evie got the feeling that he was too close. She nodded, eyes lowered. His hands were gentler this morning, turning her wrist this way and that in careful movements. It was more mottled and bruised than before, and swollen to twice the size it should have been.

"You have limited mobility, but I think it's just a sprain. I'm going to tape it up. All you can do is rest and ice it. Can you handle that?"

She shrugged. "I'm not very good with the resting part, but if you have actual freezers here I can definitely ice it."

He laughed. "Of course we have freezers. I'll have some ice sent up to you, but you can always help yourself to ice and whatever else you want from the kitchen. I trust One told you that when he took you there last night?" Evie nodded, although her stomach grumbled at the thought of food.

"Sorry for getting you up so early," he said, bent over her wrist at his task. "I'm usually up before the sun rises and I forget that not everyone likes an early start to the day. How are you finding the accommodations?"

Forcing herself to sound enthusiastic and grateful, she gushed, "It's really incredible. The way we've been living, it's nothing compared to this. I'm sure you can imagine. No running water, no electricity. No heat." She shivered at the memory.

"I think New City might be one of the few places in the world now that has a consistent supply of power," he said, his voice smug. "I'll allow myself a little bit of pride in saying that it is largely due to me." He straightened up and let go of Evie's wrist, bound tight and feeling more stable now. "Come, I'd like to show you something." He walked over to the wall of windows where sunlight had begun to pour in.

The view from the top of the hotel was spectacular in daylight. At this height there were no dull grey building to obstruct the view of the river. A large park sat between the hotel and the water. It looked as though the grass had long since died under the trample of feet. The middle of the park was dotted with brightly coloured stalls.

The embankment was lined with wooden docks, busy and full with barges and boats. It was clearly a working river, with burly men already unloading and loading crates. Bonfires lit in metal cans were crackling both on the docks and the ships.

Lachlan brought her attention to the east of the river, past the crowded buildings. The massive industrial building set on the southern bank of the river allowed the water to pass through with a crash of mist on the other side.

"That's the hydroelectric plant. Greater Havern used it to produce sustainable energy, using the flow of the river as a power source. It was abandoned at the time of the Sickness. As I mentioned last night, when it became clear to me that our society had been demolished by the Sickness, I took it on myself to organize the people to get it running again. With this plant, New City has electricity, and it's sustainable."

"That's very impressive," Evie said, and she meant it. Watching the enormous building and thinking about the machinations that must be going on inside, she wondered at what it would take to run a plant of that size, capable of producing the energy that supported them all. "Why did you want to make the city run?"

"Well, it doesn't make sense to live in a city that doesn't function, does it? Nobody else took the initiative to get things working, so I stepped in," he said, with a careless wave of his hand. He walked to his desk and Evie followed, sitting down across from him. "Having energy means that I live in a comfortable home, and so can everyone else. It gives jobs to people who need to be a part of society again. It also allows us those little luxuries that we dearly miss. A fine bottle of wine is easy to find nowadays, but a hot shower has become priceless."

"And nobody has to pay for it?"

He sighed. "There's no money anymore, Evie. It simply doesn't exist. But as I said, everyone pitches in to help. We use a barter system. It's basic but it works. I provide a necessary service to the good people of New City. In return, they provide the city with the goods and services needed, when they are needed. You can see there's a thriving trading business around the river. Our citizens bring in supplies from the surrounding countryside, where farms survived or are being re-established. It's a good arrangement that works well for everyone. It's simple supply and demand."

Evie shifted in her seat. "Well, if I am a part of New City, then what can I do to help?"

Lachlan raised his eyebrows and seemed on the verge of a smile. "What is it that you're good at, Evie?"

The question stumped her. In nineteen years, she'd learned to care for the dying and siphon gas. It wasn't much of a resume. "I used to be good at numbers," she said after an awkward pause.

He beamed at her. "I'm certain you'll be able to provide me with a very valuable service."

"What do the others do?"

"Everyone works together to ensure that the hotel is organized and efficient. There are chefs to cook meals for the residents, people that go to the market for our food, and others who clean the rooms. Many of the residents have remarkable artistic talents and help to make clothing or decorate for some of our more extravagant parties. One of the girls here used to be a set designer and you should see some of the creations she comes up with. And, of course, I employ a lot of men at the power plant — it's the main source of employment in New City. "

Evie nodded without really listening; her eyes had glazed over when Lachlan mentioned cleaners. *Did they come into the rooms at any time? Did they know about the fireplace?*

Realizing Lachlan had stopped speaking, Evie was about to respond when the elevator opened behind her. Into the room stepped a woman, taller than Evie and just as thin, with golden brown hair snaking down her back in waves.

"Lachlan, what's taking so long?" Her voice was high and sulky. She was wearing a long dress, cut low at the front, although she did not have the chest to fill it out. Instead, her clothes hung off her skinny frame, making her appear very young.

"Now's not a good time, Lia," Lachlan said with a dismissive wave of his hand, not taking his eyes off Evie.

The woman stepped towards him, her hips swaying petulantly. She was unsteady on her feet, though, and twice was in real danger of falling over. As she wobbled by, Evie saw her height was derived from the heels she was wearing, several inches higher than was safe. Lia was barely able to walk in them.

When she reached Lachlan, Lia went to stand behind him, a proprietary hand on his shoulder. Evie bit her lip when she saw her face. She was about the same age as Kit. She wore oversized clothing and had on not a stitch of makeup. The effect emphasized her youth. She looked like a child dressed up in her mother's clothes.

Lia glared at Evie with startling blue eyes. Evie could see her pupils were pinned to the point of being invisible. Evie kept her face a mask of passive interest while faced with such open hatred, but she felt pity for the girl.

Lachlan took one of Lia's hands without looking at her. "Our business is almost done, Lia. I'm assuming your wrist is okay now, Evie?"

Lia sneered over Lachlan's shoulder.

"Oh, yes," Evie shook herself. "I will go get some ice for it, but it feels much better. Thanks very much for that."

"Good. Then I want to invite you and your sister to a little brunch we're having. Go get yourself ready and be at the atrium for eleven."

"The atrium?"

He gave her a brusque smile. "It's on the top floor of the east wing. I'll see you then."

As soon as Lachlan turned his attention to Lia, she tilted her body towards him. Evie turned away, trying to hide her disgust. *He must be twice her age*, she thought as she left the office.

Chapter Seven

"So? How did it go?" Kit pounced on Evie as soon as she opened the door. Evie hooked the chair under the handle again before turning to her.

"I'm not entirely sure."

"What do you mean? Are you okay? Let me see that." Kit grabbed at Evie's bandaged wrist, making her yelp in pain.

"Ouch! Yes, I'm fine, my wrist is fine. Or was fine," she grumbled, holding it close to her with a glare at her sister.

"Sorry, I'm just a little jumpy right now. But what happened?"

Evie sat down on one of the couches in front of the fireplace. "Lachlan was just as arrogant as before. He showed me a bit of the city from his window and I think he was about to tell me how we'd be able to help out. But then this girl came in." Evie paused. "Kit, she could not have been older than you. And I'm pretty sure that they're dating, or something."

Kit wrinkled her nose. "Really? But he's so *old*."

"He's not *that* old," Evie protested. At her sister's raised eyebrow, she rolled her eyes. "I mean, he's fit for his age, I guess. But he's definitely too old for that girl. She seemed like a piece of work, and from the looks she gave me, I think she hates me. "

"So, now we know that Lachlan has a thing for young girls. One more check in the 'get the hell out' column."

"Yes," Evie said, distracted, eyeing the fireplace. "I want to show you something."

Kit gasped as Evie opened the panel of fake siding, showing her the drugs. "I took out the drugs from our hospital bags." Evie explained, brushing her fingertips over the boxes. "I don't think anyone knows about the secret panel, but I'm not sure how safe they are here. I feel certain that the room was searched last night when we were gone, but the drugs haven't been disturbed. They must have seen our other medical supplies, though."

"That was pretty smart of you. We're going to need all those supplies when we leave."

Evie gave her a look. "Umm ... *if* we leave. We still need to figure some things out, like where the hell we're going to go. But first, we have to go to this brunch."

"We're going to a brunch?" Kit shrieked. "When is this happening? Why didn't you tell me first thing? We must get ready."

No matter her misgivings about where they were staying, the news of a chance to wear something pretty perked Kit up again. Soon she was bossing Evie around, making her wear a short skirt with a flowy pink blouse rather than the jeans and T-shirt Evie had chosen. Even though she was happy to see her sister in good spirits again, Evie drew the line at wearing heels. They compromised with a pair of stylish boots. Evie felt awkward with so much of her legs showing, but Kit scolded her. "It sounds like it could be dressy. If we don't dress up we will be conspicuous. You want us to blend in, don't you?"

After many wrong turns and backtracking through the labyrinth of hallways, the girls finally found the atrium on the top floor of the east wing. The cheerful chatter of voices drifted towards them as they pushed the door open. They stood rooted to the spot as they looked around at a wide open space full of natural light. Looking way up to see a cloudless blue sky, Evie gasped at the vast skylight that covered the room, allowing the sunshine to pour through. Trees and climbing vines were displayed around benches and small seating areas, giving the impression of an elegant park. Steamy and moist, a greenhouse full of humidity, the atmosphere was perfect for the tropical plants and flowers that surrounded them. Between the trees were rough stone pathways, adding to the effect. The air was fresh and fragrant.

People milled through the trees, groups and couples mingling and moving this way and that. Voices were raised in welcome; individual bursts of laughter rang out. Some groups were boisterous, but many of the couples lingered with each other behind the limited privacy of the foliage. A waiter threaded his way through the throng with a tray of Champagne flutes; it appeared that everyone had a drink in hand.

At the centre of the sprawling room was an ornate structure reaching from the floor all the way up to the skylights. It was arranged to look like layers of elaborate netting over the windows, but a dull sheen proved that it was copper. It was a huge bird cage encircling trees and a central fountain. Birds of various sizes were flapping, squawking and soaring through the tree branches in flashes of reds, greens, yellows and silvers.

"I don't know if I've ever seen anything so beautiful in my life," Evie breathed.

"Oh my god," Kit said, matching her sister's tone. "We are so underdressed."

Evie flashed her a grin despite her tension. Leave it to Kit to worry about that.

The young women were dressed for an elegant cocktail party, wearing dresses in bold colours and elaborate hairpieces, resembling the flock of bright birds. Looking around at the girls in the room, Evie cringed. She felt so out of place. She watched as Kit pulled off the scarf that was holding her hair back then fluffed out her long blonde tresses. She then tied the scarf around her neck in a chic knot. She looked like she belonged to the beautiful people. Evie tried to smooth down the dark spikes of hair sticking up around her face without anyone noticing.

Kit's eyes widened as she looked over Evie's shoulder. Evie turned to see Lachlan approaching, looking impeccable in a three-piece black suit with a black shirt open at the collar. He was playing with his cufflinks. They twinkled in the sunlight. Evie shot her sister a look.

"Be nice," she said under her breath, "but be careful."

"I'm always nice," Kit said, a wide smile spreading across her face. "Good morning, Lachlan," she chirped at him.

Lachlan gave Kit a surprised second look but smiled back. "Good morning, Kit. How are you?"

"Much better, thanks. I was very out of sorts last night."

He gave her an understanding look and reached out to squeeze her shoulder. "I'm not surprised, what with the trauma you two went through. I'm glad you're feeling better though." He turned to Evie. "And you? How does the wrist feel?"

"Oh, it's okay." She showed him the wrapped wrist then felt silly because of course he'd already seen it. "It's holding up just fine." His gaze didn't leave her face and she looked away, uncomfortable.

"Do you know what I think you both need? A refreshing mimosa. It's the perfect drink for a sunny morning like this." He motioned to someone over her shoulder. Within seconds a waiter arrived at her elbow, offering a silver tray filled with flutes of sparking Champagne and orange juice.

The waiter was tall and thin, otherwise nondescript. He had the look that waiters have while trying to be unobtrusive, as if unaffected by the crowd around him. He wore a white suit and white gloves, like a server in a fancy restaurant.

Evie hesitated before taking a flute, it being only eleven in the morning. In her mind, it was much too early for a drink. Kit had no such compunction, sweeping a flute off the tray and taking a sip. "Oh, I haven't had Champagne in a long time," she giggled.

Rolling her eyes at her sister, who had never tasted Champagne in her life, Evie finally took one herself and watched the delicate bubbles tracing the inside of the glass. "It's been a long time since we've had anything to celebrate."

Lachlan was watching her with an amused look. "Well, then a toast to celebration," he said, bringing his glass to hers with a little clink. He then toasted Kit and tilted his glass back.

Evie brought the glass to her face, letting the fizz tickle her lips before taking a small sip. The tartness of the orange mixed with the sweet Champagne was a refreshing combination. She licked her lips and took another greedy sip. "To celebration."

Lachlan began to wander along the path, ignoring the crowd around him, focusing only on the sisters. "Well? What do you think of my atrium?"

"It's fantastic," Kit said, looking at the people rather than the vegetation.

"Evie? How about you?"

"It's stunning. I mean, it really is beautiful. So much nicer than outside." It was an unexpected delight to be surrounded by trees again, living things, instead of endless dusty plains. A surge of homesickness surprised her as a lump grew in her throat.

Lachlan gave her an understanding smile. "Does it remind you of where you're from?" She found herself blinking back tears.

"There were just … a lot of trees up north." She cleared her throat and tried to sound casual. "It already seems like a million years ago. And now here I am, in your lovely atrium." Controlling her throat and emotions, Evie looked up at him with a bland smile.

He nodded, as if he approved of her control. "I'm happy you like it."

Kit had wandered ahead on the flower-edged path, examining the people she passed. Many of them gave her interested looks, but no one approached her until Lachlan stopped one of the younger men walking by. A grey pinstripe suit gave him a certain degree of gravitas, but the effect was ruined by a patchy beard he was having trouble growing. His eyes lit up when Lachlan held up a hand to him.

"Jackson, there's someone here that I thought you'd like to meet."

Kit had turned and taken a few steps back towards them, eyeing Jackson.

"This is Kit, new to town. I was hoping that you could show her around the gardens."

Jackson gave Kit a smile and held out an arm to her. Kit gave a helpless look back at Evie, who shrugged. "Um, it's nice to meet you, Jackson." She took his arm with a strained smile. She was determined to be charming.

Jackson was already leading her away, leaning down to tell her something.

"Jackson!" Lachlan called after him. Jackson glanced back. "Behave, will you. Just show her the gardens."

The young man smiled and tipped his head.

Lachlan continued walking and Evie had to hurry to catch up to him, reluctant to take her eyes off Kit. He stopped at the birdcage. Evie's eyes were drawn up, following the path of the little birds. A particularly bright tropical bird landed on a branch close to the netting and warbled a pretty tune. Its tiny shocking blue body quivered with the effort.

Lachlan's eyes travelled up to the skylights. "The birds used to fly free in this room," he said as if telling a story. "But they kept on flying too high and hitting the glass, killing themselves. So the owners had to put in this cage, for the birds' own good. You can see there's even netting across the skylights, so they know where their limit is." He pointed above him, where a faint shimmer of copper covered the skylights. "Dumb birds," he chuckled.

Evie looked up as well, eyes flicking to follow the birds high above. "They didn't know the glass was there," she said. "They just wanted to fly free."

"Well good thing someone thought to put a cage around them, otherwise they'd all be dead," he said. Evie looked up at him, surprised to see that he was staring at her. His meaning was unmistakable, but she choked down a stinging retort about free will. Instead, she said in a neutral voice, "It was a good idea. They're safe now."

Lachlan listened to the platitude with a little smile then linked his arm through hers and led her away.

"Do most people in New City live at The Grand?" she asked.

"Many of the survivors are residents of The Grand, preferring to live here, surrounded by exquisite things, rather than finding some slum building out there, on the streets, or down at the Docks." There was a subtle distaste in how he said 'the docks'. "Wouldn't you agree it's nice in here?"

"Um, it certainly is," Evie said, hoping this was what he wanted to hear. Then she asked about something that had been bothering her. "There are a lot more women than men in here. Is there a reason for that?"

"There's a very good reason for it," Lachlan replied. "It's a matter of safety. Women, more than men, are in great danger on the streets. I make sure they all know that they are welcome here, that they don't have to be alone out there. Our world is no longer a secure place, especially for young girls." He stopped walking and placed a protective hand on Evie's arm. "Of course, you are already aware of this. Here, women are safe and free to live their lives in these peaceful surroundings. I find it complements the sensibility of the fairer sex nicely."

As before, Lachlan's attention brought up the heat in her cheeks. Evie looked at the lovely women in clothes far more stylish that she had ever had a chance to wear. *Everyone seems to be having a wonderful time*, she thought. As she sipped at her mimosa, she imagined what life would be like, surrounded by lovely things, going to lively parties every evening. It was a life she had never imagined for herself, certainly not a life she imagined existed in this world anymore. New City had so much more to offer than she had dreamed. She gave Lachlan a sidelong look, thinking about his predilection for very young women and his controlling temperament. Again she asked herself the question that had been swirling through her mind since yesterday. *Would it be worth giving up our freedom for all this security and luxury? A cage is a cage, no matter how luxurious.* She gave a sigh as she arrived at the same conclusion as she had before; *It depends on what we have to do to earn our keep.*

"We think of ourselves as family around here," Lachlan was saying. "We care for each other and keep each other safe." His arm was still wrapped around Evie's and he seemed about to say more, but something caught his attention and he exhaled in exasperation. His body went from relaxed to tense in a breath. "Evie, I apologize, but there appears to be a situation that I have to deal with. I hate to leave you here on your own, so …" he trailed off as he looked around. "Ladies!" he called to two women sitting on a bench, giggling. They both looked up when he called, faces eager and adoring.

"Us, Lachlan?" A willowy blonde stood up, showing off a spectacular grey evening gown that shimmered when she moved. Her mass of hair had been crimped and piled into a knot on her head. She slinked over to them, not taking her eyes off his face. "What can we do for you?"

Evie's stomach sank when she saw Millie saunter over as well. She was wearing a short sequined dress in hot pink, showing off long toned legs. Her face seemed to glow behind the hair that fell over one eye, straightened this morning. Despite the bitchy look she gave Evie, she was breathtaking.

"This is our new friend Evie. Can you two look after her? Something has come up." With that Lachlan released Evie with a nudge towards the women and left them, not rushing but walking with purpose, his features hardening. Evie decided she never wanted to be on the receiving end of his annoyance.

The blonde woman, although pretty, was not as striking as Millie. She had a small round face and pouting mouth. Her face was caked with thick make up and a star was painted in glitter next to her eye, which seemed garish this early in the day.

Evie felt clumsy and childish next to them. Both of them were much taller than she was, and would be even if she had been in a pair of their sky-high heels. Millie's voluptuous breasts were on display right at Evie's eye level. She was used to being shorter than Kit; now she just felt outnumbered.

"What do we have here? If it isn't the special project," Millie said once Lachlan was out of hearing.

Taking a sip of Champagne, Evie tried to look nonchalant. "What do you mean, special project?" she asked.

"Well, honey, I'm supposed to believe you're a friend of Lachlan's?" Her tone was just shy of incredulous.

Evie blushed, hesitant to respond. "I'm not sure. Lachlan offered to let us stay here, that's all. He's been very nice."

"I'll bet he has," Millie said with a humourless laugh. "You've got a lot to learn. You're way too innocent to last."

The blonde, who was still standing next to Millie, finally decided to introduce herself. "I'm Evangelina," she breathed, giving Evie a vapid smile.

"Nice to meet you," Evie said, trying to sound as though she meant it. "Do you live here? At The Grand?"

"Of course," Evangelina replied, her voice as vacant as her expression. "We all do."

"Do you like it?"

"Of course."

Millie interrupted in a lowered voice, leaning in to the other women. "It's as good as anything, I suppose. But why don't we sit down over there and watch the show?"

"What show?" Evie asked, but Millie grabbed her hand and shushed her, pulling her towards the bench. Before they had even sat down, they heard a shrill voice yell Lachlan's name.

Evie looked in the direction of the yelling. She saw Lachlan and Lia, the girl who had been in Lachlan's office that morning.

Millie nodded at the girl. "She used to be innocent too."

Evie winced as the girl screeched. Lachlan was speaking to her in a low, intense voice, but whatever he was saying was not calming her down. She looked awful, her gown bunched around her. Her long hair was tangled and her little face was puffy and blotched from crying.

"Is she Lachlan's ... girlfriend?" Evie asked, hoping she didn't sound naive.

Millie shrugged, watching them through narrowed eyes. "Sure, something like that." She paused, playing with an earring. "When he isn't otherwise engaged, that is."

Evie looked at the couple. She was unable to pick out their words but watched Lia get more and more upset, pushing at Lachlan then pleading with him.

"She hasn't learnt how it is yet," Evangelina said, watching as if caught up in a reverie. "But she'll figure it out. They always end up figuring it out."

"What do you need to figure out?" Evie's question got Millie's full attention, and she laid a hand on Evie's arm.

"Oh, nothing sweetie, nothing you need to worry about." She gave a smile that didn't reach her eyes. "Your sister, on the other hand." She gave a pointed look at Kit, who had just come walking along the path on her own, Jackson nowhere to be found.

"What about my sister?" Evie stood up to greet Kit, whose face was puckered into an irritated scowl.

"Nothing." Millie gave her an enigmatic look. "You two just watch out for each other."

"What happened?" Evie asked Kit. "You don't look very happy."

"Nothing happened, no thanks to that lout back there," Kit said, brows pulled together. "It took him approximately two minutes to try to get his hand up my skirt."

"Are you okay?" Evie asked, putting an arm around her shoulder. Pulling Kit towards her she whispered, "Don't look now, but the girl arguing with Lachlan is the girl I told you about — the one I saw in his office."

"Oh boy, and I thought we were underdressed," Kit whispered back after glancing over her shoulder.

"You didn't get along with Jackson? That's just the way he is." Evangelina said, ignoring the sisters' hushed conversation. Kit looked at her.

"I'm sure he is but I'm not having any of it. Who are you?" she asked.

Evangelina gave her name but could not focus enough to look directly at Kit. She went back to watching the fight while Kit gave Evie a questioning look.

"Don't bother with her, honeys, she's not totally here this morning," Millie said. "She's right, though, about Jackson. He can get that way. I hope you put him down like the dog he is."

"He'll think twice about pulling that with me again." Kit looked pleased with herself. "I thought coming to New City meant we wouldn't have to deal with predators anymore."

"No such luck." Millie gave her a fierce look, which soon slid into a happy smile as vacant as Evangelina's.

Evie looked around to see Lachlan turning from Lia and walking away with that same purposeful stride. Through the trees she saw Lia's shoulders slump. She crumpled then hurled herself around, grabbing the nearest glass of wine from a surprised server. She threw it back in three short gulps then took another glass and stood to the side of the crowd, looking around in contempt.

Lachlan rounded the corner and came back to Evie and the other women, slowing as he walked towards them to grab another mimosa. Millie and Evangelina rose to meet him. He looked happy and relaxed again by the time he reached them, as though nothing had happened.

"It's a lucky man that gets to spend so much time with so many lovely women," he said as he put an arm around each of them. "Millie, have you been taking care of our Evie?"

"Of course, Lachlan, I'm sure she has been enjoying herself." Millie was full of warmth and syrupy happiness that didn't suit her at all. Evie noticed a controlled blankness under the smile.

"Good." Lachlan smiled down at Evie then looked to Kit. "Jackson not to your taste?"

"Not exactly." Kit's tone was glacial.

"Too bad. He can be so friendly." Lachlan sighed, then looked to Millie and Evangelina and inclined his head towards a loud group nearby. They disentangled themselves from Evie.

"It was lovely to meet you, Evie. I look forward to seeing you again soon," Millie called over her shoulder as she swayed on her heels to a nearby group, joining in with on-the-spot laughter.

Lachlan slipped his arm around Evie. He was more enthusiastic than ever, and Evie's first thought was that the Champagne was really affecting him. "Evie, Kit, I can see you both fitting right in with our family."

Evie looked down at her outfit and snorted.

"No, really," he said with a laugh, guessing at her thought. "The two of you should stay here at The Grand, really join us. I'll give you my personal guarantee of safety, and I promise you will have a good time."

Looking at Kit with her arms crossed over her chest, Evie pondered the term "good time." She didn't like the idea of her sister with these people — all this tinkling laughter sounded false, and the boisterous jokes were vulgar.

Lachlan was watching her with a smile, expecting a favourable answer. Evie cleared her throat. "It's a wonderful offer, of course. But, as I said, I think we just need a few days to … think about it. Maybe see what's going on outside these walls apart from roving bands of thugs. There must be some good people here, aren't there? And, of course, I need to know what would be expected of us in return — how we could contribute to this 'family.' We don't want to be freeloaders and ..." Realizing she was babbling and that Lachlan's eyes had narrowed, she added, "Not that we don't appreciate it."

He looked at her for a long time then laughed. "Of course, Evie, I understand. You two have been very independent for a long time, and I'm not trying to take that away from you. Just know that the offer stands as long as you need it."

"Oh," Evie let out a breath. "I don't know what to say."

"You say 'thank you'."

"Thank you, Lachlan."

"Wonderful. Now, I have some people to talk to. Why don't you and Kit go back on up to your rooms?" He gave Evie's arm a squeeze then abandoned them. Kit and Evie looked at each other for a moment. They had been dismissed.

"I guess we should," Evie said, moving towards the exit.

"When have you ever done what you've been told?" Kit asked.

Evie didn't want anyone hear her say that she wanted to leave the party and these glitzy people, even though they had not yet had the promised brunch. Looking back over her shoulder, she saw that Lia was staring at them. The look was pure poison.

"Let's just get out of here," Evie muttered as she walked to the exit.

As soon as the girls returned to their room, Kit spun on Evie, looking mutinous. "I want to leave," she said. "Now."

"Because of that jerk Jackson?"

Kit rolled her eyes. "No, it wasn't that. Jackson is a puppy, he just needed a whack on the nose to bring him in line. But some of the people there? You can't tell me those bodyguards, One and Three, are just normal guys. And everybody pretends to love Lachlan, even though they don't. You know why you would pretend to love someone? Because you are scared of them. Everyone here seems to be scared of Lachlan. Except for maybe his creepy bodyguards," she added as an afterthought. "And Lachlan is more than interested in you."

"Does that … make you jealous?" Evie was confused.

Kit stopped her with a cutting look. "Get over yourself, much? I'm not jealous of Lachlan's attention to you; I'm frightened of it. I mean, he's dating that Lia girl? She's my age. That is not right." When Evie remained silent, she pressed. "Admit that not everything is fun and games around here."

Evie chewed her lip, thinking of Millie with her sad eyes and tough words. "It's not all fun and games around here."

"And?"

"And you're right. We should go check out the rest of New City."

Kit clapped her hands in triumph.

"I'm not saying we should leave for good right now because it's too risky," Evie warned. "But we need to get to know the lay of the land."

Kit hugged her, tone conciliatory now. "Of course. We can just go and check things out. See how bad things really are.

Maybe find a cute boutique apartment. Or not," she added at Evie's look.

"So we'll go tomorrow morning. Should we tell anyone?"

"Are you crazy?" Kit asked. "We get the hell out of here before the sun gets up, before anyone's around to stop us."

Chapter Eight

Evie and Kit woke before the sun rose. They nodded at each other in silence and got ready, manoeuvring around each other in the bathroom and closet.

"How do I look?" Kit asked as she stepped out of the closet in a bright strappy sundress, her long hair swept back into a ponytail.

Evie frowned. "I don't know," she whispered. Both girls had been talking under their breath since they woke up because Kit was afraid that someone was listening at the door. Even though Evie thought her sister was being paranoid, she kept her voice lowered. "It's a little — attention-getting, isn't it? Maybe try something that covers your body. And a hat?"

Kit pursed her lips. "You raise an excellent point. I'll see what I can do." She went back into the closet as Evie smiled a little, pulling on a baggy brown T-shirt. With her messy short hair and ragged jeans, no one would be looking at her.

While Kit was in the bathroom, Evie quietly reopened the panel in the fireplace mantel. Checking to see whether her stash had been discovered was like a tick — she couldn't help herself. By now, it was unlikely that any of Lachlan's men knew about the hiding place or her precious drugs, but she was relieved to see the rows of boxes had not been disturbed. She fingered through them, picking out a few she thought might initiate an interest.

Taking the backpack she had used for school, she loaded it with the small bags and boxes then zipped it closed.

By the time Kit was ready to leave the hotel, she had on a dark purple tank top and skinny jeans, and her hair was secured under a slouchy grey hat. She still looked fantastic, but she would not stand out. At the door they had a hushed argument over what way to leave the building.

"Let's take the elevator to the front lobby" Evie said through gritted teeth.

"But there might be someone there. We wouldn't run into anyone if we took the back stairs and then looked for a door," Kit responded in a sugary sweet voice.

"And when we get lost?" Evie tried to match her sister's tone without losing her temper.

"It will be better than getting caught by some creepy albino bodyguard."

In the end Evie agreed to go through the back. She was not as fearful about being spotted as Kit, but she figured it would be smart to know another way out. With a satisfied smirk, Kit slipped out of the room. Evie made sure they were alone in the corridor then followed her sister to the stairs. She slipped the bag over one shoulder, walking with both hands wrapped around the straps until they reached the back stairwell. Once they started the long descent, she gripped the metal handrail with one hand and pressed the other against the cold cement wall, wincing only a little at a twinge of pain from her wrist. They slipped out at the loading docks, empty of both delivery trucks and people, and finally found themselves on the streets of New City. Getting out of the hotel had been so easy that Evie felt Kit was a little disappointed.

They were covered in sweat before they even crossed the street. Evie wasn't sure whether it was nervousness or the warm, muggy weather. It seemed miraculous that fall was so mild in the south.

Kit vibrated with excitement being outside the hotel where they could spot people bustling through the streets. Evie was more wary, looking around with a watchful eye. The pain in her wrist was a constant reminder of her last encounter with the citizens of this city. The back of her neck pricked as she realized they were being scrutinized. People were leaning over balconies peering down at them, or standing in the shadows of a doorway, smoking cigarettes and watching them with shaded eyes. The girls were looked over, assessed, but no one made any move or gesture towards them. Some people whispered to each other, shooting them furtive looks, but no one spoke to them. Evie kept her head down as she walked.

"Where exactly do we go?" Kit asked under her breath after they took a few random turns around the buildings.

"I think we follow the crowds," Evie responded, nodding her head as two men and an old woman passed by. There was not a crowd exactly, but most people were heading in the same direction, towards the river. Kit and Evie followed at a discreet distance.

They came out of a narrow street directly into what looked like an open market square. "Of course, this is what I saw from Lachlan's office window," Evie said. "This is where everyone comes to trade and barter." After walking through the streets, shaded from the sun by dull stone buildings, they found the sunlight blinding for a moment. Both girls slipped on sunglasses and looked around them. Straight ahead, they could see the broad river glistening.

Evie held Kit's arm as they walked into the crowd. She felt intimidated by the press of humanity, the cacophony of voices and laughter, the general buzz of commerce.

In every available space, in no particular order, market stalls displayed their wares. Some of the stalls where sophisticated wood or metal structures. Others were little more than tents, with people sitting in front of them in camping chairs with baskets of produce at their feet. Everyone was shouting at everyone else, trying to get a better bargain.

Evie narrowed her eyes as she scanned the scene. She was right to tell Kit to change; most people were dressed in black, brown, or grey work clothes. Kit yanked Evie's arm. "Can you believe this?" she asked, breathless with excitement. "It's like going to a fair or something."

Evie laughed when Kit couldn't contain herself, bouncing and clapping like a child, but she noticed the furtive looks and steered Kit deeper into the market.

"People are going to notice us," she hissed, but it was already too late. She looked around and saw too many eyes on her. No matter which way they went, they were circled by watchful people. Evie could understand their curiosity, but she was baffled by the anger, resentment, and, in some cases, outright hostility in the stares.

"Evie ..." Kit began, looking over her sister's shoulder.

Evie turned and found herself looking into eyes that were neither angry or hostile. Dark blue eyes shone with curiosity and amusement.

"Now what do we have here?" the man said, mouth curving into a half-smile.

"I — I know you," Evie said. "You're James; you were in Lachlan's office."

A muttering went up from the people around them. James gave the circle of onlookers a sharp look. "All right, people, there's nothing to see here," he called. "Go about your business."

At his command, people dropped their gaze and shuffled off. Soon the only person left looking at them was James.

He leaned against the pole of a stall, arms crossed over his chest, and took his time looking the girls up and down. He was wearing the same T-shirt and jeans as the last time they had seen him, but the scarves around his neck were even brighter than the others. Black tattoos wound up both arms and swirled around his biceps. His dark hair was tied back with what looked like the same piece of string. The only real difference in his appearance was that the left side of his face was swollen and covered in angry-looking bruises. His eye was half closed, the skin stretched and shiny around it.

Evie gasped. "Is that — did that happen the other night?"

James gestured to his eye. "What, this? Yes, this was the result of my meeting with Lachlan the other night. I suppose I have you to thank for that."

Evie stammered in horror. "I never meant for anything like that to happen to you."

James cut her off with a good-natured laugh. "You got it all wrong. I have had a long and storied history with Lachlan. When I was brought in the other night, I was sure it was over. But you'll find that Lachlan has a, what do you call it, mercurial nature? The strangest things can change his mind. In this case, it was you. I don't know what power you have over him, but you tapped into his under-used sense of mercy and I got away with a stern talking to and a warning. And for that I am much obliged."

"That's a warning?" Kit piped up, looking at his face in astonishment.

"Around here, my dear, this is considered a beauty mark." He winked at her with his good eye.

"You mean that Lachlan was going to *kill* you?" Evie said, aghast.

"Ah, you're going to find that you're not in Kansas anymore." James looked her over once again. "And I just realized I don't know your names. I'm James. And you are?"

"Evie. And this is my sister Kit."

"Kit. And Evie." As he said their names, he paused and held their gaze, as if memorizing their faces. "Well, Kit and Evie, since you seem to be wandering about looking for trouble, and I am particularly indebted to you, please let me offer my services as guide through the city. I take it you've never been out to the Market before?"

"What makes you say that?" Evie asked, annoyed they were so obvious in their newness.

"Both of your eyes are popping out of your heads, and nobody can quite make out what you're doing here."

Evie lifted her chin. "We're doing okay without a guide."

James snorted. Kit stepped in. "Evie, don't be stupid," she said under her breath. "It would be good to have him show us around."

"Yes, but do you trust him?" Evie turned to Kit, whispering back. "Remember the first men we met here?"

"We don't have to trust him entirely, just let him show us around a bit. We could use a tour guide, and it sounds like you saved his life, so let's just take advantage of him for now."

James was watching them while they had their hushed conversation, eyes sparkling. "I promise nothing will happen to you while I'm watching out for you. There is a lot of filth living around here. You need to be careful who you befriend in this city."

Why does everyone keep promising to keep me safe, and here I feel anything but? she thought. After an appraising look at him, Evie gave a hard nod. "All right. You can show us around."

He gave her a wide grin. "Well, then, this way ladies." He gestured them forward. As she passed him, he leaned down and said in an undertone, "Make no mistake about it, Evie, you can take advantage of me any time you want."

Her cheeks flamed bright red, but she ignored him, lifting her head and continuing as if she hadn't heard. He walked between them, pointing out different sights and people as they made their way through the crowd. James took his time walking, a lazy insolent smile on his face as he spoke. Evie noticed, though, that his bright eyes were flicking over every building and every person as he passed. She suspected he didn't miss much.

"As you girls have probably figured out, this is the Market," he explained. "I just want to get us to higher ground to give you a better view." They walked up a hill just south of the market then turned and looked back. James laughed at Kit, who was gaping at the sight beneath them.

"Let me guess, you're from the country, right?" Kit shut her mouth, then laughed at herself as well.

"Well, yes, we are from way up north. But we had been to the city before. It's just seeing it like this now. After … everything."

"So you knew Greater Havern, before?"

"Not well, but we had visited a few times. It looked nothing like this. It's so dirty now. Evie was going to go to school here."

"Was she really?" James caught Evie's eye, and she looked away. She didn't want to talk about what she was once going to do. It didn't matter anymore.

He dropped the subject, bringing them back to the view. Adding an affected polish to his wrong-side-of-the-track accent, he began what he felt was a tour guide patter. "New City is the core area of what was once Greater Havern, and it's built on the south bank of the East Havern River." Like a diligent guide, he pointed to the river. "The river is deep and broad, making it an excellent transportation corridor and the easiest way to travel through the countryside to trade with farms and ranches set up over there. This area in front of us, the Market, used to be a city park, but it's been taken over by merchants. On a busy day like today, there are a lot of fresh supplies. If you're lucky, you might even find yourself some cheese." He said this in a matter-of-fact way, and Evie looked up at him to see if he was making fun of her. He gave her his wicked smile, which confused her even more.

Even though Evie had heard all this from Lachlan, she wanted to know whether James would give a different version of events. "But what is everyone trading for?" she asked. "Not for money?"

"No, not money. People trade for whatever they need — food, services, or supplies like building materials, things like that. Everyone is just trying to survive. You come to a deal for what you think it's worth."

"What do you trade with?" Kit asked.

Evie looked at him out of the corner of her eye while he turned to Kit. She was very curious to know what sort of goods or services this fast-talking man provided.

"I can provide a service here and there for those who need it." He shrugged, as if it wasn't worth talking about. "Most of the city's activities stem from the river, so there is a big Dock District just west of the Market. That's where the barges come in for a night or a week, depending on what their business is here. To the south of that is what we call the Trade District, although you'll find only services being traded, not goods. Need repairs done, you go to the Trade District."

"So the actual trading of goods takes place in the Market?" Kit asked.

"Exactly," James said. "Now, you girls are staying at The Grand, is that right?" He directed the question to Evie, his dark eyes boring into her. She only nodded, and he gave her an insolent smile, starting to walk back down the hill. The girls followed. "When you are ready to go back, you'll find it straight south of here, right in the heart of the Downtown District. Now, to continue with my guiding spiel: As you may already know, most of those stone and brick towers were built when the city was booming. The glass towers beyond them were built about ten years ago. Unfortunately, they remain empty for the most part because they take too much energy. It's still considered the nicest part of town," he said in a mocking tone.

"To the east of us is the Warehouse District, filled with, imagine it, warehouses. They were bulging with goods before the Sickness, but they are just about empty now. A few people live there and scavenge for whatever is left, but it's a dangerous place to live. I definitely wouldn't recommend going there by yourself at night. Beyond that is the Ghetto. Don't go there at all."

"Where would be the safest place to live in New City?"

He raised an eyebrow at her. "Thinking of moving out of your new digs already?"

She shook her head, not prepared to tell him any of her plans. "Just curious."

"The safest place for you is as far away from New City as possible. But it's hard to leave the city nowadays. But if you need a place to hide — I mean *live* — the Trade District is your smartest bet."

Evie remained silent, cataloguing the new information, as Kit took over peppering James with questions.

"How many people live in New City?"

"I'd take a guess and say there are about ten thousand permanent residents. Last winter there was a steady stream of people flowing in, often alone, trying to find others to help them survive. I couldn't tell you how many people from the original city survived, but New City became a gathering point, people massing here, getting themselves set up.

"Over the last six months or so, the flood of refugees slowed to a trickle, until only a handful of people were making it here. I assumed everyone else was set up elsewhere, or dead. You girls are the first newcomers I've heard of in months. It's a surprise, to be sure."

He gave them a sharp look. "Less surprising is that you're set up in The Grand already. How long did it take Lachlan's henchmen to collect you? An hour?"

"We were attacked, and Lachlan's man helped us," Evie said, feeling defensive. "What were we supposed to do?"

"I'm sure he just happened along and then helped you out of the goodness of his heart, did he? What has his boss asked you to do in return for his help and protection?"

"He hasn't asked us for anything," Evie protested.

His eyebrows shot up. "Curiouser and curiouser. Why did Lachlan take such a particular interest in you?"

Evie chewed on her lip, afraid to say what she hadn't even admitted to herself. She suspected what Lachlan wanted.

But she didn't think he would hurt her or Kit — at least for a while. The question was, for how long?

"I don't like it there," Kit said, her voice loud and assertive. Evie looked at her, trying to convey that she shouldn't say anything about their plan to leave Lachlan's as soon as they could.

"Ah, then you are the smart one," James said. "You should tell big sis to listen to you and get out while you can."

"And what, live on the streets with people like you?" Evie argued. "Constantly under attack? At least at The Grand, we're safe."

"Safety is entirely relative, I assure you. I'm sure the hot water and plentiful food more than make up for any lack of, let's say privacy, at The Grand."

"It's nice to have food and hot water," Evie said, stung by James' mocking tone.

"Here's my advice to you, little princess." James leaned down so they were eye to eye. "When choosing between comfort and freedom, always choose freedom. You can find your own comfort, but freedom is easy to bargain away and very difficult to ever get back."

"We are free," Evie protested, even though she knew if they stayed too long, they might not be able to find their way out of Lachlan's gilded cage.

He gave her a wide smile. "I'm sure you are. Nobody's watching you, keeping tabs on you at all. After all, you're just a couple of country girls. Who would be interested in you?"

"Well, exactly."

"I'd stop to look over your shoulder a time or two before you start believing that." He straightened. "Let's keep on going. I for one want to see the new goodies that have come in today."

He wandered into the market stalls with his casual, long-limbed walk. Kit followed him, giving Evie a frown as she passed. As Evie took up the rear, she fought the temptation to look back over her shoulder. Instead, she tried to relax and enjoy the market.

Kit was in a terrific mood. With James at their side, people were chatting with them. She bounced from one stall to the next. As James went through, he picked up some fresh bread, butter, and ham. The vendors would wrap up the goods and hand the parcels to James with a smile and a wave. Again, Evie wondered what he gave in return. She wanted to ask one of the merchants about that if she could get away from James.

Her opportunity came within minutes, when Kit and James stopped at a stall selling pickles. Evie wandered down the row of haphazard stalls, stopping at a fruit seller. She looked at the peaches with longing. They looked perfect — firm and fleshy — a rosy blush stealing across them. Evie could smell how sweet they were; she craved them. The old woman working at the stall turned to her. She was stooped with age. One of her eyes was milky and white, but the other looked Evie up and down with a greedy look.

"Newcomer, are you?" she croaked. Evie suspected everyone was aware of this.

"Yes, how did you know?"

"Know everyone around here, don't I? Can spot a newcomer a mile away." She continued to stare at Evie.

"Can I — can I have some peaches?" Evie stammered, trying to sound confidant.

The woman raised her tangled eyebrows and grinned. She was missing several teeth. Evie was close enough to smell her breath, which was fruity and sweet, but still unpleasant. "They are wonderful peaches, all the way from the other side of the mountains. But what would you give me for them?" She leered at Evie.

"I have insulin." Evie said, trying to sound casual, then held her breath. She wanted to do this right. "If you thought that would be worth some peaches." She was taking a gamble, but she recognized the woman's cataract and her sweet breath as signs of diabetes. Evie's mother had died of complications from the disease, so she knew something of it.

The crafty grin disappeared and was replaced by an appraising look. "Yes, insulin would be a good trade for peaches. I could do that for you."

Evie was certain she was being swindled, but that was not really the point. She reached into her bag and pulled out the appropriately labelled box.

The woman wrapped the peaches and pressed them into her hands, as if she was afraid Evie would change her mind. Then she snatched up the box and took out the vial of clear liquid, inspecting its contents with the same greedy look.

Evie tried to remain nonchalant, scratching her arm and looking around her. "So, do most people work for food around here?" she asked.

The woman's eyebrows rose again. She looked amused. "Oh, yes, everyone ends up working for New City. Be careful who you make friends with, or you'll find yourself working on your back before long." She burst into a cackle of laughter, sounding half-mad. It sent a shiver down Evie's spine. All the triumph she felt over her successful transaction disappeared, replaced by fear.

She was about to ask the woman about James when she realized he was standing right behind her, looking torn between anger and amusement.

"What are you doing?" he asked.

Evie shrugged. "Just making a trade. Isn't that how people get by around here?"

"People who know what they're doing. What are you trading with?"

"How is that any of your business?" She angled her head back to look at him.

"I make it my business to know what happens in my city. And I take note of anything and anyone of interest. And you, Evie, are very interesting. You've already been my good luck charm once, so you can bet I'm going to keep an eye on you."

Kit walked over to join them. James gave a little bow to them both. "Ladies, it's been a pleasure. Be sure to keep your eyes open, because things are not what they seem in New City." He reached into Evie's bag and took out a peach. As she opened her mouth to protest, he winked at her then melted back into the crowd. Within seconds they could no longer see him.

Evie turned to Kit, who was smiling. "I like him," she pronounced. "He has style."

"All the style of a street person, for sure," Evie said, still indignant about her stolen fruit.

"Oh, you like him too."

"I do not," Evie started to protest, but something caught her eye and she trailed off.

"That was weak, even for you," Kit said, until she noticed her sister's look. "What —"

"Don't turn around." Evie grabbed Kit's shoulder, bringing her back to face her. "Just act casual."

"Like you are right now? What's going on?"

Evie had seen Three leaning against a nearby stall, watching them. In the sunlight, his skin was so white you could see the blue of his veins and his hair reflected silver. In his smart black suit, he could not have been more conspicuous if he tried. "Three is here. I think he's watching us."

"Do you think Lachlan sent him to watch us?" Kit's eyes were wide.

"Maybe he just wants to make sure no one else attacks us."

"Oh god, Evie, don't be an idiot. I'd listen to James on this one and keep our eyes open."

They walked away from Three, trying to lose him in the crowd. Knowing he was following them made Evie aware of every move she made. "Maybe we should go back to the hotel. I'm not sure what else to do," she said. "Or do you want to go around poking into homes, trying to find a place to stay? That seems dangerous, and I bet Lachlan would know where we were anyway. What's the point right now?"

"Okay," Kit sighed. "I guess we should head back. Fun is over." Her shoulders sagged as they turned around, heading back towards the Downtown District, back to The Grand.

They remained silent all the way back to the hotel. Now they knew they were being observed, they went in through the front lobby with their heads held high. Again it was hauntingly empty. So many thoughts swirled through Evie's head she was hardly aware of walking the corridors and opening the door to their suite. But what she saw inside snapped her out of her reverie. "What the hell is that?" she said, pointing to the bed.

Chapter Nine

Laid out on their beds were two black cocktail dresses, both short and shimmery. On top of each were masks, elaborate feathered creations like those worn at the Venetian Carnival. One was dark purple, the other peacock blue. An envelope sat at the head of Evie's bed.

She opened the envelope and read the card in silence, then told Kit that it was an invitation to a party. "It's for tomorrow night," she said, not lifting her eyes from the paper. "It — it asks that we wear these dresses and masks in order to fit in with the theme." She looked up at her sister. "This can't be good."

Kit walked to her bed, plucking at the hem of the dress. "So we're being summoned to go to this party? I don't want to be surrounded by all those people, drunk and groping each other. Remember the club our first night here?"

Evie sat on her bed. The familiar feeling of panic was pressing in around her, compressing her ribs and making it hard to breathe. She brought a hand to the back of her neck, forcing herself to calm down. "I don't want to go either. It looks like things can really get out of hand at these parties." She couldn't bear to admit what she was thinking. "I don't think that Lachlan means to hurt us. I mean, the girls seem to enjoy themselves, but ... this doesn't feel right. We really do need to get out of here. Don't we?"

Kit rolled her eyes, sending the message that this is what she had been saying all along, but she didn't say anything. Instead, she picked up the peacock mask, looking at it as if it was a face. "This is a rotten place, but it's filled with such pretty things," she murmured.

Evie started to pace the room, thinking about the people they'd seen at the Market. Many looked to be in poor shape. Dirty, tattered clothes; sunken cheeks; an old look in their eyes. As she pondered that look in their eyes, it struck her that most of the people they had seen outside The Grand *were* old. *It's as if all the young people have been collected inside these walls*, she thought.

"Yes, we have to get out, before ... but nothing's changed the fact that it's even more dangerous out there than it is in here — just in different ways. We could starve or be attacked again. What we need is a safe place to escape to. And as soon as possible."

"What about James?"

Evie stilled when the mysterious man's name was mentioned. "What about him?"

"We could use him. He's the only person we know outside The Grand and he seems pleasant enough."

"So did Lachlan," Evie pointed out, but she chewed on her thumbnail, thinking it over.

Kit inspected her dress. Holding it up to her slim body, she said, "This looks like my size. How would they know that?" Her eyes flew to Evie's. "Do you think they've been in here again, checking our clothes? That is so creepy."

Suppressing a shudder, Evie nodded in agreement. She checked the fireplace then, and sighed in relief to see the drugs untouched. "Maybe you're right about James. He could be our best bet. Where did he say the safest place to hide was? The Trade District. I could go there tonight, find some abandoned apartment where we could stay a few days. We'll sneak out in the early morning and bring the drugs with us, start to trade."

"I'm coming with you."

Evie shook her head. She couldn't put her sister in even more danger. "No, you're not," she said. Meeting Kit's eyes, Evie cut her off as she opened her mouth to argue. "I need someone to cover for me. If anyone comes looking for us, you can say I'm in the kitchens or something. It would protect me, and we don't want to tip our hand before we leave."

Eyes sparking, Kit looked mutinous. Evie placed a hand on her shoulder. "Remember how Three was following us? We have to make sure they don't see where we end up going. I need you to keep watch, and potentially use some misdirection."

Kit finally took a step back and gave a tight nod. "Fine. I'll take guard duty."

That night as Evie was preparing to leave, Kit put a hand on her sister's shoulder. "Listen. Just ... be safe."

"You too." Evie ran her hand through her sister's hair. "Chair up against the door, and if anyone comes in bash their head with the fire poker." She nodded towards the fireplace. Kit smiled, but it didn't reach her eyes.

Stealing down the hallway, Evie tried to make as little sound as possible. Inching open the back exit door, she slipped into the concrete stairwell.

It was just as empty as it had been in the morning. She had made it to the sixth floor landing when a door opened below her. The sound echoed up the hollow space.

She leaned forward, peeking over the side. In the bleak fluorescent lights, she saw a bald black head. It was unmistakeable — One was headed upstairs, towards her.

Evie threw herself back from the railing, pressing herself against the wall and praying that he hadn't seen her. *Shit.* She mouthed the word in frustration. Creeping back up the stairs, she held her breath while opening the seventh level door. Beneath her, the footsteps sped up. She let the door fall shut as she dashed down the hallway, rapping on her door. "Kit," she hissed. "Let me in now." For a breathless minute, she thought One was going to find her and that something terrible would happen.

Then she heard the chair being pulled away. She shoved the door open, almost knocking Kit over, then slipped in and slammed the door.

"What happened?" a wide-eyed Kit asked.

"Shh," Evie hissed. She remained pressed at the door, peering through the peephole at the fishbowl view of the hallway. Strolling, One paused as he came into her sightline. He turned, looked at the door, and smiled. It seemed to Evie that he was looking right at her. She backed away from the door, even though he couldn't possibly see her.

Kit was standing by the fireplace, looking scared. After a few moments, Evie turned and sat down on one the chairs, motioning for Kit to sit down as well. "One is outside," she mouthed.

Kit gave the door a terrified look but sat down as well. "Did he see you?" she said under her breath.

"I don't think so," Evie breathed. The knot in her chest relaxed as the seconds passed and he didn't try to come in.

"Do you think we're being watched?"

Evie thought of One's smile and nodded. He knew she had been in the stairwell. "Maybe everyone is. But we need to be more careful." Gathering her courage, she went to the door and looked out again. "The coast is clear," she whispered. "I would try again but I'm shaking so badly I don't think I would make it. I'll try again tomorrow, really early in the morning."

She woke up before the sun had even started to brighten the sky and made it to the ground floor without running into a guard. She felt a surge of triumph as she stepped out into the cool air, but her confidence deflated when a familiar figure peeled away from the side of the building. He tossed a cigarette down on the cement and crushed it with his polished wingtip shoe.

The sight of the silver-haired man filled Evie with dread. It almost seemed as if he had been waiting for her. *Surely not,* she thought. *How would Lachlan know I would try again, and why would he take this much trouble to stop me from going out?* Disappointed and angry, she eyed the nearby alley. *Could I make it?* she thought recklessly, jutting out her chin. *Would I be able to lose him in the streets?*

But she knew that would defeat the purpose. Lachlan would figure out she was looking for a place to stay. Also, Kit would be unprotected and would be a target. Her shoulders sagged. Three made no move as she headed back into the hotel through the back door, although she thought she saw him smirk.

"It's no good," she said when she was back in the room, out of breath from climbing the stairs. Kit gave a groan of disappointment. "We are definitely being watched. I think the only time I'm going to be able to sneak out of the hotel is if I go tonight — during the party."

"Evie, you can't. It's too dangerous. What if Lachlan sees you?"

"I'll have to take my chances that there will be too much going on for him to keep tabs on me. It might be best if at least one of us is seen at the party; they might think that we're going along with them. If it's anything like the other events we've seen here, there will be enough chaos for me to sneak out unnoticed."

Evie spent the rest of the day pacing between the two rooms of their suite, distracting Kit. "You need to calm down. You're going to give me a heart attack, and I'm not even going anywhere."

"Can you help me get ready?" Evie asked "You know I'm useless at that kind of thing."

By the time Evie was ready to go, she almost looked like she fit in with the crowd at The Grand. The dress picked out for her was a comfortable bandage dress. It was a respectable knee length, but her arms, shoulders and a large portion of her back were bare. Her pale skin stood out in sharp contrast next to the inky black of the dress. Kit whistled. "If I hadn't already thought that Lachlan had a thing for you, I would now. You, my lovely sister, look hot."

Evie twisted in the dress. She could move in it, which was a benefit, but she had never shown this much skin in public. She already felt embarrassed and wished she had a wrap. She looked at the spike heels Kit was holding up and laughed. "Not on your life. What if I have to run away?"

Kit's smile faded. "Oh, I guess they're not very practical. All right, we'll go with those dressy boots you wore the other day."

Evie tied on the purple feather mask and looked at her reflection through the eye slits. "I feel ridiculous," she moaned.

"You look nice, Evie." Kit handed her a black bag. It was the one item that didn't fit with her slinky outfit, bulky with a change of clothes. Slipping it over her shoulder, she hoped nobody would notice.

Kit's eyes threatened to overflow as she fussed with Evie's hair, trying to get the pieces to stop sticking straight out from her head. "Don't let anything happen to you," she said, voice tight. "You're pretty much all I got left."

Evie gave a smile that almost broke. "Nothing is going to happen to me. You stay here and be safe, okay?" She wrapped Kit in a big hug then left the room. She waited on the other side until she heard the scrape of the chair. Steeling herself, she marched down the hallway to the elevators, taking the front exit down to the lobby. *Third time's a charm*, she thought with a grim smile. *I will get out of the hotel tonight.*

The tunnel vision created by the eyeholes of her mask gave Evie a surreal feeling, as though she was only an observer and not participating in the world around her. When she reached the front lobby, she saw that One and Three were standing on either side of the gaudy gilt doors that lead into the ballroom. She knew her smile looked more forced than normal. She wondered if they would recognize her, or if the mask gave her some anonymity. Her hopes were soon dashed.

"Evie," the black man rumbled at her. He reached out with a leather-gloved hand to open one of the doors for her. "Go right on in." His lips curled into a small unpleasant smile.

Head held high she entered, and once again was awestruck. The ballroom was decorated with over-the-top decorations. Oversized masks of gold adorned the walls, reflecting and returning the light of the crystal chandeliers that dripped down over the heads of the party-goers. It took Evie a moment to realize that everyone was dressed in black and there was not a real face to be seen.

Despite her nervousness, she smiled as she looked at the masks. They ranged from the beautiful to the grotesque, from glittering gold and black to bright reds, blues, yellows, and purples. "All the colours of the rainbow," she said to herself. But then a voice echoed through her mind: *You're going to find out you're not in Kansas anymore.* It sounded so real, as if James was right behind her. She let out a sigh and shook her head.

A large figure in a tuxedo came sweeping up to her, face covered by a black mask. There was a bird-like beak jutting out where the nose should be, and the mouth had been sewn shut with gold thread. Only a glimmer of brown through the eyeholes gave a clue as to who was behind the mask. She cursed to herself that he had found her so quickly. *He must have been waiting for me.*

"Lachlan?" she asked, uncertain.

He did not answer but led her to a small bar at the side of the room. He reached for her hand. Unhurried, he pressed it to the sewn-shut mouth as if to bestow a kiss. Something about the mannerism made her shudder, and she pulled her hand away. He held on, pulling her closer, and brought his masked face down to hers. She twisted away from the grotesque beak, stifling a scream.

The man backed away and pulled off the mask, revealing Lachlan's cropped head. He looked flushed from drinking and dancing and had a pleased grin on his face. "Hello, Evie. What's wrong, my dear? "

"Oh, Lachlan. I could hardly tell it was you," she said while pulling off her mask as well. "What do you think?"

"It's just incredible," she stammered. "I never thought I would be able to go to a party like this, not after … everything."

He smiled. "People really enjoy them, so I put on these parties as often as possible. It gives people a chance to forget their worries and cares for an evening."

"Like a big show," Evie said, watching the people as they glided and tumbled across the dance floor. Fascinated, she wondered for a moment where on earth all these people had learned to dance to the music, whether ballroom dancing was a required course to stay at The Grand. On closer inspection, she saw missteps, stumbles and a few groping hands that were certainly not in proper form to the dance. Drunken laughter rebounded off the walls and one couple fell over, knocking into a decorative mask.

"Not like a show." Lachlan caught her shoulder in a rough grasp, turning her towards him. "This is real. This is the life we're creating here." Evie's eyes widened at his forceful hands, but he relaxed, keeping a hand on her upper arm. "You look beautiful tonight."

She felt self-conscious with his hand on her bare skin. "That I don't believe." She gestured at the women who swirled around her, each one embellished in a fanciful costume, each one looking like something out of a dream.

"No, I mean it. There's something about you. You're not as …" he paused as he waved an arm around, looking for the word. "… passive, as everyone else."

She snorted then covered it with a cough. "That I *can* believe."

"I find your attitude to be fascinating. Not to mention your adventurous spirit. Your determination to leave us is remarkable."

Evie looked up at him, her wide eyes showing panic. Lachlan only chuckled. "Of course I know that you went exploring yesterday and that you tried to go again, despite all the hazards you will inevitably face there. My real question for you is, what is it that your inquiring mind is seeking out there on the mean streets?" His voice was mellow and he was swaying to the music. He didn't seem angry at all. Evie tried to figure out if he was more intoxicated than she had imagined. As if answering her question, he raised his free hand saying, "The Champagne tastes particularly good tonight. I'll have another. Care to join me?" Within moments a masked server stood before them with a tray of drinks.

Feeling off balance, she nodded and took a glass from the silent waiter, who swooped away as suddenly as he had joined them. She took a quick sip, but it seemed to stick in her throat.

Lachlan leaned back against the bar with a wistful smile. "I'm just doing my best to make this city work. But sometimes, especially in moments like these, I feel lonely. Like there's no one to talk to."

Choking on her drink, she took a step away from him, unsure of how to react. Was he using a line on her? "That can't be true," she said, a little too loudly. A few more gulps of the bubbling wine helped to clear her throat, but not her head. When she looked at her glass, she was surprised to find it was empty. "I mean, there are so many lovely people surrounding you."

He narrowed his eyes. "What do you mean by that?"

"Oh, nothing," she said, giving a forced trill of laughter. "I just mean, I'm surprised that a man like you could ever be lonely. Everyone here seems to love you."

He allowed himself a small smile, looking down into his glass. "Sometimes, though, it would be nice to have someone I could *really* talk to, not people who are just looking for something, another hand out. I would like to find someone who is loyal to the people she loves, who is willing to take risks. Someone who understands how hard things can be when you're always the one making the decisions."

"That sounds like a tall order in one person," she said, becoming more and more uncomfortable with the conversation.

He shook his head. "Don't sell yourself short. You're more genuine than anyone here. Everyone else is just pretending." Evie gave him a manic smile, wishing she could get away from him. Lachlan put his glass down. "Would you like to dance?" he asked, holding out one of his large hands.

Shaking her head, she backed away a few steps. The tempo of the music picked up so she had an excuse to say she couldn't dance that fast.

"I'm sure you'll be fine." He grabbed her by the waist and spun her into the crowd.

Evie didn't know the steps so she clung to Lachlan and concentrated on staying upright. Twirling, she saw flashes of black and gold all around her. Her head spun, whether from the Champagne or the lack of air she wasn't sure. His grip heavy on her waist, Lachlan remained a constant, holding her tight. Her instincts screamed to get away from him.

Lifting her hand, he twirled her around and she shook off his grip. His face disappeared into the crowd. She turned and was taken up in the arms of another man wearing a black devil half-mask. He dipped her then twirled her as Lachlan had done, leaving her in the arms of another man wearing an outlandish mask with a bird beak. His mouth was obscured. Was it Lachlan? She pulled away and broke his hold then swirled into the arms of a tall woman wearing a strapless black satin gown.

It was Millie. She was looking down at Evie with a huge smile. "Hi there, honey. Had enough yet?"

Evie hadn't finished her nod before Millie grabbed her arm and pushed through the crowd of men surrounding them, taking her over to the side of the ballroom. She whirled on Evie. Her smile had been replaced by a frown of concern. "Listen to me, quickly. Do not ever drink anything Lachlan gives you. Do you understand?"

Evie nodded, bewildered.

"And don't believe anything he says either. The night is about to get wild, so now is the time for you to disappear."

Evie took a deep breath. "I have no problem with that. Is there a back way?"

Millie looked around. "You can take the serving entrance, through the far back corner. Watch out for One and Three, you don't want them to see you leave."

"Thanks," Evie said.

"Just get out of here," Millie rolled her eyes then turned away from her. Evie didn't need any more prodding. Pushing through the swarm of people milling around the bar, she found her way to the serving entrance. Two waiters about to come out with more trays of Champagne looked up at her in surprise, looking like twin owls in their feather masks.

"Just need a little air," she said, staggering a little. "Is there an exit here?" One of the waiters pointed to a hallway then headed out into the party. Evie slipped down the hall and out the door with the red Exit sign, thankful she had been able to hold onto her bag.

The cool air hit Evie like a fist and she realized she had been sweating. She was in the loading dock, which looked deserted. Slipping off the bag, Evie gave one last look around then stripped off the black dress, throwing it into a corner with a sneer. She revelled for a moment in the decadent feeling of the air on her bare skin. She pulled out jeans and a sweater from the bag and dressed quickly. She began to feel more like herself again. The swirling feeling receded and she was suddenly full of energy. Alone for the first time in nearly a week, she was eager to explore.

Chapter Ten

A sound behind her made her spin. She could hear distinct noises, male grunting and female moaning, coming from the shadows. No mystery as to what that couple was doing. She shook her head and smiled despite herself; it was just like a high school party at the end of the day. Slipping down off the loading dock, she headed out onto the streets.

Relishing the freedom to move around however she pleased, Evie took a deep breath. She regretted it as soon as she did. The air carried the rotten smell of the still sun-warmed garbage that littered the streets. *This is life without garbage men*, she thought as she passed a pile of garbage taller than she was, a precarious mess threatening to collapse at any moment. Something was putrefying and it made her gag.

She started to prowl, listening for footsteps. She tried to recall James' brief description about the different areas of New City. The Grand was in the centre of the Downtown District. To the south and east was the Warehouse District, and to the east was the Ghetto, a place that Evie did not want to explore this evening, or ever. She wanted to find the Trade District, where James lived. He had said it was the safest place in the city. She headed west, hoping that was the right direction.

Worried that she was going to get lost, she tried to memorize the surrounding buildings. Most of them were the same uniform grey stone, so she looked for distinctive characteristics. One had a dark green awning; another was double the size of those next to it.

The empty streets unnerved Evie. She found herself looking back over her shoulder at imagined sounds. An occasional window was lit, but there was no sign of movement behind them. She felt far more isolated out in the empty open than cooped up inside the hotel. She wrapped her arms around herself and continued.

A sound in a doorway at her right made her jump. She peered into the darkness, but there was nothing there. Almost laughing at how tense she was, she turned back to the street, but a scraping sound behind her caused her to whirl around. Then she heard the sound of steady footsteps behind her.

She turned, looking for an escape, and ducked down an alley. There were so many garbage bags mounded on top of one another she had to step around them gingerly to avoid causing an avalanche and getting buried. She glanced back to see if anyone had followed her, but there was no one.

Coming out of the alley on the other side, she saw an open space through the buildings. She had found her way to the Market, but she wished she hadn't. It was desolate. There was no sign of the colourful stalls that had spread a cheerful design across the hills. Only purple shadows stretched across the empty park. She turned towards the Dock District, walking slower now.

A scream rang out across the park, breaking the gloomy silence. Spurred by the anguish in the cry, Evie rushed towards the sound, kicking litter out of the way. There was a grunt, then more screaming; it sounded like a struggle.

Running over the crest of a small muddy hill, she saw two men fighting. One was on his back, thrashing, while the other crouched over him. The man on the ground scrabbled his hands at the attacker's chest, but he could not get him off.

"Hey!" she yelled, allowing her instincts to overrule caution. The man looked up at the sound but didn't budge when he saw Evie.

"Help me," he shouted, cradling the fallen man's head.

She realized the crouching man wasn't attacking; the prone man was having a fit. Running to the other side of the sick man, she knelt down and grabbed his arms to keep him from flailing. His eyes had rolled back in his head, showing only the whites. There was a stream of blood-flecked saliva running down his face.

"What's wrong with him?" Evie asked, trying to keep from shouting. Gradually, the man's thrashing slowed to twitches, and the twitches turned into body tremors. His tongue lolled out of his mouth, and he became still.

What if he has the Sickness? Evie thought. *I always knew it would come back to get the rest of us.*

She forced herself to take a deep breath, examining the man. Remembering the almost peaceful deaths during the Sickness, more a defeated drowning than these terrifying convulsions, she knew it wasn't the same thing. *It couldn't be. It can't ever happen again.*

She looked across the stricken man to his would-be-helper. His eyes were wide with shock. He was dressed as she had seen others dressed on the streets of New City, in shabby loose-fitting clothing encrusted with a layer of grime. His face was filthy and unshaved. His mouth was moving, but Evie couldn't hear what he was saying.

"What is it? What's wrong with him?" she asked. Getting only a blank look in answer to her question, she looked down at the sick man and felt his neck for a pulse. No steady beat rose to meet her. She ran her hands through her hair, looking around for help. The crouching man was cowering, his head in his hands. She could hear him now, whispering "No … no … no."

"I think his heart has stopped. I'm going to try CPR." Evie shifted herself over his chest, trying to remember the steps she had learnt so many years ago. Getting herself adjusted above him, she started to pump in rhythm at his chest.

"No, no … no!" the cringing man suddenly screamed. He lunged at her, and Evie fell back with a cry of surprise. He landed on top of her, heavy, his face only inches away from hers. His pupils were so dilated she couldn't see the colour of his iris. The whites of his eyes were bloodshot, and his breath smelt foul, like something was rotting inside him.

"He. Is. Not. Dead." The man spat out every syllable, flecks of saliva sprinkling her face. She wiped at her face in disgust and scrambled away from him.

He jumped at her again, then jumped away and started pacing the length of the fallen man's body, erratic, muttering to himself. "Not dead … not dead … not … has to be done."

Evie watched him in fascinated horror.

He darted forward again and she flinched, but he was going to the body. He reached into the coat and pulled out a small bundle then slipped it into the front pocket of his own coat.

"It has to be done," he said in a loud voice, staring at Evie with bulging eyes. He scurried away in a limping run and disappeared over the hill.

Evie gasped at the callousness. She went to the prone man. He was definitely dead. She had seen enough death in her life to know. She didn't want to leave the body just lying there, but her instincts were screaming that she needed to get away from the area.

Looking up, she saw a silhouetted figure appear over another hill. Even in the deepening darkness, his silvery white hair gave his identity away. Without a second thought, Evie sprinted towards the buildings, determined to disappear in the alleys.

She heard a yell behind her and the pounding of footsteps as he gave chase. She made it to the alleys and took two quick turns, hoping she would lose Three.

Evie backed into a narrow alleyway. She was about to peer out when a hand grasped her arm and pulled her back so hard she nearly fell over. As she drew in breath to scream, another hard hand clamped over her mouth. Then she was pushed against the stone wall. She was trapped.

Heart pounding, she stared up at her captor. Returning her look were familiar deep blue eyes, clouded over with worry.

James kept his body pressed against hers but released her arm, using his free hand to motion to her to be quiet. She nodded that she understood, mouth still covered by his hand. He uncovered her mouth but kept her trapped, his arms on either side of her body.

She could hear footsteps coming towards them as Three's shoes rapped on the pavement, echoing down the street.

"Evie," he crooned, "where are you, you stupid bitch? Why can't you just learn to play nicely so I don't have to waste my time out here?" He sighed, then turned down another street. Within minutes his voice faded away.

Wide-eyed and stiff, she looked at James. "What is going on?" she whispered, so quiet it was barely more than a breath.

He cocked his head, listening for a moment, bright eyes not leaving hers. Satisfied Three was gone, he gave her a big smile. "Now, that's the question, isn't it? You've really gotten yourself into it, haven't you?" He pushed away from her, leaving her body cold without him pressed against her.

He looked as untidy as ever, colourful scarves looped around his throat, although tonight he was wearing jeans without any obvious rips in them. Brushing back some stray hairs that had fallen out of their tie, he looked at her, amused.

"Evie. You never seem to be able to stay out of trouble, do you?"

"I ... I don't want trouble," she stammered. "Why won't he let me leave?"

"Do you really want to know the answer to that?" James' amusement faded. She stared up at him for a breathless second then voiced the question that had been haunting her since she arrived in New City.

"They're all prostitutes, aren't they?" she whispered. "The women at The Grand. That's how they pay Lachlan back."

James nodded. "That's how they pay for the comfort and safety they have at The Grand. By *entertaining* Lachlan's guests. And it's how he pays the men that work for him. To keep control over the men, he needs to keep all of you pretty young things locked up."

"That's what he wants from Kit and me. He's going to ask us to join his little brothel."

"Asking would be the nice way to do it. If that doesn't work he'll turn to other, less nice ways, like demanding, blackmailing, or forcing. It's how he works."

Evie drew in a ragged breath, heart pounding. "Oh my god, I never should have left home. We were so utterly alone so I thought coming here, finding people, was the right thing to do and ..." she stopped, horrified, on the verge of tears. She tried to pull away from James, to cover her face.

"Are you all right?" he said.

"I'm fine. Don't look at me like that."

"Cause you don't look fine. You look like you're in over your head." His voice was soft.

A tear slipped down her cheek and she brushed it away, mortified. "Things just keep on getting more complicated. It's all so horrible. Why won't it stop?"

Evie felt as though her chest was going to break open, so she started talking, telling him about how scared she had been since the attack when they first arrived, her indecision about leaving the hotel, and, finally, about the man who died in the park just minutes ago. When she finished babbling, she sniffled a few times, trying to control herself. "I'm not normally like this. I don't know what's wrong with me."

She sniffed, and James continued to study her, so she turned her gaze to him. He had strong features, with high cheekbones. He was clean-shaven, and laugh lines grooved his face even though he wasn't smiling. She felt an inexplicable urge to rub her cheek against his. She was sensitive of his body so close to hers. A wave of heat rushed up over her.

"You fought off the men with a crowbar?" he said, a small smile forming on his lips.

She sighed. "Why is everyone making a deal about that? It was stupid, fine, but I didn't have a choice. What would you have done?"

His eyes held a mysterious amusement. "If I was you? I would have stayed away, never come to this place."

"And die alone?"

The laughter faded. "No, maybe not. Maybe you did the right thing."

"I just wanted to keep us both safe," Evie said in a small voice.

"And stepped directly into the fire, love." He reached up and brushed a lingering tear from her cheek. A sharp stab of desire passed through her, and she shook him off, spooked.

"Don't you dare feel sorry for me," she snapped.

He snorted and stepped away from her. "Wouldn't dream of it. Got a sob story, sweetheart? So does everyone else. In case you haven't noticed, Evie, the whole goddamn world is fucked."

"You're right, what the hell am I complaining about," she said, stung. "I'll just be on my way with my little problems." She pushed off the wall and away from him, walking out of the alley and down the street in plain view.

James followed along behind her and grabbed her arm. "I didn't hurt your feelings, did I?" Evie spun around, ready to rip into him. He grinned. "There. Glad you're feeling better. Now, what are you going to do?"

"What do you mean?" she asked, unbalanced by his changing the topic.

"I mean, now you know. You know what's waiting for you back at The Grand, what's expected of you. Are you going to stay?"

"Of course not!" she shouted, furiously shaking off his hand. "How dare you even suggest —"

"Just wanted to make sure we were on the same page, is all. You understand, not all the girls are forced into it. They see The Grand as a comfortable place. Some of the men are nice and for the most part they are willing to play along."

"I am not like that," she spat at him.

"Happy to hear it." There was a gleam in his eye. "So, the question is, how are you going to get out of this mess. Do you have a plan?"

Evie was silent for a long time, reluctant to admit how lost she was. "My plan was to find you."

He chuckled. "I'm the plan? Well then, you are well and truly fucked."

She raised her chin. "Kit and I need somewhere safe to go."

"I know of a few places — safe houses. You won't be found. I can take you there right now."

"What? No, I have to get back. Kit's there by herself. Just tell me where to go."

"You'll never find it on your own. Evie, you realize every time you sneak out like this, every time you defy Lachlan, you're goading him. He may have developed a special interest in you, but you won't hold his attention for long. No one does. The only way to stay out of his grasp is to get away from there."

Evie turned and started walking again. "I have to get back. If you think I'm leaving Kit alone there, then you're crazy."

James ran a few paces to catch up. "At least let me walk you back. It's not safe for you out here either. And ... you're going the wrong way."

Evie came to a stop in the middle of an intersection, mouth open to argue, but realized she had no idea where she was going. She turned to follow him as he turned to the right, jamming her hands into her pockets.

"Is Lachlan like this with everyone?" she asked after they walked a block in silence.

"How do you mean? Psychopathic?"

"No, I mean helpful. For the most part."

James gave her a sidelong look. "Lachlan behaves however he thinks will get him what he wants. He is a ruthless mercenary, but he also enjoys his little games. Sometimes girls will catch his eye for a moment. And although you are eye-catching, there's more to it than that. You, no doubt, are a troublesome young woman who never does what she's told."

She glared at him. "What of it?"

He gave her a wide smile with an edge to it. "Lachlan likes to be in control. He doesn't have control over you. He's going to enjoy the challenge of getting you under his thumb, among other things."

Evie suppressed a shudder. "And if he doesn't get what he wants?"

"He'll break you or he'll dispose of you. Those are the options." The smile disappeared and a grave look stole over his face.

She matched his look. "I don't like those options."

"Listen," he said, then pulled her into another alley. He spoke in an undertone. "We're a block away from The Grand, and I can't get any closer than this, not with one of Lachlan's men out looking for you. Lachlan has given me his pardon but I don't really trust it that much.
You need to get out as soon as possible. Do you understand me? Both of you. Then come and find me. I'll start checking the safe houses."

Evie was gazing up into his eyes, noticing they were ringed with thick black lashes. She could see genuine concern in them and was almost ready to trust him. She was also just about ready to kiss him, long and hard on his fast-talking mouth. She banished the thought and tried to concentrate on what he was saying.

"I can be found down by the Docks, on a big barge called the *Mary Rose*. It's the easiest way to get in touch with me. The captain's name is Bill, he can point you in my direction. I'll do what I can for you on this side. But remember; don't trust anyone."

"Should I trust you?" she whispered.

"Especially don't trust me." He reached into his jacket pocket and brought out a small folding knife. "This isn't much, but if you do ever feel threatened, don't be afraid to use it. It's not a crowbar, but it's easier to carry around. Never go anywhere unarmed, understand me?"

His face was a breath away from hers as she took the knife from him. "Why are you helping me?"

He sighed and pushed the hair back out of her face, a brusque, hard gesture. His hand remained in her hair, gripping it above her ear. "Everyone deserves a little help every now and again, and you've had none." He tightened his grip for a moment then released her. He turned to the right and pointed. "Walk straight down that street a block, you'll see The Grand to the left. Remember, you are on constant thin ice. Don't tell anyone what you saw tonight." He pushed away from her, then turned and disappeared into the blackness.

She turned towards The Grand and starting walking. Her whole body was still humming from the tension of being so close to James. He exuded an energy that she soaked up. It made her vibrate.

She turned left as directed and saw The Grand, shining like a beacon in the midst of the dull cityscape. She slowed as she approached, wondering if she should go in through the front. Deciding that would be risky, she walked around the block and went to the back of the hotel.

Something caught her eye, an object out of place with the surrounding scenery. A dumpster was overflowing with torn garbage bags, and something large and bulky was draped over the top of the pile. Clearly all of Lachlan's power and influence had not afforded him a garbage man either.

As Evie approached, keeping a hand over her face to ward off the smell and the flies, the mysterious shape clarified.

With growing dread, she realized it was the bloody, broken body of a man.

His head dangled upside down over the edge, staring at Evie with unseeing eyes. She stared back at the corpse. His eyes were already glassed over. There was something casual about his placement over the bags in the dumpster, just one more thing to be thrown out with the trash. The unfortunate man had met a violent end; his twisted limbs were evidence of that.

A sound came from the alley behind her. A surge of cold panic swept through her. She ran up to the door, praying it would be open. She heard footsteps behind her and threw a wild glance over her shoulder. No one was there. Her tangled hair covered her face. She gasped in relief when the door swung open. Without waiting for it to close, she took off to the stairwell and didn't stop running until she was tapping on the door of her room.

Chapter Eleven

There was cursing on the other side of the door as the chair was scraped away. The door opened on Kit's worried face.

"Oh my god, Evie," Kit whispered, "it was so scary here without you." As soon as Evie slipped into the room, Kit threw her arms around her. "What if something had happened to you? I would be ..." Kit trailed off as her eyes filled with tears.

"I'm sorry, Kit. Are you okay? No one bothered you, did they?"

Kit grimaced and wiped away a tear, composing herself. "The worst that happened was a group of men wandered down the hall, laughing. I was very brave and hid in the closet, just in case, but I took a cue from you." With a shaky laugh, she gestured towards the crowbar, which was now resting on the dresser. "If anyone tried to get in I was going to bean them."

"Oh!" Evie said, remembering the knife. "Speaking of weapons, here's another one to add to our arsenal." She laid the knife next to the crowbar.

"Where did you get that?" Kit asked, bubbling over now that her initial worry was gone. "What happened? Please tell me something good."

Turning away, Evie wiped her hands on her jeans, stalling. "What is it?"

"Good news first? I found James. Well, actually, he found me when I was running away from Three after a man died in front of me in the Market." Evie's voice spiralled higher and higher, so she stopped to take a breath, steadying herself.

Kit's hands were pressed against her mouth. "Oh god, are you okay?"

"Not really. James said he would help but that we have to get out of The Grand — like tomorrow. He's going to look for a place for us."

"What's the bad news, then? It sounds like what we thought."

"It's not good, Kit. Our situation — it's worse than we thought. It's what's happening here at The Grand ... all the women. They're forced, or at least coerced, into being whores. They work for Lachlan, keeping the men happy."

Kit sat down with a thud. A long silence hung between them.

"I should have guessed it," Kit said in a hushed voice. "I think I did. I just didn't want to ..."

"Sooner or later, he's going to pressure us to join them."

"That's never going to happen," Kit said, crossing her arms over her chest.

"According to James, he'll find a way to make us. And if we don't, then ... well." Her shrug implied the worst.

"But James, he'll help us?"

"He said he could find a safe house for us. As I said, he wants us to get out and join him immediately. But the problem is that Lachlan has us watched all the time. He told me he knows when we leave and even when we try to. It's all a game to him. I'm sure he is licking his chops right now at the thought of pouncing on us when we least expect it."

"He *told* you?"

"At the party. He danced with me and told me he was lonely."

Kit snorted. "Because he's a sick, sadistic creep."

"You're right about that, I'm afraid."

The skin was pulled tight around Kit's eyes, making her seem older than she was. "Evie, if Lachlan has us watched all the time, how are we going to escape?

That was the question Evie had been asking herself for hours. The only answer she came up with was that it wasn't going to be easy.

The sisters brainstormed for hours but fell into bed without any set plan, hoping that daylight would bring fresh ideas. Evie stared at the ceiling, thoughts still whirling through her head. She knew Kit was doing the same thing. She wanted to comfort her little sister but couldn't think of anything to say.

The darkened ceiling started floating and morphed into images of blood-spattered snow ...

At the sound of splintering wood, Evie's eyes snapped open. She sat up in bed. Kit was stiff under covers that were pulled up to her chin. Her eyes were wide, looking over Evie's shoulder, and she was screaming.

A hand grabbed Evie by the neck and hauled her out of bed with such force she hung in midair for a moment. She struggled to free herself but One's grip was relentless.

"Boss wants to see you," the big man said. With his free hand he pointed at Kit, who was still screaming. "You, shut up."

He threw Evie to the floor. She cried out when her bare knees skidded on the carpet. Before she had a chance to take a laboured breath, he yanked her up by the arm then laughed as she tripped on the overturned chair. It had skidded to the middle of the room when One had kicked the door in. "Let me put some clothes on, I can't leave like this," she croaked, looking down at her oversized T-shirt and tie-up sleep shorts.

"Lachlan said *immediately*," he bellowed as he began dragging her out of the room.

On instinct, she tried to grab at something to hit him with, but her fingers only slid along the walls. *Oh, god, what are they going to do to me?* she thought. *Did they see me with James? Are they going to hurt Kit? I can't let that happen. I have to get through this somehow.*

Once in the hallway, Evie jerked her arm out of his grasp. She padded next to him in her bare feet. He shoved her into the elevator and glared at her until it slid open at Lachlan's office. A few rays of early morning sun shone over the heavy furniture. Evie was relieved to see the room was empty.

"Where is he?"

"Not my problem." One stepped back into the elevator and it closed on him, leaving Evie alone, her outrage fighting with her fear.

Left alone in the room, she gave in to her impulse to stamp her foot once; after that it felt childish. Trembling from adrenaline, Evie started to pace, telling herself to calm down.

She brushed her fingers over the closed wooden cabinets that lined Lachlan's office, wondering if there were other secret hiding spaces to be found. Always feeling better when she was doing something, she decided snooping would be the best use of her time.

Stomping over to the desk, she wrenched the drawers open. Some were locked but others opened as she tugged. *What am I looking for?* she thought. *Foolproof ways to escape? Secret passageways out of The Grand. Something I could use to blackmail Lachlan with? Now that would be useful ...* The rows of files appeared to have to do with city administration. The labels were hand printed with a bold pen; it seemed quaint.

The cabinet at the back of the room held Lachlan's ample liquor stash. In a shallow drawer underneath the shelves, there was a rainbow-bright array of pills in clear bottles.

No wonder Millie told me not to drink anything he gives me, she thought as she flipped through the pills. They were unlabelled. *What kind of cocktails is he making?*

Behind the liquor, the back of the cabinet was lined with a dark mirror. Evie grimaced at her dim reflection then tried to wipe away the mascara stains under her eyes with her thumb.

The elevator doors slid open. "What are you doing?" a curt voice demanded of her.

Her heart thudded. Evie froze then took a deep breath. All she wanted to do was bolt to the elevator, but she forced her feet to stay firm on the floor. *How dare you treat me like this?* she raged at him in her head. *You said you would keep me safe.*

"I'm fixing my face, what do you think I'm doing?" She poked her head around the cabinet door and fixed Lachlan with a glare. *When caught, act like the outraged party.*

He stood at the door in yet another three-piece suit, looking astonished. She felt a surge of triumph at being able to surprise him for once. She sniffed. "Not everyone here was dragged out of bed, I see. Would you like a drink?"

She watched as Lachlan pulled himself together, bringing his face under iron control.

"Thank you, no." He sounded dangerous. As he walked around the desk, Evie circled it the other way, keeping it between them.

Standing at his seat of power, figure silhouetted by the strengthening light behind him, Lachlan seemed to inflate. Evie felt ridiculous in her pajamas and bare feet. His posturing was just a tactic and she vowed not to be cowed by him. She crossed her arms, a barrier between them.

"So when in an empty room, the first thing you do is search it?"

"Search it for a mirror," Evie clarified.

Lachlan started to prowl the room, like a tiger in a cage. He looked uncomfortable in the suit, pulling at the sleeves. "Where did you go last night?" All signs of his kind, helpful persona had disappeared. The Lachlan before her looked mean, powered by fury.

"What business of that is yours?" Her tone was biting.

"Were you selling drugs?"

"What?" Evie blinked, thrown by the question.

"Were. You. Selling. Drugs."

"No, I wasn't selling drugs. I … I left because I was scared." She cleared her throat and decided on a re-imagined version of the truth.

Lachlan stopped pacing. "Did someone here try to hurt you?" There was a treacherous edge to his voice.

"No, nothing like that. I — went out the back door, just to get some air. I was feeling dizzy after that drink." She paused for a moment, hoping for some reaction to her remark about the drugged drink. He said nothing, but gestured for her to go on. She looked down, away from his gaze, grasping for a credible story. "A body. In the dumpster. I ran and I thought I heard someone following me, so I hid." The lie slipped off her tongue like butter.

"So you didn't sell drugs to a man who overdosed and died in the park last night?"

Evie's eyes widened. "No, that wasn't —"

"What kind of drugs do you have?"

His questions were short and staccato. They set Evie's teeth on edge. *How much does he know?* She jutted out her chin. "I don't know what you're talking about."

He glared at her. "I want those drugs."

"What drugs?"

He roared and jumped at her, grabbing her arm. "Don't think playing stupid with me will help. Things will not end well for you, trust me." He bit off every word. "You think I didn't know you were trading drugs at the Market? I know everything that happens in this city. I have eyes and ears on every street corner, behind every door."

Evie levelled her gaze at him. *Apparently, you don't know everything, if you still haven't found my stash.* She waited him out.

With a sigh, he released her, brushing off his suit as though she had contaminated him. "It appears we are at an impasse. I want those drugs and I mean to get them. You understand that I can't allow you to defy me in this. I control every drug that comes in and out of here."

"If I did have some drugs, why would I give them to you? You'd probably just use them on me and Kit anyway before forcing us into prostitution."

Lachlan didn't blink at her accusation. He gave her a thin smile. "Did you figure that out all on your own, Evie? You are as smart as I thought. What? Did you think I was going to deny it? Everyone plays their part in this city, even my girls. And I had big plans for you."

"You're disgusting." Evie controlled her urge to spit at him. "I would never —"

"Never say never. A deal can always be made. What will it take for the drugs?"

Evie took a step back, weighing her options. *No point in denying they exist,* she thought. "I want safe passage for Kit and me."

Lachlan gave his crowing laugh. "You're serious?" There was a gleam in his eye. "So, the innocent little country girl does know how to play."

Evie's voice remained steady. "We leave here today, and you or your thugs will never come after us."

He eyed her for a moment. "You know I could make you tell me where the drugs are. I could do things to make you tell me everything and then some. You'd give up your sister to make me stop. I'm negotiating with you, giving you these options because I like you, Evie. I really do."

She waited him out in silence, ignoring the tears pricking behind her eyes.

He tutted at her. "No, I don't think your deal will work for me. Here's what I will offer you: No passage out of here for either of you, but I will guarantee your safety. No one at The Grand will harm a hair on your head as long as you are supplying me."

"And Kit."

He bowed his head. "And of course Kit. Evie, we don't have to be enemies. I could use a woman like you on my team. You have a particular brashness that I like. It will serve you well here. Since you seem reluctant to join my bordello, I can find some other work for you. I want you to deliver these drugs for me, throughout the city. What do you think of my proposal? Your sister safe and you get the run of the city. Isn't that what you wanted anyway?"

"Kit stays with me."

"I don't think so," he taunted her. "Kit stays at the hotel. How else can I be sure that she's safe?"

Evie tried to reason through the negotiation, thinking of the consequences. *This arrangement will only last as long as the drugs do, which isn't long. But, it could buy us time to figure out a way to escape from the hotel.* She nodded. "All right, I'll agree to that."

Lachlan stuck out his hand. As she placed her hand in his, a warning tingle shot up her spine. He shook her hand roughly.

"If anyone hurts Kit, so much as touches her the wrong way, I will flush every last pill," she said.

He yanked her towards him, bringing his lips to her ear. "If you fail to comply with me, Evie, I'll make sure she's passed to every man living in the hotel. In the city."

She jerked away from him. Holding her arms around herself, she stumbled.

He laughed. "And so it's done. Now, why don't you let me see your wrist?" He held out his hands as she stared at him. "Come on, I'm not a monster, my dear, just a business man. We live in extraordinary times, where extraordinary measures are sometimes necessary." She gave him her wrist, more out of shock than anything. He unwrapped the elastic bandage, clucking over the bruising as if he truly was the doctor he claimed to be. The expression on his face was so gentle and caring, Evie wondered if she was hallucinating. She decided to risk a question now that he seemed to be in a good mood.

"Wh - what do you need the drugs for?" she asked, her voice still raspy. His gentle expression dissolved as quickly as it had appeared.

He let her hand drop and gave her a shrewd look. "Does it matter to you?" He laughed low in his throat. "No, Evie, I don't think I'll tell you that. I'll let you use your imagination."

She returned to the room grim-faced to find Kit still in bed, sobbing. "Oh, Evie, I thought they were going to kill you," she said.

Evie bustled in, taking the chair and propping it against the broken door, this time reinforcing it with an armchair. "Kit, no one came in and hurt you, did they?"

"No." Kit took in a sodden breath then laughed a little. "I need a tissue. Are you sure you're okay?"

"There is nothing okay about this situation." Taking a deep breath, Evie told her sister about her arrangement with Lachlan. Kit started to protest but Evie talked right over her. "The thing is, we are protected only as long as we're playing by his rules. He gave me the details as I left his office for a drug deal he wants to happen tonight and he will know if anything goes awry. Lachlan's threatened to target you particularly."

Kit went to the bathroom and took a long time blowing her nose. When she returned to the room, her cheeks were dry and her brown eyes held a steely look that Evie had never seen before. "We're totally going to break his rules, aren't we?"

Evie sat back, a small smile curling her lips. "Only if you're okay with it. It's your ass on the line too. But I think we should still try to escape today — somehow."

"It should be easy now that he told us we could go out to deal for him."

Evie squirmed. "It's not going to be that simple. Um, the worst of it is that you're not allowed to leave — it was part of the deal."

"*I* have to stay here while you can run around the city? I'm a hostage. Right? That's not fair. You're crap at making deals."

"It was a smart way for Lachlan to make sure I would come back."

"Hmm." Kit started pacing the room. "So, how are we going to get me out of here?

"I find bullshit is an excellent way around most things." Evie opened the panel in the fireplace, rummaging through the drugs and going over the list Lachlan had given her.

"You know this is dangerous, right? That making deals with people like that won't end well." Kit's voice was soft.

Evie shivered as Kit repeated Lachlan's words without knowing it. "Listen, I know that Lachlan has every intention of screwing us over. He wouldn't have made this deal if he didn't think he was completely in control. So we have to change the rules of this little game without letting him in on it."

"How?"

"We are going to go on this drug deal, the both of us, then we're going to the Docks to find James, see if he has found a place for us to hide."

Kit sucked in her cheeks. "You're not leaving me behind?"

"Of course not," Evie scoffed. "We leave here tonight, one way or another. We have the whole day to think of a plan."

A soft knock sounded at the door. Evie looked up at her sister in panic and started throwing the drugs back into the fireplace, not worrying about order.

"What do I do?" Kit hovered at the door, looking panicked.

"See who it is," Evie hissed. *If it was one of Lachlan's men, they wouldn't be knocking.*

"It's a girl. She looks pretty young."

Evie sat back against the fireplace, now closed up so it wouldn't betray their secret. "Well, let her in I guess."

The chairs were pulled back and the door opened. The girl behind the door was small and pale, wearing a skimpy grey sundress. "I'm here to clean your room." She was pushing a large cart full of dirty towels; it must have been from when The Grand was a real hotel.

"We don't need you to clean our rooms," Kit said.

The girl nodded, but stayed planted in front of their door. After a long pause, Evie's eyebrows went up. "Is there something we can help you with?"

"You got drugs?" the girl asked.

"No. Why would you think something like that?" Evie controlled the urge to shield the fireplace.

"Someone told me you got drugs." The girl flushed; she was about fourteen years old. "Look, it's not like it sounds. I'm not looking to get high, I just thought that maybe you could help me out. You got birth control?"

Evie stared at her, aghast. "What's your name?"

"Dani."

"Why do you need birth control, Dani?"

Dani rolled her eyes. "Oh, you know. We used to get birth control given to us, but now they say they don't have enough. When girls get pregnant, they end up disappearing. I've never seen a baby around here, and I don't want to have what happens to them girls that get knocked up happen to me."

Evie eyed Dani, then the laundry cart behind her. "Dani, I think that we can probably help each other out."

Evie was scheduled to deliver the drugs to the Warehouse District that evening at seven, as per Lachlan's instructions. She grabbed the backpack full of the necessary drugs. Pulling on her soft leather boots, she slipped James' folding knife inside. She let the door shut with a thump behind her as she headed towards the elevators. A few men lounged in the lobby but let her pass without harassing her.

One of them looked familiar. Evie gave a quick glance back at him as she passed. He grinned up at her and gave her a lazy wave. He had a dirty bandage on his forehead. Her blood went cold. It was Ryson, the man who attacked her when she first arrived in New City.

He winked at her. "Nice to see you again, Evie. I hope you enjoyed our little game the other night. Maybe we'll get a chance to pick things up where we left off sometime."

She nearly missed the step up to the front doors. Her sore wrist gave a throb as she curled her hand into a fist. *Ryson was working for Lachlan all along,* she thought. *That bastard. We were set up from the very beginning.*

Outside, the chill air made her shiver. The evening was clouded over, thick with tension as if an autumn storm was coming. She pulled her hood up, obscuring her face. The pervasiveness of Lachlan's deception had shaken her.

She had memorized the directions Lachlan had given her to the warehouse, but she took her time in getting there. Strolling down the street, she paused every block or so, peering into a broken window or looking at a signs posted on walls. No one disturbed her as she meandered through the streets. Maybe Lachlan might have put out the word that she was now working for him so should not be molested.

As she approached the warehouse, her boots crunched over glass. Every window on the ground floor was broken and boarded up. She stopped and looked up at a faded sign; apparently coffee used to be stored here.

The door opened a crack. Evie jumped when a voice hissed at her, "Hey. Girlie." She steeled herself then pushed the huge door with all her strength. It creaked open. The space had been emptied; coffee must have been a precious commodity after the Sickness. A musty rich aroma still lingered in the air, and beans were strewn across the floor.

When her eyes had adjusted to the gloom, she saw her contact. He was not what she had expected — she had imagined someone tall and scary like One and Three. This man was scrawny and short, the same height as Evie. His eyes were bleary and bloodshot, and he looked like he needed a good night's sleep. A cigarette hung loose on his cracked lip.

She consulted her instructions. "Are you Matthew? I'm Evie, here from —"

"Shhh," he hissed at her as he came closer. "No names. Did you come alone?"

"Of course," she said, holding her breath as he approached. He smelled as bad as he looked.

"Good. You got the stuff?"

There was something in the way he said this that made Evie stifle a giggle. It was as if she had landed in a bad film noir. There was an element of the ridiculous about Matthew.

"Um, yes, I have what you need." Evie bit her lip to keep from laughing, reminding herself this could still be dangerous. She slipped the backpack off her shoulders.

"Quick, kay?" He was glancing over his shoulder.

"Here you go," she said, holding the bag out to him, her voice too cheerful for the situation.

He snatched it from her, his hands shaking. She wondered whether he was as nervous as she was. He went through the contents, mumbling to himself. "Good, good, it's all here. Fine, you can go. Get out of here." He spun around and darted back into the depth of the warehouse, slamming what sounded like a heavy metal door behind him.

She was left in abrupt silence, disconcerted. She walked back out into the evening air and headed north for two blocks. She stopped in front of a big brick building. "What was that all about?" she said aloud.

A shadow broke off from the side of the graffiti-covered wall. "If it has to do with Lachlan, it can't be good."

Evie grinned at her sister. "I saw you following me about halfway there."

"I figured. You totally sped up then. Once I was out of the building, I looped around and waited for you. I was just inside an empty shop along the route we talked about. I don't think anyone saw me."

"You got away easily?"

"It was a dream." Kit beamed, clearly proud of herself. "If you're dream consists of hiding under a pile of used towels in a laundry cart, holding on to a bag of drugs that would get me killed in five minutes. Dani took me down the freight elevator at the back and left the cart by the back door. When I was sure no one was around, I climbed out and slipped out the back door." She held up the bag triumphantly.

Evie looked at the small bag and sighed. "Maybe we should have taken more."

"I think we did the right thing by not taking everything. What if I had been found? All the drugs would be gone and we would have nothing to protect us. Now, we have something and Lachlan has nothing. That he knows of, anyway. That's one for us."

"Did you take care of Dani as we planned?"

"Yes. She was so relieved to get a year's supply of birth control pills she almost cried. What do you think Lachlan is doing with all the pregnant girls?"

Evie sneered. "I don't even want to think about it. Let's just get out of here and try to leave this nightmare behind us. We have to get to the docks before Lachlan realizes I'm not coming back and you're not in our room. We probably don't have much time. James said we could find him on a barge called the *Mary Rose*. He better be able to get us out of this mess."

Chapter Twelve

East Havern River was broad and deep at the docks. Most of the boats tied up were large and wide, but a few looked no more substantial than rafts. Most of them contained living quarters, no matter how small they were. Tents were arranged in chaotic order on the decks, and the laundry hung between them flapped in the breeze. Makeshift stoves were smoking and sending off the most amazing aromas of cooking meat.

Evie scanned the boats then cast suspicious glances around her as they pushed through the crowds. "They're all looking at us," she said under her breath to Kit.

"If you'd stop twitching like a sick cat, maybe they wouldn't," Kit replied in a breezy tone. She was still proud of her daring escape from The Grand, having recounted the whole ordeal to Evie several times already.

They slowed and came to a halt in front of a wide barge with a full-sized cabin. On the side of the vessel, in white paint, hand-drawn block letters spelled out *Mary Rose*.

"This is it," Evie called to Kit, who had walked on, more interested in the people around her than the boats.

A teenaged boy, who was leaning against a wooden post in front of the gangplank, stood up straighter in interest. He was tall and gangly, still on the verge of growing into his size. He had darker skin and a serious face, which broke into a dazzling smile that showed white even teeth at Evie's pronouncement.

"I was so hoping you were going to say that," he said as the sisters approached him. "Now, what makes you think you've arrived in the right place? Not that I'm complaining."

"We're looking for James," Evie said. "Is he here?"

"Ah — James. Yes, I believe he is around today," the boy said, looking over his shoulder onto the barge. "Are you sure you weren't looking for me?" He grinned in Kit's direction: she looked down to hide her smile. "All right then, if you must find James, who should I say is asking?"

"I'm Evie, and this is Kit."

The boy was still looking at Kit. "I'm Oliver. Do you want to come on up?"

Kit was nodding, but Evie broke in. "Maybe we should talk to James first."

"Right, I'll go see if I can find him." Oliver turned and ran up the gangplank, stumbling over newly large feet.

"We're not here to flirt, Kit," Evie said under her breath.

Kit looked up in surprise. "I wasn't flirting. He just seems so much nicer than the men at The Grand."

Evie's attention was caught by James and another man who appeared at the edge of the deck, coming down the gangplank. James moved with an unhurried grace, arrogant smile on his face as he locked eyes with her. Evie could feel her body tense just looking at him.

The man behind him was in his sixties. He had long white hair tied back in a black bandanna. His heavy white mustache drooped down his face, and aviator sunglasses hid his eyes. He had a pipe clenched between his teeth. A sleeveless T-shirt stretched over his large belly, and his arms were covered in tattoos. Evie thought he looked like a biker, a hippie, and a sailor combined. In a word: tough.

"So, you got away already?" James said as soon as he stepped onto the dock. "I honestly thought it would take you longer than that."

Evie's eyes flicked to the other man, leaning nonchalantly against the post, surrounded by the rich leathery smell of tobacco that swirled out of his pipe. He was looking each of the girls up and down with detached interest.

"Actually, Lachlan provided us with the perfect excuse to leave. I mean, he provided me with the perfect excuse to leave. We had to sneak Kit out."

"In a laundry cart," Kit announced. "And I was able to bring these with me." She thrust the bag containing the drugs at James. He opened it and both he and Bill looked inside. Bill whistled between his teeth and James' head shot up, startled.

"You have *prescription* drugs? Do you have any idea how valuable these are?"

"Valuable enough for Lachlan to agree not hurt either of us." Evie tried to sound nonchalant. "Before I left the North, Kit and I raided the hospital in the area. We had bags of medical supplies, like bandages and lots of drugs."

"You brought a pharmacy with you," he said, awed.

"Lachlan found out about them so had me trade them in exchange for Kit's safety."

James whistled. "Lachlan must have been happy to get his hands on those."

"I'm sure he would be if he was able to find the rest of them." She gave him a coy smile. "I only traded a small portion of my stash."

His eyes widened and Evie felt a thrill of triumph at shocking James.

"You've hidden them? Where?"

"Right under his nose, in my room at The Grand. The fireplace had a false back. The whole hearth is full of drugs."

He shook his head. "Do you know what those supplies could mean?"

"In a city with no hospital, I know they could mean the difference between life and death."

He gave her a grin. "Of course, they're no good to us at The Grand. But they're no good to Lachlan either."

The other man cleared his throat, a wheezy sound that came from deep within his chest. "James," he said, his voice low and hoarse. "I think you need to tell me what you've gotten yourself into."

James turned to the older man, lowering his voice. "I think we should get these girls onboard and hidden, now. Every minute we spend down here in full view we're in danger — greater danger than I realized. These are the girls I was telling you about, Kit and Evie. They were taken by Lachlan's men five days ago and have been trying to escape ever since. They've apparently succeeded, right under his nose, with valuable merchandise as well."

When the man hesitated, James pressed. "They could be an asset."

Evie cocked her head, trying to hear the conversation better. Kit had walked away a few paces, looking at the rusted frame of the barge.

The man gave James a long hard look. James stayed silent, holding his gaze. Finally, the man gave a sharp nod. His voice rose to a conversational tone again. "You might as well bring them aboard. Petra'll want to fuss, and we've more than enough meat cooking. It was a good haul this time around."

James nodded and turned back to the sisters. Kit had rejoined Evie and was watching the men with interest. "Evie, Kit, this is Bill. He captains the *Mary Rose* here. Why don't you come aboard? It'll be safer. Food is on, which I think you both could use."

Kit moved forward first, shaking Bill's hand while beaming at him, and walking up the gangplank. Evie nodded at Bill as she passed, accepting James' hand up. The pressure of his hand was reassuring.

It appeared as though a small village lived on the barge. They passed at least ten tents set up on deck, following Bill towards the large cabin at the back. James was next to her again, speaking quietly in her ear.

"These people are traders — they travel up river to the west, looking for food or supplies. Bill has a contact with a working cattle ranch, out in the prairies; he is one of the major suppliers of beef to New City."

"Does he only supply beef?" Evie asked.

"Of course not," came the gruff voice behind her. Bill had been listening. "We scavenge the countryside, don't we? Find an abandoned town, and there's plenty out there, with lots of stuff for the taking. We picked these up just a week ago." He put his hand down on several crates of cigarettes stacked precariously on the deck.

Kit turned to Bill, her eyes shining. "You," she pronounced, "are pirates."

"Kit!" Evie flicked a worried glance at Bill, afraid he would take offence.

Bill looked Kit up and down, taking in the sunny smile, and roared with laughter.

"That's it, girl," he chortled. "That's exactly what we are." Smiling for the first time since they had met, he motioned for them to enter the cabin.

Evie walked down three steps into the dim interior, careful to duck her head under the low doorframe. When her eyes adjusted to the dark and the hazy smoke, she saw that the cabin was low and made of timber beams, larger than it appeared from the outside. The front space was a massive kitchen. It housed two long tables and benches made of rough wood and two wood-burning stoves. One wall was covered with maps, some hand-drawn. At the back of the kitchen there were two doors, presumably leading to more rooms. The atmosphere, already warm and homey, was made even cozier by the mellow light of gas lamps. As enticing swirls of smoke and flavour floated by her, Evie realized she was famished.

"It smells delicious," she said to the two women bustling around the stoves. She could barely control her salivating.

"Oh, thank you sweetie," said the older woman coming towards her. She was short and compact, wearing a well-used apron over her jeans, and gave off a matronly air. Her wispy blonde hair was curled and tied back with a scarf, and she wore heavy makeup on her tanned face.

"Now, James," she said, putting a friendly hand on his arm. "What have you brought us here?" She looked at Evie and Kit through mascara-heavy eyelashes as she wiped her hand on her apron and gave them a warm smile.

"Petra, this is Kit and Evie. They arrived in New City not too long ago. Petra runs this ship; don't let Bill tell you otherwise," he said to the sisters.

"Newcomers, eh?" Petra's eyes took on a speculative look. "And just the two of them. Well, that's never going to end well, is it?" She came around the girls and put an arm around each of their waists, bringing them forward. "No matter that now though. I imagine you girls haven't had a proper meal in ages. Skin and bones, you are. Come with me and we'll get you fed up proper."

Evie and Kit ate better with the pirates than they had in a long time, as promised by Petra. The snack food they'd had at The Grand didn't come close to comparing. The table was covered with a real meal; they dug into roast beef, potatoes, and carrots. Neither girl held back and Evie's ribs were soon aching, she was so stuffed.

James didn't join them. After a quick whispered conversation with Bill, he left the table as they began eating. He squeezed Evie's arm, telling her he would be back soon. Her arm burned with his touch, even after he'd left.

The girls were joined by twelve of the pirates. "Not our full crew," Bill explained. "The rest of them are off in the city, but they'll be back before we head out again."

Besides Petra, there were three other women on the barge, each of them younger than the matron. One of the girls, Emily, was at least a few years younger than Kit. She watched them with an open curiosity, eyes bright as she sat next to Petra. A dark-haired woman with sparkling eyes was bustling at the stove, serving plates up to the pirates who clearly adored her, as she scolded and flirted with them all equally.

"That's Rebecca," Bill told Evie with a nod of approval to the cook. "She used to be a chef and decided to keep on cooking no matter what the state of the world. She can keep us well fed on a can of beans, that one."

Another woman swept into the kitchen from the back cabin. She was tall and thin, with honey gold hair she wore in heavy curls that fell down her back. Her low-slung jeans and a small halter-top showed off an amazing figure. She gave the girls a hostile glare and sat without speaking.

"Who's that?" Evie whispered to Bill, gesturing at the unfriendly girl when her back was turned.

Bill looked up. "Who? Oh, that's Anne. She's been with us for a few months now, isn't it?"

"Is she all right?" Evie asked.

Bill shrugged. "She doesn't like New City, is all. She'll get over it when we leave."

Kit was in her element, laughing and talking with everyone around her, in a way she had refused to do at The Grand. Bill, crusty as he was, already seemed charmed by her.

Sitting across from Kit was Oliver, another smitten admirer. He didn't say much, but gazed at her as she spoke, smiling.

Evie remained quiet for the most part, happy to let Kit have the spotlight. She looked around with interest. Everyone seemed to get along well, and there was a general sense of happiness and contentment at the gathering. It left her feeling lonely because she didn't belong here.

James was gone for longer than Evie had expected and she was beginning to worry that he had left them. But he did return, sauntering in with his unhurried walk as though the world moved on his time. He took a seat at the far end of the table, accepting a plate from Rebecca with a genuine smile.

Evie watched him smile. His dimples were clear even in the dimness as he joked with the men around him. He was more relaxed and casual than she had ever seen him; for once he didn't seem ready for a fight.

She noticed that Anne, the angry woman, had moved to sit near James. Twirling her long hair in her fingers, laughing up at him, it was clear she wanted his attention. Evie looked away, reaching up to feel her rough choppy hair. She tried to concentrate on the conversation next to her.

"Are you all family?" Kit was asking.

"Not related," said an older man sitting on her other side. "We're just people who've found each other after the Sickness and thought we'd do better together than apart."

As the dinner came to an end, the pirates began to leave, going about their business. Evie noticed that only the men went on deck, while the women stayed in the stuffy cabin. Thinking back, Evie couldn't remember any of the girls going outside since they had arrived.

"Do women not leave the cabin?" she asked Bill.

He turned a shrewd eye to her. "Not in New City, not if they're smart, they
don't. It ain't safe for women, as I'm sure you've found."

Anne was still sitting right next to James, their thighs touching as she laughed at something he said. The girl looked over her shoulder towards Evie with the hint of a smirk. It was a smug possessive look. A spasm of irritation passed through Evie.

"Not that I'm not grateful for that amazing meal, but what exactly are we doing here, James?" she said, interrupting him.

Anne snorted. James, distracted from her charms for a moment, looked up and cleared his throat. He got up and came around the table to sit next to Evie and Kit. Bill leaned over as well.

"I'm curious as to what's going on too," Bill said. "These girls managed to escape The Grand with a sack full of drugs and say there's more hidden at the hotel. And Lachlan is aware of this fact?"

"He knows there are more drugs," Evie said. "That's how we were able to avoid ... joining the other girls there." She lowered her voice, embarrassed. "Lachlan wants the drugs more than anything, so I negotiated a deal with him. I delivered some to a warehouse for him earlier this evening, then we came here instead of going back to The Grand. I was supposed to report back to him right away, so I figure he must have sent one of his goons to our suite to get Kit when he realized I had double-crossed him." She looked at Kit and gave her a weak smile. "I can just imagine how angry Lachlan is that we both escaped. I hope to god he never finds us."

Anne had been watching them from across the table. "You mean to say that Lachlan is after you right now?" Her eyes were wide with alarm.

The door of the cabin opened with such force that a gas lamp went out. Oliver rushed into the room and shut the door behind him. "Lachlan's men are trying to board," he said, out of breath. Every person in the room reacted, jumping up out of their seats, some crying out. "They say they're here on a legal search for unauthorized goods."

"Legal search my ass," Bill said, glowering. "Everyone knows they never actually follow through on those. They must know these girls are on board." He sighed. "I guess I can say goodbye to those cigarettes. You three, get inside." He pointed to Rebecca, Emily, and Anne. "Take the sisters in there with you and show them what to do. Take those drugs with you as well, girl! James, you better go with them. It's not worth either of our lives if you're found aboard my barge."

James gave a resigned nod and put an arm around Evie and Kit. "Come with me," he said under his breath. "Everything is going to be just fine."

"What about Petra?" Evie asked, looking at the woman over her shoulder. The stout woman was slipping a wickedly sharp kitchen knife into a pocket of her apron.

"Oh, I'd like to see them try to come after me," she said, resolute as she followed Bill and Oliver out of the cabin.

Hustled along by James, Evie went into one of the small cabins. A row of eight hammocks hung along the ceiling, with as many cots lining the walls. It seemed like an obvious hiding place, until Rebecca crouched down at the end of the room and pried at one of the wood planks. A section of the floor came up, revealing a small storage space underneath. Rebecca helped Emily in then slipped in after her. Anne gave Evie a withering look before joining them.

"Go on in," James said to Kit. He held her hands, guiding her into the small space, before turning to Evie. "Now you."

"I'm so sorry for this," she said, voice lowered so only he could hear her.

"It's my fault," he said, eyes dark. "You did exactly what I told you to do. But it's going to be fine. Just hop on down." With his arms steadying her, she lowered herself into the small space. Rebecca knelt on one side, her arms wrapped around Emily, who was clinging to her. Anne was next to them, then Kit. Everyone was bent over so they could fit into the small space. The air was stifling, holding the tension that simmered off them. Evie curled in next to Kit. There was little room available when James got in, bringing the hatch down behind him. He crouched, wrapping himself around Evie. As if unsure what to do with his hands, he placed them gently at her waist. She could feel her cheeks burn and was happy the crawl space was so dark.

"It seems like everywhere I go here, I find another secret hiding spot," she breathed, thinking of the fireplace in her hotel room.

"The Grand actually has a lot of hiding places built into it," James whispered, his light tone out of place with the tense situation. "The legend is that The Grand was built by a mob boss more than a century ago, with lots of hidden chambers, passageways, and escape routes. It was used for smuggling. The blueprints disappeared decades ago and there are probably some that will never be found. Lachlan is obsessed with finding them, but I don't think he knows about them all."

"How do you know that?" Evie asked.

Anne broke in, her tone malevolent. "You're kidding, right? Did James never tell you? He used to work for Lachlan. Up until a few months ago, he would be the one searching the cabins for hidden goods."

"What?" Evie tried to turn to look at him, but James raised his hand in alarm. A thick silence fell over them as the door to the cabin opened and heavy footsteps sounded above them. Craning her neck, Evie peered up, seeing the dark movement of people through the slats above her. Sweat broke out down her back that had nothing to do with the stifling space.

"Looks empty to me," a voice said above them. "And we were promised gorgeous girls if we came out here."

Evie felt Kit's body tense and gave her sister a comforting squeeze.

"Doesn't matter," someone replied. "We've confiscated enough goods to keep the boss man happy. Let's get out of here. Bill looks angry enough to throw us both overboard, and I don't want to push our luck."

The footsteps receded out of the room. Evie tried to move but James held her down, keeping her in place. Long minutes passed before the door to the cabin opened again. The boots overhead stopped right at the secret hatch. Two sharp knocks sounded above them. Pause. Then four knocks.

James and the women relaxed. James unfolded himself from Evie, stretching up to raise the trap door. In the dim light, they could see Bill crouching down over them.

"Well, you're safe, but my cigarettes aren't." He sounded regretful. "Come on out, they won't be back tonight."

Chapter Thirteen

"What do you mean you worked for Lachlan?" Evie demanded. They had unfolded themselves out of the small storage space, red and sweaty after being in the hot enclosed space, and had joined the others back at the kitchen table.

"It's a long story," James said, avoiding her eyes.

"I'll bet it is."

Petra placed a hand on Evie's arm across the table. "Things are much more complicated than they may seem, dear."

Rebecca made herself busy, putting together some refreshments. She set out a selection of beers and soft drinks, not cold but cool enough.

Emily sat in Petra's shadow, peering around the larger woman's soft doughy arms. Evie smiled when the girl reached for a beer and Petra slapped her hand away, offering a cola in its place without even looking at her. Figuring she needed it, Evie reached for a beer and snapped it open.

Anne sat by herself at the far end of the table, arms crossed over her chest. "I can't believe that you brought those men here."

Kit turned to her, indignant. "We didn't bring them here. We weren't followed, I swear. I followed Evie all the way out of the hotel, and no one was watching her."

"They thought that Kit was safe in the hotel, collateral for me to come back," Evie said after chugging some of the frothy liquid. "I really don't think they were tailing us."

"Be that as it may, the fact is that Lachlan's men came here tonight, and that's something we can't have," Bill said, standing at the head of the table. "They know something. I suspect this was a little fishing expedition that Lachlan ordered, and although they didn't find anything, it doesn't mean that they're not still interested. That means they could be back." He pointed a stubby finger at Kit and Evie. "I think it's best the two of you know what we're dealing with, so you understand where I'm coming from.

"Now, I have never liked Lachlan. He took power in a high-handed way when so many people were down and desperate for someone to take charge. He is greedy, manipulative and not above violence to get what he wants. We all accepted that because who isn't above a little violence in these anarchic times? We'd bring in merchandise under his nose and he'd look the other way, and we were all fine with the arrangement."

Petra stepped in, her voice full of scorn. "We got along all right under Lachlan, until we made a discovery last winter. It was the middle of February and, even this far south, freezing cold. It was all we could do to stay alive when we were out on the river. Pickings had been slim out to the west, so we had gone down river, east of New City to see what we could make of things there. We had stopped short of a regular trading area because we're not exactly welcome there. Lachlan controls much of the land to the east of the city, and we hadn't paid the appropriate taxes to be trading in the area." Petra paused, looking like she might spit for a moment. "There on the shoreline we found, nearly frozen dead, Rebecca."

Both Evie and Kit's eyes flicked to the woman standing in the kitchen. Her hands were rammed into the pockets of her jeans; her lips were pressed together in a tight line.

"Well, she was out in the cold with barely more on than what she's wearing now and no shoes. She was huddled at the edge of the river and didn't have the strength to even cry out to us. We're lucky to have people aboard with sharp eyes." Petra gave Emily a nudge. The girl tried to disappear behind her. "Emily spotted her on the shore, although how she did I don't know. Rebecca was so white that she matched the snow on the ground. But we were able to get a boat out to bring her on board, and she was lucky to have no permanent damage from the cold.

We got her nicely thawed out and now, as you see today, she's right as rain."

Rebecca looked up and finally spoke, her low voice stiff. "I'm not sure I'd describe myself as lucky, but I was fortunate to be found by people as warm and welcoming as Petra and Bill. They took me in and I've been a part of the crew ever since."

Petra gave Rebecca a comforting pat on the arm. "We've all been the better for having her with us. And Rebecca opened our eyes to some of the less desirable trade that Lachlan is involved in."

"Women," Evie murmured. "He trades in women. That's why he keeps them at The Grand, so he has total control over them."

It wasn't Rebecca who responded to her, but Anne. The girl had lost her animosity. Her eyes were blank, remembering something. They reminded Evie of Evangelina and her odd vacant looks. "Lachlan took all the women under twenty-five and housed them at The Grand. I lived there too. He said to keep us safe." She let out a bitter laugh. "Safe enough, I guess, but not from him and his men. We were one more thing to be used and traded, a good way to make some money. Simple supply and demand, he used to say."

"I don't really understand," Kit said. Her eyebrows were knitted across her forehead. "How could he just come and take people? Didn't anyone notice or do something about it?"

"He was clever about it and made sure he was discreet. He would offer girls things, even simple things like food and a hot shower, nice clothes. When you're living without these things, it's hard to say no. He likes it when we come to him willingly, but he's not above acquiring girls in other ways." Anne's tone became venomous. "Some he feeds drugs until they're so hopelessly dependent they'll do anything for more. Others, he will take as payment for an unpaid debt." Her lovely face twisted at the thought. "I was sold by my father for a case of beer. Lachlan's men came in and grabbed me, told my father his debt was paid in full. My father didn't even bother to argue. He took the beer though."

A stony silence filled the room. Anne looked down again, unable to go on. Rebecca continued. "I ended up at The Grand because I was promised safety, much as you were. It doesn't last long. Once you're comfortable, Lachlan will start to use his power against you, making you do things you don't want to do. The women in the hotel are a reward for the men who follow orders. He may dress the proceedings up with parties, music, dancing, but there's no question of what is expected of the women at the end of the night. They keep the men happy, who in turn keep on following Lachlan's commands.

"Once a girl has outlived her purpose at The Grand, either because she is pregnant or is being a nuisance like I was, she is then put on the market."

Kit made a small noise and Evie glanced over to see her cheeks streaming with tears. "The girls who get pregnant. That's where they go?" she whispered.

Rebecca gave a hard nod. "Pregnant girls go for a steep price. Everyone wants babies now; so many died in the Sickness. When you're out in the country, a fertile woman is hard to find."

Evie glanced around the group. "How did people allow this?"

"Men need wives," Petra said in her matter-of-fact way. "All those farms and ranches are getting set up. People want children to continue the work they're doing. But coming across young women after a plague can be difficult, so Lachlan brings the women to them."

"We were brought into each port along the river and displayed," Rebecca said. "People would come for miles around to see us, bartering for us with goods and supplies. Sometimes it was men looking for wives, or couples looking for a girl to do work. We were made to stand there like animals." The woman's chin shook as she fought back tears. Petra patted her hand and James pulled her in for a hug.

"Most of the girls were drugged at this point, but Rebecca would never touch the stuff without being forced to," Petra spoke for her. "She was purchased by a rancher with a cruel streak — he beat and starved her. One day in the middle of winter she up and walked away from him, without shoes on her feet. Decided she would rather freeze then spend another minute with him. That's when we found her."

There was complete silence. Evie broke it first. "Just so I have everything straight, Lachlan takes all the young women in New City, forces them into prostitution, then sells them downriver to be the wives of farmers when they are of no further use to him?"

"In a nutshell." Bill's rough voice brought her attention back to him. "We had suspected he was worse than he appeared to be in daylight, and Rebecca gave us our confirmation."

Evie turned her eyes to James. "And you worked for him?"

James cleared his throat. "Yes, I did. I ... owed him a great deal after the Sickness. I did enforcement work for him — like the men who came aboard the barge today — low level stuff mainly, roughing up those who weren't doing what they were told. I've done a lot of things in my life that I'm not proud of, before and after the Sickness, but I swear I did not know what Lachlan was doing with the women at The Grand. He made it easy to believe that everything was okay." James' gaze bore into Evie as he explained himself. He seemed so distressed that she nodded; she believed him.

"I was considered as lowbrow as they came and was never invited to enjoy the ... benefits ... some of the other men were given. There were rumours about girls being mistreated, but I was led to believe that everything was consensual. Until a few months ago." He hesitated, looking down at the table. "I was coming in to report to Lachlan. He must have forgotten I was coming, because when I got to his office he wasn't there. I heard noises though, from the wall. Screams."

"There's a bedroom hidden in one of the walls of his office," Anne said, her voice distant again.

"Oh," Evie breathed. "I had wondered if there was something like that."

James rubbed the back of his neck, jaw set in a grim line. "I went in. Lachlan was drunk and he was ... on top of Anne, beating her, hitting her over and over. I just reacted. I ran in and pulled him off of her, punching him until he was unconscious. I left him there and I took Anne. She was badly hurt. I knew we couldn't stay at The Grand. I had met Bill before in my line of work and we had a fairly good working relationship, so I brought Anne here, hoping that she might be welcome."

Evie looked to Anne, who nodded confirmation. Her lips were pressed so thin the imprint of her teeth showed through. She took a deep breath then explained. "Lachlan would take interest in a girl for a while, before moving on to the next. He propositioned me and I said no. It's dangerous to hold his attention too long. *His* girls were often sold sooner than later. But he's not a man you say no to. He ordered me to his office when he was drunk and … wouldn't take no for an answer." She ducked her head, giving James a look under her eyelashes. "James saved me. If he hadn't come, Lachlan would have killed me."

Evie took in an unsteady breath. "Oh my god, what are we going to do?"

Bill's face was grim. After a long pause he let out a ragged breath. "I suggest you and Kit go into hiding right away. James, can you help her with that?"

The look on James' face was inscrutable as he nodded; no sign of a teasing grin. "Yes. I've gotten good at dodging Lachlan's men. Not perfect, as you know, but pretty good."

"You're taking her to your place?" Anne spoke up, indignant. James turned to the girl, shifting uncomfortably.

"I think it's for the best," he said in a quiet voice.

Anne snorted and crossed her arms over her chest, glaring at Evie. "Are you sure that's what you really want?" Confused, Evie turned her head to the girl across the table. Anne's baleful glower set her teeth on edge.

Evie leaned forward and said in a quiet, steady voice. "What exactly do you mean?"

Anne snorted. "Whatever. He's told you he's a convict, right? And a murderer."

"Who, Lachlan?"

"No. James is."

James' eyes rolled up in his head as both Kit and Evie spun towards him, open-mouthed. "It is an extremely long story. I will tell you about it, but not here, not now." When Evie hesitated he placed his hands palm down on the table in front of her. "Listen, I'm not going to pretend that I'm perfect, or even remotely good. But, right now, I'm your best bet on getting through the night intact. You're going to have to trust somebody at some point."

Evie spoke to him slowly. "You told me not to trust anyone, especially you."

"I lied," he said with a faint trace of a grin. "Did I tell you I'm a liar as well?"

"And a murderer?"

A long silence hung over the group. Anne crossed her arms again, ignoring everyone. James sighed. "Yes. I'm not lying about that one."

Evie exchanged a long look with her sister. "Are you still okay with going with him?"

Kit gave her a slow nod. "Yes. James has been more honest with us than anyone else in this city. And, nowadays, in this place, killing doesn't seem that crazy. We know that." Turning to James, she narrowed her eyes. "But if you so much as try to screw us, James, I swear to god — "

Evie cut her off with a hand gesture and looked at James steadily. "Okay, that's settled. We'll go with you. We'll trust you … for now."

Kit turned to the others. "But what about all the other girls at The Grand? Is there anything we can do to help them?"

Bill cut in. "There's not much you can do for them. Sometimes the best you can do is get yourself out of a bad situation. Not that there's a good situation at all in New City, but getting you away from that man's clutches is a first step. We've had enough trouble with him over the year, but things are getting worse. It will reach a breaking point sooner than later." He shook his head and cleared this throat before continuing. "James, can I leave this situation in your capable hands? We're preparing to head out west again; we'll likely be gone for a month at the least. We simply cannot take the risk of keeping the girls on board with us as things are now." The look he gave James was a deep one, taking the other man's measure. James' deep blue eyes held Bill's, and the older man nodded. "When we come back, well, we might have a better idea where we stand. If we can, we'll take Evie and Kit with us then."

"I'll take care of them. It's best that we get out of here as soon as possible. Lachlan's already on the prowl. When are you leaving?"

"We'll push off once we have a full crew aboard, hopefully tonight. We'll try to dodge as much of the bureaucracy as we can."

James stood, turning to the sisters. "Let's get going. We move quick and figure out the details later, okay?"

Petra stood as well. "Be safe, you three. We will see you when we return." She came over to the girls and gently led them out of the cabin.

Evie took a deep breath of fresh air, sweeter after being in the stuffy space for so long. The crowd of people below them at the docks seemed bristling with danger. Which of them was reporting back to Lachlan? Evie wanted to duck back into the cabin and let the pirates whisk them away from the city.

"Come on," James said, coming up behind her. She tensed when he laid a hand on her back to usher her along; he pulled it away as if she had burned him. "We need to get moving. Follow me and don't look around you — it will bring too much attention to us." He walked down the gangplank at a casual pace, but as soon as he entered the crowd he picked up the pace, forcing Kit and Evie to trot to keep up with him.

"We're going to skirt around the Market, where fewer people will see you, but it's not exactly the best part of town."

Evie looked up at the seemingly abandoned brick building they were passing. "James, is there a nice part of town?"

He chuckled under his breath. "Not exactly. There's the bad part of town, and then worse parts of town."

"You said the Ghetto was the worst part. Right?" Kit asked from behind them.

He looked at her. "Not really. The worst is to the south, past the Warehouse District, past the Ghetto."

"What's worse than the Ghetto?" She wrinkled her nose.

"We call it No Man's Land. It's where people end up when they can't fit in with the rest of the city, can't play nice. Mainly scavengers, living off of what they can find in abandoned stores and such. Most don't last very long there. There's only desert beyond, so there's nowhere to go."

"Why would people go there?" Evie asked. "Why not live in New City?"

"They've been kicked out — exiled, essentially."

"By who?"

James gave her a look.

"Oh, I see," she answered herself. "Lachlan exiles people who don't play by his rules. How does he keep them there?"

"With armed guards. Lachlan has patrols between No Man's Land and the city. He has a monopoly on many things, and one of them is guns. He has plenty for his henchmen, but if anyone else carries a firearm without his authority, the penalty is death. Anyone can kill the person who has a gun unlawfully, and Lachlan would reward the killer."

"I know. He took our guns."

James gave her an amused look. "Your guns? You came to the city armed?"

"Wouldn't you?" she shot at him, thrusting her chin out. "Fat lot of good they did us — Lachlan's man took our truck and the guns."

James seemed to store this information away then said, "Anyway, he has patrolmen around No Man's Land, so he's able to keep undesirables out."

Or keep people in, Evie thought.

"That's barbaric," Kit breathed, looking south towards No Man's Land as if she would rescue them all. "They probably starve to death."

James nodded, his face somber. "It has a way of keeping people in line."

"And if that doesn't work, use a bullet," Evie said in a fake cheerful voice. Both of them gave her a look. "Sorry, not funny." She waited a moment before lowering her voice, speaking to James. "What Anne said, back at the *Mary Rose* ..."

James stopped, pushing his tangled hair back from his face. "Listen, I know you probably have questions, but it really is a long story. I would rather not talk about it right now."

She paused. "I just wanted to say that it's ... all right. I understand."

"Oh." He gave her an appraising look. "Well. I promise I'll tell you about it when the time's right." He forged ahead of them, but she could see his jaw was tight.

They walked in silence until Evie noticed they had left the grey streets behind. This neighbourhood had smaller buildings of rough unpainted timbers and steep pitched roofs. The doors were wooden and had once been painted in garish reds and blues, but these had faded to nothing more than faint chips of colour.

"This is the Trade District," James said in a quiet voice. "It is the oldest part of the city, so most of the buildings are several hundred years old. This is where most of the trade in New

144

City happens. More and more merchants set up shop here as they get enough supplies."

Wrought iron lanterns with electric bulbs flickered as they passed the narrow passages. There was nobody on the street at this late hour. Once or twice there was a sign of life in windows above them, but nothing distinct. Evie rubbed her arms to warm them. There was a chill in the air; she was feeling colder than she had since arriving at New City. She paused to look around, feeling as if she was in an entirely different city. "I thought that people traded at the Market."

"Does Bill have a shop here?" Kit asked.

James lowered his voice to a whisper, so the girls strained to hear him. "No, Bill sells to the merchants in town, strictly under the table. He doesn't want to get tied down with all the bureaucracy it takes to become fully legitimate in New City."

"Bill mentioned bureaucracy as well," Evie said. "You mean like going through Lachlan?"

He smiled at her. "Exactly. To become a New City merchant, you need to pay a tax on your goods to the city, which is Lachlan. Bill decided a long time ago he didn't want to do that, so he finds a way around it."

"How does Lachlan feel about that?"

"Well, usually Lachlan tries not to get too involved in some of the underhanded trades going on because it's not worth his while. Bill makes sure he's never caught. But you can be sure he's being watched."

"I guess we didn't help with that."

James' tone sharpened. "No, but neither did I when I brought Anne there. But there are things going on in the city Bill can't ignore, and he's made his decision as to where he stands. As of right now, I don't believe Lachlan knows that Bill is harbouring Anne. If he did …" he trailed off, shaking his head. He stopped in front of a brick building and said brightly, "And here we are."

Chapter Fourteen

They had stopped in front of a four-storey walk-up. The brick
was dark and crumbling in patches, giving a sense of history to
the place. With its intricate stone Victorian façade, it looked as if
it had been built centuries ago. Small and squat, it had just
enough room for three apartments on each floor. An iron fire
escape climbed the side of the building. The effect was quaint and
Evie was charmed just looking at it.

"Your new home," James said, then led them away from
the building.

"But ..." Kit started as Evie followed after him.

"Shh," James hushed her, taking them to the far side of
the next building. Behind a dumpster there were stairs leading
down to a basement door. "I never use the front door," he said
to Kit. "When trying to avoid being picked up, it's much better to
use a little bit of stealth. Besides," he turned to her with a wink.
"This is much more fun." James gripped the handle of the rusted
metal door with two hands and pulled, bracing one leg against the
wall. "It's a little stiff, but you just need to use some muscle and it
will give," he grunted, his efforts rewarded with a slow creak as
the door opened.

Once in the building, they found they were in a damp
dark space, with the overpowering smell of mould around them.
A few rectangular windows were caked with dirt but let in a small
wedge of milky light. Evie blinked, trying to see her surroundings.

"I don't think this space was used much even before the Sickness," James said as he walked through the dark with confidence. "The building we're in right now was an office. It leads to the parkade of our building."

In the dim light, Evie could see stacks of boxes along one wall. A few pieces of abandoned technical equipment littered the floor. She passed an ancient photocopier and an overhead projector. She put her hand on it as she passed and smiled. "This reminds me of school."

James grinned at her. "I never was much for school myself."

"You don't say." She raised an eyebrow at him. They followed his dim form to a door, which opened easily. The parkade was just as dim, but Evie could see six cars. They seemed to be patiently awaiting their owners.

"Do these still work?" Evie asked. By habit, she itched to know how much gas was in each tank.

"If you know how to hotwire them, I guess," he answered. "I've never checked."

"Do you know how to hotwire a car?"

"Why, because I'm a criminal?" James' tone was sharp.

Evie was taken aback. "No, I didn't mean it like that. I was actually thinking, well, it would be a good skill to have. I kind of wish I had learnt before — everything."

He gave her a long look. "I could teach you." At her incredulous look, he grinned again. "I am a criminal, after all. It comes in handy when you're stealing cars."

"Is that what —" Evie cut herself off before she asked James what his criminal trade had been. "I'm sorry, that was rude."

"Yes, it was, but I'll forgive you. I have stolen cars in my day, from time to time. I can pick locks too. I bet you'd want to learn that as well."

Evie's eyes lit up. "Could you teach me?"

Kit broke in. "Not to interrupt the burgeoning crime spree here, but I'd love to see where I'm going to be staying."

"Come this way. You guys can get all set up, then we'll figure out the next step." James walked up a cement stairwell that led into the entrance of his apartment building. The floor was covered in a faded oriental carpet, and the walls were lined with wood wainscoting. Two doors in the lobby led to the ground floor apartments, and large double front doors led to the street. A polished wood staircase spiralled upwards, curling back on itself at each landing. James started climbing the stairs, the girls behind him. The ancient wood creaked under their weight. There was a stale dusty smell in the air, but it was not altogether unpleasant. Evie liked the place; there was a warmth to it.

On the fourth floor, James led them to a door to the right of the stairs. "Here we are," he said, stopping in front of a door where tarnished metallic numbers proclaimed it to be Suite Eleven. He turned the handle and the door swung open. "When I moved in here I checked all the apartments — this one wasn't locked, but the keys are inside."

The girls followed him into the small foyer, feeling as if they were trespassing. "There's heat, electricity, water, the works," he said.

"How does that all work?" Evie asked. "Does Lachlan provide that to everyone?"

James nodded. "The hydro plant sends electricity to every building in New City."

"But Lachlan doesn't know whether the buildings are occupied or who lives in them. Right?"

"No, he doesn't. You don't have to register or tell anyone where you're living, although I'm sure that Lachlan would love to have that information. But I am fairly certain he knows about the other occupant of this building. I'll introduce you later."

Evie looked horrified. "Someone else lives here? Is he going to be okay with us staying here?"

James laughed. "*She* will be overjoyed to have you. Don't worry about that. Just get yourself settled first and I'll be back in a little bit."

Kit had already disappeared around the corner. Evie turned back to him. "All right. James, I ..." she stopped, biting her lip.

"Yes?" he asked, an expectant grin on his face.

"You've done a lot for us. It was really good of you."

James slouched against the wall and gave a nonchalant shrug. "I guess I'm just a natural at the heroics. Enjoy your new home." He shut the door behind him as he left. Evie turned into the apartment and slipped off her shoes, the way she used to do in her own home.

Kit was exploring the small galley kitchen. She had opened the fridge and was gazing at the soft yellow glow emanating from it. "It will be nice to have our own place."

"Well, who knows how long this will be ours," Evie said with a heavy sigh as she sat down at the counter. "We're on the run now. From the guy who's in charge of the whole city." She covered her face with her hands and starting laughing, because it was too ridiculous.

"Well, life has certainly been anything but boring, wouldn't you say?" Kit shut the fridge and spoke in a matter-of-fact tone. "I'm going to enjoy this while I can. Look, I think we can even have separate bedrooms," she said as she wandered down the hallway. "I call this one!"

Evie looked around with appraising eyes. She walked into the living room, feeling the soft carpet under her feet. There was a layer of dust over everything. The furniture was basic and clean in neutral colours of browns and beiges. What it lacked in personality, it made up for in functionality.

The kitchen was equipped with a large double sink, a microwave, and matching stove and fridge. She looked through the cupboards and pantry. The shelves were stocked with glasses, china, utensils, and cans and boxes of food. Even the fridge wasn't quite empty; there were a few jars and bottles. Evie went through these, deciding most would have to be thrown out.

As she began taking the jars out, she thought about the former owners of the apartment. Looking into their fridge was like taking a glimpse into their lives. Who enjoyed pickles, and whose soy sauce was that? What happened to them and where did they go? It looked as though they had stepped out for a holiday. *Thankfully they didn't die here*, she thought with a shiver. She looked around the small living room for more clues. A few travel books were arranged on some shelves and art in muted colours hung on the walls. There were a few photos of a couple in their forties. *They look happy*. Evie picked one up, wondering how their story ended.

Following her sister's voice, she walked down the hallway to the bedrooms. She smiled as she saw that Kit had chosen the master bedroom. It had an enormous four-poster bed and an ensuite. Of course. Kit was rummaging in the closet. "Evie, guess what? There are clothes here. They are a bit old for us, but we'll be able to wear some of them."

Evie peeked into the walk-in closet. Clothes were hung in tidy rows on either side, one side with feminine dresses and blouses, the other with suits in navy, black, and charcoal grey. "Does anything fit?"

Kit held up a shirt to her frame. "A little big, but better than nothing. It's a shame we had to leave all our clothes behind," she lamented.

Evie sat down on the floor of the closet. "Kit, I'm sorry, about all of this. It's like everywhere I go, I step into it a little bit more."

Kit settled down next to her, abandoning the oversized clothing. "Evie, honestly, nothing makes me happier than being out of that hotel. Away from Lachlan."

With a sad smile, Evie looked at her sister. "You never did trust him, did you? From the very beginning. It's like the first time you met him, you knew exactly what he was."

"I think Lachlan can pretend to be very charming, and I think he set out to charm you. But neither of us felt right at The Grand, and you figured out what was going on before it was too late. Thank god we're out before we had to do anything … like what happened to Anne and Rebecca." Kit shuddered.

"Yes, we're lucky that way." Evie looked out of the closet, through the window at the blackness outside. "Who knows how long our luck will last."

James returned an hour later. Evie sat up quickly when she heard the soft tap on the door and quelled the fluttering that had stirred in her belly. Unlocking the door was a small pleasure. She opened the door with a flourish.

James looked down at her. The flutter was back. His wild hair looked as if he had run a brush through it, and he was wearing clean jeans. His face was still as wicked as always, down to the sharp grin aimed right at her, but somehow he looked different. He was holding a pile of clothes. "I come bearing gifts," he said.

Kit shrieked from behind Evie and pushed her out of the way to grab the bundle from James' arms. "What is this? Is this denim?" She ran into the living room with her prize.

"Why don't you come in?" Evie said, gesturing him in.

"I'd love to," he said formally, walking past her into the foyer. At close quarters, Evie could smell his soap smell — clean and sharp.

Once they were in the living room, she stepped away so he couldn't distract her any more than he already had. Kit was laying out jeans on the floor, along with T-shirts, skirts, and long-sleeved sweaters. "Where did you find all this?"

"There was a boutique store down the road. There isn't much left, it had been picked over, but I thought I would grab what I could." He sounded apologetic.

"It's wonderful," Kit said, ecstatic. "These are name brands! Here, Evie, you're short. You can have these." She handed a few pairs of jeans to Evie.

"I grabbed what I thought you might need," James said with a shrug, now looking embarrassed.

"It was great of you," Evie said. "Can I get you something? I can offer you ... water."

"You can offer me more than that," he said. Reaching up into the cupboard over the microwave, he pulled out a bottle of whiskey. "Want some?" he asked, as he took out a glass.

"I don't see why not." She sat down at the kitchen counter with him, taking the proffered drink. Kit ignored them both as she categorized the clothes. "I take it you've been here before? Is this where you bring all the ladies you rescue?" She was teasing, but he looked down. "Oh, I'm sorry, James. I didn't mean to bring up what happened with Anne. It's just ... you know your way around."

"I swept all the apartments when I came in here. I like to know what's around me, what I can use. And, obviously, where the booze is."

Evie took a swig of the drink, coughing at the strength of it. "And the resident of the building? Another lady you've rescued?"

"In fact, she rescued me."

Evie raised her eyebrows. "There must be a story there."

"Not really a story. I had brought Anne to Bill's, but he wouldn't let me stay there. It was the right decision," he said as Evie's eyebrows shot up again. "All he knew was I worked for Lachlan, had given him a hard time in the past, and had shown up with a girl who was seriously harmed. For all he knew I was setting him up. It was wonderful that he took Anne in at all, for all the danger it brought to his whole crew.

"So I was out in the streets, and I knew that Lachlan's men were after me. I was spotted near the Docks and made a run for it, dodging through the streets like we did today. The Trade District is the best place to get lost in. Lachlan's men were close behind me and I was running out of options. I looked over at this building, and a woman was beckoning me towards her. I didn't think twice, just barrelled in and locked the door behind me before anyone came around the corner. Marjory, she's the lady who lives here, is one of those people who would never hurt a fly and doesn't leave her home very often, so she isn't hassled very much.

"Later that day, some men came to the door to ask her if she'd seen anything. She played dumb, as it were, and the men finally got tired of asking and left. She's an unlikely person to be harbouring a fugitive, so they didn't suspect her. I've been here ever since, and Lachlan's men have never tracked me down. Mind you, I take precautions. I never use the front door, I try to come and go at unpredictable times, and I take different routes to and from the apartment. One and Three have seen me in the city now and again, and — as you know — dragged me back to The Grand one time, but they have never been able to follow me here, before or since my 'pardon'."

Kit bounced up next to them, full of energy. She'd listened to part of James' story. "Can we meet Marjory?"

"She keeps odd hours, so she might still be up right now. We can go check."

Down on the ground floor, at the suite marked Two, James tapped at the door. "Marjory?" he called in a low tone, trying to determine whether she was up. He turned to the girls as they waited. "I hate that she's on the first floor," he whispered. "It seems too out in the open, I'm always afraid some junkie is going to break through her window. But Marjory likes things the way they are and she insists on staying. She's not the type of person you can argue with for long. You'll like her," he said to Evie, who made a face at him. He was about to tap again when the door was flung open.

Standing in the doorway was the shortest, roundest woman Evie had ever seen, as wide around the middle as she was tall. She beamed at them all. It was impossible to figure out how old she was; her soft face was unlined and ageless. She had an enormous motherly chest and a round belly, giving the impression of a female Santa Claus. Her sensible brown dress fell to her calves and her feet were strapped into sturdy black shoes. She simply stood in the doorway with her enormous smile and looked at them.

"Marjory." James stepped forward. "I've brought some people to stay here, if that's okay with you. They're in one of the top floor apartments."

Marjory looked at James with an exaggerated expression of disbelief. James took a step back and gestured to the girls. "This is Kit, and Evie." They waved in turn.

Marjory's face shone with happiness, her sunny smile returning and her eyes filling with tears. Her facial expressions were over the top, comical even, but easy to read. Evie got a sense of great gentleness from her. She approached each girl in turn and placed a fleshy hand on her cheek. She looked into their eyes for a long moment as if searching for something, then nodded in confirmation. All the while she never spoke a word or made a sound. Evie's brows came together in confusion, and she looked to James with an unspoken question.

"Marjory doesn't speak," he said in a voice they could all hear. Marjory bobbed her head up and down in acknowledgment of this. "But she understands everything that's said, in many languages actually, and is the smartest person I have ever met."

Marjory flushed pink with pleasure. There was an easy affection between James and Marjory; he was even more relaxed with her than with the pirates. She ushered them in and showed them around her apartment. It was an inviting place, with books stacked on every possible surface. In some cases, books made up the furniture, as impromptu stools or side tables. Marjory had been reading when they interrupted her, judging from a cup of tea and open book lying next to a comfortable chair.

Kit fell in love with her when she brought over a plate of homemade cookies. Both girls dug in with vigour. "Oh," Kit groaned as she bit into one. "I haven't had a fresh cookie in a year. This is so soft. I can't believe I'm eating a cookie. Forget everything else that's happened, today is officially the best day of my life."

Evie looked at Kit, who was eating the cookie with long chews, savouring each bite. She had her eyes closed and there was a blissful smile on her face. Despite the fact that she was clearly enjoying herself, her little sister looked exhausted. There were dark smudges under her eyes, and her sixteen-year-old face seemed to be lined with wear. To Evie, it was a sharp reminder of how harrowing the day had been — of all they had been through since they'd arrived in New City. A wave of exhaustion swept over her and she knew they needed to rest now that they were safe. They could deal with everything else in the morning.

She looked over to James and Marjory. They were having a conversation, with James speaking quietly and Marjory gesturing in sweeping motions. They both looked up at her when they noticed her watching them.

"I think we're going to head upstairs. We're both pretty tired and a little bit overwhelmed."

"Let me walk you up," James said, standing up.

Too tired to protest, Evie and Kit said goodnight to Marjory, Kit thanking her profusely when she pushed an enormous bag of baked goodies into her hands.

As they walked up the stairs, Evie's legs didn't want to cooperate. She supported herself with the rickety railing, forcing her feet to move. She couldn't remember ever feeling so drained of energy. Kit's feet were also dragging, her cookie-inspired euphoria already worn off. James walked behind them both, silent.

"Where is your apartment?" Evie called back to him as they rounded the last turn to the fourth landing.

"Back there, on the third floor." He pointed down the dark hallway they had just passed.

"And nobody else lives here?" At the shake of his head, she asked, "Don't you find it lonely?"

"Most buildings are pretty abandoned in New City. You get used to it. And, after the crush at The Grand, the emptiness is more than welcome."

Evie stopped in front of Suite Eleven and looked at him, her eyes dark and serious. "Why are you letting us stay here? Aren't we putting you in danger?"

James shrugged, looking away from her, impassive. "I'm in no more danger than I was before. I told you, Lachlan doesn't know where I am. I figured I could at least share my haven with you." He looked down at her, a small smile curling one side of his mouth. "Besides, maybe you'll make it a little less lonely."

Kit snorted. "You've probably bitten off more than you can chew."

James' eyes never left Evie's. "Of that I'm sure," he said, his voice soft and promising. "Think of it as my gift to you. Take it and enjoy." He started to walk away down the hallway. "I'll be back tomorrow to check on you."

He was halfway down the stairs when Evie called out in a small voice, "Thank you."

She didn't know whether he heard her until a faint "anytime" came floating back up to her. Her mouth curved up, her private smile, as she closed the door behind her and gave the lock a satisfying snap shut.

Chapter Fifteen

For the next month, Kit and Evie did not leave the apartment. James visited them every day, bringing them food and checking to see if they needed anything, but he insisted they didn't leave. He was even concerned with them getting too close to the windows. "You don't want to be seen by anyone," he explained one day, drinking coffee at the counter in their kitchen. "There are informants everywhere. If someone spots you, they could report to Lachlan."

"Are Lachlan's men still out looking for us?" Evie asked.

He shrugged. "No more than usual, since you were always sneaking out of The Grand. No, there aren't any armed men searching for you," he said with a laugh at her annoyed look. "But it's not safe out there for you and Kit."

Evie controlled her urge to pout. "Well, what are you doing out every day? Is it safe for you?"

He gave her a hard look. "Safer for me than for you." When she continued to stare at him, he sighed and covered his face with his hands. "I have business around town. You have no reason to be out where anyone can see you."

"What do you do out there now that the pirates have left?" said Evie, finally asking the question that had been nagging at her all week.

"A little of this, a little of that. Kit, what are you making over there? It smells delicious." The change in topic was deliberate. Evie seethed at his dismissal and vowed she would bring it up later.

With so much time on their hands, the girls turned to exploring all the other apartments in the building. They were all as dusty as their own had been, but there was no evidence of rotting food or decomposed bodies. Lachlan had obviously been very thorough when he ordered a general clean up and removal of all corpses for burning. Grudgingly, she admitted to herself that she appreciated his effort.

Kit found a few items of clothing to add to their collection, and Evie looked for prescription drugs. All the medicine cabinets were bare, which made Evie realize that Lachlan's men had probably taken more than bodies from the apartments. Her thoughts went to the stash of medical supplies at the hotel, and a worry filled her; Lachlan had probably found it by now.

Marjory's suite was by far the most interesting. With all the books in her home, Evie had assumed the silent woman was an avid reader, but that was an understatement. Her spare bedroom was covered in books, some precarious piles reaching to waist height. She used another apartment to store those she couldn't fit into her own place.

As they explored, which Marjory encouraged them to do with enthusiastic gestures, they found the piles were organized into categories, containing everything from French classic literature to world history to books on gardening. It was as if a library had been emptied. Evie suspected that was exactly what had happened.

Marjory communicated to the girls that she was delighted with their company, through her overt facial expressions and hand gestures. When they were discussing any serious topic, Marjory would join in. Slipping on tiny reading glasses she perched on her nose, her hand flew over a pad of paper in a tight concise cursive. Her education and intelligence were clear from her insightful comments. After some persuading, Marjory admitted that she used to be a professor of sociology at the Greater Havern University. When pressed about why she wouldn't speak, she always remained silent, both in words and writing.

The girls started to spend the days in her cozy apartment. Kit curled up on an overstuffed couch with an enormous book in her lap, looking perfectly at peace. She still had the ability to be content doing whatever it was she was doing at the time. If she was wrapped up in a book, she could remain there for hours.

Evie was happy to see she was reading a broad range of books, from literary classics to tomes about history and philosophy. Marjory had started to leave books out that she thought Kit might be interested in, and then would engage her in conversation about them, asking pointed questions. It was providing Kit with a well-rounded education. Evie had been worried and a little sad that Kit never finished high school, not that it mattered, not that there was any high school any more, but still. Being with Marjory turned out to be even better than public education.

When she was not reading or engaging the girls in conversation, Marjory puttered about in the kitchen, flipping through her immense collection of cookbooks and then baking something delicious. Evie, restless, often watched.

"You should open a restaurant," Evie said to Marjory one day as they enjoyed her latest creation, shortbread sprinkled with a tiny portion of sugar. Evie rolled her eyes as she bit into the flaky pastry.

Marjory giggled and handed her a napkin. She jotted down a note, then pushed the paper towards Evie.

You're sweet. But even if I opened a restaurant, who would come?

"Are you kidding? Anyone who tasted these, for one."

"I'd come," Kit called from the living room.

Marjory smiled again, but it was a sad smile.

"Could you teach me?" Evie asked, hesitant. "It's just … cooking is something I've always wanted to do but never really got a chance to learn."

Of course. What would you like to make?

Evie thought about it. "Well, isn't it hard to get all the ingredients you need? Does that affect what you make?"

Somewhat. Baking is easier; a lot of the ingredients are non-perishable and so can still be found. The other ingredients — milk, butter, eggs — James gets for me at the Market. Other items are harder. Marjory paused for a moment then brought her notepad back to her as an afterthought. *What I wouldn't give for a piece of cheesecake.*

Evie smiled. "When I was little, my mom made this big dinner for the family. I forget what we were celebrating but it really stuck in my mind. It was a roasted rack of lamb, I think. She told me I wouldn't like it, but I loved every bite. I always wanted to try that recipe someday, but ..." she trailed off with a shrug.

Lamb is hard to come by. But I'm roasting some chicken tonight, why don't you help me with that?

Evie spent the day in the kitchen, mainly getting in Marjory's way, but the result was a delicious chicken, roasted in spices and juice, along with potatoes in oil. Kit and James exclaimed over Evie's obvious culinary talent while she blushed and told them to shut it.

James opened up in the weeks the girls were confined to the building. Instead of the diffident delinquent he was out on the streets, he was helpful, and he did not try to hide his adoration of Marjory. He became much easier to get along with. And so did Evie. Now that she wasn't being chased through the streets, she started to enjoy his sly sense of humour. Despite her original misgivings about him, she was now able to take his merciless teasing without getting defensive. As the days passed, she recognized that she finally trusted him fully, even though — or maybe because — he had not tried to deny he had killed someone.

She also began to realize she had been foolish to ignore his advice about how to stay safe in New City and resolved not to lash out at him when he told her what to do. While she still chafed when she felt she was being controlled, she knew that he was just trying to keep her and Kit safe.

They became a tight-knit group. He taught them how to pick a door lock using only bobby pins. Kit started to bug James about letting her cut his hair. He would run his black-tattooed hands through his unruly mane and tell her it was just part of him.

Evie found he was becoming more of a distraction to her. Every time he came into the room it brought about that treacherous longing to touch him. From the looks he gave her, holding her gaze for too long and standing just a little too close, she suspected he felt the same way.

Despite their comfortable set up, and her vow not to rant against James, Evie was becoming impatient with the enforced confinement. "This is ridiculous," she snapped one day during the third week, pacing the length of the living room. "Are we never going to be allowed to go outside again?" She whirled around. "Do you know that people who are kept inside all the time develop vitamin D deficiency?"

Kit had been watching her pace in silence, but she laughed at this. "You and your vitamins. I'm sure we'll be okay. And we're going to go out again, at some point. We just need to wait for the pirates to get back …"

"And then what?" Evie growled, impatience making her bad tempered. "They certainly weren't jumping at the chance to help us out before. Did you notice how vague Bill was and how quickly he got us off his barge?"

"Come on, Evie. You know James will persuade Bill to take us."

"And what do you think James is out there doing all day long?"

"I'm sure you have nothing to worry about," Kit said. "He doesn't seem to stray very far from here. From you, in particular."

"That's not what I meant." Evie glared at her sister. "I mean, where does he go? How does he keep himself busy all day?"

Kit shrugged, less bothered by the questions that were eating at her sister. Evie sighed, looking out the window that she wasn't supposed to be near. "I've been thinking about going back to The Grand," she said, forgetting her decision to try to accept James' guidance.

"What?" Kit stood up at this announcement. "What for? To turn yourself in to Lachlan?"

"No, I'd go in secret. I have to find out whether Lachlan has found our drugs or not. He knows there are secret hiding places all over the hotel, so he'll soon have figured out there is one in our suite and that I hid the drugs there. He has probably had the place torn apart by now, looking for it, but there's a chance he didn't find it. I have to try to get the drugs back. They could be really important to us. Especially if we wanted to leave New City, it could be the difference between life and death."

"Going back to The Grand could be death," Kit shouted, eyes round with anger. "It was sheer dumb luck we were able to get away without being hurt. You can't go back there, you heard what Lachlan does. Is still doing. You might even put James and Bill in more danger. Lachlan could torture you and make you tell —"

Evie sat down on the couch, defeated. "Okay, okay, I know. It was a dumb idea. Sorry. But, we can't just sit here forever. I'm going crazy."

"Crazy is right." Kit sat back down in disgust. "We're waiting for the pirates to get back. I know that they'll take us with them, away from New City. Don't you dare go anywhere until then."

Evie stormed out of the apartment. "I'm going down to see Marjory," she called over her shoulder.

"That better be all you're doing," Kit called after her.

At the ground level, she was going to rap on Marjory's door but was drawn to the large double front doors instead. They were solid wood, with no windows around them. It made the lobby dark even in the middle of the day, but protected them from the watchful eyes of passers by. Evie trailed her hand along the door handle, itching to go out. Surely there wasn't a group of men just sitting in the streets, waiting to grab her.

She sighed and let her hand drop. *Be sensible. Going out would be as dumb as going back to The Grand, you idiot,* she told herself.

"Going somewhere?"

Evie jumped away from the door, startled, whipping her hand behind her back as she spun to see James coming up from the parkade. "I — no. I wasn't going anywhere. I'm just curious, but I wasn't going to do anything."

James looked at her skeptically. "You just can't seem to keep yourself out of trouble."

Evie smiled despite herself as she thought, *You could be right, James. You would have a fit if you knew what I was planning ten minutes ago.* She considered telling him, but said instead, "Some might call it a character flaw. I wasn't going to go anywhere, I promise. I wouldn't put Kit's life in danger, or Marjory's. Or yours." She looked up at him, her smile fading as she absorbed the heated look he was giving her. For the first time since she met him, she saw a blush spread over his sharp features.

"You must be bored out of your mind," he said, breaking eye contact with her. "Come on. I know what will help. You need a drink." He started to walk up the stairs, not waiting for her. She hesitated for a moment then followed.

Instead of continuing up to Evie's apartment, James turned off at the third floor and headed to his apartment. She had never been there. She had always thought he wanted to keep this place separate from them. Curious, Evie followed him into his kitchen, looking around.

His home was a similar layout to Kit and Evie's above him, but immaculate, barely lived in compared to their sprawling mess. There was little colour in the room, only various shades of white and beige. It appeared that he had not touched the place since he started living there, keeping it exactly as he'd found it. This may be where James put his head down at the end of the day, but it was not home.

"Do you want some wine?" he asked.

"Is booze how you deal with everything?" she teased him.

"Not everything, but it certainly has a way of taking the edge off, don't you think? You know, end of the world and all." His back was turned to her as he rummaged in the overhead cupboards. James had shrugged out of his usual tough leather outerwear. From this viewpoint, he was giving Evie an excellent view of his denim-clad backside. He turned around with two glasses and an expectant look. Her eyes flicked back up. "What? Um, yes, wine is good."

"Perfect." He took out a bottle of red and popped the cork. "That is such a great sound," he said as the wine glugged into the oversized glasses. He lifted his glass to hers, and they toasted silently.

He took a deep breath and led her over to the couch. "This is relaxing. It's nice to have a safe house, isn't it? So hard to always sleep with one eye open."

She nodded. "I've been sleeping so much better since I got here. I could never relax at The Grand. I was never sure who was going to come barging in during the night."

"Good instincts. Anyone could have, and eventually would have."

Evie shuddered, remembering One ripping her out of her bed. "I'm so glad we're away from there."

162

"Did you ever trust Lachlan?" James gave her a careful look from behind half-closed eyelids.

"No, not really. Not enough to ever relax around him. He scared me, truthfully, from the very beginning. But I was so grateful to him; I thought he had saved us. He pretended to care about us, and I thought that I *should* trust him. How about you? Did you ever trust him? I mean, before you knew what he was capable of?"

James took a deep drink of his wine. "I trusted him once. More than anyone. He saved my life." He put the glass down, staring into it.

Evie stilled. "During the Sickness?"

"Yes, but not because I was sick."

"Does this have to do with what Anne told us?"

James gave a self-deprecating smile that didn't reach his eyes. "That I'm a convict? I didn't think you'd forget that." He picked up his glass again and settled back against the couch. "I was in prison when the Sickness hit. By the time anyone realized the extent of it, there was an outbreak among the prisoners. The guards fled and left the inmates to die.

"It was a cesspool, every cell with at least one rotting body. The stench was amazing, as were the clouds of flies. My cellmate died early; he started coughing then just didn't get up one day. I watched as he decomposed day to day."

Evie choked on a horrified gasp, picturing the vivid scene James was remembering behind his blank eyes. She picked up her wine and took a swallow, trying to ease the knot that had formed in her chest.

James continued, "I don't know why, but I didn't get sick. Everyone else died around me, and I was left. I ... I thought I was being punished. I was starving and I started to envy my cellmate. I thought of ... ending things. But the will to live was stronger.

"I think two things saved me in those weeks. The first is I had just gotten there. I hadn't been in prison a week before the insanity started. I was still strong; it was too early for them to have broken me. My cellmate on the other hand — he looked dead before he even got sick. I don't even remember his name now.

"The other thing that saved me was the leak in the roof over my cell. I complained about it when I first arrived, but the leak wasn't fixed. The guards just gave us some buckets to catch the drips. That month was particularly wet and the rain gushed in. After the water stopped working, I was able to drink the rainwater. That's what kept me from dehydrating.

"Still, I wouldn't have survived for long. One day, a man came into the prison looking for survivors. I didn't have the strength to call out, so I banged my water cup against the metal bars until he found me. I collapsed after that, and when I woke up I was at The Grand."

"That was Lachlan? He rescued you?"

"Yes, he was organizing the body clean up of every building in Greater Havern, as it was still called then, and that included the prison. They torched the place afterwards; it was easier than dragging all the bodies out to burn them. I was the only guy he found alive. He let me stay in the basement of The Grand and told one of his underlings to look after me. As soon as I was back on my feet he gave me a job helping out with, as he put it, 'the administration of New City.' I thought that I was being given a second chance. I think that's why I ignored so much of what was going on right under my nose. I promise you I never touched a girl while I was at the hotel, but I wasn't exactly paying attention either. I trusted Lachlan because — like you — I was grateful to him and felt I owed him."

"He gave you every reason to trust him."

James shook his head. "When I look back on it now, I can't believe I thought I could start over. I should have known he saved me because he thought I was a thug. He just wanted me to do his dirty work."

"But you're not like that. You're not violent or awful, like some of his men."

"What do you think I am, Evie? A murderer with a heart of gold? Lachlan wanted men to do the sort of work that he'd rather not muddy his hands with." His tone was bitter. "He should have left me there to rot. I wasn't far away."

"Don't say that," Evie said. "Nobody deserves that."

"Maybe I did. I really was nothing better than a thief from as far back as I can remember. In and out of juvie. I stole what I could. I would hurt those who tried to hurt me, and more besides that. And I killed a man. He didn't deserve it."

They sat in silence for a long time. James swirled his wine, deep in thought.

"I didn't mean to," he said finally, still watching the purple liquid swish. "It was a burglary gone wrong. No one was supposed to be there. It was an in and out job, easy. Something I couldn't say no to. But he was there." His tone was bleak. "A man, the owner of the home. He wasn't supposed to be, but he was. He surprised me, came at me with a baseball bat. I didn't think, I just shot him."

A long silence stretched out in front of them. James nodded. "I should have been left to rot in that prison. Instead, Lachlan got me out to steal from others on his orders. He wanted someone like me on the streets. I never carried a gun again though." He looked up at Evie, an odd hopeful look on his face. "I'll never kill anyone again. I'll never forget it, and wish I could take it back."

"But you're helping people now. You helped Anne, and you left Lachlan once you knew what he was. And you helped me. Us, that is."

His face was twisted, haunted. He looked at her without seeing.

"I took a life. Do you understand how that makes me feel Evie? You have never killed anyone. You can't possibly understand."

She took a deep drink of wine then looked him straight in the eye. "But I do understand, James. I really do. "

Chapter Sixteen

James sputtered into his drink. He gave her an incredulous look, but didn't say anything.

Evie paused, in part pleased that she had surprised him, but also dreading recounting her tale. "It was this past winter. Kit and I were alone, we had been alone for months, and it was so cold. A blizzard had blown in, which wasn't at all unexpected, but we still weren't prepared for it. Stupid of me, really. We had been snowed in for two days, trying to keep warm by the fire even though the firewood was soaked through so produced more smoke than heat. I was afraid we wouldn't be able to get the truck out afterwards, that we wouldn't be able to get more food, that we would slowly starve or freeze there. It was horrible." She shivered as she remembered the dark frozen days.

"It was the afternoon of the third day and there was no sign of the storm breaking. But I heard something else outside, over the blowing snow. Two men had snowmobiled up to our house. I have no idea what they were doing out in weather like that. They could have died." Her voice caught. James reached over and took her free hand, giving it a squeeze. She didn't squeeze back but kept his hand in hers. "We couldn't believe it. We had not seen other people — living people — for months. We were beginning to think that maybe we were the only survivors, anywhere, so we were thrilled to hear those machines.

At first we thought maybe these people were coming to rescue us.

"But, something was wrong. I knew almost immediately. They had all kinds of fancy gear on and they were laughing and singing. I figured they must have gone crazy. A whiteout like that can do that to you. I told Kit to hide in the basement and I got out my father's guns.

"I surprised them when they came up to the door, welcoming them with the business end of a rifle. They were so drunk that even from behind the screen door I could smell it coming off of them in waves. They said they were looking for shelter. I didn't know what to do. I told them they could stay in our shed and I could share some provisions with them if they needed food, even though I didn't have much. But I wouldn't let them come in. One of the men, he became ... unpleasant," she said with a twist of her mouth. "He tried to force his way in. He told me I owed it to humanity to entertain him and his friend. I kept on telling him no, and even his friend backed off and said they should leave, but he just kept on. He went to the front window and said he would break it if I didn't invite them in. I told them ..." her voice faded as she remembered. "I told them," she started again, voice gaining strength, "that if he tried, I would shoot him. I told him, and he laughed at me. He said I wouldn't shoot, that they were the best I could hope."

"What did you do?" James' normally hooded eyes were wide.

She stuck out her chin. "I shot him in the chest. It was messy. There was a lot of blood. It didn't kill him right away. He started coughing blood and collapsed. The other guy picked him up and dragged him to their snowmobile, all the while yelling at me not to fire again. There was so much blood. It left a trail in the snow covering the front lawn. It disappeared when the wind blew more snow over it."

After a long pause, James said, "Did he die?"

She shrugged. "I don't know for sure. His friend took off with him on his snowmobile, propped up in front of him. But it was in the middle of a blizzard and even if they found the hospital, there was nobody there to help them. I'd say there is one in a hundred chance that he survived." Shaking her head, she met his eyes. "I don't know why I try to kid myself he had even that much chance of making it. I killed him."

"How do you feel about that?"

"I don't regret it," she said in a cold lifeless voice. "I would do it again in a heartbeat. When I think about how he laughed at me, how he made me feel helpless, how they could have hurt Kit. And me.

"I promised my father, just before he died — that was a year before we left to come south here — that I would survive and take care of Kit. That we would keep on going. If that makes me a cold-blooded killer, then so be it."

James gave her a sad smile, so different from his usual grin. "What happened to you was different. You were protecting yourself. Besides, things are different when order breaks down. You have to be able to protect yourself like that."

"Are you telling me life is cheaper when there are so few of us left? That his life was worth mine and Kit's safety? Because there's not many of us; you'd think we'd be taking better care of each other." She took another deep drink of wine, draining her glass. James refilled it when she set it down. Evie felt more tired than she had in a long time, a bone-weary exhaustion that had nothing to do with physical exertion.

"When no one's going to take care of you, you have to take care of yourself," James said, voice tinged with pity and understanding.

The look she gave him was fuelled with anger and grief. "I told you I would do it again in a heartbeat. I know you wouldn't. That makes me worse than you, I think. But I don't regret it."

He shifted towards her on the couch, leaning into her. "When it comes to us, there's no worse or better. Just us. Anyway, thanks for not thinking I'm a monster." He brought his mouth down onto hers, tasting sweet and fruity like red wine. Evie started to pull away, but he pulled her into him, his hands at her waist, and kissed her more deeply. His mouth moving over hers unhinged her; she leaned into him, into his warmth, finding her balance there with him. When he released her she was reeling. She sat up, breaking out of his embrace.

"I should go," she said.

He was looking down at her, his eyes simmering. "You probably should," he whispered. She got up and headed out of his kitchen, his apartment. As she left, she saw him pouring another glass of wine for himself. "I'll see you tomorrow," he said.

"The pirates are coming back," James announced as he walked into Marjory's apartment, where the girls had been curled up all afternoon.

Kit sat up with a cry of joy. "When? Are they going to be here today?"

"This afternoon." James laughed at her enthusiasm. "I've just been at one of the trade houses and heard that some smaller boats passed by yesterday. They are faster than the big barges, so they usually get here a day ahead of the *Mary Rose*."

"That's great news." Evie sat up slower than her sister. Her mind was already spinning, thinking about what it meant that the pirates were returning. "Do you think that maybe they'll let us join them now? Or at least get us out of the city?"

"There's still a lot we need to figure out, but that was the original plan. We'll speak with Bill tonight about that." James' voice sounded stiff and formal. It had been five days since he kissed her, and since then they had been unfailingly polite to each other, but she had taken care not to be alone with him. It was driving Evie nuts.

"Are they considering leaving New City forever? It sounds like Bill is getting impatient with trading here. Maybe they want to settle somewhere out west?"

His smile faded as he shrugged. "That's the question I'm sure everyone is asking."

Marjory sat by, listening and watching with a gentle smile on her face. She had stated many times that she had no interest in meeting the pirates, in leaving the shelter of her small apartment, no matter how much the girls told her she would enjoy their company.

"We have to get ready," Kit said. "We are going to see them, aren't we?"

James looked uncertain. "That was the plan. We'll go after dark though. Less chance of being spotted."

"Okay, that doesn't give us a lot of time." Kit went over and grabbed Evie. "Come on, let's go."

"We have all afternoon," Evie said, laughing as she allowed her sister to hoist her out of her comfortable chair. She was as excited as Kit to get out of the stifling apartment.

"I'm going to the Docks to meet them," James said. "I will come back to pick you up and take you there. Evie," he paused, giving her a meaningful look. "Don't even think about leaving without me."

"Wouldn't dream of it." She gave him an arch smile.

Hours later, after enduring Kit's chatter and endless muttering over the state of her hair, Evie was pronounced good enough to be seen in public. The sisters met James downstairs near midnight and followed him through the parkade, coming up behind the dumpster. They followed him through the darkened streets, keeping within the Trade District along back roads and alleys. Both girls wore dark bulky clothes and had their hoods up. They looked like everyone else in New City now. Kit stayed pressed at Evie's side.

Twisting out of one alley, they came face to face with a group of men loitering in the empty road. Kit was closest to them and stepped back with a gasp. Evie kept her head down, pulling her sister into her.

"Now what have we here?" said the closest man, walking over to them with a leer. "These wouldn't be the two girls who have mysteriously gone missing from The Grand, would they? Word is there's a big reward to the man who brings them in."

Evie drew back, forcing Kit back with her. Adrenaline crashed through her system as she had a flashback of their first encounter with men in New City.

James stepped in front of the girls, leaning down to the shorter man so their heads were even, speaking in a low voice. "I'm pretty sure the reward wouldn't be worth it for a man like yourself."

"James!" The man backed away a step, startled. "I didn't see you there. Sorry for —"

"I'm pretty sure you didn't see anything here at all, Dan," James said. Evie watched as the group melted into the shadows of the surrounding alleys until only the one man was left.

"Of course. I didn't see anything at all. You can count on me, no worries." Dan backed away a few more paces before turning and hurrying after his friends.

"What —" Evie whispered.

"It's nothing," James said, turning to take her arm, hurrying her along. "Just a bit of bad luck is all. We'll survive it."

"But what if they report back to Lachlan that they saw us? They clearly know who you are."

"They won't," he said. "Not if they know what's good for them."

They emerged at the Docks on the west end and kept their heads down as they walked along the pier to the *Mary Rose*, ignoring the men that swarmed and shouted around them.

Relief flooded through Evie as she ran up the gangplank and stepped onto the deck. "We made it," she whispered to Kit, who was still gripping her arm. "I thought those men were going to drag us back to The Grand."

Evie's nervousness melted away as friendly people swirled around her, laughing, talking, flirting. Under the cover of darkness, the female crewmembers felt safe enough to leave the cabin and join the men on deck. Drinks were being passed back and forth and it seemed very much the beginning of a party. The pirates must have done well. Evie found herself comparing this scene to the glittering parties she had witnessed at The Grand.

The pirates were much rougher than the people at The Grand. Living off the land and the occasionally misappropriated cargo, they had gotten used to taking care of themselves and each other. Their smiles were real, though, as was the way they enjoyed each other's company.

James had left her side to speak with one of the burly men, and Kit skipped off when she saw Oliver. Feeling conspicuous on her own, Evie looked for someone to talk to. She spotted Bill sitting to one side of the crowd, drinking a large mug of beer. She wound her way through the moving bodies and sat down next to him.

"Hello Bill. James told me you had a good trip."

"He's right. We came back with enough beef to feed a healthy portion of New City, which will go a long way to funding our next few trips."

"Can I ask you something? Why don't you have electricity on the boat?" she asked. "I've seen other boats hook into the grid when they arrive at the Docks."

"The price is too steep of us, is the reason for that," Bill said, glowering at her from underneath his bushy eyebrows.

"You mean being under Lachlan's control." He didn't answer, only took a deep draught of his drink. "I prefer the bonfires," she continued. "They're warmer and more useful for cooking."

He squinted at her and grunted, taking another long slug of his drink. He reached over and filled another mug from a pitcher and passed it to her. She took a long drink realizing, nose-deep in the fumes, that it was whiskey, not beer as she had thought. Sputtering on her mouthful, she lowered the mug and wiped her mouth. Bill had the grace to pretend he hadn't noticed. She took a more cautious sip and enjoyed the warmth spreading through her throat and chest.

She held the glass mug between her hands as silence settled between them. Risking an occasional glance in his direction, she wondered about Bill. His natural state was to growl and complain, but there was a soft side underneath his crusty exterior. The only person she'd seen getting under that shell was Kit, but she had that effect on everyone. Looking for her in the crowd, Evie realized Bill wasn't the only one affected by her bright charm, as she was once again surrounded by a chattering group of young men.

Evie preferred Bill's gruff company. Before the Sickness, before the world changed, he had travelled around the globe, or so James had told her. He had visited places and seen sights that she would never be able to see now. Some probably didn't exist anymore.

She cleared her throat and interrupted whatever deep thought was occupying him. "James mentioned you do business with a cattle ranch out west." She took his squint as tacit approval to continue. "What's it like out there?"

Setting his mug down, he sat back on the bench, looking as if he were about to tell her a tale. "It's something to see out there. They're like a bunch a' cowboys from the Old West. They don't got no power out there at all, so they make do the way everyone used to before we had it. Funny to watch them, though, since half of them don't have a clue what they're doing."

"How can they run a cattle ranch if they don't know what they're doing?"

"Well, they do the best they can. A lot of it is common sense, some of it just trial and error. All of them came from the city, though; none of them have any experience as ranchers."

"Why did they decide to do it, then?"

"After the Sickness, many set out looking for … god knows what. Answers, maybe. These people found a cattle ranch, and maybe that was answer enough for them. The owners were dead and the cattle were starving, horses running wild. They saw something they could fix, so they did it." He reached for his mug, taking another long drink of whiskey. "There's all kinds of establishments like that, setting themselves up across the prairies. I'm sure elsewhere, as well." He glanced up at her. "I've only been out to the west as far as the mountains. While you were up north, did you hear of any other settlements, farther afield?"

Evie shook her head. "Nobody in my community survived, other than Kit and I. We drove all over, but we never saw another living person until we came to New City. Other than a few raiders," she added quietly. "Of course, there weren't very many people up there to begin with."

Reaching into his pocket, he pulled out a wilted hand-rolled cigarette and a grubby book of matches. He lit it and inhaled deeply, thinking over what she'd said. "That makes sense. Not as many survivors, and harsher winters to get through." He pointed his nicotine-stained finger at her. "You and Kit both survived. I've seen this before — a pair of siblings surviving when the rest of the family don't make it. Whatever protective gene you have, Kit must have too. Strange how that works."

"I guess it makes sense." Because Bill was for once forthcoming with his answers, likely due to the amount of whiskey he had consumed, she kept up her line of questioning. "Do many people leave the city, to set up new communities like that?"

Bill frowned, weighing his answer. "In the beginning, yes. People would come to New City and then leave again, venturing out into the world. Modern-day pioneers, trying to find something better. In the last few months, though, no. Very few people leave New City, once they've set up here."

"Because of Lachlan's influence? He controls people that much?"

Bill shrugged. "Lachlan can do whatever he wants, so it seems. No one's going to stop him. Then again, maybe people like it here and see no reason to leave. It's cushier than out west, at the very least."

"You can leave though."

"Well, we never got set up here in New City. We come in for a few weeks, sometimes a month at most, to trade, then we're off again."

"Is that why you don't try to deal with Lachlan?"

Bill fixed her with his bright blue eyes, still very alert despite the whiskey. "That's one of the reasons, yes."

"Are you going to leave the city for good, set up in the West as well?" He hesitated for a moment, so Evie rushed on with the question she had been burning to ask. "Are you going to take us with you?"

Instead of answering, Bill gestured to the tall figure that had walked over to join them. Evie, usually happy to see James, cursed inwardly at his timing. *Why won't Bill answer me on this?* she thought in frustration.

"What are you two talking about, so serious?" James asked, smiling.

"The price of power," Bill said straight-faced. "Now, why don't you take care of your girl here, so that I can be left alone to smoke in peace?" Bill got up, hiding a small smile under his shaggy mustache.

The only light came from the flickering flames of the bonfires nearby, hiding Evie's flush at being referred to as James' girl.

"How are you doing?" he asked as he settled in next to her.

"Good. It's nice to be back here. It feels more like a home than anything in New City." He nodded and Evie got nervous in the silence between them. "Can I get you a drink?" She grabbed the whiskey and made a motion to pour it for him.

He flashed his wide smile. "Evie, that's the best offer I've had in a long time." He collapsed down next to her, stretching out his long legs so they were right next to hers. She could feel the warmth from his body, welcome on the chilly night. James took the mug she poured for him and took a grateful drink. He closed his eyes and leaned his head back against the packing crate behind them. The tension of the last week dissolved and Evie found herself relaxing. Studying him, she saw deep shadows under his eyes. He seemed about to fall asleep.

"You must be hungry. Why don't I grab some food for you?" She started to scramble up, but he reached out and grabbed her waist, pulling her back down and settling her in front of him. He left his arm around her, holding her close.

After having more whiskey than she should have, she didn't mind others seeing them like this. It was the most comfortable thing in the world to be curled up with James in the firelight, her back to his chest, watching people dance and talk. In companionable silence, they took occasional sips from their mugs. She laid her head back on his shoulder and could feel his steady heartbeat. Thinking he had fallen asleep, she glanced up to see his eyes were half closed, glittering in the firelight.

"James," she said softly, wondering if he was in the mood to talk.

"Hmm?" he responded, drowsy with the warmth and whiskey.

"You've been to the parties at The Grand, right?"

That woke him up. The mention of The Grand caused him to tense as he became more alert. "I've certainly seen one or two in my time. Usually just there to keep men in line. Why?"

"They bothered me right from the start."

He snorted. "Well good. They should bother you." James sat up straighter and picked her up with him, settling her more comfortably in the circle of his arms. "Tell me what you're thinking, Evie. I love hearing what's going on inside that beautiful head of yours." He said this with his face in her hair, his breath tickling her ear. The hairs at the back of her neck prickled as a shiver passed through her whole body.

"Everyone surrounding Lachlan was so lovely and elegant, and everything seemed perfect there, like there were no cares in the world. But you could tell something was off; something was false. Do you know what I mean? Smiles were too wide, laughter too loud, as if everyone was an uneasy actor in a play. Even before I knew what was going on, there was a sense of something dark lurking behind the sparkling people."

She paused for a moment, trying to put the rest of her thoughts into words. "Of course, everything that Lachlan is doing at those parties is horrible, the whole thing is. But there's more. It's as if the Sickness never happened. I think, deep down, that's why they're all there. To pretend it didn't happen."

"Ah." James relaxed against her.

"It's as if they're ignoring the fact that the world changed. Almost like living in an alternate reality. Bill told me about the people setting up farms and ranches, even though they have no idea what they're doing. He called them modern pioneers. It seems like they're thinking ahead, to the future. People living in New City, though, I feel like we're living off the back of our past, scavenging the refuse of a lost civilization.

"But it can't last. I saw that up north. At first, it seemed like there were lots of supplies left, but they will eventually run out, and no one is creating anything new. What will happen to all the fancy parties then? I came to New City to survive, to take care of Kit and myself, and I'll do what it takes. But why are we so concerned with electricity when the food is about to run out? Ignoring reality in the long run isn't going to help us survive. Working the land, trying to make something more lasting, that seems more ..." she trailed off, running out of steam as she struggled for the appropriate word.

"Honest?" James supplied.

"Maybe. It's honest to work for your food. I like the idea of it. But it's also smart. You don't have to rely on anyone else."

"So do you want to go west, set up a farm, Evie?" She could tell he was smiling from his voice.

"Maybe I will set up a farm." She couldn't help smiling too. "What about you? What would you do if you left New City?"

"If you set up a farm, you'd need some strong masculine types to do the grunt work for you. What'd you say, Evie? Can I be your labourer?" Wrapping his arm around her, he slid his other hand down her thigh, surprising a laugh out of her.

"James," she shrieked. "You're drunk! Get off me!" She tried to squirm out of his grasp, giggling.

James was laughing too. "Come on baby. I'd muck out the stables for you. What else do you want in a man?" He wiggled his eyebrows at her.

"Stop it, someone's going to see us," she hissed.

"Why would they be looking at us when there's so much more to be looking at?"

"What do you mean?" He had stopped wrestling her and was looking over her shoulder with a mischievous smile on his face.

Following the direction of his look, Evie gasped. Kit had broken away from her pack of admirers and was now in a dark corner of the deck, wrapped in the arms of a boy a foot taller who could be no one other than Oliver. They clearly had no compunctions about being seen.

"That little hussy," Evie whispered, starting to giggle again. She looked up at James' face. "I knew Oliver had a crush on her, but I didn't know she felt the same way."

"I don't think Kit knew about it either, until she drank a bottle of wine tonight."

Evie leaned back, giving a dramatic sigh. "My little sister, drunk, shameless, making out with strange pirates. What kind of influence have I been?"

"I'm sure you've been a wonderful influence on her," James murmured. His face was so close to hers, she couldn't focus on him. It only made sense to close her eyes and lean into his lips.

James kissed her softly, pressing his lips gently against hers. All too soon he pulled away with a sharp breath. She made a small sound of loss, wanting his lips back on hers.

"Evie, love, it seems you've gotten yourself a bit drunk as well."

"So?" She leaned in towards him again, craving his warmth.

"So," James said as he shifted away from her, planting a kiss on her forehead, "I'm absolutely terrified of your temper tomorrow morning. I don't want to go through another standoff between us. "

When she opened her mouth to argue, he stopped her.

"Listen, I need to go. I actually should have left a while ago. I have some business in the city. Bill will walk you and Kit home tonight. Don't you dare go by yourself." He gave her a warning look.

She bobbed her head in assent. "Don't worry, that little gang on the street was enough to warn me away from wandering the streets alone tonight. Or ever."

"Good. I will be back at the apartment tomorrow. I'll come and see you." He got up to walk away, leaving Evie wondering whether he would ever tell her what this "business" was.

"James?" she called after him. He whirled around, his face nearly hidden in shadows. "Be careful."

Even in the dim light she saw his grin. "Always," he said firmly. And then he disappeared.

Chapter Seventeen

Evie's eyes flew open to the sound of someone banging on the front door. It took her a moment to get her bearings. At first she thought she was back at The Grand, being summoned to see Lachlan once again.

She sat up, relieved to see she was in her apartment, alone in a room flooded with sunlight. She had forgotten to close the blinds the night before.

"Oh, shoot," she said as the events of last night came flooding back. *The party on the pirate's boat. Bill walking her and Kit home in the early hours. Kit unable to contain her good mood, dancing through the empty streets. As much as Bill tried to stop her, he was less cautious than he should have been, at one point even starting to chuckle along with her before telling her to pull her hood up again. And then there was James, and the memory of his warm lips on hers.*

She took half a second to get lost in that memory, until the loud knocking brought her back and she realized it was James banging on her door.

"Ladies, don't tell me you're still asleep," he called out cheerfully. "It's almost noon, time to get up."

Evie got to the door and rearranged her face into a scowl before opening it. His face lit up in amusement. "Good morning, Evie. Oh, now don't look at me like that. You look like an angry bear cub."

She started to laugh with him, unable to keep up the pretence any longer. He pushed past her into the apartment, making himself comfortable in the kitchen. He set down a thermos and opened it, releasing the rich smell of coffee. "How are you feeling?"

"Not bad, for all that I woke up about five seconds ago. I'm not even going to ask how you are. I don't believe you ever actually sleep."

"Sleep is for the sane. But even sane people don't need to sleep for half the day." That comment was directed at Kit, who had just come stumbling out of her room. Evie's first thought was that she hoped she looked better than her sister. Kit's long hair was hanging tangled over her face and it looked as if her legs were made of rubber. She collapsed onto a kitchen chair and sprawled forward onto the table, resting her head on her folded arms and groaning.

"Kit, I have a present for you," James said, placing the thermos next to her, along with a mug. "You're going to need it. I talked to Bill this morning and he said that if you're going to drink all of his wine you're going to have to work for it. He wants to see you at the barge this afternoon, ready for some hard work."

Kit groaned again, but from where Evie was standing she could see the corner of her mouth turn up into a smile. Clearly, Kit had not lost her good mood of last night, despite the hangover.

"I put about eight extra shots of espresso in there," James told Evie. "She'll be up in no time. And as for you."

She arched a brow at him. "Did you come here today to mete out punishment?"

"That's exactly what I'm doing. Are you hungry?"

She pressed a finger to her lip, pretending to contemplate the question. "I could be persuaded to eat."

"Excellent. I'll give you some time to get cleaned up, then we'll go to lunch."

Evie arched her eyebrow at him again. "Oh, so now that the pirates are back, we're allowed out again. What's that all about?"

As he passed her, he reached out and grabbed her side, making her jump. "Well, some things are starting to come together. It could change everything. I'll tell you about it soon."

Kit exploded from the kitchen, "Why does Evie get lunch and I have to work?" She was already pouring coffee into the mug.

"Evie didn't drink Bill's good wine."

Kit grumbled but didn't say anything.

"So, you think I need time to get cleaned up?" Evie asked him.

"You still look like an angry bear cub. I'll be back in a bit to pick you up," he called over his shoulder as he left the apartment.

Evie sat down next to Kit and folded her legs under her. She took the mug from her sister and took a long sip, making a face at the strong thick liquid. "Oliver?" she asked her sister.

"James?" Kit shot back in the same tone.

Evie shrugged and got up. "Well, I need to go make myself pretty. You better get ready to work."

She winced. "You think he means it?"

Evie grinned at her. "This is Bill we're talking about. Of course he means it."

Evie indulged in a hot shower and used some perfumed soap. She even took time to shave her legs. She examined herself in the mirror for a long time, looking this way and that, taking extra care with her makeup. It had been so long since it mattered what she looked like, but today she felt like it mattered very much.

She would have worn something feminine, if she had the choice, but her wardrobe selection was limited. Anyway, she now realized the wisdom of wearing the same sort of shapeless clothing as everyone else in order to be indistinguishable at a casual glance. After everything she had seen, she knew it was dangerous to be attractive when out in the city. With a sigh, she grabbed a pair of baggy jeans and an oversized sweatshirt. Underneath, she put on a tight-fitting tank top. Even if no one saw it, she knew that she was wearing it.

As she came out of the bedroom, Kit rushed past her. Clearly the espresso James had given her was working. She was dressed like a boy in a long-sleeved shirt, with her hair piled up under a baseball cap.

A rap on the door announced James as he walked into the apartment. He was wearing his signature scarves looped around his neck, which she was starting to consider his uniform. Unlike everyone else, he seemed to be declaring his identity. *But that doesn't make any sense,* Evie thought as she greeted him. *He's on the run from Lachlan as much as we are.*

"Are you girls ready to go?" he said, looking Evie up and down without comment. She wished she hadn't put the sweatshirt on already.

"You mentioned something about lunch?"

"I did," he said, holding up a duffel bag. "I, ah, asked Marjory to throw some stuff together for us. I thought we could have a picnic, make a day of it." He was hesitant, as if unsure of her reaction. As Evie watched him, the memory of his lips on hers flashed over her skin and a lump caught her throat. James' colour deepened, as she realized she'd just been standing there staring at him.

"That sounds wonderful," she said, voice wavering. "Do I need to bring anything?"

"The only thing you need to bring is your lovely self. I'll take care of everything else."

"I like the sound of that."

Once Kit was ready to go, Evie locked the door of the apartment behind them. They wound through the alleys of the Trade District, cutting in through buildings. Evie had grabbed a large windbreaker with a big hood that she brought up over her head. "Are you sure this is safe?" she asked James.

"Nothing is really safe right now," he said, voice lowered so Kit couldn't overhear. "It will be good to get Kit on the barge — Bill's men can protect her, so she'll be okay there. As for us, we are heading out of the city. There are no guarantees, of course, but I know places where Lachlan's men don't patrol, and I know how to get there without being seen."

"Where are we going?"

"You'll see."

After they dropped Kit at the *Mary Rose* and watched her bound up the gangplank to greet the pirates, they turned west and started heading away from the Docks. As they crept through the streets of New City Evie's heart was thudding so loud she was sure it was audible. They sneaked through an abandoned strip mall that backed onto a forested wilderness park. Once they had slipped behind the natural screen of trees, James relaxed and slowed down.

The grittiness of the streets faded; they were walking along a path, a narrow trail through the trees that led to a river. The wild grasses were invading the crumbling asphalt, and dandelions were popping up through the cracks. From this perspective, Evie could see how New City was really only the downtown core of Greater Havern. She wondered how far out the ruined city stretched, with its empty yards and dead streets. The towering buildings of New City were no longer visible. The only manmade structures to be seen were a few big houses set back from the river.

"This must have been a very upscale suburb, you know, before," she said.

"Yes it was. Not that it did any of the richie richs any good once the Sickness hit." James looked at the homes disdainfully.

The path through the trees opened up again, to show a clearing overlooking the river, an idyllic place that exuded serenity. The grass was dotted with late wildflowers of pink, purple, and orange. This part of the river was shallow at the banks and Evie could hear the water bubbling over rocks. The trees were beginning to turn gold and red. The effect was calming.

"I feel like I can breathe here," Evie said, turning to James.

"Yes, it's nice to occasionally get away from the smell of filth."

She took in a deep breath, realizing he was right. The smell of garbage in New City was so prevalent it became a part of the atmosphere, so she hadn't immediately noticed how sweet the air was.

"Do you come here often?" she asked James, who had been watching her breathe in and out like a dying fool.

"I don't really, no. I used to — a long time ago, long before the Sickness. Coming here makes me sad more than anything. Brings back old memories."

"Then why come here now?"

He shrugged. "I wanted to see it again. I used to love watching the boats go by when I was a kid. Anyway, I thought you might like it."

"I love it. It reminds me of home a little bit, but not in a sad way. Oh look, a squirrel." She pointed up into the trees. "You never see animals in New City."

"Or any plants."

"Not growing wild, anyway," she said, thinking of the cultured loveliness of the trees that grew in the atrium of The Grand. She nodded her approval to James. "This is the perfect place for our picnic. We are going to eat here, aren't we?" She couldn't mask the eagerness in her voice.

James laughed. "That was the general idea. Are you hungry?"

"Do you even need to ask?" She skipped over to him and grabbed the bag. It was so heavy she nearly dropped it. "Yikes," she stooped under its weight. "What did Marjory pack for us? An entire turkey?"

Opening the bag, she found on top a large flannel blanket. Moving it aside, she saw plates, cutlery, wine glasses, a bottle of wine, and jars and containers full of food.

"This is very … sweet of you."

The awkwardness was plain on James' face. "I heard that girls like that kind of thing."

Evie was rummaging through the bag. "You thought of everything. Or is this Marjory's work?"

"She helped me out with a lot of it. So, you like it?" He looked uncertain.

She took his hand. "James, this is really *really* nice. Thank you."

"Well, I know you like to eat a lot, so I figured it would probably go over well."

The uncertainty gone, he started teasing her again. She bit her tongue to hold back a tart comment. No one had ever taken her on a picnic, and she thought it was perfect. And entirely out of character for James, who seemed more at home in a seedy alley than a riverside meadow. Grabbing the blanket she spread it out on the flattest patch of earth. As she laid out place settings, James took a corkscrew to the wine and poured them each a glass.

"Oh my, wine instead of coffee for my first drink of the day. You are leading me astray. Never mind, here's to your health," she said

"And yours."

They brought their glasses together, the glass making a dull tink. It made her smile.

"I feel as if we're celebrating something."

"I think we all deserve some festivity in our lives," he said, his eyes a brighter blue than usual as he looked at her.

"So, what are you celebrating today?"

"Today, I'm celebrating meeting you, since you probably saved my life that first night. Best thing that's happened to me in a long time." James leaned towards her, until his face was inches away. Before he reached Evie, her stomach interrupted them with an impatient rumble. She burst out laughing.

"You must be starving. You haven't eaten since last night." James busied himself digging in the bag, laying out the food. It was gorgeous. There were hunks of Marjory's sourdough bread, fresh cheese, pieces of roast chicken, and a salad full of beans and fresh vegetables, thanks to the pirates' latest haul. The meal had been prepared with such care she felt tears pricking her eyes.

"You really like it then?" James asked after she had eaten more than her share of the food. James had made sure her plate was always overflowing, and she was happy to oblige him by eating it all. Their conversation turned to speculation over Kit and Oliver's romantic prospects. Evie felt that Kit was simply enjoying herself, not forming any serious attachments. James was less certain.

"Oliver is a serious guy," he said. "He has his head screwed on tight and doesn't go into anything lightly. I don't know Kit very well, but she doesn't seem the type to have a fling with a guy like that."

Evie nodded. "She might like to flirt and have fun, but she wouldn't consciously hurt anyone. I'm not sure I like it very much though. Kit is so young; she doesn't need to be forming that kind of relationship right now. She's never even dated before."

"Maybe not before the Sickness, but we're in a new world now. You and Kit are very lucky to still have each other. Most people lost every single person in their lives. Now they struggle to find new people, create new families. I've noticed that relationships form quickly now, and with more intensity than before. It's as if ... people are our lifelines." His voice was quiet and deeper than usual. He looked at Evie. She wondered who he had lost in the Sickness. A girlfriend? A wife? Had he escaped from prison to find his loved ones lost to him forever?

As if reading her mind, he asked, "So how about you, Evie?" He studied the contents of his wine glass. "Any boyfriends?"

She sighed, relaxed enough to allow her mind to drift back to a time that seemed to be in a different dimension. "No one ... special."

"No one? I have to say I'm surprised. I thought you would be breaking hearts all over the place."

She looked down, a coy smile playing across her lips. "Well, maybe there were several special people. I used to have a lot of fun, back in the day. Nothing serious though. It was always more fun to see one guy one week, than another the next. I could never settle on just one person."

When she glanced up, she saw James had moved in closer to her, a mischievous look on his face. "So, you were a heartbreaker. I knew it." She could feel his warm breath on her skin and then he was kissing her. She opened her lips, letting his tongue explore the inside of her mouth. He responded with enthusiasm, causing Evie to spill the remains of her wine over his shirt. He ignored it, pulling her in closer. She brought her hands up to either side of his face, tangling her fingers in his long hair.

He lay back, bringing her down with him. His fingers ran up her back, then down again, long fingers teasing and exploring. She buried her face into his neck, tracing the line that ran down to his collar with her mouth. He groaned and rolled over, looking down on her, brushing the hair out of her face. Leaning in, he stopped abruptly, hovering over her face. "Evie. Are you a virgin?"

Embarrassed, she pressed her face into his shoulder, hiding from him. "Um. Yes, actually. I was waiting for the right guy, the right place. I thought I had all the time in the world for ... everything. And then, I had waited too long."

"Maybe not," he whispered, finding her mouth again. He kissed her deeply then broke away. "You might have to remind me how to be a gentleman."

Still self-conscious, she grinned at him, feeling like a child. "What about you?"

"Me?" He gave a little laugh. "No, not for a long time. I had a chaotic childhood and even more disturbed teenage life. I never knew my mother; she took off soon after I was born, although her family kept an eye on me. My father tried to look after me but he worked out of town, on an oilrig, so I was shuttled between relations and friends, whoever would let me sleep on their couch for a few months at a time. At some point, child welfare caught onto this and I was shipped to different group foster homes. All of us kids there, we'd form gangs. There were never really any rules. We thought we had the run of the streets. School was optional, but the drugs weren't always. It was a wild, fast way to grow up. We all started having sex in our early teens — there didn't seem to be any reason not to — and the girls were just as eager as the boys. But we never talked about love, none of us wanted to get married or anything like that. I guess none of us really knew what love was."

"I'm so sorry," Evie said, sad at the thought of James as a little boy, hardening year by year.

He shrugged. "It wasn't all bad. I finally found a fairly permanent place to stay, with my mother's brother, when I was sixteen. He had lived on another continent for years but decided to come home. As soon as he got settled, he took me in. He was a fascinating man, really intelligent. He saw the sorry state of my education and tried to teach me the basics. In some ways, Marjory reminds me of him. Of course, he was also a thief, so there's a big difference there. He started taking me on jobs before I was eighteen, I suspect so I could take the fall if anything went wrong."

"That's horrible."

"That's life. Who can say how far I would have gotten in New City if I hadn't been raised into that life? But maybe it was all meant to be." He paused then added softly, "Maybe I was meant to meet you."

"Maybe." She smiled up at him. "Maybe it's right that we find something good in the midst of this horror show. I'm so happy right here. It feels wrong to be this happy, after everything."

"It's what we deserve," he said. The statement reminded Evie of Lachlan, of his attitude about how they should be living after the Sickness. A chill passed through her.

"Are you okay?" James noticed her shiver. "Are you cold? Come here." He pulled her towards him, tucking her up in his arms. She gave an inward smile. She wasn't cold but she wasn't going to say a word, being exactly where she wanted to be.

Once James deemed her to be warm, he sat up and poured more wine.

"Will we see any boats going by today?"

James made a face as he sipped. "I doubt it. Not as many boats are trading with the West these days."

"Why is that? What about all the farms being developed out there? It would make sense to get as much as possible from those people."

"Yes, it would definitely make sense, but Lachlan is making it difficult. He has complete control over trading to the east of the city; he has a company that sends ships to all the farms and ranches there. He didn't bother with the farms west of the city until he realized traders like Bill were doing well out there and so were becoming his competitors. So now he's taxing the traders so heavily it's hardly worth their while to continue with the western trade. He sends out his men to harass those that don't toe the line, so the timid are giving up. He aims to shut down his competitors and take over the western trade himself."

"Simple supply and demand," Evie murmured.

"Something twisted like that," James said. "Lachlan's trying to set up a monopoly on all trade in the city, an empire, really, and only a few renegades like Bill are doing anything about it. It's easier to play his game."

"But even if a captain has not paid the taxes, Lachlan doesn't stop the boats from coming in, right? You said he looks the other way," she pointed out.

"No, he doesn't stop them from docking. But his spies try to find out who buys from Bill and the other renegades and then intimidates them — the customers and the traders. That's why Bill sells his goods underground, away from Lachlan's greedy reach. Many people like what Bill is doing, but only a few are willing to defy Lachlan openly."

Evie thought about the broken body in the dumpster next to The Grand and shivered again. James didn't notice this time, lost in his own dark thoughts. "Bill is thinking of moving west, permanently. Maybe even going over the mountains."

"The river runs into a lake at the foot of the mountains, effectively ending any way of travelling by boat. Wouldn't that be a very dangerous journey to make without reliable ground transportation?"

"It sure as hell would."

"I wonder," she said thinking aloud, wondering whether she would want to be on the boat.

"What?" James asked.

"I still wonder how Lachlan has such influence over everyone in New City. It confuses me. I mean, he's a powerful guy, but you talk as if everyone owes him their lives around here. What exactly gives him so much power?"

"In a way, the people do. They have come to rely on him for most of their basic needs, like electricity and water, and to feed their habits. Lachlan deals in all kinds of very nasty stuff, not just prostitution and human trafficking. He'll take what people need then use that need to make them his."

"Like drugs. He must want those I left behind very badly. I'm really worried that he has found my stash." She paused for a moment. "Think of how useful they would be to us if we were heading out west. I've been wondering whether there's a way to go back into The Grand and take them — if they are still there."

James chewed his lip, considering. "Of course they would be useful. But there's no way you're going back to The Grand. That would be suicide. "

"But, I could help —"

"Absolutely not!" His voice was sharp. "It's too dangerous. We'll figure out another way."

She mulled it over in her head, eyes open but unseeing as she tried to imagine how they could pull it off. Her fingers absently twirled through her short hair. "Maybe we could sneak in one night, just dash in and out. The pirates could hardly deny us room on their ship with something as valuable as that."

James threw his hands up in exasperation. "Haven't you been listening to me? Didn't you listen to what Anne and Rebecca told you? How could you not get how serious this all is?" James ran his hands through his hair, brushing it away from his face. "People are dying everywhere you look. Don't you understand how this works? Lachlan is the one and only drug lord in New City. He must have been right pissed to have some pretty little thing, a ward of his no less, start providing medicine to people. I saw you in the Market that day. I thought you had only one or two packets of drugs with you, but Lachlan would immediately have suspected you had more. He could have ended you then, or set you up in his stable of girls. Those drugs were probably what protected you. But no matter what happens, things are not going to go well for you and Kit if he finds you trying to get them back. "

"I was just trying to help," she said petulantly, irritated at being treated like a child.

He shook his head then leaned back, trying to relax again. "Things are going to get better. It won't always be like this."

Evie stared at him. "How do you know?"

He glanced away. The slightest hesitation gave away his evasiveness. "Well, things can't always be this bad, right?"

She narrowed her eyes, thinking hard. *He sounds so confident. What does he know that he's holding back from me?* "Is something going to happen? Soon? Does it have anything to do with where you go all day?"

He shrugged, sitting up, a rare frown crossing his features. "I don't know what you mean."

"Of course you do. I might be a simple country girl, but I'm not stupid. You've been on the run from Lachlan ever since you rescued Anne, but you don't have any problem hanging out in crowds of people — they all seem to know you well enough to keep you fed. Why hasn't anyone turned you in?" She grabbed the edge of one of his scarves, flipping it up into his face. "You certainly aren't trying to hide on the streets, not really. You act like you're trying to get attention. Why don't the men on the streets hassle you, or me when I'm with you? You're protected, that's clear. But why? There must be something bigger going on here."

He refused to face her. "I can't talk about it."

She turned away from him, lips pressed together. "I thought we were past these games." She sat up, the mood ruined. She started gathering up the dishes, packing them away in the duffel bag. He followed suit.

A heavy tension settled between them. Neither of them knew how to break it, so they walked all the way back to New City in silence. As they entered the city proper, she viewed the place with wary eyes, more resentful of the tall grey towers then before. The smell was overwhelming, thick in her nostrils. It made her overly full stomach turn. She could see The Grand in the distance rising above the other buildings. It seemed as if the wide windows of the penthouse were watching her every move. She felt as if the hotel was just a prop, a stage setting for the play Lachlan was directing.

They were as covert getting back into their building as when they left. James made sure no one was watching the side entry before they went through it. Evie brushed past James as they reached his floor and continued upstairs without a word. Tired and angry, she just wanted to be alone and safe in her own home.

Two steps into the suite she froze. It took her a moment to figure out what was out of place.

On the kitchen table, next to the thermos and mug Kit had left there, sat a tall bottle of Scotch. Evie didn't know anything about Scotch, but this dusty bottle looked very old. And expensive. Underneath it was a note. She picked it up with trembling hands, feeling the heavy weight of the creamy paper as she read it.

I saw you left the city today. I'm happy you've come back. – L

Chapter Eighteen

Evie was shaking when she banged on James' door, anger forgotten. She held the nasty note in her hands. "James, it's me. Open the door quickly!" she yelled, looking around her nervously.

The door opened, a quiet rasp as the handle turned. James stood in front of her, and something deep inside Evie, low in her belly, turned over. Distracted, she forgot what she was going to say.

He was wearing a pair of jeans riding low over his hips and nothing else; his broad shoulders filled the doorframe. Evie ran her eyes over the long lean chest that tapered down to a smaller waist and flat, hard stomach. A faint hairline trailed from his belly button down past the waistband of his jeans.

He raised an eyebrow at her and put his hands on his hips, which made the sinewy muscles roped around his arms stand up. "You've come to ream me out? Evie, I'm sorry I haven't told you everything. I just feel that you're already in this too deep. I want to keep you away from some of it. I guess I'm trying to protect you."

She pulled her thoughts back to their dire situation and gave a bitter laugh. "Too late for that," she said, holding up the note. "Lachlan knows. He followed us, somehow. He knows where we are." Her voice took on a note of pleading.

"Fuck," was all he said as he pulled her inside and threw the deadbolt in place. He read the note then crumpled it tight. "Dan, that bastard, he must've snitched on us."

"Someone could have followed Kit and me home last night. We were ... less than careful. Now that I think about it, it must have been that. God, I've been so stupid."

James was shaking his head. "I thought I was so clever, dodging him this whole time, but now he knows."

"He didn't know until I got involved."

James gave her a sharp look. "Is that supposed to make me feel better?"

She shrugged. "At least we know who the weakest link is. If it weren't for me, you'd probably be safe."

"If it weren't for you, Lachlan would likely have killed me the night he caught me, so don't beat yourself up."

Evie shuddered. "I hate the thought of him in my apartment. He didn't even break in, it's like they had keys or something."

"They could have picked the locks, but it certainly doesn't make me feel any safer." He paused, considering. "I wonder who he actually sent? He wrote the note, it's his hand writing, but Lachlan wouldn't do this himself."

"What difference does it make? It's the same thing; Lachlan is telling me he can get to me in my own home and can pick me up any time he wants to. Why isn't he? What sort of game is he playing now?" Evie paced along James' cramped kitchen. "Could it be that he hasn't found the drugs yet? Maybe he's trying to get me to come back, to reveal the hiding place, but ... it doesn't make any sense." She looked up at him. "Why doesn't he just grab me then? And Kit and you too?"

"It's all about the power to him." James spoke softly, running his knuckles over his jaw as he worked it out. "You have power over him, and he hates that. This ... little game he's playing is to unsettle you, to unsettle us. He thinks he has all the time in the world, and we have no way to fight back." He turned to her, mind rapidly shifting gears. "We should go check on Marjory. She might have seen something."

Evie looked up, wide-eyed. "Do you think she's okay?"

"She'll be fine. She's an old woman who can't even speak – they have no reason to harm her."

"Except that she's harbouring fugitives, or whatever we are." With a nod, James paused only long enough to throw on a clean T-shirt, then they rushed down the stairs.

James gave a soft tap at the door. It opened within moments. Marjory did not look her normal jovial self and didn't greet them with a smile and a hug. Instead, she looked shaken. She nodded her head, motioning them to come in, then closed the door firmly. She walked into the sitting room and looked up at them, eyes wide.

Evie sat across from her as James put his arm around her. "Marjory, are you all right?" The mute woman nodded. "Some men came to the apartment today. Did you see them?" Again the wide-eyed nod as she pointed to the window with a view of the street. "Did they come to talk to you?" She shook her head.

"Nothing was broken," Evie said. "So how did they get in?"

Marjory mimed the turning of a key.

"They have a key?" Her stomach sank when Marjory nodded again. Lachlan could just let himself into people's homes. He really did own everything here. "Marjory, do you know who Lachlan is?" She gave a jerky nod. "Was he one of the men who came here today?"

A shake of the head. For what it was worth, Evie was a little relieved. Somehow, sending men into her home wasn't as bad as him being there himself.

"How many were there?" Evie started to feel like she was interrogating Marjory, but she didn't seem to mind. She was upset and wanted to communicate. She held up two pudgy fingers, then mimed they were large, puffing out her cheeks and swinging her arms around a large girth.

"Two big men. Hmm. Was one of them black and the other an albino?" Marjory gave an eager nod. *The bodyguards, One and Three*, she thought. *Why had Lachlan sent his two best men to leave a bottle of Scotch and a message? No, not a message, a warning.*

Marjory was watching her with a wary look. She didn't like this any more than they did. She wanted to be left alone, and her privacy had been invaded because of Evie.

Evie sank down on the couch, burying her face in her hands then running them through her hair. Marjory perched on the overstuffed armchair facing her. "It really is just a game to him. What have I gotten us into?" Evie said.

Marjory reached out and patted her knee, sympathy in her eyes.

"It's not your fault," James said.

Evie snorted. "This is entirely my fault. The question is, what on earth are we going to do about it?"

"There's something I need to show you. In the city." James sounded reluctant. He turned to Marjory. "Are you going to be okay here alone? Or do you want to come with us?"

Marjory crossed her arms, settling back in the couch with a stubborn look on her plain face. "I think that means you're staying here," James smiled at her. "Brave lady. We'll be back in a few hours."

Marjory saw them to the door. Before Evie left she gave the older woman a hug, gentle and tender. Evie found herself missing her mother, a rare feeling, and leaned in for a moment. Allowing herself one breath, she pushed away. She heard the door lock click behind her.

"Where are we going?" she asked.

"There is more, so much more, that you don't know. This is important. I need you to understand where we're coming from."

"Where who's coming from?"

James hesitated then shook his head. "It's best if I show you something first. I'll tell you everything while we walk. We're going to the Warehouse District."

Evie was close to a jog to match James' frenetic pace. Filled with a nervous energy, he was talking at a pace to match. "After Marjory took me in, part of me was afraid that I would be caught and killed, but a bigger part of me didn't care. Not after everything that I'd seen and done at Lachlan's. It wasn't just the women; it was how men were treated as well. Everyone suffers when Lachlan's involved." He gave her a sad smile. "I started to ask who the hell we were. So very few people survived, and those that did were completely untouched, unharmed by the Sickness. Have you ever wondered why? Why us? What did we do to deserve this?

"And yet so many survivors seem hell bent on making sure they don't last long. If you could see what they are doing to themselves." He stopped in front of a dumpy warehouse. It was more dilapidated than anything else in the area, and that was saying something. With a jolt, she realized they were no more than a block away from the building where she had delivered her drugs. "You need to see," James said as he pulled up a utilitarian garage door and motioned for Evie to enter.

She ducked down to clear the low metal entrance. He followed her in and allowed the door to fall shut. She winced at the noise and blinked in the darkness, still adjusting from the stark sunlight. When the shafts of light seeping in from around boarded windows eventually revealed her surroundings, she recoiled and backed into James. He grabbed her arms to stop her from running out. She stared at rows and rows of identical metal frame beds. This was a hospital. It looked like a war infirmary, dark and dirty, with patients crammed in shoulder to shoulder. There was a dreadful sense of familiarity; the groans and the smells. Instinctively, she covered her nose to avoid inhaling the odour of antiseptic and anesthetic — and the stench of sickness and death. Evie was suddenly back at the North Pine hospital, where everyone she knew had died in front of her. Even the darkness was familiar, as they had worked long after the electricity had gone out. She shrank into James, turning her face from them.

"What is this?" she whispered, her face concealed. "Why have you brought me here? Is it the Sickness?"

"No." James turned her around with a sigh. "These are the people who survived the Sickness. This they've done to themselves."

"They made themselves sick?"

"They had help along the way, trust me. And they're not sick, not really. This is just another way that Lachlan ensures absolute control in New City. He puts on elaborate parties, as you know, and provides plenty of cheap drugs and booze. They numb themselves, forget their loss. It makes them imagine life is good, no matter what. Until the drugs run out."

"So once the guys are hooked, Lachlan threatens to withhold the drugs. Right?"

"Yes. Unless you give him exactly what he wants, whatever it is at the time. Luxury goods, slave labour, someone's daughters. He's created a generation of addicts who want to turn off their minds. They'll do anything for him."

"That's hideous." She thought back to everything she had seen in New City. "That man in the park, the one who died, he ..." she trailed off, not sure of the question.

James shrugged. "I can't be sure about it, but it sounds like an overdose. It happens a lot around here. As soon as they get their hands on something, anything, they'll use it all. I'd say a lot of them would be happy to go that way."

A man was hurrying towards them, down an aisle of beds. He was short with a halo of springy curls around his head. His face appeared to have once been plump, but now collapsed in on itself.

"This is Gregory," James said as way of introduction. "He's a doctor. He oversees this ... care facility, I guess you'd call it. He got it set up several months ago. Gregory, this is my friend Evie. She has also managed to piss Lachlan off."

Gregory gave her a short nod, but his face was stern. "I don't want any trouble here, James. It's hard enough keeping your involvement secret, but if it gets back to Lachlan that a woman was here ..." he trailed off, his voice suggesting ominous consequences.

James laid a hand on Gregory's shoulder with an easy smile. "No worries. I just wanted to show her the place, explain what we do a little bit."

"Well, be quick about it. I don't want you to rile my patients up." He took off down the aisle again in quick, short steps, throwing Evie one more annoyed glance over his shoulder.

"Come over this way," James said, taking her to one side of the building, where weak sunlight trickled in from a row of windows set high up in the wall. She walked behind him, looking down at the beds. There were so many. Some moaned and twitched. Others, worse still, were covered in oozing bloody scabs. A few were strapped down, like in an old-fashioned asylum. Patients stretched and screamed against their bonds.

Those worse off lay in their beds, staring. They were skin and bone, with hollowed-out cheeks. Their skeletal fingers twitched, scratching on the thin material of the sheets, a dusty-dry whisper. They looked like the living dead, their eyes showed no flicker of light in them. *Row after row of intentional zombies*, she thought. James spoke in a low voice next to her.

"It looks terrible, but it's for their own good." James said, seeing the appalled look on her face. "If we don't strap them down, they'll tear their own flesh off. It's only until they come out of their withdrawal."

"These are the people whose luck has run out?"

"They're the people that Lachlan had no more use for or wanted to punish. Most are just found on the streets, homeless, in extreme withdrawal. Some of the worse off here, though, have probably been given drugs cut with other toxic products. They don't always survive. Some come back from the brink and have the strength to keep on living. A few men have even stayed on, helping feed and care for the others." There was a note of pride in his voice.

"What does Lachlan think about this care facility?" Evie asked.

"He looks the other way, for now. It's in his best interest to keep the streets cleaned up. Having addicts roaming around hardly adds to the appeal of New City. Keeping this side of things hidden away means no one has to think about it. But he's starting to lose patience with the facility. With a lot of things going on in the city."

Evie snorted. "Why? Are you getting in the way of his plan to kill everyone who won't do what they are told?"

"Lachlan just wants to control. Killing is a means to the end, but I don't think it's one he prefers. He needs people. I think he's starting to think our facility makes him look weak."

"It makes him look like a monster," Evie said with vehemence. She watched as James walked away from her, checking a man's chart, which appeared to be a series of short scrawled notes on scrap paper. She followed a few steps behind, mind churning.

Without thinking, she began talking to the patients, seeing if there was anything she could do for them. It was an instinct left over from caring for those at her home hospital during the Sickness.

Most of the men ignored her, seeming not to see her at all. A few watched her with greedy eyes. She avoided those, starting to feel conspicuous. She reminded herself this was no ordinary hospital. She was surrounded by a group of addicts who had not seen any drugs, or any women, for a long time. Looking around for James, she pushed down the wild feeling of panic.

The man next to her let out a hoarse wheeze. He was one of the men who looked dead, with large staring eyes. His face was sunken in, covered in a stiff scraggly beard that stuck out in every direction. He was mumbling, so she leaned over his bed, trying to hear what he was saying.

"What was that?" she whispered, not wanting to disturb the people around her. Looking into his bloodshot eyes, she searched for some spark to show he was alive, human.

"Hhhrrn ..." he gurgled.

"I'm sorry, I don't understand." She reached forward as if to touch him, but found her wrist snatched up in someone else's grip. Whirling around, she saw the man at the next bed sitting up and holding her wrist hard. Dark eyes glared at her, nearly lost behind his shaggy hair.

"He called you a whore," he said in a harsh nasal voice. "A whore walking amongst us, without any shame. How dare you show your face after what you've done." He spat the words at her.

"Me?" she squeaked. Twisting her wrist, she struggled in his painful grip. "What did I do?"

"What you all did, you worthless cow!" He yelled so loud he looked apoplectic. "Leading us into temptation, taking us away from the light. We're being punished for the sins of our flesh and you dare to ask what you did? Are you here to tempt us again, you little slut?"

"I assure you I have no inclination —" Her reasoned retort was cut short when the man yanked her forward and wrapped his hands around her throat, throttling her. Evie struggled and tried to hit him. Her body convulsed of its own volition, desperate for air. Clawing at his face, she felt her body sink, getting weaker. She looked into the scowling face; he looked far away, his eyes glittering in hatred.

And then it was over. An arm flashed in and punched the man under his jaw. His eyes rolled up and the pressure at her throat released, allowing Evie to fall back and draw in gasping breaths. James jumped onto the bed with a syringe in his hand and plunged the contents into the man's neck.

Evie choked on a breath. "What the fuck!" she tried to say, but her voice came out as a wheeze.

"Tranquilizers," James explained. "We should go." Other patients had started to stir, agitated by the action. With James' hand firm on her upper arm, they ran to the door. They scrabbled to pull it up, then crawled underneath and into the glaring sunlight.

He turned to her, patting her arms, her face, her tender throat. "All good? Are you able to breathe okay?"

She leaned over, her hands on her thighs, nodding. "Yes. Just give me a second." Her voice was hoarse, as if she'd been screaming for hours, but it still worked. She cleared her throat and winced.

He placed a hand on her back. "How do you always manage to get into such trouble?" His voice was gentle; it had lost the urgent edge.

"Wrong place, wrong time, I guess. That was the first time I've been accused of causing a plague, though." She gave a weak smile, letting him know she was okay. Relief was coursing through her, making her feel giddy, like she wanted to laugh and cry at the same time. She giggled, smothering it when she saw the exasperation on his face.

"It's not funny. You could have been really hurt."

"It would be what I deserved, really. Punishment for tempting men with the sins of the flesh and all that." She started laughing but choked it down when she heard the note of hysteria. "It's comforting to know that even after the world ends, we still have crazy religious nuts shooting off their mouths."

James grimaced as he hugged her, his hand at the back of her neck, pressing her into him. "You're the crazy one. Or maybe I am for taking you in there. I'm surprised you didn't cause a riot.

"Listen, all of this, it's just a part of what Lachlan does to people. And a lot of us have had enough of it. People like Bill, and Gregory. There are enough people, I think, to cause major problems for Lachlan, to throw him off his game. Maybe even topple him. Now that would be sweet."

"Are you planning something? Is that what you've been holding back from me?"

After a long pause, he nodded. "Yes. There's a … I guess you would call it a revolution. I'm a part of it; I've spent the last few months organizing the people of New City to fight back against Lachlan. I've been waiting for the right pieces to fall into place. To get enough support from the right people."

"Like the trades people."

"Exactly. The merchants and trades people who want to legitimately set up shop in New City are starting to see my way of thinking. With their support, I think we could do a lot of damage to Lachlan's reign. I think it's time you got to know the real underworld of New City."

"It sounds exciting," she said, smiling at the prospect.

"You don't know the half of it," James said dryly.

Evie bit her lip. "We should get to the barge. I need to see Kit." He nodded and they started walking. Her immediate relief faded away as she thought of the bottle of Scotch sitting on her kitchen table; there were still problems to be dealt with.

"Where does he get the drugs?" she asked. "For the addicts."

"The actual drugs that these guys are given? He's been manufacturing them."

"For his latest batch, some must have come from the medication I delivered for him, right?" She reached up and found a straggle of hair at the back of her neck to pull on, twisting it around her finger. She thought of the man who died in front of her, the men lying near comatose in the metal beds, probably better off dead than alive. Eyes glittering in hatred at her. "I'm a part of this too."

"Evie, no." James stopped and looked down at her. "You didn't know; you are not responsible for this."

She lifted an eyebrow. "Maybe, maybe not. But what would Lachlan do if he got his hands on the medications that I left at The Grand?"

"Evie, forget it. You're not going back there. You are going to leave this place for good, I swear it."

She gave a firm nod, sticking her chin out. "Yes, someday we'll all be safe again. We'll do more than survive; we'll start living again."

His grin flashed. "Sounds good. Let's get to the *Mary Rose*."

She linked arms with him and they set out at a brisk pace. They arrived at the barge and ran up on deck, hearing a few surprised hellos called out to them. Evie barely acknowledged them, focused on finding her sister. "Where's Kit?" she called out, and someone motioned towards the cabin.

Evie dashed into the cabin, squinting against the sudden darkness. She found Kit sitting at the far end of the long table, chatting with Petra and Rebecca. They looked up as James and Evie approached.

"Are you okay?" Kit asked.

"I was going to say the same thing to you," Evie said, giving her sister a hug. "You're fine, right?"

"Of course. Evie, what's going on?"

"It's Lachlan. He knows where we are, he was in our apartment today."

Both Kit and Rebecca gasped. Petra had a grim look on her face. "I'm going to go get Bill," she said, pushing her heavy frame up from her seat and waddling out of the cabin.

"Did he hurt you?" Kit asked.

"No, some of his men came in while we were out. Marjory saw them. They left a message for me."

Bill came into the cabin, Petra close behind him. "So, you've been flushed out. What do you expect me to do about it?" His face was set in stony lines, a fat cigar clenched between his teeth.

Evie turned to Bill, heart sinking. She had been hoping that they would offer to shelter them, but even she could see the risk that the pirates would be taking. "Safe passage," she said, her voice wavering. "When you leave the city, take us with you. You can drop us off somewhere, maybe at one of the settlements you told me about."

Bill raised his eyebrow, taking his time as he looked both of them over. "And what's in it for me?"

Kit made a small sound of anguish and Evie felt her insides squirm. *If he doesn't take us, we'll have nowhere to go,* she thought. "There's ... the drugs. Stashed away at The Grand. You have to admit they would be useful." Her voice was strained with desperation.

"Can't deny that."

"Evie, you can't," James burst in. He turned to Bill. "We can't go back there."

"Maybe I could," Evie said, jumping on Bill's interest. "Like I said, I could sneak in —"

James whirled on her, anger and fear in his face. "And when Lachlan finds you, cripples you then gives you to his men, how are you going to get out of that one?"

Evie glared at the ground, knowing James was right.

Bill took the cigar out of his mouth, blowing out a long stream of fragrant smoke. "As it happens, we have decided to leave New City for the foreseeable future," he said. Petra gave a grim nod. "Lachlan's tax men have gotten a little too nosy about our goings-on in the city, and it would be best for us to be leaving. We do better trade out west anyways, without having to deal with psychopathic dictators."

"Will you take us with you?" Kit asked.

"Of course," Rebecca said, rubbing her arm while giving Bill a dirty look for making the girls wait. "There was never any question about that."

"True enough," Bill said, scratching his beard. "But there is still this idea of the drugs that Evie has hidden away, that's interesting. Could be good for trade. Not to mention our own needs."

"And guns," Evie said at a sudden thought.

"Nobody has guns in New City," Bill told her.

"Because Lachlan confiscated them all, right? He must keep them somewhere."

"The garages," James said in a soft voice. "I've seen them — a whole arsenal. I've never been given one; he rarely lets any of his men take them. He prefers knives."

"I would love to have my hunting rifle back," Evie said. "Think of the game we could live on."

"There's no way," Petra said in a furious voice. "I'll not have you send these girls into that hotel, only to be taken up by that man."

"No," Bill said, considering. "I wouldn't want that to happen. But some interesting points have been raised. Be that as it may, we will be sailing out shortly, within the week. You three will have to keep yourselves out of trouble for that time, do you think you can manage it?" Kit and Evie nodded, while James flashed a relieved grin.

"And Evie," Bill continued. "You are not to go to The Grand under any circumstance, is that clear? If you want to live on my ship, you follow my rules. Understand?"

"Yes, sir," she said.

"James, you watch out for her. I am putting her safety in your hands — again. You are responsible for her until we sail. Is that clear?"

He snorted. "As if I could possibly handle her." At Bill's glare, he cleared his throat. "Yes, sir."

As they walked out of the cabin, James put his arm around Evie. "This calls for a celebration."

"How do you celebrate in a city full of pimps and addicts while being hunted down by a maniac?"

"Turns out, if you look hard enough, there are a few places left to have some genuine fun."

"Genuine fun? I've heard of this, I thought it was a myth."

"Not entirely," he said. "I'll show you tomorrow." He stopped when Anne came up to them. She was dressed as always in a skimpy shirt, her long hair falling down over her shoulders.

"Evie, could I speak to you for a moment?"

Evie gave James a bewildered look, but said, "Of course," and followed the older girl back into the cabin. Anne spun around once they were inside.

"Look, there's something I wanted to warn you about."

"About James?" Evie was confused.

"What? No. James is fine. Before, when I blew up, I didn't really mean anything. Me and James, we … never were anything. He never saw me like that." She looked down, her tone indicating she was still a little mad about the fact. "No, it's about Lachlan. He's not going to let you go so easily."

"I know he likes to play these weird games, but we'll be gone soon. He won't know I'm leaving."

Anne shook her head, her hair swaying with the movement. "It won't be like that. He will come after you. He's not crazy, unless you tell him no. It will go better for you if you don't defy him."

"Why are you telling me this?"

She shrugged. "In case you're taken. Just keep it in mind. Lachlan doesn't do violence for the sake of violence. He uses it to control people, the way he uses everything to control people. You've proven to him he doesn't control you yet. That's why he has such a hard on for you and that's why he won't let you go."

"We just have to get through the week."

"Well, good luck with that. But remember what I said."

Evie turned, shaken, as James walked into the cabin. He was carrying a bundle of blankets. He looked at the two women. "Everything all right?"

Evie nodded, trying to ignore Anne's warning. "I'm fine. What do you have there?"

"Obviously we can't go back to the apartment," he said, handing her a blanket. "You and Kit can sleep in the back, with the other girls. Anne, can you show her?"

"What about you?" Evie asked. Anne made an annoyed noise in her throat, making James grin.

"I'll be sleeping out on the deck with the men. The fires keep it warm enough at this time of year. Are we on for tomorrow?"

"Yes. Are you sure it's safe?"

He shrugged. "As safe as anything is right now. We'll go to a place that Lachlan doesn't know about."

"Hate to break up this little flirtation, but I'm going to show you where you'll stay," Anne said, stalking away from them. "You can have your date tomorrow."

James winked then turned to leave the cabin. Evie hugged the blanket to her and followed Anne to the back of the cabin. A swell of hope started to form in her chest. If they could only get through the next few days, they were going to be fine.

Chapter Nineteen

That night Evie slept heavily, curled up on an air mattress next to her sister. When she woke up, light was streaming in from a small window and Kit's large brown eyes were on her.

"Good morning." Kit's usual cheery greeting was tempered by a serious tone.

"Hi." Evie sat up, looking around them at the empty cabin. "I guess we slept in."

"Make that *you* slept in. I've been up for a while and I thought it was time to wake you."

"Listen, I'm really sorry. We've had to leave everything behind us again."

"Evie, it's not your fault." Kit reached out and brushed a strand of hair out of her sister's face. "It was only a matter of time before Lachlan found us. And I feel safer here than anywhere."

"And you get to be closer to your new boyfriend here," Evie said, smiling.

Kit flushed and gave her sister a shove. "All right, that's enough out of you. I saved you some breakfast. The pirates eat early, and Bill said this better be the last time you think you're going to sleep in. We have a full day ahead of us."

"What are we doing?"

"You have a date to get ready for. And I need to work my magic on you."

Evie's stomach gave a nervous flutter at the thought of going out with James. "Sounds like you're the boss. Lead away."

Stuffed full of a hearty breakfast of eggs, cheese, and bread, Evie followed Kit into one of the back cabins, ready to get into "date shape." Kit pulled out a large bag and starting to take out a dazzling array of bottles, beauty products, and instruments.

"Good god, you could open a salon and spa with all of this," Evie said. "Where on earth did you get it?"

"Um, a salon and spa," Kit said, looking a little guilty. "It's close by. It was all just sitting there. Oliver took me there yesterday, when I said something about wanting good shampoo, and I may have taken a little bit more than shampoo. Everything was just so shiny." Kit's hands passed over all the products greedily. She looked very pleased with herself.

Evie raised her eyebrows. "Oliver took you there to get shampoo?"

"Well, can you blame him?" Kit swung her head around so that her long blonde hair fell in a perfect sheet as she flashed a brilliant smile. Evie had to admit, she looked straight out of a hair commercial. "The pirates have rigged this room to bring up water from the river, so you can shower and everything. It's just a little cold."

"So, what's first?"

Kit sat her down and got to work. Evie found herself brushed and scrubbed and exfoliated. Even before the Sickness, she had never been much for beauty products. That was always Kit's domain. But it felt wonderful being clean and polished. Feeling more feminine than she had in a long time, Evie admired her nails, newly shaped and painted. Then Kit started tsk-ing over her hair.

"There's nothing we can do to save it?" Evie guessed.

"Um, no." Kit tried to sound optimistic. "It's not that bad. But you just hacked away at it, there's still clumps sticking out everywhere. I can't believe I haven't done this before." She rummaged in her pile of products and found a pair of scissors. Closing her eyes, Evie told herself it couldn't get any worse than it was. After snipping away like she knew what she was doing, Kit attacked with sprays that made her cough. She stepped back to judge her work.

"It will do," was the final pronouncement.

Evie turned to look in the mirror and thought it would do more than that. Kit had shaped her hair into a long pixie cut, with bangs sweeping across her forehead and pretty wisps that framed her face.

"You will not touch until tomorrow," Kit said as she smacked Evie's hand away before she touched it. "You're just going to ruin it. Now, skin products."

Kit continued her primping through the afternoon. By the time she was ready, it was close to five, when James had said he would pick her up. Peering into the mirror, Evie barely recognized her reflection. She looked like someone much better looking.

"You are really good at this. You should go into business," she declared to her sister, tilting her head one way and another.

"Oh right, it'll be the first post-plague beauty salon. That's exactly what people need." Kit tried for sarcasm, but ended up sounding sad instead.

Evie put her arm around her. "Hey, everyone deserves to be a little pampered now and again. Even plague survivors."

Kit still looked watery and brushed away the subject with a wave of her hand. "It's too bad you don't have anything nicer to wear," she said, looking at the tank top and jeans, which were now Evie's only clothes apart from a shapeless sweater.

"James said it didn't matter what I wore." Evie tried to sound optimistic, but she wasn't pleased at the idea of wearing clothes that were getting riper every day she wore them.

"Okay," Kit said, sounding unconvinced. "It's just a shame, is all."

"You've already made me look fantastic." Evie grabbed her hand. "I'm sure it will be fine. Besides, James has seen me look much worse than this."

But Evie reconsidered when she went on deck and laid eyes on her date. Instead of his usual battered clothes, he was wearing a dark grey suit, fitted to show off his lean tall frame to its best advantage. His normally tangled hair had been brushed out so it was shining, tied back with a leather tie.

"You look really pretty," he said, with a bashful look he seemed to keep reserved only for her.

Evie narrowed her eyes. "What is this? You said to dress casually." She took a step back. "I would change if I had anything to change into."

James laughed and then winked at Kit. "Kit already told me about that, so I'm going to take care of it."

"Kit knew about your plan, did she?" Evie raised her eyebrow.

"She also said it was time for you to get a grown up dress, so we have a stop to make before we're ready to go to ... our final destination."

Evie stood between James and Kit, both smirking. She wanted to be exasperated because they were both so smug, but somewhere along the way she lost the battle and started to laugh.

"C'mon," James said as he pulled her towards the gangplank. "You're going to have to trust me eventually."

"All right then." Before leaving, she put on the same windbreaker she sported yesterday, pulling the hood up around her face, careful not to muss her hair. "Lead away."

Heading west into the Trade District, James turned into a small wooden building, really no more than a glorified shack, that Evie otherwise wouldn't have looked twice at. He led her downstairs into the basement, to a passage that went underneath the road. "Where are we going?" she asked, reaching out to grab his arm as the corridor became darker around them. She pushed back the hood from her face to see better — no one was going to see her down here.

"Don't worry. These are services passages for this part of the city. They go for kilometers; they bypass The Grand, where Lachlan's men usually patrol."

"Just so we're clear, you're taking me through the sewers."

She felt, more than saw him grin. "Not sewers. Service routes. City maintenance would use these back in the day. While some storm water runoff will come through here, it's not connected to the sewage system."

"You sure know how to show a girl a good time," she muttered, taking wary steps as he led her down yet another stairwell, leading into a dank, dripping walkway.

He laughed. "Hey, what did you expect from New City's underground?"

"Why haven't we taken this way before? It must be safer."

"It is safer. But can you blame me? I try to avoid taking girls I like down into the sewers until I really know them."

"Aha! So you admit that these are sewers."

"Really clean ones," he insisted.

They walked steadily south, before coming to another stairwell leading upwards into another building. This structure was much more ramshackle than those in the city's core. Blinking in the light as she came out of the building into the sun, she looked behind her, seeing the skyline of the city in the distance.

"Where are we?" she asked as they started down the middle of the deserted road lined with other empty commercial buildings gaping at them through their jagged empty windows.

"We've left New City," James said. "As you can see, there's no power here."

"Does anyone live here?"

"No one we want to meet. This is No-Man's-Land. Remember I told you about it?"

"Didn't you say it was worse than the Ghetto?" Evie drew back in alarm. "Is it safe to be here?"

"For the most part, it's safe. It's a ghost town. Anyone living here is worse off than even the poorest people in New City."

"I wouldn't think that's possible." Evie shivered, despite the sun that still slanted down on them, thinking of twisted corpses and screaming junkies. A soft noise behind them, like paper rustling, made her twist around to glance behind her. "What was that? Do you think someone's following us?"

James looked around, alert but not concerned. "I doubt it. I've been here loads of times and I've never had any trouble. I've never seen anyone else down in the sewers, and Lachlan doesn't need to worry too much about people escaping the city this way. There's nowhere we can go from here."

"Because of the desert?"

"Yup. If anyone was looking for a way to escape New City, this wouldn't be the way to do it."

Evie arched an eyebrow at him. "It will be easier to get away on the river, won't it?"

James shrugged. "Listen, it would be great to just sail out of the city, never looking back again. It just doesn't happen very often anymore — not since Lachlan really started taking over. Maybe we're just kidding ourselves that anything can change." His tone, unusually bleak for him, made Evie reach out to take his hand.

"I think that we're going to be able to do it. We can take out Lachlan and waltz out of the city, no problem." Her light tone made James look up, gifting her with a grin. "Besides, won't it be wonderful to get away from these depressing streets? There's nothing that I'll miss here."

James cleared his throat. "Like I said, it just might not be that easy. And besides, not everyone wants to leave the city."

"What do you mean? You don't think we'll be able to get away?" Evie turned to stare at him. James grin was strained this time.

"We'll figure something out," he pacified her. Putting his arm around her and hugging her into him, James spoke into her hair. "It's remarkable what you can achieve with a little luck, some creativity, and a whole lotta balls."

She snorted. "We just have to have balls to get out of this?"

"A whole lot of them." He nodded wisely. "Happily, you are, no offence, the ballsiest woman I know, so we should have no problems there. Now, tonight, no more dark thoughts. We are going to have a great evening. But first you are going on a shopping spree — right here."

James stopped in front of a department store that looked like it had once been elegant. Now, the stucco walls were coated with a layer of grime. A large sign edged with lights sat dark, most of the bare bulbs broken. The building was as empty as all the rest.

"Why do I feel like you've done this before?" she said to him. "Do you take all your dates shoplifting?"

"Not for a very long time."

She smiled at his teasing tone as they went into the abandoned store through the broken display window. Inside, the dim light showed glass and debris liberally scattered on the floor around racks of clothes. She followed him as they picked their way through the debris, careful not to slip on shards of glass, over to the ladies department.

He looked around then headed into the gloom, stopping in an area crammed with racks of dresses. "Now, pick out something nice for yourself."

"Aren't you the gentleman," she murmured as she started to look through the dresses. Shopping this way was fun; no need to worry about whether anything was affordable. She did take a surreptitious peek at some of the price tags and choked at the astronomical prices.

"Did you find anything you like?" he asked.

"I'm just considering the heart attack I would have had if I had to pay for these." Flipping through a rack of silk floor-length gowns, she dismissed them as too formal for anywhere James would take her.

"It certainly makes it easier when you don't have to pay for them."

She held up a vintage black and white polka dot wrap to her body. "So, all of these beautiful, expensive things are just lying around for the taking?"

"Everything that isn't pillaged stays right where it is, until it rots or falls apart."

She fingered a chiffon shift in sparkly champagne. "That's sad. Soon everything will be gone."

He reached over to squeeze her arm. "Don't get upset. We'll make more — eventually. Maybe not quite this nice," he said, nodding at the dress, "but we will make things again. Now, go try some of these on and I'll be right back." James turned and headed into the dark interior of the store.

The thin light coming in from the front was washed out at the change rooms, where everything looked like shadow on shadow. Evie found herself holding her breath, listening for warning sounds so she would know if someone was sneaking up on her. She wished James would come back.

Groping a little as her eyes adjusted to the dimness, she tried on several dresses and dismissed them. She had to go down a size from what she used to be — a year of surviving on whatever food they managed to find had diminished her bust and waistline.

"Yes," she whispered, as she slipped the perfect one down over her hips and twirled in front of the mirror. It was a black sleeveless sheath that fit like a glove, showing off what little curves she had left, in comfortable stretchy material. The front draped just under her collarbone, while the back plunged down open past her waistline, tapering to a point just above the swell of her hips. Fine chains of pale gold crossed the back, holding the dress in place, pressing coolly into her skin. The hem fluttered just above her knees. It was edgy and sexy, and a shade over on the side of daring, which was exactly how Evie was feeling.

Kicking her way through piles of clothing, she headed back to the front of the store, where she had seen the shoe department. It was a disaster, having suffered the brunt of the looting because it was close to the display window. Shoes were piled together in small mountains of straps and heels. After some digging through the rubble, Evie managed to find a matching pair of black shoes in her size. She sat to slip off her battered sneakers, gliding the shoes on over her toes. They were higher than anything she'd worn before, held on with a delicate strap around her ankle. She stood up and tested her balance, trying to not fall flat on her face. After a few test runs, she decided she was ready. She held onto her sneakers, knowing she would need them to get back to the city.

At a low whistle from behind her, she spun around. She smiled to see James looking at her, a look of unadulterated masculine appreciation on his face.

"You look incredible."

"Well, I couldn't go out with you looking prettier than me." She blushed as he came closer, unable to keep his eyes off her skin.

"No, we couldn't have that." He drew close but didn't touch her, keeping himself a breath away. "I got something for you, to finish your look." He held out his hand and she opened hers as a reflex, feeling him twist a necklace into her palm.

Holding it up to the light, she saw it was a delicate chain, made of interlacing hoops of hammered gold.

"I love it," she murmured, holding it up to the light. "It's beautiful."

James' intense look pierced the gloom. He took the necklace from her and turned her around until her back was to him. His fingers brushed against the nape of her neck, and she felt his warm breath on her shoulder as he attached the chain. His nearness created the now familiar liquid, sinking feeling in her belly.

A dull thud came from somewhere deep in the blackness of the store. It sounded as if something had been knocked over. Her nerves were already searingly raw; the jolt pushed her over the edge. "What was that?" she gasped.

"Sounds like we have to go." James grasped her hand and pulled. Running to the window, Evie tried to keep up in her stilettos but was falling behind. Tripping over a box, she fell into it and started giggling nervously.

"Evie," James growled, running back to wrap an arm around her. "What are you doing?"

"I'm sorry, it's just — doesn't this make you feel a bit like were running away from security after shoplifting? It all seems so ridiculous."

He looked down at her, his exasperation etched into his face. "I wouldn't know, actually, I've never run from security. I was always too good for that."

"Well of course I've never run from store security either. Or shoplifted. Obviously," she said, looking shifty. "But you don't think Lachlan had us followed, do you?"

"Even if it isn't Lachlan, it could be a junkie looking for a hit, who hasn't seen a woman in months."

"Right. Let's get out of here. Just slow up a bit, I'm useless in these heels. Unless someone gets within kicking range." She did a mock karate kick with her shoe-clad foot.

James looked at the killer point. "Those are dangerous. You could poke someone's eye out with that. Let's try to avoid hand to shoe combat for the moment, though. It might ruin my dinner plans."

"Okay, let's go." She allowed James to manhandle her out of the store, still pulling her with more haste than her feet would have liked. Once outside, she quickly changed back into her comfortable sneakers, then they ran back to the subterranean service passages, Evie holding her fancy shoes by the pointy heels. It suddenly occurred to her that she had left her jacket in the store in their haste to leave; she chided herself for her carelessness.

When they finally got back to New City, she realized they were heading towards the Docks. "Are we going back to the *Mary Rose*?" she asked, suspicious.

"Not quite, no." James took her hand and led her down a tight alley. There was no lighting back here and the pavement was uneven and cracked. She clung to James to avoid a sprawling fall. He brought her up short in front of a plain back door. The painted metal was peeling and rusted, chained shut. It looked as if it hadn't been opened in years.

"It looks like it's closed," she whispered.

"It's not," he said, reaching forward and pulling the door towards him with ease. The chains were not connected, only arranged to make it appear so.

"Tricky," she said, walking in front of James, his hand on the bare skin at the small of her back.

A wall of noise and smoke hit her at once. The room they had entered was large and high, with wooden beam rafters crossing the soaring ceilings. Along the back wall was a long bar, with old-fashioned beer taps lining the counter. A man stood behind the bar, chatting with a few men who sat there on stools. A dirty mirror behind the bar barely reflected anything in it.

Wooden booths lined the walls around an open space in the middle of the room. It was packed with people, both men and women, milling around, holding drinks and toasting each other. The odour of stale beer lingered in the air, underlying the smell of cigarette smoke that circled the ceiling. Laughter peeled through the room.

"James," she hissed at him. "Did you get me all dressed up to take me to a bar?"

Chapter Twenty

James grinned at her. "Is that a problem?"

Evie tossed back her head and laughed. "Are you kidding? This is fantastic!"

"That's the spirit," he said with a laugh, putting his hand on her lower back again as though drawn to it like steel to magnet. "How about we find a table?"

Walking slowly along the battered plank floors, Evie soaked up all the noise, the talking and laughter floating around her. It struck her that this was the complete opposite of The Grand. It wasn't polished or beautiful, it smelled of old booze and smoke, and most of the people were far from good looking. It suited her a great deal more.

James stopped at a small booth, hidden away from the main crowd behind a wooden stairwell heading upstairs. A single candle illuminated the table, flickering in a pool of wax, casting shadows across their faces.

"How romantic," Evie said as she squeezed into the back of the booth.

"That's why I brought you here." James leaned in and kissed her. "Now, can I get the lady a drink?"

"Ooh, okay. I'll have whatever you're having." She watched James walk away, enjoying the view, towards the long bar at the back of the room. He stopped to chat with several people along the way, before being greeted warmly by the man working behind the bar.

Evie sighed, overwhelmed with happiness. Tonight, she was young and beautiful. Everything else could wait until tomorrow.

Curious, she glanced around, taking in the solid woodwork that looked beaten and weathered. She was unsure whether this was due to a lack of maintenance over the years or whether it was the style the designer wanted to achieve. The mellow flickering light cast by candles and gas lanterns created a cozy atmosphere, and the many hidden booths gave it an air of intrigue. She wondered briefly why the proprietors did not use the available electricity. *They must not be big fans of Lachlan's*, she thought.

She looked at the sunken dance floor in the middle of the room and thought about the last time she had danced. It seemed a lifetime ago. The wooden surface was covered with scuffs and dents, as if hundreds of people had danced there over the years.

As if hearing her thoughts, someone began to strum a guitar. She turned her head to seek out the musician. She wasn't the only one; several people got up and wandered over to check out the action. The night's entertainment was about to begin.

Evie stood up too, eager to see more, and peeked around a column to get a full view of the entire bar. On a raised platform on the edge of the dance floor, three men were getting set up with instruments; a guitarist, a fiddler, and an accordionist. She smiled as she recognized the fiddler; it was Oliver.

The men started to play something light and airy, but quick and reeling, and soon a crowd of people was swinging around the floor. She clapped her hands along to the music as others were doing, until a flash of blonde hair caught her eye. Kit had just walked to the edge of the dance floor, pint in hand and swaying to the music.

Evie's eyes narrowed as she left the booth. She walked towards Kit and tapped her on the shoulder. Kit spun around, giving a big smile when she saw her sister.

"Oh, Evie, you look beautiful. I really do good work. And that dress!"

"Kit, what are you doing here?" Evie tried not to be swayed by her sister's happiness.

"Oliver said he'd take me here, since James is taking you. Isn't it fabulous? Isn't Oliver a great player? Let's dance." With her happy rant, she skipped into the crowd, immediately being swung up by a burly man and laughing as she tried to keep her beer upright.

Evie stepped onto the dance floor but found her way blocked by James, holding two pints.

"Hey, you moved," he said. "Where are you going?"

"I need to go have a word with a minor over there," she said, trying to march forward.

"Okay, but Evie, could you just hold these pints for me for a second?" He thrust the glasses into her hands and she took them automatically, looking up at him in surprise.

"Sure, why?"

James put a firm hand around her waist and directed her off the dance floor. "So I can escort you back to our table." Burdened as she was by the beer, her choice was to spill it over herself or go with him without a struggle.

"You're tricky," she said, making a face at him, laughing underneath it.

"And I can't believe you fell for it. Don't worry about Kit, she's fine here. She has several large beefy guys looking out for her."

"It's just …" Evie sighed. "She's drinking. In a bar."

"So are we." He took a tankard out of her hand and brought it to hers with a soft tink. "It's not like there's any drinking laws any longer. Or police to uphold them. And people are looking out for her. All you need to do tonight is relax and have a good time."

"I guess I could do that," she said as she sat back down in the booth. She laughed when James squeezed in next to her on the one side so they were pressed against each other.

"Now, where was I?" He leaned in to kiss her.

"Food!" Evie exclaimed, dodging him. A small boy had come over to their table with a plate overflowing with enormous double-layered sandwiches held together by toothpicks but threatening to burst open. Next to them sat a pile of enormous pickles. "Is this dinner?"

James leaned back, letting out a long breath as he did. "This is dinner. It seemed like a good idea at the time."

She grinned. "It still is a good idea. Ooh, is that roast turkey in there? These look really good." She picked up a half, needing both hands to keep it together.

"They are really good. Unfortunately, there's no deep fryer around so we'll have to forego the fries tonight."

Evie swallowed her mouthful and closed her eyes, dreamy. "Do you know what I would kill for? Some of those deep-fried cheese sticks. Remember those?"

"Really?" He made a retching noise. "Those things are awful, all fat and grease. Now, give me a chicken wing any day."

"Which of course have no fat or grease. Nope, nothing but freshly fried cheese sticks. I want one right now."

James sat back, looking at her under hooded eyes as he took a big bite out of a pickle. "You mean to tell me that if you could eat anything in the world, it would be a disgusting piece of fried cheese."

She contemplated the question for a moment. "No, not if I could eat anything in the world, I'll agree there are better things. If I could have anything, just one thing, it would probably be … eggs Benedict. With smoked salmon."

"Now you're talking. You know, Marjory could probably whip some up for you, if you ask her nicely."

"Ooh, do you really think so?"

"Well, minus the smoked salmon. I haven't seen any of that for ages."

"Still," Evie said as she munched on a pickle, thoughtful. "The thought of Marjory's egg bennies is almost better than an illicit pub in the middle of New City."

"Almost better," James agreed and looked around him. "Nice place, isn't it?"

"It's very unexpected. I had no idea places like this still existed."

"It's always been a bar," James explained. "I used to come here when I was younger, we would sneak in. Someone had the great idea of opening it again, largely for the traders who pass in and out of the city. There are rooms upstairs for those looking to get off the river for a night or two."

"An inn for pirates?"

"Something like that."

"And what does Lachlan think about his competition?" Evie arched one eyebrow at him.

"He wouldn't like it, if he knew." She shot him a skeptical look and he laughed. "Okay, yes, he most likely knows about this place, or knows that it's a place for the traders to kick back. He doesn't come here though, nor do the people who work for him. It doesn't do a huge amount of business and he probably wants to leave well enough alone."

Evie looked at the many large men circling the dance floor and heaving pints back at the bar. "I wouldn't want to cause waves in here either. Is that why there are women here?"

James nodded. "They're mainly the traders' women."

She shot him a dirty look. "That's so sexist, like they belong to them or something."

He put up his hands in surrender. "I didn't mean it that way. It's mainly women who live on the river, or who are well protected, anyway. You'll notice none of them are very young, either, other than you and Kit. Petra will come down here occasionally, although I don't see her tonight. You can't miss her; she's dancing on the tables in no time."

Evie's eyes got big at the thought of Petra hauling her considerable bulk up on one of the sturdy tables. "I would like to see that!"

After taking a sip of beer, he continued. "What Lachlan likely doesn't know is that this place is used as a front to bring in and store smuggled goods."

"So you mean a trader can smuggle his loot into the storage rooms, or somewhere, and sell stuff from here, without Lachlan knowing?" He nodded as Evie pondered this. "Is there a tax on goods leaving New City? Do you have to smuggle things out as well?"

"It's not regulated." He gave her a suspicious look. "Why? Are you thinking of getting into the smuggling business now?"

Her face was a study in wide-eyed innocence. "Depends on what I was smuggling out."

James frowned. "Are you considering getting into more trouble than you already are?"

She batted her eyelashes, the picture of innocence. "Me? Get into trouble? Perish the thought. Now," she said, artlessly changing the subject. "I want you to tell me all about Captain Bill and the pirates."

James regaled her with tales about Bill, how he gathered a crew around him with his gruff manner and the deft way he smuggled supplies into the city. "He has a loyal crew," he said of the people on the *Mary Rose*. "They would do just about anything for him, because they know he'd do the same."

"How did people join Bill's crew?"

"Most of them came together a few months after the Sickness started," he said, taking a long drink and settling in closer to her, looking out over the heads of the crowd as he spoke. "Men, mainly, who knew their way around a boat. Before the Sickness, Eastern Havern River was mainly used for pleasure crafts. Now, fuel's so valuable that it seems like a myth, and the river became a better shipping route. Anyway, Bill started using his old barge to transport goods. He needed a crew, so he signed the guys up when they came to him. Since then, others have joined, usually people who have nowhere else to go. Although, most people in New City have nowhere to go anymore. Lachlan has seen to that."

He took another sip of beer. "Just last month I rescued a young boy who had been stabbed in the chest. I brought him to Bill."

"He was stabbed in the chest?" Evie repeated, aghast.

"Well, not deep. It was more of a really bad scratch. But he was just a little guy, and wailing in the streets. I'd seen him before, wandering the streets alone. His father was an addict, had abandoned him for drugs, I guess. He turned up dead, overdose, not too long after that. I got the kid to the ship and Petra was able to patch him up."

"I haven't seen any children on the ship," Evie said.

"I think he lives on a farm now. A barge isn't really a suitable place for kids to grow up; they're more underfoot than anything. You'll notice there aren't many children in New City. Almost all of them died in the Sickness. They were the first to get sick, the first to die."

"Yes, I had noticed," she murmured. "It was the same way at home."

"Well, now children are precious. There are more than enough people wanting to adopt orphans, so this young guy was taken in by a woman who had lost her two children in the Sickness."

"That's so sad."

He shrugged. "Depends on who you ask. That little boy is probably better cared for than he's ever been. And that woman has some solace; she has someone to live for again."

The thought of the mother and child finding each other in this world brought unexpected emotions rising in her throat. She missed the unconditional certainty of having one person in the world who would always love her the way her father did. She tried to flash a brilliant smile at James, but it was a little wobbly.

"Can I ask why you've stayed in New City? After leaving Lachlan's service, why did you stick around, knowing that you're a hunted man? Why do you still stay? You hate it here."

Sighing, he put down his glass. "I don't hate it here, not all of it, anyway. I've never been anywhere else, to tell the truth, so I don't know much about what's beyond the city. I was street trash long before the Sickness ever hit.

"If," he started, then corrected himself. "No, *when* things change around here, someone's going to have to keep an eye on things. Make sure another Lachlan doesn't just rise up to take his place. I could do that. Since I left The Grand, I've helped a few people. It's something I never did before, helping people. It's like surviving the Sickness has helped me be a better person. Maybe I was meant to stay and help out here."

"Here in New City? It seems like a lot of people don't want to be helped. They'd rather forget about life and fade away. Maybe you shouldn't be wasting your time on the people who don't even care." Her mouth twisted down, betraying her emotions. The brief bubble of happiness she had been feeling for the past few hours imploded. *Who am I kidding?* she thought. *There's no way that we could work out. That I could escape from this hellhole with Kit, and keep James too.*

He let out a bitter laugh. "Well, at least you're not pessimistic about everything. Maybe you're right; maybe everyone who survived is a lost cause. Hell, this whole city is a lost cause. But don't you think that everyone deserves to know at least one person is willing to care for them?"

She played with her glass, turning it this way and that in her fingers as she thought about it. "I understand what you're saying. But to stay for the people here? It seems like they are throwing away a second chance at life because they'd rather be too high to feel. A careful observer might say that by sticking around when you are a hunted man, you are throwing your life away right along with them."

"Are you a careful observer?" His eyes glinted at her.

She pursed her lips. "I have been known to be observant."

His smile reached his eyes, warming them. "I've noticed that about you. And if not New City, then what, Evie? What life are you planning to set up?"

"Well, I've thought about it a lot."

"Of course you have." James sat back, his arm slipping around her shoulder. "So tell me, where would you like to go?"

She looked at him, eyes wide. "Have you ever been west of the mountains?"

His eyebrows shot up. "I haven't, but I hear it's nice."

"Lush valleys, orchards loaded with fruit, mild winters and hot summers. Lakes filled with fresh water everywhere you look."

"It sounds wonderful, if there was any way to do it. From what I've heard, it would be suicide to try."

"We get to the foothills by boat."

"And then ..." he prompted.

"I don't know," she said. Looking out into the bar, she watched the figures twirling around the dance floor. Kit wasn't with them anymore, but was sidled up to the bar with some of the men. "We steal bikes and use them to get across the passes. We wouldn't be the first to do it, I bet."

"You don't know that and it's a bad idea. I've heard stories about crossing the mountains. The people who settled in the passes have become animals. They stop anyone trying to cross on the main routes." His sneered in disgust. "There's even been rumours of cannibalism."

She gave him a look. "You can't be serious. How is that possible?"

"Maybe they're urban legends, but are you willing to risk it? There is no doubt that there are bandits in the forests there. Not everyone is looking out for the good of humanity, Evie."

"Now who's being pessimistic," she said, glaring at the table.

"I didn't mean to destroy your dream, Evie, but you need to use your head. You don't always think about the consequences of what you do."

She stiffened. "You think I'm foolish."

He took her hand in his. "Nothing like that. You are just so full of possibilities, like anything can happen if you just decide to do it. But it doesn't always work out like that."

Evie grumbled a little, still feeling as if she had been chastised. "I don't see anything wrong with being that way. I thought all it took was balls to get away from here."

"You also need a good solid plan. One based in reality, preferably."

She gripped his hand, looking him straight in the eye. "You want a better life than this, though, don't you?"

"Of course."

"And you do believe it is possible?"

James took his time answering. He finally squeezed her hand. "It's not as simple as that."

"That's okay. We'll figure it out."

He stilled, barely breathing. "We?"

She bit her lip, not realizing until this second how much she wanted to keep him with her. "I thought you might change your mind. About staying? There are other people who need you."

He put his hand on the side of her face and leaned in. "Who might these other people be."

Screwing up her courage, she said. "Me. I need you." And she closed the space between them to give him a warm kiss.

James kissed her back, then sat up. For the first time, his smile didn't reach his eyes. "You make it sound so easy. I wish I had your confidence."

"Well, you better get confident, because I'm counting on you to help us get out of the city. You're the smart one here. I'm just the foolish little girl who rushes into everything."

He smiled and leaned in to kiss her again, but they broke apart in alarm when someone started shouting over the din of conversation and laughter. The music came to a jarring halt as everyone in the bar turned to the door, muttering to each other.

Evie peered around the side of the booth and gasped. James grabbed her by the arm and yanked her down. "It's Lachlan's men," she said, loud enough for him to hear her over the yelling. She recognized the rat-faced man standing at the door with four other toughs she had seen at The Grand. It was Ryson. "I thought you said they didn't come here," she hissed.

"They don't."

She cringed as she heard Ryson's whiny voice straining to be heard above the shouting. "Everyone just stay calm. We're not here to cause any trouble. We just came for the girl."

Chapter Twenty-One

Evie looked up at James as panic flooded through her. "Oh god. They must have followed us again. They know we're both here. What are we going to do?" Before James had a chance to reply, she grabbed his arm. "Kit is here. We have got to get her out before they see her."

"Kit is fine," James whispered to her through gritted teeth, tense with anger. "You need to worry about you right now. You have to stay hidden, do you understand? They could be just guessing you're here; I'm sure no one followed us."

She nodded then grabbed him as he started to leave the booth. "Wait, where are you going?"

"I need to go take care of this," he snapped, eyes darkened to nearly black. "Let me go. Don't even think about going out there."

"Are you mad at me?" The words tumbled out of her mouth and she bit her lip, realizing how it sounded.

He let out an exasperated breath. "I'm not angry with you, Evie, I'm in love with you. It's not the same thing, although it sometimes feels that way." He grabbed her up by the arms and jerked her to him, kissing her fiercely. She held him to her as hard as she could but he broke away.

"Wait, what? Don't go."

"I have to. Do as you're told for once and stay here." He got up and began to saunter towards the dance floor. The traders shuffled aside to clear a path for him.

Evie stayed crouched behind the booth as she watched James walk out of her line of vision. *He loves me,* she thought, her head spinning with a mix of terror and exhilaration. She held her breath as she waited for something to happen. Some of the traders were yelling at the intruders, but they fell silent as they watched James approach Ryson.

"Gentlemen, what can we do for you?" James said calmly, with just a hint of mockery in his voice. The sudden silence was eerie. Evie couldn't stand not being able to see what was happening, so she crept around the booth until she could peek out the side.

James stood in the middle of the dance floor. Lachlan's men were facing him, fronted by Ryson. The weaselly man looked straight at James, while the other four looked around them menacingly.

The pirates, now gathered behind James, began murmuring to each other and shifting their weight, uneasy and alert. The musicians had disbanded, their chairs abandoned at the edge of the dance floor. Evie did a quick sweep of the floor for Oliver. He was standing near the back of the group. Kit was nowhere to be seen; Evie's heart eased slightly at the thought she might have left already.

"We have no issue with you all," Ryson called out, puffing out his chest. "Just give us the girl and you'll be allowed to carry on with your business as usual. We know she's here."

"Oh, we'll be allowed to continue business, is that it?" A burly, bearded man taunted, bristling at Ryson's tone. He took a step forward and looked down at Ryson, who barely came to his shoulders. Evie realized it was one of Bill's men. "How very gracious of you, thank you kindly." His voice dripped sarcasm as he moved a little closer to James. He looked as though he would like to cause some damage.

As if his movement was a signal, the rest of the pirates clustered around James. Several of them slipped knives into their hands, and the bartender gripped a length of iron. There was a moment of electric silence; no one moved or said anything. Ryson's eyes twitched back and forth over the group facing him.

The next move was his. He would either diffuse the situation or light this powder keg.

"Guys," he said with a short laugh, trying to sound consoling. "This really shouldn't be necessary. We don't want to interfere with your business; it's small fry to us. All Lachlan asks is that you don't interfere with his. There is no need to react like this when all we want is one little whore."

She felt more than heard it when James punched Ryson in the face, causing his head to whip back, blood spurting from his nose. The two groups launched themselves at each other. Badly outnumbered, each of Lachlan's men pulled out a gun. This didn't stop the traders, who barrelled right past the weapons. James kicked Ryson's gun out of his hand the moment he brought it out. A few shots were fired, but no one fell. Bodies collided, knives flashed, flesh smashed into flesh. A gun slid across the floor. Eyes widened in horror, Evie felt as though they were moving in slow motion.

This fight, this outpouring of aggression had very little to do with her, in reality. She was just the catalyst. The fight had been coming for a long time, over nothing less than the struggle to survive in the city. Lachlan had intruded too far into the traders' affairs, and they were going to fight back.

Paralyzed with fear, her eyes flicked over the room. A flash of blonde hair caught her eye — Kit was still there. She was peeking around a booth, the same as Evie, watching the action anxiously. Evie wanted to catch her eye without drawing attention to herself, so she crawled forward on her belly and waved frantically at her. It took several exhausting minutes, but Kit eventually looked over and her face lit up with relief, then worry.

"Get. Out." Evie mouthed, pointing towards the bar. She had seen several women dash behind the tall wooden counter, so she figured it was the best place to hide.

Kit looked confused, and she watched Evie's mime several times before her forehead cleared with understanding. Then she shook her head, her worried eyes finding Oliver in the crowd again. Evie glared at her but was ignored.

Evie sighed as she sat back, desperate to make Kit leave before she was spotted. Slipping her shoes off, she gauged the distance between herself and Kit. Peeking around the corner again, she determined the men were otherwise engaged and took a deep breath, running down the line of booths, crouching down the whole time. No cries of recognition followed her. Getting to the back, she ducked behind the bar. Nobody was hiding there, so she figured there was a back exit.

Behind her table, Kit was gaping at Evie, aghast that she had run across the bar.

"Kit," she hissed. "Get over here." Kit bit her lip as she looked back at the men, trying to decide if anyone would see her. "Hurry!" Evie hissed a little louder. Kit rolled her eyes and dashed to the bar as Evie made room for her. They sat for a moment in silence, clinging to each other, listening for a shout from one of Lachlan's men. Nothing happened. They let out a breath as one.

"Kit, listen to me," Evie whispered. "You have to get out of here. They don't know you're here. Leave out back, the other women must have left this way. I'm pretty sure it will take you to the back alley. Go out and find Bill, tell him what's happening and stay on the barge."

"Are you crazy?" she whispered back, furious. "Oliver is out there."

"Kit, don't be stupid, this isn't the time for heroics. You need to leave now and keep yourself safe. Remember what Lachlan threatened to do to you if we disobeyed him? You cannot be caught."

Kit got up on her knees and thrust her face close to Evie's. "Why is it always do as I say, not as I do with you?" she hissed. "When are you ever going to take your own advice? Or didn't you notice that those men are after my only sister? Do you think they're here for your health?"

Evie sat back as if she'd been slapped. "Kit, I didn't think —"

"What? You didn't think that I care about you? Didn't think this might affect me just as much as it affects you?"

"I just want to keep you safe." Evie's voice was small.

"Well, right back at you. How about this? I'll leave if you come with me."

Evie gave her an anguished look. Kit saw her face and nodded in satisfaction. "Well, if we have that all figured out now, let's watch what's going on."

Realizing Kit wouldn't leave short of sheer force, Evie crept along behind her and they peeked around the edge of the bar. The pirates had the advantage – three of Lachlan's men were on the floor, unmoving. Another was taking on two traders at once, his gun nowhere to be seen. James had the better of Ryson and was hitting him repeatedly, backing him into a corner. Most of the pirates had stopped to watch what was going to happen. Evie had to bite back a cheer and gave Kit a squeeze.

A roar went up from the pirates when the two traders took out Lachlan's man. Distracted for a moment, James looked around and Ryson took the opportunity to back away from him. He straightened and reached into his jacket, pulled out a second gun, and fired two shots in the air. The sharp cracks got everyone's attention, and an unnatural silence fell over the bar.

Ryson grinned and aimed the barrel so it was pointed straight at James' head, close enough that he couldn't miss.

"That's enough," he said again, his nasal voice husky. "We're not here to fight you. We just came for the girl and then we'll leave you in peace. Evie!" he called out, taunting her. "I know you're here. Come with us, and you won't be hurt. That's more than I can say for your boyfriend if you don't come out."

"Evie, do not come out," James yelled, not taking his eyes off Ryson. "Don't worry about me."

In one quick motion, Ryson darted forward and hit James at the temple with the butt of his gun. James swayed then collapsed face down on the floor. The pirates shouted and started forward, but Ryson screamed, "I will shoot him if anyone comes closer!" The men fell back a few steps, looking murderous.

Ryson stepped forward and placed a foot on James' back. A pool of blood was forming under his head.

"Evie, I'm not joking," he yelled, his voice breaking. "I will put a bullet in your boyfriend's head if you don't come out this instant."

Scrambling to get up, Evie found herself jerked back.

"What are you doing?" Kit whispered, fear in her eyes.

"I have to, Kit. It's me they want. I'm not going to let anyone die because of me."

"But —" Kit's eyes filled with tears.

"Listen to me." Evie grasped Kit in a hug as she started to cry. "I will be fine. You need to take care of Oliver, and James.

Go to Bill's and stay with him. I will be fine," she repeated. "But we both have to be strong. Okay?" Kit nodded against her shoulder.

The sound of a gun being cocked turned Evie's blood icy. "Time's up," Ryson snapped. "James dies, and so will everyone else in this room unless you show yourself."

"No!" Evie yelled, standing up and stepping away from the bar, her arms over her head. "Don't shoot anyone, I'll go with you." She walked towards Ryson, ignoring everyone else but him.

He nodded in satisfaction, bringing the gun away from James' head, pointing it at her instead. "Good. We'll be off then." One of Lachlan's men had staggered to his feet. A hand closed around her arms as he moved behind her. Some of the traders made a motion to step forward.

"Stop!" she said, enraged. "Everybody stop." Jerking her arms out of her captor's hands, she sneered at Ryson. "I am coming with you. But you have to give me a minute." She spoke only to Ryson. He looked as though he might argue. She stared at him, chin tilted in defiance, determined to leave on her own terms. Ryson finally shrugged a bony shoulder. "Take a minute, then."

She walked to James before Ryson could reconsider and knelt down at his side. The blood was seeping from the cut on his head; his eyes were closed.

"James," she said, quietly, putting her hand on his cheek. "James, wake up." *Please, please, please let him be all right,* she thought. *Let him wake up.*

He stirred and let out a weak groan. Evie laughed, out of sheer relief. "That's right, now I need you to look at me." She took her hands away from his face as he shifted his body around, bracing himself so he was half sitting up, looking at her. His face was pale, one side slick with blood, and his eyes were unfocused.

"Evie ..." he started to say, his voice trailing off.

"Shh," she hushed him, moving her face in close to his. "I have to go, James, but I'm going to be all right. I need you to make sure that Kit is safe, that's the only thing that matters now. Promise me you'll take care of my little sister."

"Evie, no." He shook his head, more in confusion than anything. "You don't have to do this."

"I do. Take care of yourself, James." She stood quickly and turned to Ryson and his one remaining thug. Feeling as though she were in her own nightmare, she heard herself say, "I'm ready to go."

The man who had grabbed her arm a few minutes earlier reached for her again, but she wrenched away. She walked towards the door of her own volition, with her eyes facing straight ahead.

"Evie, don't do this," she heard James scream behind her. But she didn't look back.

Chapter Twenty-Two

On bare feet she marched along with the men towards The Grand, refusing to let any of them touch her. Nothing was said. All the time her mind was working furiously: *Was James going to be all right? Could Kit be kept safe? What was going to happen to her now?*

She heard music pumping from the ballroom long before they reached the hotel. The men led her inside, taking her through the main level entrance, opening onto the dance floor. Once again the room was alive with a mass of grinding, dancing people. In the flashing lights it was difficult to tell one individual from another; they looked like one enormous wriggling being.

Evie curled her lip. There were so many people here, bought and paid for by Lachlan, scrambling to forget their lives as quickly as possible.

She was led through crowds of people cackling with each other, ordering drinks from scandalously underdressed waitresses. It was all so fake; so staged. Evie could see signs of unsatisfied cravings in some of the men, sweating, scratching, eyes nervous and darting over the beautiful people. She figured they would not last much longer. They would be thrown out on the streets to fend for themselves, or thrown in the trash like so many before them. Such a waste.

By the time Evie and Ryson had twisted their way through the crowd to Lachlan's table, Evie's revulsion had fuelled her anger and drowned her terror. She stood looking down at Lachlan and his entourage in a controlled silent rage.

He was surrounded by his women and several men who had likely paid for the privilege. The table was covered with glasses of different coloured drinks; everyone was laughing a little too hard. Lia was standing behind Lachlan, her body draped across his shoulders. Her little-girl face was close to his ear, whispering something, and his mouth was curled in a smile, but he was not really paying attention. His eyes were hard and alert, snapping to Evie as she approached. He dismissed Lia with a wave of his hand, sitting forward. She straightened slowly, peering malevolently at Evie from behind her curtain of hair. Her fingertips remained on his shoulders.

When she felt she had Lachlan's full attention, Evie raised her eyebrows. "You summoned?"

"Evie," he said, his voice smooth, his polish in place. "So lovely to see you. Do have a seat." He motioned to an empty chair that had been placed behind her.

She ignored it. "I'll stand, thanks."

His jaw tensed. Lachlan looked like he might argue the issue, but instead relaxed back into his chair. "Have it your way." He looked her up and down slowly, relishing in her discomfort. "You clean up nicely. I suspected you would. I only wish I had been the one to bring out this side of you." He sipped on a drink, sucking it through his teeth. "Since I wasn't, I can at the very least enjoy the results."

Evie wasn't going to play. She hated his eyes on her; she felt too exposed. "Are you getting to the point anytime soon?"

He narrowed his eyes but he ignored her comment. "But what's that on your arm?" he asked in mocking concern. "I hope that nobody had an accident tonight."

She looked down involuntarily. Her left hand was smeared with blood, the stain travelling up the outside of her forearm. James' blood. It stood out on her pale skin, appearing to glow in the unnatural light.

"So much blood," he taunted. "Has someone been hurt? I do hope it isn't serious."

Evie folded her arms over her chest and stared down on him. Her silence infuriated him more than anything. He dropped his false concern, leaning forward, his eyes flashing. "You want me to get to the point. You are a little bitch. That is the point. Did you think you could just walk away from me?"

She hesitated, unsure whether the question was rhetorical. His silence simmered, so she finally answered. "I want no part in this life."

"Well, that's where we're going to have to disagree. Because *this*, darling little Evie, is your life. This has been your life since the moment you came to The Grand. Stop kidding yourself; it's time you came back here to stay with us."

"I don't want to," she responded. It was a childish answer and several people sniggered. "I didn't have a choice in coming here, and I don't want to stay."

"You think this is a matter of choice?"

She stuck out her chin and glared at him. "No, Lachlan, I think this is a matter of business. Everyone here is bought and paid for, isn't that right? Well, I never accepted any payment from you, not for what you're asking."

He raised an eyebrow at her and laughed. "Don't be such a child. You had no problem moving right in. It's not my fault you didn't read the fine print."

She stepped closer to the table and leaned forward, bringing her face down to Lachlan's level. "Yes, it damn well is," she hissed. "You can't buy someone without telling them."

"You were bought and paid for with a comfortable room. Nobody comes into my city without paying a price. You're nothing but a little girl who doesn't like the consequences of her actions."

"What consequences? You gave me a place to stay so now I owe you my life? How exactly does that work?"

Lachlan sat back, reaching up to play with Lia's hand at his shoulder. "You want me to tell you exactly how this works? Let me spell it out for you. You are mine. You will stay here, at The Grand, for as long as I choose for you to stay. You will stay by my side whenever I say so, and you will do exactly what I tell you to do, with whomever I tell you to do it. And you will enjoy it."

Shaking with disgust, Evie tried to keep her voice steady. "For how long, though, Lachlan? Until the next batch comes along, I'm assuming. What happens to me then? You own me, so you sell me. That's how it works, right? Will I go to the highest bidder, or do you just have a catalogue for your customers to pick girls out of?" Her eyes flicked up to Lia, who looked like she was sucking a lemon. "How about you, sweetie? Has he made plans for you to be sold down river to a farmer? It will happen soon, you know. I guess that wasn't in the fine print either," she spat.

Lia looked ready to spring across the table at her, but Lachlan was smiling. "I take advantage of the commodities I have." He reached out with his other hand and fondled the thigh of a nearby girl, whose smile was frozen on her face, eyes blank and unfocused. "So what?"

"The world collapses and you take advantage by starting a slave trade, and your only answer is, so what?"

He shrugged.

Evie shook her head and straightened. "A lifetime of slavery in return for a warm bed. I think one of us is getting a better deal."

He looked up and smiled. "You want better payment. I always enjoy negotiating. Tell you what, here's the new deal. For your lifetime of slavery, I will stay away from that delicious little sister of yours. I'm giving up a lot here, Evie, because Kit would make an excellent addition to my collection."

Evie went to slap him, but her arm was restrained by one of the men behind her. "If you ever so much as touch my sister, I swear I will kill you." Her voice was a growl as she strained against her captor.

He didn't flinch. "And, I think I'll let James live as well. You'd like that, wouldn't you? Even you have to admit that's a good deal. Two lives for the price of one. All you have to do is give yourself to me. And, of course, the drugs."

Evie stilled, and the man behind her let her go. She looked down at Lachlan, slowly shaking her head, stalling for time as her mind swirled. *Has he really not found my stash?*

"Is that a no?" he said with a little laugh, looking at her in wonder. "I thought I knew you better than that. You don't want to save your sister and your boyfriend? Seeing as you're such a martyr, are you sure you can take the consequences of that decision?"

She stood there, frozen, unable to form the proper words.

He sighed. "I won't make you answer right now, although this offer won't be on the table forever. I want you here, Evie, and will have you, but it means so much more to me if you walk through that door willingly." His tone became gentle, solicitous. "Listen, I'm not a bad guy. I'll give you time to think about it. One day to say your goodbyes, and then you come here, tomorrow at sunset — not a minute later. I will be expecting you, and you have my word your sister and the convict will remain safe, unless you don't show up on time." With that, he dismissed her by turning his head and resuming his conversation with the man on his left.

Rough hands grabbed her arms and Ryson started to shuffle her towards the exit. A figure at the back of the group standing around Lachlan's table caught Evie's eye. It was Millie. As Evie passed, Millie looked up. Evie's words caught in her throat as she gasped. The woman had been badly beaten, her beautiful face disfigured with the swelling. One eye would barely open and her lips were contorted. "Oh, god, Millie …" Evie said, trailing off. Millie's one tired eye rolled away from her as she shook her head, not saying anything, as Ryson continued to hustle Evie away through the crowd. In her shock, she could barely keep one foot in front of the other, so it was a hidden blessing that Ryson and his buddies were all but carrying her.

Evie was deposited at the front doors. Ryson gave her a shove and sneered. "Too bad you don't have a crowbar now, eh, princess?" he taunted before following his friends back into the lobby. She limped down the front stairs on her swollen feet then stood looking back at the hotel in a daze. She couldn't believe that Lachlan had let her go. Relief, fear, and humiliation churned inside her. She wanted to laugh and scream at the same time. She aimed her emotions at the man who had tricked her into this living hell. "You bastard!" she yelled at the closed door. "Tell your boss he can't play with me like a half-dead mouse. I'm not going to come crawling back. He doesn't control me. He —"

Someone cleared his throat behind her. She spun around, instantly regretting her bravado. The white-haired bodyguard, Three, appeared from the shadows. "Evie," he said in his high voice. Goosebumps broke out along her arms at his sinister tone. "That was quite the outburst. I take it you aren't planning on coming back. Talk to me a moment."

"I'd rather not," she said, giving him a disgusted look and turning to leave.

"I could offer a word of advice. Something you might need, when the time comes."

"What do you think you could possibly tell me?"

"Just that if I were you, I would be here tomorrow with a smile on my pretty face. I don't think you'd like the consequences if you didn't."

"Yah, your boss already made that pretty clear to me."

"I just don't know if he made himself clear enough. Lachlan can sometimes be a little too subtle. I think the deal he offered you was entirely too lenient." Three took a thin knife out of his suit jacket. He started to play with it, watching it flash as he twirled it around his fingers. Evie backed up a few steps, putting distance between them. He continued. "Me? I thought he could be more obvious. I like to send a message that will really hit home. In fact, I already have. I'd love to hear what you think of it when you find it."

"What are you talking about?"

"I left you a message. At *home*. You'll see." He caught up the knife and put it away, smoothing down the front of his jacket. "Can't wait to see you again." He turned and went back into the hotel, letting the door slam shut.

Evie started walking, feeling off-balance after the threatening conversation with the cruel man. *What did he mean, a message at home?* she thought. *The apartment? That's the only home I've had in this place.*

Her body reacted before her mind caught up with the thought; a swooping feeling of panic crashed down on her and she began running through the streets. *We didn't all leave the apartment. Someone never left.*

She ran all the way to the apartment building, trying to quell the feeling of dread. She threw herself against the unused front door, praying it was not locked, and went sprawling into the lobby as it crashed open. Not only was the door unlocked, it was not completely closed.

"Marjory!"

Her apartment door was ajar, a crack of light peeking out. "No," she breathed, her heart crashing in her chest at the thought of what she would find. The apartment was trashed. Every book Marjory owned had been thrown about the main room, lying in messy heaps. A lamp had been overturned and was struggling to function. The flickering light and crackling of electricity added to the sense that Evie had entered a nightmare, leaving reality behind. Marjory was not there.

Perhaps she had seen them coming, was able to get away or hide before they got in. Evie's mind was already ahead of her, imagining all the places Marjory could be now, how she had to let her know they needed to leave the city.

As she moved towards the hallway, the only sound she could hear was the buzzing of electricity; it seemed to come from behind her eyes. She saw the foot first, sticking out from the bedroom door, wrapped in a practical sturdy shoe. Staring at the foot, Evie approached against her will. The leg was exposed. It wasn't like her at all. Her body was sprawled out on the floor, as if casually tossed there. She was lying on her stomach, arms pinned underneath her body.

"Marjory," Evie whimpered, falling to her knees at Marjorie's side. She scrabbled at her jacket, struggling to flip her over, in case she was just hurt. *We can find a doctor, it's going to be okay.* Evie finally rolled her onto her back and faced the staring blue eyes. Her kind face was frozen in an expression of horror. Evie was unable to look away, her face a mask, matching Marjory's.

Her arms had now fallen to her sides. Blood was on her right hand, and under the nails. She had fought back.

Trembling, Evie reached out to touch a cheek. Still warm. Evie moaned, realizing this must have just happened. While she fought with Lachlan at the club, Three had sent a thug to do this. He even stalled her outside the hotel, making sure that his message was ready for her. *The consequence of my actions.*

Staring down at Marjory, she sat for an age, tears flowing down her cheeks. Reaching up she closed the bright blue eyes, stroking her hair, wishing life back into her. She folded both hands over her chest, placing the left over the right, hiding the blood.

After a time, something caught Evie's eye, on the floor near Marjory's head. Detached and curious, she got up to see what it was. A note, on Lachlan's heavy stationery, folded in half. It was pinned to the carpet with the bloody needle of an empty syringe. Realization hit and Evie looked back at Marjory, moving the hair off her neck. The only mark on her body was one pinprick of blood where she had been injected, in the side of her neck. With what, Evie could only guess. Maybe one of her own drugs had been used to kill this dear woman, the drugs she had purposefully stashed in her truck before coming to New City, thinking they would help her, and others, survive. She let out a wail and covered her face with her hands. Even in her worst nightmares, she could not have imagined what a terrible chain of events she triggered that day.

Evie ripped the note from the floor and unfolded it with shaking fingers. A single line, sealing her condemnation.

SHE WASN'T PART OF THE DEAL.

Chapter Twenty-Three

She ran blindly, leaving the note, leaving Marjory, leaving the apartment. The chill air hit her face like a slap, bringing her up short, before she keeled over and threw up in the filthy gutter. She lay in the deserted street, sick and exhausted, unable to move. She didn't know how much time passed before she was able to pull herself up, stumbling, clutching a lamppost to stop herself from falling. When her head cleared, she started walking. There was no thought as to where she was going or what came next, other than putting distance between herself and her guilt.

The buildings crowded in around her, dank and claustrophobic. She wound her way through one alley after another, unknowing and uncaring. A loud laugh, rough and male, from a nearby doorway brought her back to her senses. Looking down at herself, she was almost surprised to find she was still wearing a scrap of a dress. She folded her arms around herself, feeling her shaking body, surprised at how cold she was. Her bare feet were bloodied — when had that happened? She needed to find shelter.

She ducked down the next alley, away from the boisterous voices. Passing by a storefront office, she peered through the broken windowpanes. It seemed empty; a haven from the cold wind. The door was open, so she walked in, gingerly stepping over the broken glass that littered the floor. She gritted her teeth against the pain when she wasn't careful enough.

The office had old-style cubicles everywhere — some still had computers sitting at them, as if waiting for the workers to return any day. The thought faded almost before it registered, and she focused on studying her surroundings. Judging by the tropical escape posters that cheerfully lined the walls, it used to be a vacation travel agency. A getaway for when life was both more complicated and infinitely simpler.

She walked through the central floor space towards the back, finding an office with a big desk and a couch. "The boss's office," she said to herself in a monotone, half expecting someone to invite her in. There was a blanket thrown over the back of a chair; she wrapped it around her, grateful for the warmth, and curled up on the couch. Once she was there, with those small vestiges of security around her, she let herself cry. She sobbed into the hard wood arm of the couch for what seemed like hours, finally escaping into the blackness of sleep.

For whatever comfort unconsciousness offered, Evie's dreams were dark, amorphous, and disturbing, causing her to drift in and out from one nightmare to the next. Finally, she woke with a start, eyes wide in alarm as she tried to figure out where she was.

The panic faded as reality came crashing back, and already she missed the oblivion of sleep where at least the nightmares didn't last forever. She sat up slowly, thinking only of Marjory; what her last moments of life must have been like.

Looking around her, she forced herself to take stock of her immediate situation. She was in the back office of a store somewhere in New City. Judging by the weak light trickling in from the front, it was some time in the early morning. She was wearing a very small, very thin dress and had lost her shoes in the bar. Her feet were blackened with filth and streaked with blood from numerous cuts; she winced as she tried to put her weight on them. She would need to find shoes before she went anywhere.

Concentrating on one task at a time, she began to poke around the large office and found a washroom with a toilet and sink. The water was thankfully running, so she soaked the dirt and tiny shards of glass off her feet and washed her hands and face. A further search found a closet with some personal belongings, including some shirts and sweaters. She took out an oversized cardigan, grateful that it would keep her warm and restore her modesty, and a pair of beaten up sneakers. They were bigger than the size she took, but her feet were so swollen they only just fit.

Heading out of the building, she blinked in the few shafts of watery sunlight that made their way down to ground level. Disoriented, she stumbled through the streets again heading towards the Market. She was thinking clearer now and needed to see Kit with her own eyes, to know she was okay. She didn't want to face her yet, to have her know what she did, that she had caused Marjory's death. Her thought was to walk near the barge, see if she could spot her.

As she got closer to the Market, more and more people surrounded her, going about their daily business. She expected everyone to stare at her, to point, to know, but she was paid little attention. *That's a benefit of living in New City*, she thought. *No one thinks twice about a person stumbling down the street, unfocused and disoriented.*

All too soon she was wandering through stalls and tents being set up. Snatched bits of overheard conversations told her the main gossip of the day was the brawl at the traders' bar. From what Evie could gather, a few people were seriously injured. She prayed the damaged men were Lachlan's and, more than anything, that Kit and James were all right.

She stood to the side of an anonymous market stall, a merchant selling a sorry selection of wilting harvest vegetables. From this vantage point she was hidden but had a clear view of the *Mary Rose* and the people around it. There was an enormous stack of crates on the dock nearby; it seemed as if the pirates were loading up.

She knew there weren't scheduled to leave yet. Maybe the fight had changed their minds. There was no sign of Kit, so she walked a few steps closer, craning her neck in a futile attempt to see above the deck. Perhaps she could get someone's attention, have a private word to find out whether Kit was still safe.

She sensed him before she saw him, a tingling along her spine. Her eyes sought him out and she saw James standing on the other side of the docks, surrounded by packing crates. He looked wild and disheveled as he stared at her. *He knows about Marjory*, she thought, dread tightening her stomach. *He blames me for her death.* It was obvious by the look in his eyes as he stared her down. His face contorted with rage, and with hatred. No one had ever looked at her that way before, and her breath caught in her throat.

For a seemingly endless moment they started at each other, a moment of hate and fear, then she took an involuntary step backwards, then another. His eyes widened as he realized before she did that she was going to run, and he started towards her. She hesitated for just a second, then spun and fled.

Pushing away from the stall, she elbowed her way into the crowd, hearing angry shouts behind her and feeling clutching hands trying to stop her. The pain in her feet was forgotten as she wove between people and stalls, too terrified to look back and see him right behind her, catching up. There seemed to be hundreds of hills in the former park, and just as many hostile people. For the first time since arriving in New City she felt her salvation lay in the alleyways and buildings of the Downtown District.

Fueled by desperation, she sprinted across an empty street bordering the Market. She let out a sob of relief when she reached the sanctuary of the dull stone walls and garbage-filled streets. Ducking down one alley then another, she lost herself in the labyrinth. Finally slowing down, she clutched at her side. She was empty; the last run had used up everything she had.

A noise from behind her made her gasp. She spun around. No one was there, but she still limped on to the next street. That was her mistake. James was waiting for her there. He grabbed her. She felt her feet leave the pavement before she hit the wall, hard. The wind rushed out of her body and she would have curled up in pain, only James was holding her immobile, pinned against the wall. She could only let out a wheeze, robbed of air, and look up at him.

He was clearly out of control. His eyes were red rimmed and bulging in fury, and his lips were pulled back in a snarl. The ugly cut on the side of his forehead was pulled together with a coarse black threat, and a detached part of her mind wondered who had stitched it.

"What were you thinking?" he screamed in her face. "What happened? How could you — after everything I've done for you, this is what I get?"

Evie winced away from his face, too close, and his words. "I didn't know what was happening. I didn't know what would happen."

"What did happen? You were taken to Lachlan, and now you're all of a sudden wandering around, free? What, did he just decide that he wasn't interested in you anymore? Tell me one thing, Evie, the truth for once. What deal did you make with Lachlan? Did you know that Marjory was going to pay the price?"

"No." All she could manage was a desperate whisper. In her shame and her fear, she began to cry. "No I didn't."

"Don't lie to me! I know!" He thrust a crumpled a piece of paper onto her chest. She didn't look at it and didn't have to. She knew it was the note. She knew what it said. She shook her head.

"I didn't know," she choked out. "I didn't. Lachlan said he would save your life, and Kit's, if I agreed to go back and whore for him." She could barely get words out. "But I didn't agree to anything, I swear. He gave me a day to decide. I didn't know." She was pleading with him to understand, to alleviate her guilt.

James let out a roar. He brought his arm back. She closed her eyes and tried not to flinch away. She deserved worse.

He hit the wall instead. She felt the impact next to her face. Her eyes flew open as he groaned, but he didn't pull back. Instead, he put his bleeding broken hand around the back of her neck and pulled her roughly to him, holding so tight she could barely breathe. She leaned in, desperate to be close to him, burying her face into his shoulder, comforted despite her anguish.

His mouth was right next to her ear. "Do you really believe that?"

She let out a sob into his shoulder and collapsed, held up only by his arms. Crying freely, she shook her head.

"Do you think her death is your fault?" His voice was cold.

After a breath, she nodded, without looking up.

"Good," he said fiercely, and she started crying harder. He held her like that for a long time, as if reluctant to let her go. Finally, he spoke again, intense. "Do you know what the worst part was, for me? When I went to the apartment, desperate to know if you had somehow managed to get away, the first thing I felt, the first traitorous thought I had when I found Marjory's body, was that I was relieved it wasn't you. It sickens me."

He let her go, slowly. She stepped away from him, leaning back against the wall. "Wait," she pleaded. The contempt was clear on his face, but he raised an eyebrow, waiting for her to continue. "Please, just tell me. Is Kit okay?"

"Of course she's okay. You told me to take care of her. Before you left with his men. Willingly."

"They were going to kill you!"

"You could have made another choice. You could have done something different."

"That's not fair!"

James made a noise of disgust and turned his back to her, walking away, leaving her still pressed against the wall.

There comes a point when there are no tears left to be shed; no matter how sad or painful the situation, crying is no longer an option. Evie had reached that point. Crying wasn't going to solve anything. She walked through the streets again, this time with a sense of purpose. She had made of mess of things, but there was still a chance she could save the two people she loved.

Nobody stopped her or so much as looked in her direction. It didn't matter anyway. She had been found and there was no more point in hiding.

She limped into the apartment and averted her eyes as she passed Marjory's half-opened door. Walking up the stairs was agony, and she bit her lip to keep from whimpering.

The door to her suite was wide open. The apartment had been torn apart. Every object in the living room was broken; the soft furniture had been slashed open. Same for the kitchen, even the tiles had been smashed. She stood in her former home, reeling from the destruction that surrounded her. Debris was scattered across the floor of the ruined apartment, and she had to pick her way around it. *They must have been looking for the drugs*, she thought, *At least I know for sure they didn't find them at The Grand.*

It was a relief to find that the bathroom was relatively untouched. The cabinets had been torn from the walls, but the tub and shower were intact. She let out a sigh of relief when she found the water was still running. She got undressed, letting out a cry as she peeled off the huge shoes. Her bleeding feet had scabbed over, and removing the shoes reopened some of the wounds.

Turning the water as hot as she could make it, she lifted her legs over the edge of the tub and set her feet under the scalding water, biting her lip against the pain. The heat hurt but felt good. When she felt strong enough she turned on the shower, standing under the pounding spray for a long time, wondering when she was ever going to feel clean again. She washed the product out of her hair, the makeup off of her face, the blood off of her hands.

Stepping out of the shower, she wiped steam away from the mirror, staring at herself, naked and unmarked. Evie looked back, the girl who not too long ago had lived in a small house up north, who had dreams and a family that died along with everything else. The same girl, and yet so changed. There was no way to go back.

She stuck out her chin at her reflection. *Keep on moving forward*, she thought.

She dressed quickly, finding plain white underwear, baggy jeans and a T-shirt. She left her face bare and her hair air-dried and messy. Looking at the clock, she was surprised that it was only nine in the morning. It felt much later. Lachlan wasn't expecting her until the evening. For the moment, she could escape.

Walking into the living room, she picked up the bottle of Scotch and a glass and brought them over to the couch. A one-time present from Lachlan, she figured she might as well reap the benefits from her employer. Even though the pillows and cushions of the couch were slit, she managed to make a nest and get comfortable. Settling in, she poured a glass and downed the fiery liquid in one gulp. She drew in her breath and hissed at the burning as it hit her throat, then she poured herself another. And another. In no time she was in a deep boozy sleep. She had escaped, even if only for a few hours.

Chapter Twenty-Four

Her recollection of what happened next was hazy, as if it was only a lovely dream interrupting her sleep. A hand was stroking her hair. Her eyelids fluttered open. James sat on the edge of the couch with her, leaning over, tracing the tear tracks on her face.

His eyes were still raw and he looked as exhausted as she felt, but he looked calmer. He no longer crackled with rage, but was a soothing presence, hand in her hair.

She struggled to sit up. Her eyes never left his. "James, I'm so sorry." Her voice was hoarse, the words barely discernible. He nodded and pulled her in for a close hug.

"I'm sorry too."

Her eyes fell closed with relief as she wrapped herself around him, warming herself against his body.

"Let's not stay here," James said as he untangled himself from her, holding out a hand to help her up. She cried out when her feet hit the ground. They had swollen even more in her sleep and could barely hold her weight. The pain was an unwanted intruder, imposing itself on her moment of relief.

"What's wrong?" James asked.

"My feet ... aren't doing so well." He crouched down and picked one up tenderly, inspecting it. He tsked.

"What a mess! What did you do? Dance barefoot on broken bottles?"

"Not entirely by choice," she said.

Without another word he scooped her up into his arms, carrying her out of the ruined apartment. She let herself relax into his shoulder, for the first time in years allowing someone to take care of her.

Walking into his own apartment, he carried Evie to the bedroom. He jostled her as he laid her on the bed, waking her. She looked up at him with a frown, unaware she had drifted off to sleep again.

"Don't give me that reproachful look," he said. "It's not my fault you keep on passing out."

"I am not passing out. I'm enjoying several lady-like naps."

He snorted. "Lady-like naps and a bottle of Scotch. And here I thought you were a lightweight. I'm impressed." The brief levity faded from his eyes. "I want you to just rest here. I'm going to fix up your feet. They're in pretty rough shape. Are you hungry?"

She shook her head. The thought of consuming anything right now caused her stomach to churn. He grinned. "I didn't think so. I'd give you something for the pain, but you've already taken care of that."

When he left the room, Evie sat up and looked around. The blinds were shut tight against the daylight, lending artificial darkness to the room. She couldn't see a clock anywhere and began to get anxious, wondering how much time she had left. "What time is it?" she asked with more force than she intended as soon as James came back with a bowl of water and some bandages.

"It's almost noon," he answered in alarm. "Why?"

Still time. She relaxed back into the pillows, putting her head down again. "It's disconcerting, not knowing."

He went to the window and opened the blinds, allowing daylight to flood in. Then he came to the end of the bed. "There's nothing worse than not knowing."

Her eyes flicked to his and held his gaze. She knew he wanted to ask why she was free now, even though she had said she had to go back. *Please don't ask me yet*, she thought, not wanting to get into the details until she could think straight again.

He put the bowl down next to her feet. "This is going to hurt a bit, love. There's some glass in your feet that I need to get out. I'm no expert, so you're going to have to bear with me. It's probably best that you just try to relax."

She looked down at his hands. The knuckles of one were opened where he had smashed his fist against the wall, but they were clean. As she reached down to touch him, he took her hands in his. "Just lie back," he whispered.

She did as he suggested, resting her head back into the pillows and closing her eyes, encouraging herself back to sleep. It didn't work, it never does, but she was determined to keep her face blank, or at the very least not cry out.

It was difficult. The hands at her feet were gentle, running a washcloth over the various wounds. But the water stung, and when he dug for pieces of glass with tweezers she had to grit her teeth. Clenching and releasing her fists, she willed the rest of her body to remain relaxed.

She opened one eye cautiously. James sat at the edge of the bed, intent on the task at hand. The tip of his tongue peeked out at the edge of his mouth.

Finally, she felt a soothing balm being rubbed into her skin, and she let out a small sigh of pleasure. The cool cream made her feet tingle as the sharp pain left them. She wiggled them, testing. "That is much better," she said.

James looked up and smiled, as if so focused on the work he was doing he had forgotten she was there. "I'm happy to hear it. You should be able to walk on them now without too much pain. You were just pushing the glass in farther before." He wrapped her feet in long white bandages, giving them a mummified look. Once he was done, he gave them a gentle pat. "That's all I can do for you." He moved the bowl and tweezers to the side table then came back and sat on the edge of the bed. The atmosphere in the room was suddenly awkward.

He cleared his throat. "I'm really happy you came back here. I figured this is where you would be."

She gave a tight smile. "I didn't really have anywhere else to go. Have you seen Kit?"

He wouldn't meet her eyes. "She's fine. I was able to sneak a message to her that you're okay. She's with the other women, on the boat, and she's angry with you, but she's fine for now."

Her chest tightened. "What do you mean, *for now?* What's going on, James?"

"That fight caused a lot of damage, and some of the men got hurt. The pirates are planning to leave tonight, but it's more than that. People are angry right now, and that anger is directed at Lachlan. He's gone too far, and it's rallied everyone to our cause. This unrest is ready to boil over. Now is the time to fight back. Tonight."

"You mean, all of you? The revolution, it's going to happen tonight? The pirates too?" Evie's heart was slamming in her chest. *Kit!*

He nodded. "The pirates too. The *Mary Rose* is getting special attention from Lachlan's men. The women are hiding and are scared. He has men on the docks with guns, with orders to shoot first and ask questions later, but they haven't caused much trouble yet. It's almost as if … everyone is waiting for something."

She struggled up to a seated position as Lachlan's words echoed through her brain. *Tomorrow at sunset – not a minute later.* "They're waiting for sunset. That's the time Lachlan gave me to get back. If I'm not back by then he's going after you and Kit."

James listened in silence, his jaw clenching tighter with every word.

"I'm going back to The Grand." She said, her voice like steel. She stuck out her chin at his incredulous look. "Like I said, he promised me that you and Kit would be safe if I did. I don't believe him, I'm know he'll come after you eventually, after he has made me show him where the drugs are, but I can buy you more time to … do what it is you plan to do. I'll be on the inside and if Lachlan is with me, he won't be paying attention to what's going on outside."

He was silent for a long time. "Evie, this is stupid. We are not talking about this. You go to Lachlan tonight and you are as good as dead. He won't let you leave."

"Now it's you who is not listening. If I'm not there at sunset, his men *will* get onto the *Mary Rose* and find Kit. They'll go after you as well. It could derail your whole rebellion before it even begins."

As James considered this, she continued in a quiet voice. "Everything is at stake tonight. You realize I could do more than just escape from The Grand tonight."

Realization washed over his face, but he didn't look happy. "The drugs?"

"The drugs. And the truck. And the guns. Wouldn't you rather go out west with an arsenal?"

"Yes," he said, drawing out the word. "I'd rather do a lot of things with an arsenal."

"Well, here's what I was thinking. It would be great if your revolution started just as I got to The Grand; that would distract Lachlan, allowing me to get away from him and get to the drugs."

"I'm well ahead of you, my darling. We've got a few surprises up our sleeves that will do more than distract Lachlan."

"And you think it will get his men out of the hotel? The more men you get out of The Grand, the fewer I will have to contend with."

"The fewer *we* will have to contend with," he corrected her. She gave him a quizzical look and he squeezed her hand. "You didn't think I'd let you take on Lachlan on your own, did you? We'll have men in The Grand as well."

Evie wanted to protest, but was too relieved to put up a fight. James got up and started pacing, working the plan through again in his head.

Finally he sighed, settling back down on the bed next to her. "I think that this could work. I can move the time we strike forward. To sunset. We'll know where Lachlan is at that time … he will be with you," he ended grimly. He ran his hands through his long hair, making it stick out in wild tangles. "I don't have to tell you that if things go wrong … you could be giving up a lot, Evie."

She nodded. "I understand the risks."

"I hate that. Listen, your priority is to get out of the hotel alive. Don't go looking for trouble. If that's even possible for you. I don't think Lachlan has figured how much of a handful you can be, yet. When do you have to go?"

"About half an hour before sunset — it could take me twenty minutes to hobble there from here. I can't risk being even a second late."

The light in the room was still strong and bright from the sun, a long way from sunset. "Sunset it is." He stood up, awkwardly looking away. "I guess I'll let you get some more sleep. You have had … a long night." It sounded like he wanted to say more then stopped himself. He turned to leave.

"James?" Evie said, very quietly, in case he didn't want to hear. Her heart was thumping so hard she could see her chest throbbing. He did hear, though, pausing at the doorway, not saying anything. "Would you stay with me please?"

He turned to look at her, an anguished look on his face. "Are you sure?"

In response, she moved to one side of the bed to make room for him. He hesitated for one moment then nodded. He crawled onto the bed and sat next to her, seeming large and awkward, as if he didn't know what to do with his arms.

She reached for him, taking his hand in hers in a tentative gesture. He wrapped both his large warm hands around hers.

"You're freezing." It wasn't until he said it that she realized he was right. Her hand felt like a block of ice in his and her body was chilled through. "Here, get under the covers." He lifted back the plain white sheets, allowing her to slip inside without catching her feet on anything. The cover was warm and heavy, pressing down on her body. It was even better when James slipped under the covers with her as well, folding his body around hers. She pressed her face into his neck, letting his skin warm her freezing nose. He wrapped one of his hands around the back of her neck, pulling her in closer.

Moving her face a little, she looked up and kissed him. He kissed her back, hungrily, leaving her breathless and wanting more. His hands, tight on her body, began to move of their own accord, under her shirt, taking in all of her skin. She made a small noise of surprised pleasure. He stopped, watching her, seeking answers.

"Evie, are you sure?" He let the question linger between them.

"Yes," she said, reaching up to kiss him. "I want you to be the first."

He let out a shaky breath. "We don't have to."

"The time for waiting is over."

He looked as if he were about to argue, so she pressed against him. "No more talking," she ordered as she sat up and straddled him. She looked down on him from this position and peeled off her shirt. She sat before him, bare physically and emotionally, her eyes on his face. She reached down and started to pull off his jacket. He allowed her to take it off but made no move to help her. He wore nothing underneath. She wanted nothing more than to run her hands over the broad expanse of his chest, so she did. James took in a sharp breath.

"Evie?" he asked, voice hoarse.

Her lips curved into a smile. She craved him, wanted to be as close as possible. She lay down, pressing bare chest to bare chest, and took his lips in hers again. "James," she said. "I am in love with you too." And then she showed him how much she loved him.

Hours later, she lay in bed, cuddled in James' arms. She had yet to get out of the bed. James whispered that he had to leave for a while to tell the men about the change of plans. She smiled to herself, thinking about him. She dozed off, exhausted from grief, and worry, and James.

He slipped back into bed later in the afternoon, a wry grin on his face. He told her the men had agreed to the changed time, then he pressed a plastic cylinder into her palm.

She held up the small bottle of pills, raising her eyebrows at him.

"What are these?"

"You're not the only one with access to drugs in this city. These are some powerful sedatives. They'll dissolve in liquid. If you could drop one into Lachlan's drink, it would put him out of the picture for a few hours. And get him out of our way."

She gave an angry smile. "A taste of his own medicine? I like the sound of that. You make it sound easy."

"We both know it won't be." He caught her gaze and held it, and silence grew. The air was heavy between them.

She felt now that there was a countdown ticking over her head. The past few hours had been a blissful reprieve from her nightmare, but they did not change what was going to happen. Her mind started to work again, picking up speed, in contrast to her body, which felt satisfied and boneless, content to lie there for a lifetime. But the clock kept on ticking.

"James?"

"Hmm?" he said, eyes half-closed but trained on her face.

"If anything ... happens ... to me tonight ..." she started, and he rolled over to kiss her, silence her.

"Nothing will happen to you tonight."

"But it might," she whispered, trying to keep her face in control as she fought back a rush of tears. "If something happens, Kit needs to be kept safe." She blinked back the feeling of loss she felt as she spoke. "I made a promise, a long time ago, that I would keep her safe. That has to happen."

James ran a hand over her face, rolling his thumb over her cheek as he kissed her. "Kit will be safe. And so will you."

"I'll always be yours. No matter what happens." She reached up and brought him back down to her, relishing the feel of his mouth on hers, his body pressed to hers. "What time is it?" she whispered. The thought that sunset was drawing near sent a stab of panic through her.

"We still have a little time." His eyes were intense as he pushed her back down onto the bed.

An hour later she rolled out of James' arms and found her clothes, which were still scattered over the floor. She dressed quickly then sat on the edge of the bed looking at him. His lashes brushed down on his cheeks. He looked like a little boy in that moment. It broke her heart to think she might never see him again after tonight. "You should be with me," she whispered, wishing he would hear her. Reluctantly, she shook him awake.

He stirred, then his eyes flew open. He took in her appearance, dressed and ready to go, and frowned. "Trying to sneak out on me, are you?"

"Like I could sneak away from a thief like you. It's time for me to go."

He sat up, pulling the sheets around his still-naked body. "Evie, if there was a way you didn't have to do this ..."

"There isn't. And you have things to do to. Time's running out."

"I know. Time to get everyone in place."

He gave her a look she had never seen before, holding all the love and fear of the day. A lump formed in her throat. "James. Tell me we'll see each other again."

His beautiful grin was strained. "We'll see each other again." His words were as hollow as his smile.

"Okay then," she whispered, blinking back tears.

"Evie, if anything goes wrong ..."

"Yes?"

"Give 'em hell."

She smiled and straightened up. "Will do." She stood and left, trying very hard not to look back.

She walked upstairs to her old apartment, padding on her newly bandaged feet. They were sore and aching, but she could live with it. Carried tightly in her hand were the drugs James had given her. She emptied the bottle, putting the pills loose in her front pockets, hoping no one would find the tiny, powerful drugs. She twisted her short hair back away from her face with long pins.

Going to the front closet, she found her soft leather boots, the ones she had slipped a knife into weeks ago. She felt the lining, smiling grimly when she felt the hard edge of the handle still there, and slipped them on. It was all she needed. Nothing else in the apartment mattered; it would probably stay there forever and rot like everything else. It was time to move forward.

Chapter Twenty-Five

The sun was hanging motionless in the sky as if reluctant to leave the horizon. The daytime warmth had dissipated, leaving behind cool clear air. The smell of garbage seemed less prevalent. She folded her arms around herself, hugging tight as her feet took reluctant steps towards The Grand.

The walk took less time than she had imagined. All too soon she was standing in front of the doors. She looked up at the building for a while. When she had first seen it, all lit up and shining, it had seemed so breathtaking, a spotlight of glamour in an otherwise grim world. Now, it seemed gaudy and overdone. Fake, like everything else in it.

The front doors swung open and she straightened her shoulders. Her heart thudded in her chest as One stood in the doorway, grinning down at her. She overcame the urge to sneer at him, keeping her face carefully blank. *Show time now*, she thought. *Best to not piss off anyone until it really mattered.*

She walked into the hotel, nodding at the large black man. He didn't say a word, only gestured her in and closed the doors behind her. She followed, quickening her pace to keep up with him, as he walked up the grand staircase to the second floor then down a corridor.

The hotel was eerie in its quietness, no music, no voices floating around, no false trills of laughter. The silence pounded loud in her head, matching the beat of her heart.

The elevators came into view ahead and at the sight of them she slowed, hesitated for one second. *This is it.* The black man glanced back at her, noticing she was lagging behind, and said, "He's in his office. He wants you to join him there."

She nodded and swallowed hard. Staring at her brassy reflection in the elevator door, she wondered how this place had ever impressed her.

The doors slid open and she stepped in with her head held high, refusing to look contrite. She turned to see One smirking at her. "Enjoy your stay at The Grand," he taunted.

She paid him no attention, not trusting herself to make a scathing comeback. The doors slid shut on his smug face, bringing with it a fresh wave of panic. "The penthouse it is," she whispered and pressed the button. As she rose through the building, her anxiety level rose with her. She had only a few more seconds to herself, then she had to fake it harder than she ever had before. She closed her eyes, breathing slowly. *I'm not ready for this,* she thought.

The elevator glided to a stop and let out a quiet chime. As the doors slid open, she opened her eyes with them and made herself smile, just a little. Lachlan wouldn't buy beaming happiness right now, but if she acted nervous and just a little excited, it would play to his ego.

She stepped into the office, uncertain, looking for him. Lachlan was not sitting at his desk but standing at the far side of the room, looking out the window over his small kingdom, his broad back to her. He was wearing the navy blue pinstripe suit, classy and tailored as always. She waited for him, not saying a word.

He turned then, a warm welcoming smile on his face. His tie was off and the pale blue shirt loosened. He was holding a drink in his hand. Evie had eaten nothing that day, and the sight of the amber liquid made her stomach roll. Fighting queasiness, she looked him in the eye and gave him a timid smile.

"Come in," Lachlan said, sounding happy, content. She walked towards him, trying to keep her face friendly and open. *You are insane,* she thought. He looked relaxed, as if all was good in the world. No sign that he understood how sick his games were. Her eyes started to burn so she looked down, hiding them.

She would play the shy girl and hope that Lachlan took her reticence for nerves, not hatred.

Glasses clinked and she glanced up to see him pouring another drink for himself and one for her. She wondered if he tried to slip anything into her drink, as she would try to with his. At least she was expecting it. Lachlan came towards her, drinks in hand, and she struggled to keep control of her voice.

"Lachlan, I'm … here." She stopped, not really sure what else to say. There was a certain awkwardness in presenting yourself to your would-be captor and pimp. The etiquette was hazy at best. *The less said the better*, she decided, and stopped there.

"Evie." He smiled down on her. "I am so happy you are here. You have no idea …" He stopped himself, letting out a short breath. "Well, it's wonderful to see you anyway." His eyes were alight with warmth and affection, even love, as he said this.

She gave him a tentative smile. "Will you …" she started, not wanting to make him angry. "Will my sister be safe now?"

"Of course she'll be safe. As soon as I knew you've joined us here, I made sure of it." He crossed the distance between them and put his hand to her cheek.

She flinched away from his touch, a tiny gesture, an automatic response, but he noticed. He froze, eyes narrowing. "You should have this." His tone was icier than before. He pushed the glass into her hand and she took it on reflex.

He stood over her, waiting for her to drink. Left with no choice, she brought the glass to her mouth. The fumes were heady, making her head spin. *I definitely should have eaten something today,* she thought as she pressed her lips tight on the glass, allowing the liquid to splash harmlessly against them. *There is no way this isn't drugged.* Faking a cough, she pulled away sputtering.

"I'm sorry," she said, breathless. "It's just this is very strong."

Lachlan smiled again, warmth returning to his face. "It's some of the best. From now on, you'll get nothing but the best."

Evie smiled at him, taking another small close-mouthed sip, pretending it went down easier that time.

"Sit down, Evie, and drink up." Lachlan gestured to the chair behind her and she sank into it, relieved to not be standing face to face with him for the time being. He sat at the edge of the desk, looking down on her. She took another drink, causing him to beam. "I'm afraid you've caught me at a busy time."

You'll be a whole lot busier in a few minutes, she was thinking, but she gave him another sweet smile and said, "I did? I'm sorry ..."

"No, no, it's not your fault, it's just, this city. Sometimes the work it takes to make a city run is overwhelming." He turned away from her, pointing towards his desk, covered with papers, charts and blueprints. As he turned his back, she took advantage of her position to splash some of her drink onto the carpet, watching as the liquid was absorbed. Some came dangerously close to Lachlan's shoe and she let out a small gasp.

"Really?" she said, to cover this. "I have no idea how you run all of this. It seems very complicated to me." She made her voice small and breathy, like some of the girls she'd seen at The Grand. Her drink half-gone now, she pretended to be a little happy and a little dreamy. She let her eyelids droop and put a half smile on her face, letting her foot nudge closer to Lachlan's covering the wet patch on the carpet. She felt the squelch under her shoe. His smile had lost some of its warmth — he looked smug and calculating.

"No, I don't expect that you would understand what I have to put up with, the control it takes to make sure everything is orderly." He shook his head with false sadness.

Do you mean how many innocent people you have killed? She thought, looking into his smirk. *How many people you keep drugged, or manipulate into slavery?* Her eyes were burning into him and she dropped her gaze at once. She held onto the glass with both hands to keep from shaking.

"No, I have no idea." She aimed to keep her voice light, a little desperate. "You must have a lot of power to be able to govern a city like this."

He wandered around the desk as he spoke. "It's not just power, you know. To stay on top, to keep the respect of the people, you need to have something more. Intelligence, yes, and a work ethic. The ability to see into the future." He stopped his slow walking, looking out the window again at the oncoming darkness, basking in the glow of a spotlight that she couldn't see.

Her gaze was fixated on the desk, where he had left his glass right in front of her. It was just a matter of leaning forward to reach into it. Evie kept her eyes level at his turned back as she reached into her pocket with her left hand, stretching her fingers to catch three of the loose pills. If one could put him to sleep, maybe three would kill him. She brought them out and leaned towards the desk, heart vibrating. She put her glass down next to his, like it was a casual thing. He was not paying attention, continuing to talk as if to himself. She dropped the small white pills into his glass. The fizz sounded like fireworks to her; she was terrified he would hear.

" ... you need to be special," he continued, "it takes dedication to run a whole city, to be responsible for this many people. But I always knew, especially after surviving ..."

What was he talking about? She wasn't listening, couldn't concentrate over the beat of her heart, so loud Lachlan must hear it too. She picked up her glass, lifting it off the desk just as he turned around. She froze when he looked at her, then lifted the glass up as if toasting him. "You really are a special person," she said, allowing the dreamy expression to slide over her face again. "I've never met a man more intelligent than you. Or more powerful." *Was he actually buying this?* She could barely believe the smug look plastered over his face as he walked back to her, picking up his glass and clinking it against hers. He took a long swallow as she watched, her eyes over the rim of her glass as she pretended to sip. *Drink up, you bastard.*

Lachlan let out a satisfied breath. "You know, I was so right to bring you here, Evie. You're a sharp girl. You have been misguided in your friendships," he gave her a pointed look, "but you've certainly come around. I knew you would see reason."

Biting her lip, she controlled the satisfied look that wanted to creep onto her face as he took another healthy swallow of the drugged liquid. "You're right, I have been misguided," she said, standing up and twisting her fingers nervously in front of her. "After everything you've done for me, I've been so ungrateful. I mean, I just want to make things up to you." She looked up at him from under her eyelashes. "I'm so sorry, Lachlan," she whispered.

Saying his name acted like a spur to him. He reached out and grabbed her, pulling her in. His lips were on her, kissing her, hand behind her neck. There was nothing soft about the kiss, it was hard and rough and needy, and she had to force herself to open to him, allow him to kiss her as he wanted.

He released her and she stepped back with a shaky breath. His hand was still on her neck, a proprietary gesture, as he smiled at her. "Yes, soon, you can make it up to me." He took a long drink of his Scotch, finishing it. Evie felt a bubble of triumph in her chest. He leaned in again, but stopped in annoyance when the phone gave a shrill ring. Leaving Evie, he stomped to the desk.

"What?" he snapped. "The — what? Are you sure? But how did they ... fine then. Fine. I'll be down to take care of it."

He put down the phone with a sigh. He smiled at her, trying to regain that relaxed command he had before, but she could tell he was flustered. "I'm afraid we'll have to wait just a little while. There are a few pressing concerns that must be dealt with immediately."

"Pressing concerns?" she asked in her airhead voice. "I hope they're not very serious."

"It's nothing, nothing. I have a room ready for you, why don't you go there and wait for me. Here," he said, finally walking away so she could breathe again. As his back was turned, she fought the urge to rub at her lips. "Take another drink. Go, enjoy yourself and relax. I'll be down very soon." He poured a drink and pushed it into her hand. She gave him what she hoped passed for a sexy smile.

"Where do I go?"

"I'll have someone show you." Lachlan went to the room to the left of the office and spoke to someone in low tones. He returned with Three. Evie was shocked, unaware someone had been listening to them. Her stomach clenched in a moment of panic when she wondered whether he had been watching her, but he would have likely stopped Lachlan from drinking the drugged Scotch if he had.

"Please take Evie to her new suite," Lachlan was saying to him. "Then get back here at once." The white man gave her a smile that didn't reach his eerie translucent eyes. She followed him to the elevator, wishing she could thrust a needle into his neck.

He took her to the fourth floor and stopped in front of one of many generic doors. "This is your room now," Three told her in his high, sibilant voice. He looked her up and down, slowly, causing her to squirm under his crystal eyes. "You should put something else on, something pretty," he said finally. "You'll find everything you need in here."

She gave him a withering look and entered the room. He shut the door behind her and she heard him turn the key. She looked down in surprise to see that this room had a lock, only it was on the wrong side. *Thank you James, for your Introduction to Criminality courses*, she thought as she walked around the room, exploring her new prison.

The suite looked like the other one she and Kit had stayed in, except that a king-sized bed sat at the back of the room, partially hidden by a half wall. She shuddered and looked away. A walk-through closet led to the washroom on the other side. Putting her glass down, she walked slowly through the closet, flipping through the clothes that filled it. All women's clothes, some lovely, some glamorous, some like costumes. It was like a high-end Halloween store. There were wigs and scarves around one side. All the better to dress up in.

Walking to the mirror in the bathroom, she saw a girl in grubby clothes and scruffy hair. She didn't look like one of the girls here. There was an unopened toothbrush sitting on the side of the sink. She pried it from its case and brushed her teeth, trying to get the taste of Lachlan out of her mouth. She spat, watched the foam swirl down the drain. A trickle of panic started to seep in. She didn't like being locked up. She picked up the glass of Scotch and played with it, swirling it around and holding it up to the light, watching the amber liquid as it rose and fell. The walls pressed in on her but she forced the feeling back, dumping the contents of the glass into the sink. She wasn't helpless.

She turned back to the main room to examine the locked door. Lachlan wasn't taking any chances that she would be able to get out. A smug smile played on her lips as she took a pin from her hair.

Kneeling, she examined the lock, slipping the pin in. Before she had a chance to work it out, she heard a rustle from the other side of the door. Her head shot up. *So soon?* she thought. *Lachlan should be feeling the effects of the drugs by now, or is he too big to be brought down by them?*

As the lock slowly clicked, she sat back on her heels, pulling out the small knife from her boot. The weight in her hand gave her comfort. She'd kill Lachlan herself if she had to. She took a steadying breath, preparing to fight.

The door opened, and she stared in shock at the figure there. "You're not a part of the plan!" she gasped.

Chapter Twenty-Six

"Kit!" she hissed, trying to show how angry she was without making any noise. "What the hell are you doing here?"

Kit rushed into the room and shut the door carefully behind her. She turned to Evie with a triumphant smile. "I'm head of the rescue committee!"

Evie stared in disbelief at the outfit Kit was wearing. A tiny halter-top and equally tiny short shorts, all in a stretchy silvery fabric, that barely covered her at all. Enormous silver thigh-high boots finished the outfit. She wore a long red wig that fell straight down her back. She looked like some kind of sex-bot. The platforms on her boots were several inches high, enhancing the height difference between the two and forcing Evie to look up at her little sister, which did nothing to improve her mood.

"Kit," Evie said through her teeth as she reached over and grabbed Kit's arm. "For real. What are you doing here?"

"Ouch! Watch it." Kit pulled away from her, anger sharpening her features. "I couldn't let you be the only hero around here. James got a message to the pirates about what was going down tonight, and Oliver told me. I can't believe you were just going to make me hide in a cupboard, patiently waiting to see if Lachlan's men would come to get me, while you were out here dealing with this freak show. You think I wasn't worried about you, after watching you being dragged out of the bar, not knowing what was going to happen to you? And now, what if something goes wrong and you end up here for the rest of your life? Which you deserve, by the way. Why do you keep on thinking you can take on the world by yourself?"

"The whole point of this was to keep you safe," Evie said, voice shaking. She leaned down, tucking the knife back in her boot and trying to control her fury. "Now you just come waltzing into the lion's den, serving yourself up on a silver platter."

"You're mixing your figures of speech."

"Do not test me." Evie's voice was dangerous and low. "How did you get in here, anyway?"

"Waltzing in is pretty accurate. We came in through the back, the loading area."

"You just walked in?"

"Yup, just walked in the back. James and Oliver were dressed the way Lachlan's men dress, you know, in nice suits? And I pretended to be a scared little girl, like they were just bringing me in. We lucked out and didn't run into anyone. I went into one of the rooms and put on the first outfit I found."

"How did you know where I was?"

"That was easy. I just asked. Nobody realizes who I am. I walked right up to one of the men and asked where you were and he told me the room number. Actually," she said with a fake pout. "I'm not sure he even bothered to look at my face at all."

Evie smiled at this, starting to relax as she saw Kit wasn't hurt. "Who's we? How many?"

"Well, five of the pirates, including James and Oliver, of course. James is leading them down to the garages, where the arsenal is stored. Oliver followed me and is waiting in the stairwell. James will join us once the other men are in place."

"And Oliver was okay with you coming here?"

Kit's eyes were serious and Evie wondered what happened between the two of them. "Well, no. But I told him I was going, with or without him, and he would be able to keep an eye on me if it was with him. Besides, I know my way around the hotel a lot better than him."

"Hmm," Evie gave a grudging nod, agreeing this would have been the way she'd go about it.

"But we don't have a lot of time, so I'll explain as we get ready," she ended impatiently. "You can't make a daring escape around here without a costume. You'll be noticed more like that then dressed up like the rest of the girls." Kit led her by the hand to the closet. She delved into the closet, pulling out a minuscule scrap of silver fabric. "Here, we'll match. Like a theme."

Evie gave the dress a doubtful look but dutifully stripped. "Nobody stopped you from coming in?"

"Well, there just aren't very many men around The Grand tonight because — well, you know why. The action has started already."

"I know!" Evie exclaimed. "Lachlan got a call while I was in his office. He didn't say what was happening, of course, but he was really rattled. What did they do?"

Kit jumped a little in pleasure. "You should see it; they started setting fires at sunset, all at the same time, all over the city. All of the buildings are Lachlan's. And they are taking over the power plant."

Evie stared at her. "Oh, he's going to love that."

"You should see it. His men are scrambling everywhere. It's not like there's a fire department or anything."

There was a muffled *boom* from outside and all the lights flickered for a moment then returned to their regular glow. Evie thought her heart stopped for a moment, but then it came crashing even harder in her chest.

"Oh my god, Kit, are they using bombs?"

Kit was looking out the window, trying to see. "I guess so." She turned to her with a little well-how-about-that smile. "Okay, you look good! Let me do your makeup."

Evie sat down in front of her sister, anxiously looking towards the door. "Do we have time for this?"

"Don't grumble. We have to give James time to get to our old room. You need to be unrecognizable. I don't want anyone to figure out who we are. We'll be able to walk right out of here." Kit picked up a brush and starting dusting powder on Evie's face, a look of concentration creasing her forehead.

When she was done fussing, Kit turned Evie's face towards the mirror. Heavy black eyeliner shadowed her eyes and her lips were pale. Kit pulled a wig onto Evie's head, pulling it down tightly. Evie now had long, brunette hair with a heavy bang. She couldn't recognize herself.

Kit was gazing at Evie's reflection as well, in contemplation. Her fingers were tangled in the long fake hair. She held a strand of it up. "You know, Evie, I understand why you did it, but sometimes I miss your long hair."

Another boom sounded in the distance. Evie looked at her in the mirror. "Not the time to discuss it. We have to get out of here."

"Right." Kit flashed a grin. "Let's flee." She handed her sister a pair of high heels in glittery silver.

Evie glanced down at her bandaged feet and grimaced. "No more heels. This is an escape, Kit, not a gala. I'll stick with the leather boots and hope no one will notice."

"Fine, then, but you look ridiculous."

Evie forced herself not to roll her eyes. "Yes, it is the boots that make me look ridiculous. Are you ready?"

Before Kit could answer, the door burst open. Both girls froze as Lia stalked into the room, a look of malevolence making her face glow. Her long dirty hair hung in her face and she wore a black silk dress.

"Well, well, well," she said, her high little-girl voice dripping hate. "What do we have here?"

The shock of seeing her was wearing off. Evie rushed to the door and peeked out to the hallway. Lia was alone, for now. No sign of Oliver either, which was good; she didn't want Lia to know about him. She turned and closed the door silently behind her.

"Lia, listen, we don't have a lot of time," she said to her in a low urgent voice, trying to make her understand. We are leaving here tonight. We're getting away from the city, from this place. You can come with us. You could have your life back."

Lia's face was alight, but not from the words she was hearing. Evie didn't think she was even listening.

"Two sisters for the price of one," she chortled, gloating. "Lachlan's going to have a field day with you. And I was the one to stop you. I'll be rewarded, maybe he won't even ..." she trailed off.

"Won't what? Won't literally sell you down the river now that you've become inconvenient?"

Lia glared at them with absolute hatred. Evie continued, "You could have a better life than this. You don't have to do anything you don't want to. We'll take you away from this. Lachlan will never hurt you again."

This galvanized Lia. Her eyes flared. "Lachlan is a great man, what do you know of it?" she spat.

Evie was taken aback. "Sure, okay, but ..."

"Do you know where I was before Lachlan?" Lia advanced on Evie slowly, hissing in her venomous voice. "Dirty, starving and alone, living on the streets, family dead, scavenging what I could find and barely making it. It was Lachlan who found me, fed me, took care of me. I was nothing without him. And now look at me." She smoothed her dress down her thighs. "I'm his and he is mine. We love each other."

"Lia, he's getting rid of you. How much can he love you if he's willing to do that?"

Uncertainly flickered across her face, making her seem more like a child. "I ... was behaving badly. I was wrong. He was right to punish me. But now, he'll see, I'm the one he can count on, the only one that's really loyal. Now that certain *distractions* are out of the way." She became so angry she choked on the words.

"Lia, no." Evie realized she was losing her. That she had never had her in the first place.

"Shut up!" Lia shouted, her shrill voice reverberating around the room. "You think you can just show up here, take what's mine? I'll make you pay for that, you slut." Lia slapped Evie hard across the face, small nails digging into her cheek. The pain was unexpected and Evie reeled back. Kit stepped forward as if to grab Lia, but the girl dodged aside, shouldering Kit out of her way as she grabbed the door and yanked it open.

"She's getting away! Help! Somebody help me! She's getting away!" Lia screamed at the top of her lungs. Her words echoed down the empty hallway. Evie looked at Kit, frantic, knowing that anyone close by would hear. Evie lunged for Lia, grabbing her by her long hair. She pulled back sharply, causing her head to snap back and cut off her alarm cries.

Lia jerked around and threw herself at Evie, but she was ready this time, side-stepping her as she tripped her, forcing her down. Lia's feet got wrapped up in the long sweeping skirt of her gown. As she struggled to get up, they heard footsteps running down the hallway at full-tilt towards the room. Evie reached for the knife in her boot, ready to fight.

The door swung open and Millie stormed into the room. She looked like a gladiator dominatrix in black leather and boots strapped all the way up her legs. Her curly hair was loose and wild around her face. She glowered into the room, fury in her eyes, looking every inch an Amazon.

"Where is that bitch?" she growled.

Kit was looking at her wide-eyed. "Good timing," she said.

Evie stared at the tall women, unsure why she was here. Millie stalked into the room, looking like a panther about to strike. She went straight to Lia, who had righted herself and was glaring at her.

"What do you think you can do to me?" Lia spat.

Millie slugged her in the face, just above the jaw. Lia made no sound, but dropped like a stone, lying motionless on the ground. Millie turned to the sisters, cradling her fist to her chest.

"That felt good," she said with a smile. "Really good. How are you doing, Evie?"

Evie let out the breath she'd been holding with a whoosh. "Millie ... what? Are you ... what are you doing here?"

"I saw Kit come in and ask about you. Nice job, by the way," she said with a nod to Kit, "Very daring. Nobody expects that around here. It's funny the men never really notice us girls. Well, not, you know, as people. We see a lot, though. Lia saw you come in and followed you with a smirk on her face. So I followed and saw the little bitch listening at the door. I owed her that," she tilted her head to Lia's body on the floor, bringing her fingers up to her own cheek. Her face was still swollen from her beating.

Millie whirled around to the sisters. "All right. The important thing is to get you out of here, tonight. Lachlan's planning to kill you after he gets what he wants from you, and it's likely someone heard Lia. I'll tell you how to get out of here."

"Better yet, you'll show us." Evie grabbed Millie's wrist. "We are leaving the city, for good tonight. You're coming with us."

Millie stared down at her, a slow smile spreading across her face. "Sounds like a great idea."

"But first, we have some unfinished business." Evie turned to Kit. "Where is Oliver now?"

"He should be in the stairwell at the end of the hallway, keeping watch. He didn't come with Lia's shouting, so I'm hoping no one else heard. We'll meet him in the stairs. James knows where we're going."

Millie opened the door, peering out to make sure it was clear, then stepped into the hallway. Kit was next and Evie brought up the rear. She closed the door and locked it from the outside, getting one last look at Lia's body lying on the floor. She couldn't help hoping that Lachlan would be merciful if he found her in the locked room. Lia may have been a vile little girl, but that was the point. She was only a child and had been perverted by everything she'd been through. Evie didn't blame her; she didn't know any better.

"Where are we going?" Millie whispered.

"Upstairs, to our old room," Evie said, grim and determined. "Lachlan has something of mine, and I want it back."

Chapter Twenty-Seven

Evie, Kit, and Millie crept down the seventh floor hallway, listening for any voices or shouts of recognition. All was quiet. They slipped into Suite 713. Oliver kept watch in the rear stairwell, waiting for James to join him.

The place looked as though a bomb had gone off in it. Furniture had been ripped apart, stuffing scattered over everything. All of the girls' belongings littered the floor, torn and shredded. "They took all the medical supplies," Kit said, pointing to where they had left them.

"It's okay," Evie whispered. "Everything is okay as long as they haven't found the stash of drugs." She approached the fireplace, heart in her throat. It looked as though it had been gouged with crowbars; wood chips from the carving were all over the hearth. But the secret door was not open, so surely Lachlan's men had not found it. *Maybe they just didn't hit the sweet spot.* With gentle fingertips she pressed at the woodwork, finally feeling the panelling ease under her hands. When the door swung open, Evie sighed with relief. The piles of pills were exactly as she left them. "Everything is here!" she shouted. "Kit, are our duffel bags still here? Can you grab them?"

"That won't be necessary." Out of the closet stepped Ryson, followed by two large men Evie didn't recognize. They each held guns, pointed at the girls.

"Run!" Millie yelled, but it was too late. Evie, kneeling at the fireplace, wasn't quick enough to get up. Her feet protested the movement and the deep cuts reopened. One of the men came and scooped her off her feet. Her wig had fallen over her eyes, obscuring her vision, but she could tell Kit and Millie were still in the room.

Kit launched herself at Evie's captor, grabbing him from behind, fingers clutching at hair, nose, eye sockets, whatever they could reach. He cried out and his grip on Evie loosened. She fell to the floor, landing on hands and knees. She struggled to turn over but was wrestled down on her stomach, arms wrenched behind her back at an impossible angle. She screamed as heavy metal encircled her wrists. Handcuffs. Pushed face down again, the wig over her face blinded her. She wiggled her body around until she could right herself without the use of her hands. This was so awkward it seemed to take forever, but she eventually made it to her knees and shook the hair out of her eyes.

Kit and Millie were receiving similar treatment. Millie was pressed against the wall as one of the men handcuffed her hands behind her, and Kit was sitting on the broken couch, twisting her arms in a futile attempt to free herself.

The man standing over Evie grabbed her by the arm, forcing her up onto the couch next to Kit. Millie was thrown to Kit's other side and all three of them glared up at the men. Evie found herself sneering into Ryson's weasel face. He looked down on her, fury burning in his eyes.

"You've gotten quite the promotion, haven't you, Ryson?" Evie spat at him.

"All thanks to you and your little friends," he responded with a humourless smile. "I knew that if I waited long enough you would come back to find the drugs. I'm smarter than you think I am, princess. Now I have everything."

"You have nothing," Evie said, holding her head up high. "You're nothing but one of Lachlan's lackeys and always will be. You think he'll give you the keys to the city because of this?"

"Maybe not, but I'm hoping he gives me your sister."

Evie's mouth twisted in disgust, but she refused to speak to him again. Next to her, Kit stared straight ahead.

Ryson continued, "Or maybe he'll give me this traitor here. I've always wanted to have a go, but she was kept for the higher-ups. No more, I bet."

"I'd like to see you try me," Millie growled, eyes darkened with rage. "You'd be dead before you knew it. If you were lucky."

Ryson grabbed her face, and she jerked her chin out of his grasp. "I really wish we didn't have orders not to hurt you girls," he said with a malicious smile. He wiped the sweat off his brow. "That's not going to last very long. Lachlan is on his way now."

The other men grinned at them but didn't get any closer. They seemed tense as well. "Pack up those drugs," Ryson snapped at one of them, who started piling the pills into a black sack he carried with him. His gun was set to the side and Evie eyed it, gauging the distance to it but realizing that it would be useless to her while she was handcuffed.

A fraught silence fell over the room as they waited for Lachlan to arrive. Millie sat still as a statue, but her eyes were wide. Her body was so taut with tension Evie was afraid she was going to break. Her fear was palpable. Kit meanwhile was struggling against the handcuffs, with no thought to the men standing over them. Evie sat still, trying to breathe through her panic, to relax. Until they could get away, there was no need to expend any energy. They would wait, Lachlan would come, and she'd figure something out then.

Footsteps sounded down the hallway, furious and loud. Evie felt a sweat break out down her back. So much for being relaxed.

Lachlan stormed into the room. Evie had never seen him look like that. Normally he was calm and collected, in control of himself and everyone else in the room. Even under the effect of drugs or very annoyed, he was still always the master of himself.

The control had slipped away, as if the real animal was showing itself from behind the polished veneer. His face was red; the colour travelling all the way up to his closely cropped head. Veins stood out along his neck and forehead, bulging to the point that they looked as though they might burst. He was sweating and breathing hard, as if he'd been running. His clothes for once were dishevelled and his eyes were glaring in fury.

He stalked towards the girls then paced to and fro in front of them. Ryson's two sidekicks retreated to the open door, standing on either side of it. Their faces were neutral and their gaze unfocused, but Ryson's eyes were on Evie, watching her with interest.

In a sudden move, Lachlan grabbed the coffee table between them and threw it out of the way. It flew halfway across the room. Evie flinched and Kit cried out in surprise. Millie managed to maintain a cool look on her face, although her body was wound so tight it could have been that she simply couldn't move. Or maybe she was used to Lachlan's displays of temper.

Without the minimal protection that the table offered, Evie felt as vulnerable as she ever had. Lachlan approached her first.

"You." He pointed a finger into her face, shaking with fury. "I don't know how you did it, but somehow, I know this all goes back to you."

She gazed up at him with wide blank eyes. "What goes back to me?"

He gave a cry of frustration and slapped her across the face. She fell into Kit, not being able to balance herself with her arms. The blow stung more than it really hurt. Evie was surprised at how little force he had put behind it. She sat up with Kit's support and watched him through wary eyes.

Lachlan laughed a little and staggered. "You slut," he said, pointing vaguely over her shoulder. "Don't lie to me."

Evie felt a surge of hope. Were the drugs finally kicking in? She controlled the urge to smirk. They were still handcuffed, and he was still a very dangerous man, no matter what tranquilizers were coursing through his blood stream.

Lachlan was still rambling. "You set fire to my city, my plant, you little bitch. Everything is falling apart, and it's all because of you." He wandered over to the window, where the flickering of flames was reflected. A building nearby must be on fire. Evie had a sudden thought and prayed that The Grand itself was not burning; too many people would get hurt.

Lachlan was staring out the window, face ghoulish in the dancing light. "Don't know how you did it," he muttered and pushed away, staggering towards the women again. He stopped in front of Millie, grabbing her hair and forcing her head back to look at him. "Millie." His voice was soft. "Wasn't I good to you? How could you do this to me? What did I do to deserve your betrayal?"

275

She remained silent but met his eyes in an unblinking stare. He hit her across the face, a hard backhand. Evie gasped at the suddenness of it. Somehow Millie remained seated and whipped her head up to meet his eyes again. This time her look was undiluted hatred. Lachlan hit her again, on the same place on the cheek, this time with his fist. Millie fell over and righted herself slowly, painfully. She sat with her body erect, proud, but kept her eyes down.

Lachlan moved over to Kit and looked down on her with an expression of contempt. "And Kit," he sneered. "The pretty little sister, always keeping to herself. You don't like bodies, do you? Shame you'll soon become one. I could throw you on that pile of corpses you were so concerned about and set you on fire — while you are still alive." He grabbed her hair and yanked her head back as he had with Millie, inspecting her. "So very pretty though. And young. Do you know how much I'll make off you if I sell you?" His face was inches away from hers, as if he would kiss her, but instead he spat in her face. He stepped away and Kit sat up, spittle running down her cheek. She was shaking, but Evie was certain with anger, not terror.

"Never has any little girl given me as much trouble as you." Lachlan was back to his ranting now. Evie assumed he was speaking to her, although he was looking wildly around him, as if dizzy and trying to orient himself.

Kit's bare foot rested on Evie's and she nudged her, trying to tell her something. Evie had been focused on Lachlan and his ranting but now looked around and immediately saw what had excited Kit. The two men guarding the door were gone, and so was the bag of drugs, leaving Ryson and Lachlan alone in the room with them. Neither man had noticed yet, they were too focused on the three of them. It would have to stay that way.

"What are you going to do?" Evie blurted out.

"What?" Lachlan snapped, as if surprised she was able to speak. His eyes went to her then slid out of focus. He shook his head, frowning.

"I — what are you going to do with us? I mean, we tried to escape. And we killed Lia." A lie, but Evie wanted him mad and out of control. It would be worse for them if he came to his senses.

"Lia is dead?" A frown wrinkled his face.

Evie nodded. "Her body's downstairs."

If she had been expecting him to fly into a fury about this, Evie was mistaken. Lachlan sneered and gave a short bitter laugh. "That, I should thank you for. Saved me the trouble. Another slut who was more trouble than she was worth."

He looked up at Evie and gave her a sadistic smile. The tranquillizers were really affecting him now. Insanity lit his eyes. She stared back at him, trying to keep his attention, forcing herself not to let her eyes flick to the doorway as they desperately wanted to. There was movement in her periphery — were the guards back? Ryson noticed, and he walked towards the door to investigate. Evie willed Lachlan to continue focusing on her instead of turning to look at the door.

"Now I will have to deal with you. I am going to enjoy this." He leaned towards her. He was so close Evie could not see the manic look on his face. He pulled a syringe full of a clear liquid from his pocket. His mouth brushed her ear as he whispered, "You're not going to enjoy it at all, my dear. I'll make sure of that." He bent down and kissed her, hard. Unable to move, she tried to clamp her mouth shut, but his hands were strong at her jaw, forcing her mouth open, forcing his tongue inside. He pulled away from her slightly and she heard the whisper of the cap sliding off the syringe. He brushed the fake hair away from her neck, leaving it exposed. His eyes were inches away from hers, dilated so she could see only black.

"Goodnight, Evie," he whispered. "Dream of all the things I'll do to you while you're asleep."

She let out a moan of disgust and did the first thing that came to mind — she butted her head against his. The pain was sudden and sharp; she reeled back, wincing. The blow surprised Lachlan long enough to keep the needle out of her neck.

Kit lashed out nearly at the same time, kicking Lachlan. Her foot made solid contact with the side of his knee, causing the leg to give way under him. He fell to his knees with a grunt. He cursed at her, but the angle he was kneeling at put him directly in front of Evie. She took advantage of her position, bracing herself against the couch as she kicked him in the face. There was a crunch as Lachlan's head snapped back and his body followed. He fell onto his back, blood spurting form his nose and flowing over his face.

"Bitch!" he screamed through the blood, but that was all he got out before a man in a suit was on him, kneeling on his throat. Evie looked up, for the first time allowing herself to believe that they might just get out of this. James was looking up at her.

"Where's the syringe?" he yelled. He was holding Lachlan, as the man flailed under him, grabbing at him and trying to pull him off.

Evie scanned the ground for it. "Next to his leg." The syringe had fallen from Lachlan's hands when she had kicked him. Now it lay close to the couch. She tried to push it forwards, manoeuvring it towards James while avoiding Lachlan's thrashing limbs.

James saw it and lunged to grab it, releasing Lachlan for a second. The bigger man came up swinging, hitting James in the back of the head. James went down, falling forward from the force of the blow, nearly landing on top of the syringe. James grabbed it and twisted back to Lachlan in a lightning movement, seizing him by the throat and thrusting the syringe into his neck, emptying the entire thing with the push of his thumb.

Lachlan's eyes rolled back in his head, so immediate it would have been comical if it weren't so frightening. He fell backwards hard and lay spread-eagled, limbs twitching. James just sat looking at him, as if unable to figure out what had just happened.

"James," Evie said, breaking into his trance. He looked up at her then stumbled towards them, leaving Lachlan behind him, forgotten. James grabbed Evie, half picking her up as he held her against him, close enough to be painful but not nearly close enough.

Evie was sobbing, not realizing she had started. She didn't notice she was falling apart until her face was pressed into James' shoulder as he told her everything was going to be all right.

"I was so scared," she was saying. "You could have been killed."

"You were scared for me?" James pulled back, looking into her eyes and brushing dark brown hair out of her face. "I was supposed to be the rescue committee. You're the one who thought she could take on this whole enterprise on her own."

She smiled through her tears. "Maybe I needed just a little bit of help."

He raised his eyebrows. "Just a little bit of help? I'm surprised to see you admit even that. But help you certainly did get. The traders are pulling this whole city down around us." He shook the smile off his face, took on a serious look. "So we don't have much time. We're leaving now."

"Okay," Evie said. "But please no more handcuffs?"

"Already on it," Oliver called from the door. Ryson's body was stretched out on the floor, halfway in the doorway, and Oliver was searching through his pockets for the keys. He had already relieved him of his gun. In his suit Oliver looked less gangly and much more manly. Kit's eyes were warm on his. "The other guards are unconscious and tied up in another room, where hopefully they won't be found until we are out of here." He unlocked Millie's handcuffs first then moved on to Kit. He handed the keys to James as he leaned down to kiss Kit.

Evie turned to help James free her. As soon as the handcuffs fell off of her wrists, he pulled her in for a rough hug and she threw her arms around him. She was looking over James' shoulder directly at Oliver. Suddenly she stiffened and asked, "The bag of drugs. Do you have it?"

Oliver held up the sack with a triumphant grin. "Thank god," she whispered, and sagged back against James with relief.

Millie was up and pacing the room, rubbing her wrists. "Is Lachlan dead?" She sounded hesitant.

Evie watched as James turned his face away, not meeting anyone's eyes. Going to the body, she reached down and pressed her fingers to Lachlan's neck. There was no pulse.

"I think so," she said quietly. "There's no heartbeat."

Everyone stilled.

Millie's voice broke the silence. "Good." Her voice was cold as crystal. It seemed to sum things up nicely.

James met Evie's eyes, looking defiant and vulnerable at the same time. His feelings were plain to her. *He had vowed he would never kill anyone again.* "It was the right thing to do," she assured him. "James, I had already given him enough sedatives to kill him. He might not have survived the night anyway." He looked away, giving a strained nod.

The lights in the room flickered and went out, leaving them in the dark. "They must have really taken the plant," Oliver said, walking to the window to look out. The planes of his face were lit up from the glow outside. "There's no electricity anywhere."

A sense of urgency overtook the group. "We have to get out of here," James said as he pulled Evie out of the room.

"Wait," Evie called. "What about all the other women?" She turned to Millie. "Is there a way to get them away from the men, so we can talk to them?"

James gave her an exasperated look while Kit watched her with a blank face, the barest of smiles playing at her mouth.

Millie gave Evie an intent look. "You want to bring all of us?" she asked.

"I'm certainly not leaving you behind."

Millie shrugged, as if she was a curiosity. She thought about it. "Right now most of the men are gone, trying to put out fires. I expect some of them are actually helping to start new ones," she said with a smile. "Most of the girls have the night off so will be in their rooms. On the third floor."

"Show me. We need to get them together."

Chapter Twenty-Eight

Knowing the elevators were no longer working, they rushed down the hallway to the back stairwell. It was pitch black so they had to feel their way down the concrete steps, gripping tightly to the railing.

"I think this is it," Millie whispered when they had gone down four flights. She found the door, opened it a crack, and peeked out. Faint light shone from the emergency exit sign. "Yes, this is our floor."

They ran down the hallway, stumbling against one another in the dark, banging on the doors and yelling for everyone to get up and out of their rooms. Heads poked out of every door, faces clouded by confusion. Picking up on the urgency of the cries, everyone followed, stopping just long enough to slip on some shoes and throw on robes or sweaters over their pajamas. A few clutched flashlights.

Evie stopped at the end of the hallway, a small sitting area where a cluster of benches sat around a window. The women gasped as they looked out at the burning city and then began screaming, drawing together in fear.

"Why the hell are we standing around here?"

"Why aren't we getting out?"

"Where the fuck are the guys?"

"Oh my god, we're gonna burn alive!"

Evie jumped up onto a bench in front of the crowd so everyone could see her. The flickering firelight outside lit up the outline of her face in an eerie glow. Millie and Kit came and stood by her side.

"Everybody, please," she cried, but the girls continued to cry out, ignoring her. "People!" Evie screamed, putting all the power of her lungs behind it. The din finally died down as the crowd realized she was speaking to them. "Listen to me," she continued when she could be heard. "Don't panic! The hotel is not burning, but you need to listen to me!"

"What's going on?" a girl in a robe and slippers shouted. "What happened to the lights?"

"Lachlan is dead!" Evie shouted over the questions tumbling at her. The silence was so sudden that she reeled in it. "His men are gone — they are trying to put out the fires — and the lights are out because the power plant has been taken over."

"Who has taken over? One woman yelled. "Will they give us power again?"

"I don't have time to explain everything. I'm here to tell you that you can leave New City, tonight. You can leave and you can be free."

"What do you mean?"

"I mean, you can leave the city if you want to. You don't have to stay at the hotel, working for these men. There is a barge leaving the city tonight — within the hour — heading out west. You can come if you want to, choose to live however you want."

"No one will sell you to the highest bidder," Millie yelled, seeing the cynical looks directed at Evie. "No one will tell you who to screw and beat you if you refuse. No one will pump you full of drugs so you don't even remember who you are."

There was a deafening silence. Evie was baffled; she had expected a rousing cheer.

"Maybe we don't want to leave with you," said a tall girl at the middle of the crowd. "Maybe it's better here, where we know we'll be taken care of. Maybe it's better to have food and running water and heat in the winter, than anything you're offering."

"Don't you understand?" Evie cried in frustration, "You might not have those things forever, even if you stay here." When no one responded, Evie sighed and continued, "I'm not trying to force anyone. This is your choice. Yes, leave New City and life might be hard. But it will be your own life."

The girls stood watching her, shifting, whispering to each other and watching Evie with uncertain eyes. James moved towards Evie, while the girls he passed pulled away. She bent down to hear what he was saying.

"Evie, don't be crazy. Bill won't have room to take all of them," he said, so only she could hear him.

Her eyes flicked up, looking at the resentful faces around her. "I don't think we're going to have to worry about all of them. But Bill has some room on his barge, at least to take us west to the next surviving township, the next settlement. These women have a right to leave the city on their own terms, if they want to."

He gave her a quick kiss on the cheek. "Always the warrior, aren't you. You won't rest till you save the world. All right then, gather your recruits but be damn quick. Things are ... well, all sorts of things are happening outside. I'll go down to the garages, give the signal to head out. We'll meet outside, at the rear doors, as soon as you can get there. I'll leave Oliver here with you to help get everyone out."

The young man moved closer to Kit and gave a solemn nod to indicate he understood.

With a quick grin and his usual grace, James manoeuvred through the crowd. Evie turned her attention back to the girls.

"Millie, is it true that Lachlan's dead?" someone called.

"It is true, I saw it with my own eyes."

"What are you going to do?"

"I will never be a man's slave again. I'm leaving tonight, to start a new life." Standing tall and proud, Millie looked more like an Amazon than ever. The atmosphere brightened and there were some cries of assent.

"Evie, for heaven' sake, we haven't got all day. We need to get going," Kit said, looking around anxiously. Evie glanced outside, following her sister's gaze, seeing the firelight was glowing stronger.

"Who is coming?" she yelled. "We leave *now*. I'm sorry to throw this at you, but the barge won't wait for us so you need to make the choice now." She jumped off the bench as four girls stepped forward. She looked at the others searchingly, but they hung back, looking wary.

Then a young brunette wearing flannel pajamas and sneakers pushed her way through the crowd. "I'll come with you. I hate it here." She turned to the other girls. "You all despise it too, don't try to deny it."

Evie flashed the girl a smile as several other women followed her.

"Okay, anyone else? This is your last chance!" she shouted, hoping for a few more recruits.

Some of the girls hanging back started yelling in protest. "Wait! What are we supposed to do?"

"You should get to ground level, just in case. Stay in the lobby as long as you feel safe there."

One girl let out a ragged gasp of fear, collapsing against the wall. Another sat on the bench, shaking and crying.

Evie turned to her small group and hustled them in front of her. Doing a quick head count, she saw nine girls, including Kit and Millie. "Get to the back staircase. We're heading out towards the loading dock!"

In the eerie glow of the firelight outside, the group ran down the hallway, some stumbling in their slippers. Evie jogged next to Oliver, who held the bag of drugs slung over his shoulder.

"Okay, everyone follow Oliver. Plan is, we're leaving out back by the loading docks. We have people there waiting for us with a truck. They will take us to the docks. As I said, we're taking a barge out of here tonight — if we make it in time."

They took off down the stairs, and Evie and Kit brought up the rear. As they turned to go down the last flight of stairs, Kit reached out and grabbed Evie's hand, squeezing. Evie felt emotion swell up in her throat and had to swallow it back. She didn't have time for feelings right now.

When they finally stumbled out of the hotel, some of the girls wrinkled their nose at the smell of garbage around them. Evie wondered how long it had been since they had been outside at all.

Waiting for them was a giant, mud-spattered vehicle. Evie had never been so happy to see her old truck. One end of the bed was piled high with guns and boxes of ammunition. *James is going to need to keep those away from anyone he doesn't trust if he wants to bring justice back to this city*, she thought grimly. Two traders sat in the front seat and James stood next to it.

"Quick, everyone!" he called. "Get into the bed of the truck. Pile in, fast as you can. I've just heard from another one of my men that some of Lachlan's crew, led by One, are heading back to the hotel — and they are armed."

Oliver was already placing the bag of drugs into the bed and holding out his hand to the first girl.

"No!" a high voice called from behind her. Shots rang out over Evie's shoulder. She spun around and ducked, an involuntary reaction to the noise, and several of the girls cried out.

She turned to see Three standing at the entrance, an assault rifle pointed towards them. "Stay awhile. Anyone who tries to leave now will be severely punished. If you come back now, though, you won't be hurt."

The girls pressed into one another, cowed. Only Millie was walking forward, back straight, eyes on the ghost-like man.

"Don't believe him," Evie called, coming to stand in front of the girls. "Nobody is safe with him."

"If you don't come now, you will be found and brought back alive. You've never imagined pain like what I'm prepared to inflict if you don't come back. Right. Now," he said, forcing each word through gritted teeth. "Come back, girls. You don't want to get lost out there in the world."

"No!" Evie screamed. "Get into the truck!" The girls started surging forward, eager to climb in and get away from Three.

"You think you can just drive away from all this, Evie?" Three said. His voice had a singsong quality. He sounded insane. "Some people can, maybe." He took aim and shot. Evie's eyes slammed shut, but she wasn't hit. The girl who was trying to climb onto the truck bed fell to the ground like a stone, eyes staring. Screams and sobs erupted from the terrified women as they scattered. James and Oliver herded them behind the truck to take cover, all the while yelling at Evie to get out of the range of fire.

"Oops, I missed," Three said, staring Evie down. "And I liked that one. She knew when to keep quiet. I never could remember her name though. Pity about that."

Evie felt a blaze of fury fire through her. She reached into the truck for the first two rifles she could get her hands on, praying they were loaded. She felt Millie by her side and nodded as the tall woman took one of the rifles from her.

"Go," Evie yelled to the drivers, and the truck started to pull forward, slow enough that the women could continue crouching behind it, using it as protection from the gunman. Evie slid the safety off the rifle and kept it trained on Three's head.

He stared at her with bulging crystal eyes. "At least I can take you out," he said as he brought his gun up and fired. Evie heard a cry beside her but didn't flinch as she pulled the trigger. She found her mark the first time and Three fell back against the wall, part of his head missing. "That's for Marjorie," she whispered, unable to look away from the terrible damage she had inflicted. Her momentary daze was shattered as she felt Millie falter. James was right next to her, then, catching the tall woman as she crumpled.

"Is she hit?" Evie screamed. "Where? Where is it?"

"Here," James said, keeping his voice calm. "She was hit in the arm. Millie, can you talk to me?"

She nodded and coughed. "Yes," she said, her voice weak. "I'm okay, I think I just need to sit down."

"Here." James lifted her up so she was sitting on the bed of the truck. "Hold on. We need to boot it to get to the boat," he yelled at the remaining women. Fuelled with fear, they jumped into the back of the truck unaided, trying not to crush Mille. "Evie, get in now and stay next to Millie."

Evie scrambled up beside Millie on James' command, putting her arm around her ally with care and holding her tight. "You are going to be okay," she whispered as the truck started to speed, causing them to sway against each other. Millie took in a sharp breath of pain, but nodded.

Only burning buildings lit their way. The flickering glow made it seem as though nothing was real, although Evie's pain was real enough when hot ash floated down, burning a hole in her thin dress through to the skin underneath. She bit back a cry.

Several times, men trying to put out fires spotted them and shouted at the truck, but the driver didn't stop. One man started to chase them, but Evie fired two warning shots above his head. He dove for cover and didn't come out.

286

At last they were driving over the dark hills of the market, away from the burning city. They slowed as they arrived at the docks. Nothing was burning here, and the fresh breeze coming off the river was a relief. The *Mary Rose* was at the pier, crates all packed up and ready to leave.

Everyone piled out of the truck as soon as they stopped. Many of the girls were still crying; others looked around at the boats bewildered. Evie still held her rifle in clenched fists and noticed that Millie hadn't let go of hers either.

Bill and Petra stood at the base of the gangplank, along with Anne. The group stopped in front of them, afraid and uncertain. Even Kit, Evie, and James were nervous about what sort of reception they would get. No one spoke and Evie felt her stomach churn as she realized Bill might turn them away. Then one of the women recognized Anne and ran to her. The women embraced, and the tension was broken.

Bill raised his eyebrows at Evie and Kit's improbable costumes, then nodded his head towards the crowd of women who looked as though they were going to a pyjama party.

"Deal was I'd be taking two extra bodies, you and your sister," he said. "Now, I can count. This is nine goddamned bodies."

Panic washed over Evie. "Bill, you have to take all of us," she said, hating the pleading in her voice. "We don't have time for this. Lachlan's men will soon figure out where we are and they will —"

"What do you mean?" Bill raged. "Does Lachlan know they're gone?"

Evie lifted her chin and met his eyes. "Lachlan is dead, so he isn't thinking anything, but some of his men are looking for whoever started the fires, and they are bound to go back to The Grand, and when they find out what happened, they will come to the docks and —" Her voice trailed away as she became aware that all the men on the *Mary Rose* were leaning over the rail of the barge, listening to every word. She looked Bill in the eye and lowered her voice. "You don't have to take us very far, just get us out of the city to someplace safe." She stole a look at the crew. It was plain they did not share their captain's reluctance to shelter the women. "I don't think your men would mind," she whispered.

Bill looked at the men and nodded. "No, I can't deny you that. Actually," he said with a frown, "they'll probably begrudge me if I don't allow it." He nodded, decided.

He stepped forward and bellowed, "I'm Bill, captain of the *Mary Rose*. You are all welcome to come aboard, we are leaving just as soon as we get some of those guns on board."

A cheer went up from the boat, but the women were now looking more uncertain than ever. They muttered and shifted amongst themselves, uneasy. Anne was trying to draw a few girls forward. Kit had helped Millie out of the truck and they moved to the front of the group. Millie looked at Evie with a question in her eyes.

Evie got the message and turned back to Bill. "We are helping these women out of a bad situation. Nobody is to be touched without her consent. They're not here for that, Bill."

The crusty old captain smiled at Evie for the first time. "You have my word. I'm not Lachlan." He walked over to the women. "Know this," he shouted. "You are all under our protection, whether it's on this boat or out in the world. I can offer you food, clothing, and shelter, but no one will expect *that* sort of payment, and no one will hurt you here. You are safe, and free, from now on."

Millie stared him down for a few tense moments, before giving a short nod. "Thank you," she replied so that everyone could hear her, her voice husky. "It means a great deal to us."

Bill nodded and gestured to the gangplank. "Welcome aboard."

Millie stepped on first, assisted now by Anne. The other women, some smiling now, surged forward and were helped aboard by eager hands. Oliver helped Kit up the gangplank, passing the bag of drugs to her as he went.

Soon, all the women except Evie were on board. Now that her mission had been accomplished, she realized she had not seen or heard James since she began her negotiations with Bill. Searching for him in the crowd, she spotted him still standing next to the truck, keeping a close watch on the contents in the back.

One of the pirates approached him. James leaned down to talk to him, then, at a glance from Bill, he nodded. The pirate began to pick out some of the guns and ammunition. James helped him and also unloaded two large canisters of gas. After a quick handshake with the pirate, James spoke to the man behind the wheel, who nodded and pulled away from the Docks, towards the Trades District.

He's bringing the arms to the men over there, who really need it, Evie thought. She smiled and gave James a small wave when he looked for her. He came towards her with a smile and put his arm around her, allowing her to sag into him.

"You did good tonight," he said.

"You weren't so bad yourself," she said, walking towards him and gasping at the sudden pain in her feet. Now that the adrenaline was draining away, she could feel every cut and bruise.

"Get on board, Evie. We don't know how soon ..."

"I know, I know," she whispered as he slipped his arm around her, supporting her weight. He got her on board and found her a crate to sit on. Only then did she realize she was still clutching the rifle. She uncurled her stiff fingers from the barrel and put it down.

"James," she began, but could not go on. She looked up at him, eyes brimming with tears. She knew that her next word had to be goodbye, but couldn't bear to say it.

"Evie, I can't go with you." His voice was raspy. She nodded, unable to speak. The motion spilled her tears over the brim; they fell in streams down her face. It seemed so unfair, to have come so far together, only to have to part.

"I have to go," she choked out. "We can't stay in New City."

He shook his head. "No, you can't. I wouldn't let you if you tried. This place is going to be chaos now. We'll do what we can — I'll do what I can — to get a fair system running, but there's a long road of anarchy before we get there. It's not safe for you here."

"I wish you could come with us."

He fell to his knees in front of her, taking her in his arms and burying his face in the crook of her neck. His eyes were dry; only his shaking shoulders betrayed his emotion.

Evie stroked his hair, closing her eyes and relishing feeling him against her for the last time. "But this is where you're supposed to be. You're going to help so many people. You'll get this city back on track, you and the others, and you'll make sure no one tries to take over the way Lachlan did. But James, what you did tonight was amazing. Don't ever think that it was anything less than heroic. You saved my life and you saved many others as well. Don't ever forget that. Now you have to keep on going."

He sat back on his heels, still only a breath away but so she could see his tear-splotched face. "How am I going to do that without you around? No one else can put me in my place quite like you can."

Her watery smile shook but held. "Don't worry; I'll try to keep track of you and what's happening in this city. There will still be boats coming and going. I'll try to get a message to you that we're okay, as soon as I can. And you must try to get a message to me. Okay? And I'll be back, of course I'll come back, someday. And you better have this city in shape by then. I'll have words for you if you don't."

His grin came quickly and faded just as fast. "I'll look forward to it."

"But right now I need to go somewhere that Kit and I can be safe. Somewhere where trees grow everywhere and the air is clean."

"I know. I never expected you to stay."

"Then you're stronger than I am because I wanted nothing more in the world then for you to come with us." Evie started crying again. "But I know I can't have you. Not now." She closed the gap between him and gave him a long kiss. She poured everything she couldn't say with words into her lips, praying that the moment would simply last forever.

But it didn't. She broke away. "I'll always be yours," she whispered to him. Then stood up, bringing him with her.

"I'll be here, Evie. You can count on that."

She stepped away from him. "Tell me we'll see each other again," she commanded.

His crooked grin was a promise. "We'll see each other again."

A shout rang out from the darkness. Three men were running along the docks, shouting to Bill that he should not leave.

"James!" Bill yelled. "We are casting off. Are you in or out?"

290

"Out, unfortunately." James turned and ran towards the railing then leapt over, landing on the docks in a roll. Reaching for her gun, Evie dragged it up and aimed it at the approaching men, firing a shot above their heads. They jumped out of the way, stopping their pursuit for the moment.

Evie stood, heart in her throat, watching James as he straightened. He looked back at her, standing with his hand upraised in a goodbye. She couldn't see his face; his dark silhouette was backlit by the fires that still burned in the city. Then he turned and ran in the opposite direction, away from the trio. He was lost to her then, and Evie let out a jagged breath.

Evie stood leaning on the rail, watching as the city slipped away from them. How different it looked from when she had first seen it. It had seemed so new and modern, a beacon of hope when they'd first arrived. But New City had been an illusion. It was built on a lie, creating a shadow of what the world once was. Now it was dark and silent, save for the few buildings that still crackled and flamed in the night. Her heart sank as she heard gunfire, the jarring staccato warning of more danger to come.

Turning back to the deck of the *Mary Rose,* she took in the scene before her. The women were being settled in, with Petra fussing over them. Some of the men were offering them warm clothing and bowls of something that smelled delicious. Millie's arm was already bandaged, and she was chatting with another woman. Nobody seemed tired. Several fires were lit and the atmosphere was cheerful and festive. The women had come out of their state of shock and were almost giddy with relief at their escape. Evie smiled, but gave an involuntary shiver.

Kit came up and stood next to her. She wore a large hoodie that came to her knees, probably Oliver's. Purple smudges under her eyes betrayed her exhaustion. "I'm sorry. About James, that he couldn't come."

Evie looked down. "He's where he's supposed to be."

"What about us now? Where are we supposed to be?"

Evie smiled then, a real smile at the thought of what could be ahead of them. "You know what? I have no idea. It's time for us to head out and see what we find. What do you think?"

Kit wrapped her arm around her sister, resting her chin in her shoulder. "I think that sounds like a good idea."

Acknowledgements

New City has from the very beginning been a labour of love, and it has come together with the help of many people over time. Thanks very much to my editor, Pat Kozak, for her time and dedication in refining this work into something I am truly proud of. I appreciate all you did to bring out the best in my story and help me find my voice.

Thank you to Heather Grab, for all the time you took to read, and reread, and give thoughtful comments. Your sharp eye for character and different perspectives took this novel to the next level.

Thank you to Cathy Helms at Avalon Graphics for creating my exact vision for a gorgeous cover design.

Thanks to Allison Barr, for being such a great inspiration and for all the support, and for indulging my occasional procrastination.

To all my family, thanks for the love and support you've shown me over the past few years, through both the hard times and the good.

To Zacharie Magnan, I don't even know how to thank you for the love and support you provided in bringing this dream to reality. Without you, I would not have pushed myself as far as I have.

Made in the USA
Charleston, SC
27 February 2014